The CONSORT

THE ASCENSION SERIES

book three

USA *Today* Bestselling Author

K.A. LINDE

PRONUNCIATION GUIDE

Ahlvie Gunn: *Al-vee Gun*

Aralyn Strohm: *Air-uh-lin Strahm*

Aonia: *A-own-yuh*

Aubron: *Ah-bruhn*

Aurum: *Are-um*

Avoca: *Ah-vok-uh*

Barkeley Iolair: *Bark-lee I-o-lar*

Basille Selby: *Bah-seal Sel-bee*

Benetta: *Ben-ee-tuh*

Braj: *Brahj*

Byern: *By-urn*

Caldreva Anamarya: *Cal-dray-vuh Ann-uh-muh-ree-uh*

Caro Barca: *Car-o Bars-uh*

Ceis'f: *See-es-ef*

Creighton Iolair: *Cray-tun I-o-lar*

Cyrene Strohm: *Sah-reen Strahm*

Daufina Birket (consort): *Daw-feen-uh Bur-ket*

Edric Dremylon (king): *Edge-rick Drem-lin*

Elea Strohm: *El-ya Strahm*

Eleysia: *El-a-see-uh*

Emporia: *Em-por-ee-uh*

Eren: *Air-en*

Haenah de'Lorlah: *Han-uh d-Lor-luh*

Haille Mardas: *Hayl Mar-dus*

Huyek River: *Hoo-yik Riv-er*

Indres: *In-dress*

Jardana: *Jar-don-uh*

Jesalyn Dremylon Iolair: *Jess-uh-lin Drem-lin I-o-lar*

Jestre Farranay: *Jest-ray Fair-uh-nay*

Kael Dremylon (prince): *Kayl Drem-lin*

Kaliana Dremylon (queen): *Kal-ee-ah-nuh Drem-lin*

Keylani River: *Key-lahn-ee Riv-er*

Krisana (Albion Castle): *Kris-on-uh*

Leif: *Leef*

Maelia Dallmer: *May-lee-uh Dal-mer*

Malysa: *Muh-liss-uh*

Matilde: *Muh-tild*

Merrick: *Mer-ick*

Nit Decus (Byern Castle): *Nit Dake-us*

Reeve Strohm: *Reev Strahm*

Rhea Gramm: *Ray Gram*

Serafina (domina): *Ser-uh-feen-uh*

Shira: *Sheer-uh*

Vera: *Veer-uh*

Viktor Dremylon: *Vick-ter Drem-lin*

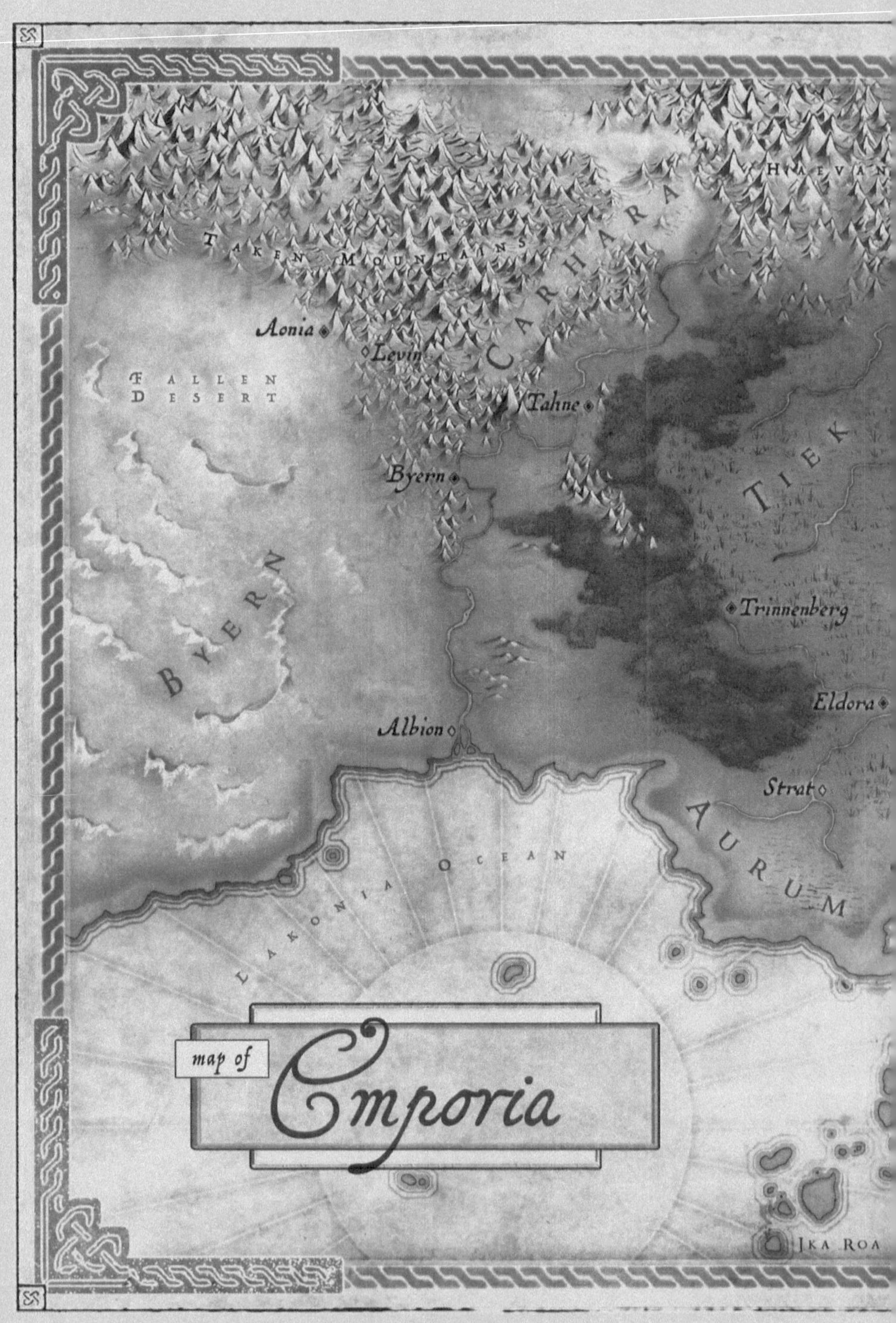
CARHARA
HAEVAN
TAKEN MOUNTAINS
Aonia
Levin
FALLEN DESERT
Tahne
TIEK
Byern
BYERN
Trinnenberg
Eldora
Albion
Strat
AURUM
LAKONIA OCEAN
map of
Emporia
IKA ROA

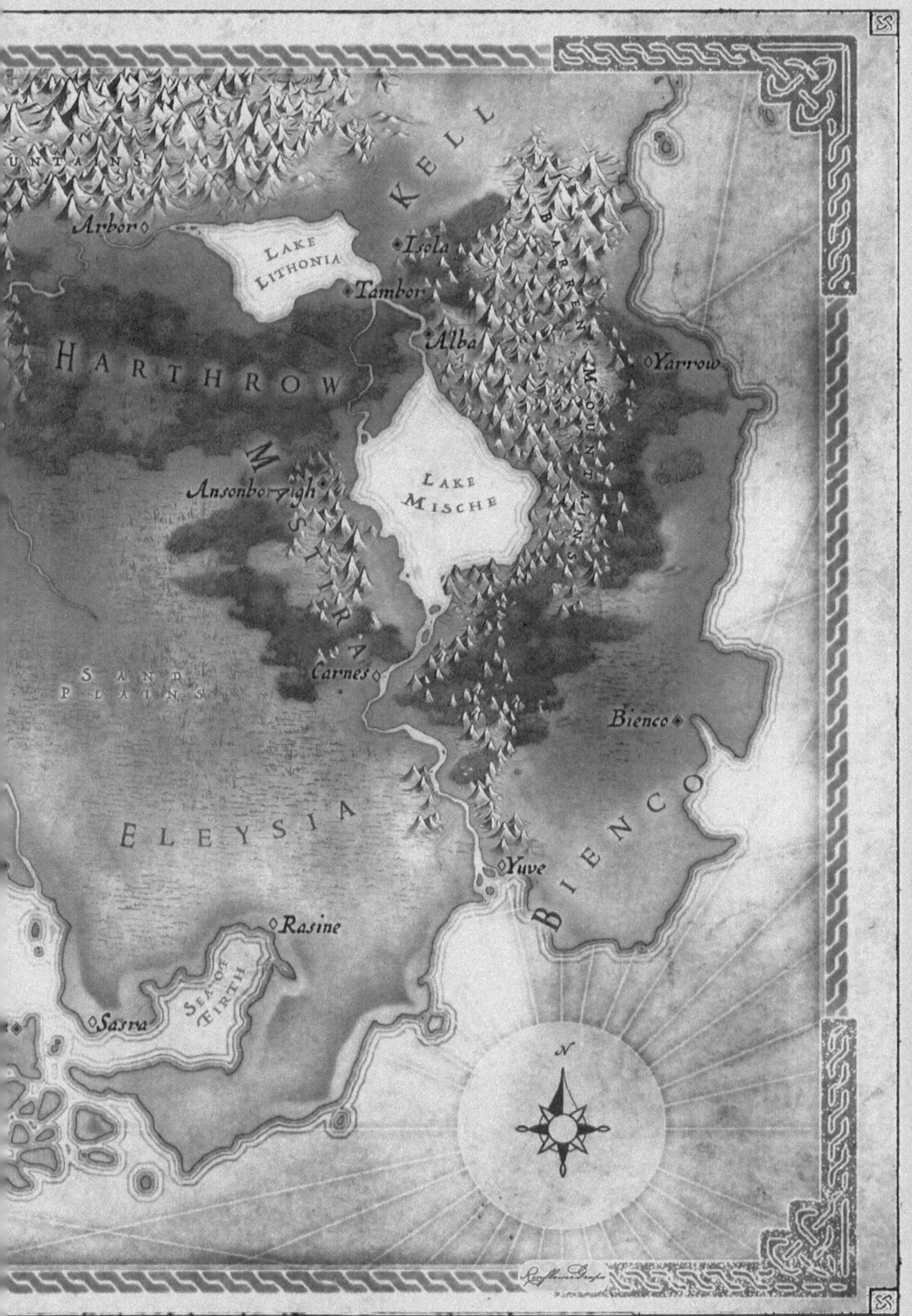

KELL
BARREN
MOUNTAINS
HARTHROW
Arbor
LAKE LITHONIA
Isola
Tambor
Alba
Yarrow
Ansonborough
LAKE MISCHE
MISTIRA
SAND PLAINS
Carnes
Bienco
ELEYSIA
BIENCO
Yuve
Rasine
SEA OF FIRTH
Sasra
N

Prologue

"Lysa, don't!" Benetta cried, reaching for the giant circular diamond in her sister's hand.

"I'm just looking at it," Malysa said.

Benetta rolled her bright blue eyes to the ceiling. Malysa was never entirely innocent about anything she was doing.

"Father said that we were not supposed to touch that. Can't we go back to the parlor and wait for Camilan to get here?"

Malysa scrunched up her nose. "I don't want to marry that pig."

"I know you don't."

"Then, stop trying to make me into the perfect daughter." Malysa threw her long braid over one shoulder and glared with fiery determination. "If you're so set on Camilan, then *you* marry him."

"Well, I can't. You're older," Benetta reminded her.

"That's right. I am."

Benetta sighed. There was no point in pushing Malysa when she was acting like this. Father had refused them access to the academy. Malysa was still sulking. *What use was their magic if it was only to be used for menial tasks, like tidying the house and baking fresh bread?*

"Seventeen years of magic school was not, nor will it ever be, enough for me. If I'd gone to the academy at seventeen, like I was supposed to, then I'd know how to make this work," Malysa said. She lobbed the priceless diamond at Benetta, who gasped and caught it in her hands.

"We all have a place in this world."

"My place is ruling everything," she snarled. Her magic flared, black and wicked, before receding quickly. "I am so tired, Benny."

Benetta took a deep breath and then held the diamond back out to her. "Come on. Maybe, if we practice together while we can, we'll find our own place."

"You really think so?"

"Anything is possible."

Malysa looked as if she was going to argue before she gently placed her hands over Benetta's. They stared into each other's eyes, light meeting dark, and then entwined their magic together around the diamond. Benetta giggled as they held it, cocooned in the shimmery gold magic. But Malysa stayed perfectly still and silent. Her eyes were unfocused, as if she were very far away.

"Lysa?" Benetta asked.

"Do you hear that?"

"Hear what?"

Benetta tried to release her magic, but Lysa held on.

"The humming."

Then, a shock wave blasted through them, obliterating their father's study. Benetta screamed and tried to duck, but she couldn't. She couldn't move at all. She and her sister were connected by the diamond, spinning in a circle and picking up speed. She screamed, but the wind carried it away.

They were lost. They had done something truly horrible. Their Father had said not to touch his things for a reason. The diamond wasn't just some beautiful new bauble for Lysa's wedding.

Then they landed roughly. Benetta's knees buckled beneath her. She clasped her hand around the diamond as her knees hit the hard stone. Malysa had toppled over a foot away from her. Her mouth was open, her dark eyes wide.

"What just happened?" Benetta asked. She righted her dress, brushed loose dirt from her knees, and pulled her dark brown hair to one side.

"I...I don't know," Malysa admitted.

They were at the foothills of great towering mountains with a swirling river cutting down the mountain pass. It looked like an elbow as it moved in an L-shape off and away from the mountains. The earth was green and lush as far as the eye could see. Smoke blew in further down the river. Benetta could just make out the roofs of houses. A small village of some sort.

"Where are we, Lysa?"

Malysa shook her head. "I've no idea. We should go find out."

"I've never seen this river or mountains like this. We've seen all the maps in Father's study. This doesn't feel like home."

"I know. It's not."

Malysa was already tramping down the side of the mountain, toward the village. Benetta had no other choice but to follow her. But her fear only mounted as they entered the strange, small village. The houses were made out of hard wood and thatched with straw. Children were playing a game with a ball in the dirt and stared up at them with eyes as large as saucers as they passed.

A group of men approached them from what appeared to be the center of a poorly constructed square. Many of them were carrying wooden weapons; only a few had steel.

What kind of place had we been transported to?

"Greetings," Malysa said.

"Don't come any closer!" the man in the front shouted.

"We mean you no harm."

"You drop out of the sky like a tornado, come at us with your shining light, and expect us to believe you mean no harm?"

"Shining light?" Benetta asked curiously.

"Your bodies are glowing!" another man yelled.

Benetta and Malysa glanced at each other and then laughed. These people must not have magic. *How odd.* That natural glow came from magical use. They could diminish it if need be, but they never had to do it before.

Just then, two women barreled through the men and splayed their hands out. They both bowed low.

"Our apologies," one woman said. "These fools do not recognize when they are in the presence of gods." The woman snarled at the men. "Kneel to the goddesses."

The men looked dumbstruck and then began to kneel to them.

"Oh no," Benetta started to say.

But Malysa cut her off. "All is forgiven," she said to the townspeople. She tilted her head up and released the full weight of her magical powers into her brightness. "You may stand."

"Welcome to the great city of Byern," the second woman intoned.

Benetta's eyes widened. *This is considered a city?*

"We are honored to have your presence among us," the first woman said.

"We are pleased to be here," Malysa said with a wide smile.

"Come. We have accommodations for you and are truly privileged to house ones so great," another woman said.

Benetta shot Malysa a nasty look but followed her into the nearby inn where they were immediately shown to the nicest room. They had to wait a full twenty minutes before the women would leave them be. And only after Malysa agreed that they would come down for dinner.

As soon as the door closed, Benetta whirled on her sister. "What are you doing? We're not gods, Lysa!"

"Obviously, Benny," Malysa said with a laugh. "But how else were we going to explain to these simpletons what had happened? Let them think what they want to think. We'll eat some dinner, and then we'll use the diamond and get home before Father even notices. You do still have the diamond, right?"

"Of course I have the diamond, but this is absurd. We don't even know where we are. What kind of place is Byern, and how can they call this a city?"

"No idea, but it hardly matters. We'll be gone before we have to find out anything else."

"We don't even know how to use the diamond."

"Details," Malysa said dismissively. "We're the most powerful magic users of our time. We'll figure it out."

Benetta scowled. "Well, did you bring anything else with you?"

Malysa patted down her dress and then pulled out a handful of gold coins. They were about half the size of her palm with the profile of their mother, the queen, on them. The motto of their people gleamed around the edges. "Just some money I filched from Father. I was going to buy that blade at the market."

"You are incorrigible. Those won't help us at all."

Malysa stuffed them back into her pocket. "Stop worrying. It'll be fine."

"Can we just go now?" Benetta begged.

"Benny, come on. How amazing would it be to be gods? In this land, we could be anything. We could rule the world, just like we always wanted to."

"Like *you* always wanted to."

"Here, there are no forced marriages. There are no responsibilities and restrictions. We can choose how we live our lives. We can choose to be gods in this land. We can enlighten these people to the ways of magic. Just think of all the good we could do," Malysa said with an eager light in her dark eyes.

"But what about our families? What about our *lives*?"

Malysa sighed. "Can't you see what it could be?"

"All I see is everything we've lost."

"Fine," Malysa said with a shake of her head. "Let's get back then."

Benetta retrieved the diamond from her pocket and held it out to Malysa. Like before, they intertwined their powers and reached for the diamond. Benetta stared until her eyes were dry and aching, but nothing happened.

"Why won't it work?" she groaned.

"I don't know. We're doing the exact same thing as before."

Benetta tried to be transfixed by the diamond, as she had last time, willing it to transport her back to her world, to her friends and family, to the life she loved.

But it did nothing.

"What will we do?" Benetta whispered.

"We'll keep trying," Malysa said, reaching out and grasping her sister's hand. "But, in the meantime, we will play our parts."

"You want us to be gods?"

"Isn't it obvious, Benny?"

Benetta raised an eyebrow.

"We are Doma, the first in this land, and Doma have always been gods. Now, it is our turn to rule."

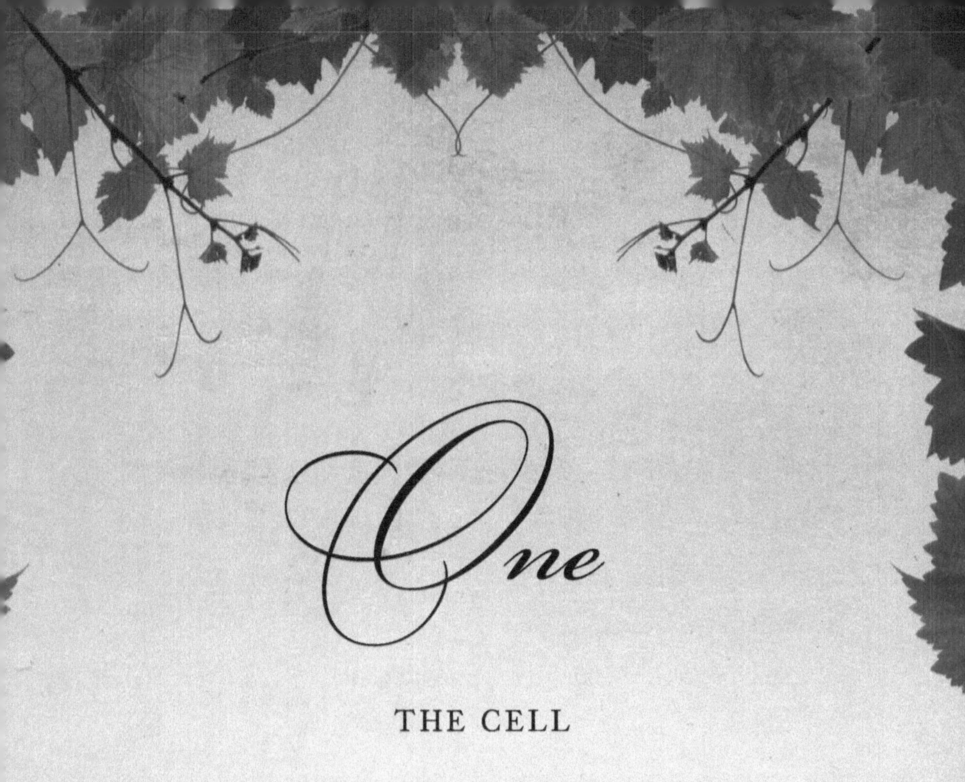

One

THE CELL

Darkness.

Hazy. Blurry. Grainy.

"*...do what I say!*"

Cyrene had heard that voice before. Somewhere. Distantly.

But, when she tried to grab on to it, to hold the precious knowledge, it flittered away, just out of grasp, like a butterfly.

"*She needs more. Do you hear me?*"

More.

No, she didn't need more. She'd had enough.

She tried to peel her eyes open, but nothing happened. She felt *nothing*. No pain. No control. No powers. A total absence of anything whatsoever. There was just shadows and the nothingness of her body. If she still had a body at all.

A door creaked open. Iron against hard-packed dirt. The sound clawed at her, but she couldn't place it. Her mind had once been a bottomless place. Now, it only held black depths, wisps of smoke, an abysmal vortex of nothing.

"Turn her over," the unfamiliar voice rasped.

"Creator, she looks ill."

"Well, it's hard to feed her when you keep her like this."

"We have to. You don't know what she could do."

"What are you going to do? How will you force her to stand trial like this?"

"Stand down," the voice growled.

It cut and broke, like taking a hammer to glass.

"Yes, Captain."

Cyrene's mind jolted on that word. *Captain.* Yes, she knew a captain. She had known one once. An image pieced itself together. The first image she could conjure. A face. A beautiful face. Tan, strong jaw, light hair falling into dark eyes, perfect lips, that smile.

Dean.

Her heart broke at the memory. Of the perfect man she loved. Of his ring on her finger. Of his hands on her skin. Of all the promises wasted.

Prince Dean Ellison of Eleysia. The orphaned prince. Alone now but with eleven sisters. His parents…dead.

Dead at the hands of an assassin. Her mind tried to shield herself from it. Not an assassin. Her friend. Maelia Dallmer. Her first friend at court, back at home in Byern. A place she would never see again. Because Maelia had killed them. Slaughtered the king and queen of Eleysia in their sleep.

Cyrene croaked, feelings rushing to her all at once. Pain. Lacerating pain.

Not physical. All emotional. All heartache and guilt and remorse and grief.

"She's waking up. Hurry up!"

"She can't be waking up. That last dose could have knocked out a grown man for a week!"

"She's not any regular person."

"Dean," Cyrene rasped, getting the word past her closed throat.

Heavy hands pushed her shoulders down hard into the ground. She couldn't move. Her mind was working, and she'd managed one word, but beyond that, she felt frozen, paralyzed. A headache was starting at the base of her skull and right behind her eyes, as if her head were about to crack open.

Someone clamped fingers over her nose.

"Drink this," said the other voice.

Not Dean.

He hadn't said a word since she called out to him. *How could I think he would?* When she had been implicated in killing his father and mother. When he had trusted her, and then his world had shattered. Even if she'd had no knowledge of Maelia's actions…she had brought Maelia to the island capital city of Eleysia. She had brought Affiliates to their homeland for the first time in years when they were banned from the city, and in turn, she had brought death.

Liquid was forced down her mouth, and she swallowed to keep from drowning on the potion. She choked and sputtered, but he didn't stop until she finished. Then, when he was through, he finally released her.

She tried to move. Tried to think. Tried to grasp at the fleeting memories that hovered at the front of her mind. But whatever she had been thinking before, whatever grief had hit her full in the chest, was dissolving.

For a moment, she mourned the loss of her mind. In the next, she was thankful for the sedative to numb the pain…to numb her from the world. Because a part of her did not want to live in it anymore.

Sunlight.

Just a small stream.

Cyrene felt it on her skin, bright like a beacon on the sea. It warmed her face, pushing away the darkness, calling to her.

Light.

Not the absence of darkness but its playmate. Always reaching out to grasp the other, to hold it for a few more seconds each day. Constantly chasing. An endless game of tug-of-war. For, without one…how could there be an appreciation for the other?

Cyrene shucked off the darkness like a heavy blanket. She peeled it back from her head where it'd lain on her eyes, down her body, and all the way to her feet until she felt the weight of it release her. Though her heart remained heavy, whatever had held her underwater no longer remained. She must have burned it off with fever, for her skin was clammy. Her neck still slick with sweat.

Slowly, she opened her weary eyes and raised one dark blue eye up to the shaft of light breaching her prison cell. Her pupil shuttered to a mere pinprick. Warmth infused her, and she drank it up, letting it fill her to the brim.

No more.

She'd had enough.

She refused to ever feel so weak again. To ever let someone force her into nothingness. To ever have to claw her way back to sanity.

Even if she no longer knew which way was up or down, where her heart lay, or the bleakness of the road ahead, she knew that she was not weak. She had never been weak. She would *never* be weak.

And Dean had made a grave error in believing her to be so. To bringing her to her knees in such a manner.

With trepidation she hated feeling, she eased onto one elbow and took a shuddering breath. And then another. She was alive. That was what mattered right now. They hadn't killed her without a proper trial, like Maelia. Though…Maelia's crimes had been evident. Blood on her hands.

Cyrene snapped her eyes shut and curled in on herself again.

Blood. Creator. *Blood.*

How had I let this happen? How hadn't I seen what my friend intended? She had seen the effortlessness of the way Maelia held a sword but assumed it had come from the training of having two Captains of the Guard as parents. Maelia never confirmed or denied that. She had seen the way Maelia blended into crowds so seamlessly that no one remembered seeing her, but Cyrene had just thought people had shoddy memories. She should have seen the fierceness hidden under the meek girl she had known as her friend. Should have known the deception that would follow. The assassin waiting to strike in their midst.

She shuddered once more at the thought and then let it slide to the back of her mind. She couldn't process it all yet. Slowly, she moved into a sitting position with her back against the rock wall and looked around.

She was in a dark prison cell. Alone. She had been knocked out and drugged to keep her from accessing her magic. She should not have been awake. That much, she knew.

Dreamily, she remembered the other person saying they had given her a stronger dose. A sedative, she assumed. *But what could numb me so completely? What could cut me off from my powers…from myself?*

A question for another time. First things first, she needed to find out how long she had been down here and how to get out. It couldn't have been that long, or she would have already stood trial…or been killed. Surely, the Eleysian court would be calling for her head.

The prince's betrothed had turned traitor in the course of an afternoon. Uproar and commotion and fire and brimstone. She was no longer their prized and cherished soon-to-be princess, as she had been for that one glorious afternoon.

So, why am I here still?

Dean.

She crushed the idea. No. Dean would not save her. The way he had looked at her. No, she doubted very much that Dean cared whether or not she lost her pretty head.

But the weight on her finger held her fast.

Why had he not removed my engagement ring? The exquisite stone glinted up at her in the meager light. If he truly did not care for her life, then this should be gone. But she didn't know the answer to that question. To any of her questions.

Cyrene ran trembling fingers through her matted hair and tried to find some semblance of her old self. The proud, honorable girl who would bring on a hurricane to stay with the man she loved, who would stop it to save his life. A piece of that girl had broken off while she lay on the prison cell floor.

Love was foolish and weak.

Love was destruction.

Love was utter ruin.

Pride, honor, power, control. These things were worth cultivating. Worth living and dying for.

She knew that now, where she had not known it before. Things would be different this time.

Two

THE VIAL

Cyrene heard the stomping of boots as they came down the dusty hallway, toward her cell. Keys clattered against a man's leg. But a fresh smell breezed toward her—lumber and soap and sandalwood. A scent she would remember anywhere. Dean.

But is he coming to try to subdue me again or to take me away?

She hurried to her feet and casually leaned back against the opposite wall. She picked at the sand and grime that had caked under her fingernails and strove for nonchalance.

When Dean finally reached her cell door, he startled in surprise at finding her standing and clearly coherent. She didn't look up, but she could just make out his appearance from the edge of her peripheral vision. He looked haggard and worn. Though he was clean, his clothes were rumpled. Mud caked his boots. This was not a man who had been at ease since his parents' tragic deaths. If she was not so furious, she would have felt sympathy. Instead, she felt nothing.

"You're awake," he said hoarsely.

"How astute of you," she bit out.

"You…you aren't…"

"Clearly, I'm not supposed to be awake, yet I am."

His eyes bore into her so fiercely, it was nearly impossible to avoid his gaze, but she didn't look up. She wouldn't give him the satisfaction.

"Cyrene, I…"

"When is my trial?" she snapped.

"Your trial?"

She sighed and gave in, looking up into his piercing eyes and immediately wishing she hadn't. He was gorgeous. Her stomach fluttered to life, and she cursed her heart for yearning for him.

"Yes. You accused me of a crime. I'm to stand trial to plead my case," she said slowly, as if he were dim-witted.

"You won't stand trial."

"Excuse me?" She straightened considerably, giving off the practiced air of royalty.

Dean didn't shrink from it, of course. He actually was royal and had been raised as such. The youngest and only son of the king and queen of Eleysia. Eleven older sisters—a fact he knew all too well since he would never be in line for the throne of the queendom.

"You're too dangerous to stand trial. We're keeping you imprisoned until we decide what to do with you," he said simply.

Cyrene's stomach roiled. *How dare they!* "And how long have I been imprisoned thus far?"

He looked sheepish. "Two weeks."

Two weeks. She'd lost two weeks to that sleeping draught. Two weeks without Maelia. Two weeks without knowing what was coming next and where her friends were. Without her powers, which she still couldn't access, Avoca couldn't reach her through their magical bond. When she and Avoca had been bound together, it gave them the power to intertwine their magic as well as provided them with a tether to the other person. But the tether was silent, as were her abilities.

And she had sent her friends Ahlvie and Orden back to Byern to deliver a letter to King Edric, who had been prepared to send an army to Eleysia to retrieve Cyrene. She'd thought the letter would stall Edric from doing anything rash, but if not, she had believed the storms would keep him away. Now, in her current predicament, she wasn't sure what would be worse— Edric coming for her or abandoning her.

"Two weeks," she finally intoned, her voice flat. "You've held me captive and drugged with no trial for two weeks."

His face seemed to harden at that as he remembered where he was. "Yes. And we will keep you here longer until we figure out what to do with you."

"What to do with me," she repeated.

"You were an accomplice to murder!"

Cyrene stretched a slow catlike smile onto her face. She had been with Dean for months. They had met in the Aurum woods with neither the wiser of who the other was. He had not been a prince in that moment, and she, not a Byern Affiliate that he would have otherwise despised. He had completely accepted her, trusted her, believed in her…loved her. And, now, with that one horrible sentence, everything fell apart.

"And you smile," he spat as anger suffused him.

"Do you truly believe that?" she asked calmly.

"What else am I to believe? You invaded my country, waited out your time until you had our complete trust, and then sent an assassin in to do your dirty work. Affiliates were never welcome in Eleysia. Now, I understand why."

"You're a fool."

"She claims I'm the fool!" he cried, throwing his hands out in frustration and turning from her. He ran a shaky hand back through his hair and then solemnly looked back at her. "Yes, perhaps I am a fool…for loving you."

Cyrene swallowed, refusing to wince at the accusation, even as her heart ached. With considerable effort, she straightened and walked as steadily as possible toward Dean.

"Cyrene…do not take another step closer," he warned.

"Or what?"

If she had her magic, there would be nothing he could do to her. He wasn't quick enough to subdue her again. He had only been successful the first time because she had been so shocked when she heard of the murders and Maelia's involvement. But she was not going to let him know that she couldn't access her powers. Whatever was in that potion had definitely dampened her innate ability…or else…

No. She didn't want to think of the other possibility. That she might have burned out her powers entirely.

"Cyrene," he growled out again.

She stepped right up to the iron gate that separated them. His scent was even stronger there. She just wanted to bury her face into his shoulder and hold him. The strain and pain and grief were evident in the lines of his youthful face. Something primal in her woke up at his nearness. She needed to keep herself in control. He had put her behind these bars after all.

Cyrene slowly reached out and tenderly touched his cheek. He flinched but let her touch him. She dragged the pads of her fingers down his cheek and curved toward his mouth. Her thumb stroked across his lower lip, and he took a sharp breath before taking a step backward.

"Think," she whispered, her hand still outstretched toward him. "Just think, Dean. You know what I'm capable of. Why would I have sent an assassin to do my dirty work? Why would I've even bothered? Why wait *months* in Eleysia when I could have done the job by the Eos holiday and returned home, if that were the plan? Why would I have agreed to marry you, made love to you after the betrothal, and then saved you from certain death on the water? Why would I have allowed you to incapacitate me in the first place if I had known what I would be returning to that day?"

Dean never responded. He just stood there, captivated by her ocean-blue eyes, and she dropped her hand.

She sighed heavily. "If you truly believe that I had a hand in this, take me to trial right now. Prove my guilt."

"I can't do that."

"And why not?" she growled, unable to keep the bitter anger from her voice.

His eyes locked on hers, and she saw something soften and then harden once more before he said, "Because you are safer in there."

Cyrene laughed hoarsely. "Safer? In a prison cell?"

"My sister…Queen Brigette needs no proof of your guilt. She will try you before the council and sentence your death without blinking an eye."

"So, you have left me in here to rot?"

"I have left you in here to *live*."

Cyrene shook her head. "This is no life."

With a flourish, Dean produced a small green vial from the inside of his jacket pocket. Cyrene recoiled. She hated to admit that the thought of another potion frightened her. She knew that her abilities fought off illness and injuries at an alarmingly fast rate, which was likely how she had been able to rid her body of the potion that had knocked her out. But that didn't mean it didn't scare her that something like that was even possible.

"Drink this," he commanded, shoving it toward her.

"I will not."

"Cyrene, don't be so difficult."

"I will not drink another thing you give me unless I see *you* drink it first," she spat.

"Just drink it!"

"Let me stand trial," she shot back.

"If you stand trial, you will die."

"Wouldn't that make you happy?"

His anguish was clear in that moment, but he didn't respond. He slowly bent down and placed the green vial on the floor of the prison cell. "Drink the vial. Don't drink the vial. It's up to you, Cyrene. But make up your mind before the moon rises full tonight."

Dean took a step back and then another before turning and striding away.

"Or what?" she called out to him.

But he didn't respond. He just kept walking.

Whatever semblance of control she had been holding on to left her as his footsteps echoed softly down the hall and then disappeared entirely. She slammed her hands against the iron grate and wrenched at the door. She pulled and tugged and pushed and kicked at it, desperate for something, *anything* to happen.

Just get out of the way.

The last time she had been trapped, she had used her magic to burst through the door and knocked down several stone walls past the door. No such luck today. At the time, Dean's sister Alise had left her alone in a locked room. Alise had hated Cyrene for her happiness with Dean, for Alise was in love with a man she was not allowed to marry. A commoner turned military rival of Dean's. Robard.

At the memory of Robard, the life left Cyrene.

Because it was not just the king and queen and Maelia whose lives had been forfeited that day two weeks ago; Robard had died, too. No, not died. Killed. Dean had killed him.

Robard had snuck aboard the vessel where she and Dean were celebrating their engagement. Robard had intended to kill them that day, out of jealousy or spite. She would never truly know what his insane motivations had been. All she knew was that, when he had attacked, Dean had not hesitated in taking down his friend.

And worse…Cyrene had felt the magic in Robard's blood call to her. She shivered at the thought. Even in her bedraggled state, bereft of her own magic, she could distinctly remember the dark call. She didn't know what it meant that dark magic sang to her.

Had I been so weak after starting and attempting to stop a hurricane in the span of an hour? Or did I truly long for that?

Her mind turned to what she had seen in her fever dream after halting the hurricane and passing out. Two thousand years ago, Viktor Dremylon had overthrown the evil Doma court and their leader, Domina Serafina. At least, that was the story Cyrene had been told all her life. Now, she knew that Viktor and Serafina not only had loved each other greatly, been separated because Serafina had magic and Viktor did not, but that they had also performed a Creator-cursed act. Together, they had slit the throat of Viktor's firstborn child and used the strong blood magic to bind themselves together for all of eternity.

Like called to like. A magical and nonmagical person could *never* be bound officially, as Cyrene and Avoca had been bound. But using dark magic to perform the ceremony and entangling the pure, untainted Doma magic with blood magic was unthinkable.

Had that driven Viktor to kill Serafina? Was that how he had defeated the most powerful ruler in all of history?

Cyrene's head spun, and she slowly lowered herself to the hard stone floor. She had not fully recovered yet, and she was pushing herself.

Her eyes darted to the green vial. It seemed so inconsequential. It could kill her. Poison.

It seemed beneath Dean. He'd had the opportunity to kill her, and he hadn't. For two weeks, he had kept her alive and safe…albeit imprisoned and incapacitated.

She mulled over his words. He'd accused her of being an accomplice to murder in one breath, and in the next, he'd claimed she was safer where she was.

So, which is it? Am I a danger to the throne—a traitor and an assassin? Or am I someone to be kept safe—alive and healthy?

Cyrene palmed the vial. She considered it like an enemy would. *Am I an enemy to be disposed of?*

No. If she were an enemy, they would want it to be public. This vial was a way out. It would be too easy like this. They would want to make a spectacle of her. Like they had with Maelia. She knew that much.

But she didn't know why Dean had given this to her. *Had he planned to give it to me himself but hadn't been able to because I was awake?*

Cyrene cursed under her breath. She didn't have any answers. She just had to decide whether or not she trusted Dean.

She gritted her teeth and remembered the bite of the butt of his blade against her temple. The way he'd drugged her. The way he had held her imprisoned.

No, she didn't…couldn't trust him.

But, as the moon started to rise toward its zenith, she realized she had no one else to put her faith in. No one to help her. No one, not even herself. Just this little green vial. And Dean.

Cyrene unstopped the cork on the vial and took a big whiff. She coughed gruffly as the cloying sweetness enveloped her senses.

Creator! Guide my hand.

She glanced once more at the moon and then tipped back the vial.

Three

THE DEAL

Cyrene was swaying.

Back and forth. Back and forth.

That was all she could feel as she was jolted awake. Then, everything came to her in a rush. The vial.

She bolted upright and screamed at the top of her lungs. But the scream was muffled through her gag. Her eyes widened in horror as she observed her predicament. Her hands and legs were knotted, trussed up like a prized turkey. A blanket had been hastily thrown over her body. It obstructed her view of where she was or was headed, but she could already tell by the swaying that she was on a boat.

A boat? How did I get on a boat? Why am I no longer in prison?

Out of nowhere, a hand shoved her backward, and she wrestled with her captor. She tried to scream again but had no luck through the gag.

"Quiet you!" hissed a disembodied voice from above her. "How the hell is she awake?"

"I have no idea." Dean's crisp voice cut through the humid night.

"She's supposed to be dead!" the man said. "You just said you were dumping the body."

"And we are," he said evenly.

Cyrene seethed. *Dumping the body! He had thought that the vial of liquid would kill me! What had I been thinking? How could I have trusted him?* She had been an idiot, and now, she had no idea where she was or where they were going. Now would be a great time for her magic to come back to her.

The blanket was yanked over her head, and a man peered down at her. She recognized him at once as Dean's personal guard and Maelia's former lover, Darmian. He was the one who had caught Maelia with blood on her hands…literally.

"Shut your trap, or we're going to be noticed. Then, you'll be in real trouble," he growled out. His voice was gruffer than she remembered. His face harder. He must be taking Maelia's death hard…or he just hated Cyrene now.

But she didn't stop wriggling or attempting to shout for help. She doubted she could get away so easily without her powers, but she wasn't going to give up without a fight.

"Listen here, you want me to knock you out again? We're all out of puffer fish liquid since you burn it up faster than humanly possible. So, shut your mouth, or I'll make you!"

Then, he threw the blanket back into her face, and she stilled.

Puffer fish liquid? What in the Creator's name is he talking about? Is that what Dean had given me? She knew puffer fish were extremely poisonous. She didn't think that her magic should have been able to resist the toxin, but apparently, it had its uses. Even if she couldn't reach it.

She didn't relish the thought of being knocked out again. She'd rather be alert to witness what they were up to, sneaking her out and dumping her body in the middle of the night.

Then, taking one soft breath through the gag, she closed her eyes and reached for her powers again. Whatever Dean had given her might have died out, but her magic was still held at bay.

Then…like the soft flutter of a butterfly's wings, a tiny source opened up within. Not much. Nothing that she could really do much with. Not like before when she had been working with her tutors, Matilde and Vera. But, still, she had enough to tug on her bond with Avoca.

Feeling the bond brought a wave of relief. Her fear had been that she'd burned out her magic and would have to suffer a life without it. She couldn't imagine that life now. But the power was still there, just numbed from the amount of energy she had used and whatever Dean had given her.

An answering call came almost immediately, like a beacon in the night, and Cyrene knew she was not alone. Avoca would find her. She was sure of it. After Cyrene had saved Avoca's life from the Indres—evil wolflike beasts—she had forfeited her life to Cyrene and now owed her a life debt. Even without their bond, Avoca would go to the ends of the earth for her. And Cyrene felt the same way for her Leif sister.

As soon as the tug came to her, the boat rocked hard, and Cyrene listed toward the edge. Without her hands free, she nearly tumbled over the side. Arms roughly grabbed her around the middle and hauled her back to safety. The blanket fell from her face, giving her the first real glimpse of where they were.

Her mouth dropped open, and her eyes rounded.

"No," she tried to yell into her gag.

Darmian kicked her side to silence her. She grunted and started to squirm around, trying to sit up, as she stared at what was before her in horror.

As far as the eye could see were Byern warships.

Cyrene's heart sank. She hadn't known whether she would feel better or worse if Edric came for her…and now, she knew for certain. Worse. Much worse.

She had left Byern and given up her place. She had agreed to marry Dean and become an Eleysian princess. The last thing she wanted was to return home.

Yet it called to her. She could feel a pulse on the ship nearly as strong as what she held with Avoca. A pulse that sang to her.

She wanted to ignore it. She knew that it had to do with the illegal binding of Affiliates and High Order to the Byern throne and lands. But this somehow felt different, more precise. It wasn't her lands or the Dremylon throne calling her. It was one Dremylon in particular.

Without knowing why, Cyrene leaned into the bond, like bathing her face in sunlight. The king. It must be Edric.

She had told Dean that she did not love Edric, but the truth was that whatever was between them was more than that. Not love but connection. A bond she had felt the very first day she gazed up into his face at her Presenting ceremony. Though, at the time, she had not known what the electric zap that passed between them was. She now knew. And it called to her.

With him so near, she had no idea how she had ever believed their connection diminished.

If anything, it felt stronger.

They rowed right up to the side of the first ship. It was enormous, ten times the size of the barge they had ridden in on the trip down the Keylani River for procession and significantly bigger than the vessel she had come into Eleysia on with Dean. Of course, Eleysian vessels were more for stealth. Their navy was beyond reproach.

In the moonlight, the ship seemed to glow supernaturally. The dark wood planks were from the Hidden Forest on the banks of the Taken Mountains near her home. The sails were white and crisp. A Dremylon flag in the traditional green and gold flew high overhead with the *D* in flames. It was magnificent.

But this amount of force from Byern baffled her. *Edric had sent dozens of warships just for me?*

"Untie her hands and feet," Dean said coarsely. "But watch her. She's cunning."

"Aye," Darmian mutter.

He hauled Cyrene to her feet with one easy tug of the ropes on her wrists. He withdrew a wicked-looking knife and sliced the ropes, as if they were made of butter. As he worked on her ankles, she removed the bindings, rubbing her wrists to soothe the chafing.

Her eyes darted out to the water. *How far out are we? Could I swim away from here and get back to Avoca?*

"Don't even think about it," Dean said.

She glared at him. Her mouth was still gagged, so she couldn't even retort, but if looks could kill…

A rope ladder descended from the top of the ship, and Dean reached out for it.

"Prince Dean," Darmian said at once, "let me."

"You stay behind Cyrene. Don't let her do anything…stupid," he said, his eyes remaining on Cyrene.

As if she were prone to doing stupid things. Well, she supposed that wasn't entirely inaccurate.

Dean scrambled up the rope ladder, as if he had been born to do it. Darmian, who still had the scary knife in his hand, edged her forward with it. She wanted to reach up and yank the stupid gag from her mouth, but the way Darmian was eyeing her, any small movements might get her disemboweled. And she didn't care how fast she could heal; she wouldn't come back from that.

Cyrene reached out for the ladder and wrestled it into place. The stupid thing shook and moved with Dean above her.

"Go on," Darmian growled.

She sent one more withering look his way, hiked her dress up, and then stepped out onto the ladder.

It was hell.

How Dean made this look easy, she had no idea. No wonder female sailors wore pants. How could they manage this in fine dresses? Not that she was wearing a fine dress. And she wouldn't mind hacking it off with Darmian's blade right about now. It tangled between her legs and tried to trip her with every step she took. She might like sailing, but climbing a moving rope ladder was not her forte.

When she finally made it up to the top, two men grabbed her beneath her underarms and unceremoniously hauled her onto the deck. She stumbled a step and then righted herself. Her hands went to her gag, and she wrenched it out of her mouth. She had to remain confident, despite her fury and…fear.

If they were to drop my remains, then why am I on a Byern warship?

"What is the meaning of this?" she demanded at once.

Dean shot her a look that told her to hold her tongue, but that was another thing she'd never really been good at.

She took in the deck before her. Even in the moonlight, she could make out a half-dozen sailors standing in a semicircle, facing her. All of them were in the Dremylon green military uniforms. No one answered her question.

"Where is he?" Dean growled impatiently.

"He'll be up when he's up," a woman spat out in a fierce tone.

She had one arm at her side and the other resting on a broad sword. Cyrene had every confidence that the woman knew exactly how to use it.

"He?" Cyrene snapped.

She already knew whom they were talking about, of course. Dean was selling her out. Handing her back over to Byern rather than giving her a proper trial and proving her innocence. Now, he wouldn't even look at her.

"Who is he?" Cyrene stalked across the deck toward Dean and made it with only a few inches between them before a hand encircled her wrist.

"Stop right there," Darmian said.

She'd been so set on Dean, her anger burning so bright, that she didn't even hear Darmian climb onto the deck behind her. She also hadn't even realized that she had grasped her magic. Her skin tingled from the raw energy coursing through her system. It was more than the bond but still feeble and diluted. It crackled and spit, as if it were reaching down into a once-bottomless well and finding it lacking.

"Leave her be," Dean said, calm and collected.

Darmian released her, and Cyrene extinguished her magic at the same time.

"How could you do this?" she demanded.

"There was no other choice," he told her flatly.

"There is *always* a choice."

"Do not stand there and lecture me on what I should be doing with you, Cyrene. Be glad you are not dead."

"And why did you not just kill me? Why poison me and abandon me to this fate?" She flung her hand at the Byern sailors, who shifted uncomfortably at the display.

His eyes found hers across the short distance, and she saw nothing there. Not a glimmer of the man she loved.

Was he so grieved that he couldn't think clearly? Was he so mad that he had no remorse for handing me over to the very people I had been escaping all along?

Byern refused magic. Magic did not exist in her home. And, worse yet, King Edric's very ancestor, Viktor Dremylon himself, had extinguished it and set to wipe it out from the rest of Emporia. If she set foot on Byern soil once more, she would be hunted down and forced to fight for her life.

What Dean was doing was as good as killing her.

"If you keep asking me why I did not kill you, you will make me regret not doing so," Dean said harshly.

Cyrene took a step back in shock. Her heart was already broken and shattered into a million pieces. A darkness settled back into her heart and reminded her why she should not care or hope. Maelia was gone. And, now, Dean was gone just the same.

She refused to cry for him. She just yanked on the ring on her finger, the ring *he* had given her, and pulled it off. She took a step toward him and thrust her hand out. "Fine. If I mean nothing to you, then you will want this back."

Dean stared down at the glinting ring reflecting the moonlight in her open palm. Then, he reached out and covered her hand. She thought he was going to take the ring and be done with her for good, but he closed her hand around the ring and shook his head.

"Keep it," he said hollowly.

She was about to argue when a commotion drew her away from Dean. The sailors all snapped to attention, and Cyrene's heart stuttered. She was about to come face-to-face with Edric for the first time in nine months. The last time she had seen him, she had agreed to come to his bedchambers … and then she had abandoned Byern to go to Eleysia and discover her magic. She'd never even gotten to say good-bye.

She steeled herself for what was about to happen and felt Dean stiffen next to her.

The figure appeared at the top of the stairs, clothed in all black from head to toe. A deep velvet cloak billowed behind him with a cowl that rose up and obscured his face from view. He looked impenetrable and foreboding. The darkness actually seemed to lick at the sleeves of his black tunic, as if the night were accepting him as its own.

Cyrene wasn't breathing by the time he came into full view and tugged back the cowl to reveal his all-too gorgeous face, that mussed dark hair, and the piercing blue-gray eyes.

She gasped. "You!" she cried, her hand going to her mouth.

"Oh, how I've missed you," Crown Prince Kael Dremylon said with a sharp, knowing grin.

Four

THE BOAT

Cyrene whirled on Dean. "How could you do this?"

She noticed he didn't look exactly comfortable. And how could he? Kael Dremylon was their mortal enemy. And Dean was handing her over to Kael, despite all the reasons not to. Foremost being that Kael had some kind of powerful dark magic and had tried to *kill* Dean the last time they were within a few feet of each other.

"Cyrene," Dean whispered.

"Enough of that," Kael said with a truly dangerous smile. He fixed his eyes on Dean. "I have what I came for, and *you* have what you came for. It's best that you leave."

"You'd better hold to your word," Dean said.

"Of course he's not going to hold to his word!" Cyrene shrieked. "Do you know who you're dealing with? Do you know what you're doing?"

"I promised to let you leave," Kael said easily to Cyrene. "And I held to that until it seemed time to bring you home."

Cyrene sneered at him. "Bring me home? Like a prize?"

The last words Kael had said to her slithered into her conscious, unbidden.

"You'll remember and know…it's all your fault. Everything that happens. You'll remember, and you'll come back to me."

She shook her head, not wanting to think about what that meant. She remembered all-too clearly that night on the docks when he had compelled her mind. The black tendrils that had seemed to pull her toward him, the fogginess that had clouded her senses when he touched her, and the desperate need he'd induced.

Black magic.

Dark magic.

Blood magic.

It was the only thing that made sense.

Yet, as much as it terrified her, the spark was still strong between them. And the longer she stood there, the more she felt her defenses weakening.

"Ah, but you decide if you are a prize to be won. Or has that changed?" Kael asked. His eyes went to the ring she was still clutching in her hand.

She wanted to hide it behind her back, but she wouldn't give him the satisfaction. She slid it back into place. If it infuriated Kael, then all the better. It didn't mean anything. She and Dean were over. They had been over as soon as he ordered her to be knocked out.

Dean ground his teeth. "Just remember our deal. I have the terms in writing. Stick to them."

Kael stuck out his hand. Dean looked down on it with apprehension before taking it in his own. Kael's smile grew, and a shiver ran down Cyrene's back.

"You have my word," Kael said.

Dean wrenched back his hand, and it looked like it took considerable force not to shake it. "For all that's worth."

His eyes cut to Cyrene's, and he opened his mouth, as if he was going to say something, but she turned her back on him. Betrayal was the name of the game. She didn't have to sit back and listen to what he had to say.

"Cyrene, I…" Dean said softly. Boot steps sounded against the wood planks, and she thought that was all, but then he said loud enough for her to hear, "I am sorry."

She closed her eyes against the sting. He was sorry. *He was sorry? Creator. What good did that do me?* She was still trapped aboard a Byern vessel with Kael Dremylon, bound to return to a place she had sworn off.

Sorry wasn't enough. It wasn't even close to enough.

She waited until she heard the signs of him and Darmian descending down the rope ladder and into their little boat before facing the facts. She was heading home with Kael Dremylon as her escort. She could see no plausible way to escape it.

Finally, Cyrene dragged her eyes up to Kael's. The blue-gray orbs were dancing brightly in the moonlight. He seemed amused. But, as much as her magic had changed her in the time they were apart, it was clear he had changed as well. He might be her sarcastic, flirtatious prince, but there was a darkness around him now. And with the increase in his powers came the stronger call to hers.

"I assume you've had a trying time. Should I show you to your rooms?"

Kael asked.

"I learned my lesson about allowing you to escort me to my rooms a long time ago," she said, reminding them both of the time he had tried to take advantage of her on the night of her Presenting ball.

Kael bristled at her tone and stepped toward her. She stilled and took a quick breath, as his nearness made her want to edge toward him.

"We must be on our way." His eyes crawled over her body. "And you require some freshening up."

Cyrene stood ramrod straight and glared at him. Of course she looked like a wreck. Hurricanes and dungeons had that tendency. She humphed and then strode past him, in the direction from where he had originally come. Kael chuckled softly and then followed behind her. As soon as her feet hit the stairs to go below decks, the ship came to life above her. It was as if every sailor had been waiting for their cue to begin.

The one problem was that the ship was as massive on the inside as it looked on the outside. The first set of stairs led her on a long corridor, and there seemed to be many more sets of stairs to bunks and stores and ammunition and more below. She would never find her room at this rate. And she desperately needed somewhere to be alone with her thoughts.

"Are you going to allow me to help, or are you just going to walk around, dressed like that, with a ship full of military-trained sailors ogling you?" Kael asked from directly behind her.

She could sense him even before she had heard his voice. If she backed up a step, she could press herself against him and feel that electric pull take over.

Kael took that step for her, and suddenly, his solid chest was against her back. His hand fell to her waist. He seemed to breathe her in. And all she could do was stand there and shiver. Because just that one touch jolted her system, yet, at the same time, it made her completely forget where her mind had been spinning toward. And forgetting felt so nice. So wonderfully nice.

"Well?" he breathed.

"My rooms," she said softly.

He turned her around to face him and took her hand in his own. "Ah, yes. Now, this is much better."

Her eyes were hazy as she stared up into his beautiful face. Deadly but beautiful. "What is?"

"I do love how feisty you are, Cyrene," he said, pressing a lock of matted hair back from her face. "But I never thought how much I would adore you…pliant."

A voice in her head told her to say, *Well, don't get used to it,* but she didn't. She didn't say anything. Her mind succumbed easily to nothingness.

She just followed Kael down the long hall and to the end of the row. He opened a door for her, and she walked easily inside.

The room was as immaculate as anywhere she had ever stayed while traveling with Edric. Lush and overdone, as was the Byern style. She had gotten used to the simplicity of Eleysian clothing and decorations…the simplicity of it all.

She tried to force the thoughts aside. Thinking of Eleysia was dangerous territory.

And the pain of it all snapped her out of whatever numbness she had been feeling.

She whirled to face him. *What had Kael done to me?*

"Is this what you want?" she asked. "Pliant? You never seemed the type."

"I'd prefer to have you naked on my bed."

Cyrene rolled her eyes. "Well, nothing has changed then."

He bristled. "Hasn't it?"

His magic filled the room, practically choking her. She could feel it all around her, touching her skin, pushing through her hair, and obstructing her vision. It cleared away almost instantly.

"Oh, yes, you have all this new dark magic now," she said. Cold, emotionless.

She stalked toward him but found herself held in place. She had thought he had eliminated all of his magic, but she was encased in something. She couldn't move a muscle. She couldn't feel a thing. Her magic was on the fritz, but still, she pushed at the bounds of whatever held her. *How is he even capable of this?*

"Let me go," she commanded through gritted teeth.

His fingers caressed her cheek. "Magic is neither good nor bad, dark nor light, Cyrene," he said with that same sly grin she had grown accustomed to. "It is how you use it that defines you. Not how it uses you."

"I'll take that into consideration," she said. Her eyes were on fire. "After you let me go."

He twirled his wrist, and all restraints were eliminated. She stumbled forward into him, and he easily caught her.

"It could have been fun, you know."

"Ugh!" she groaned. "Get off of me. That is *never* happening."

She glared up at him with all the pent-up anger from her journey to Eleysia at her fingertips. She had been hunted by Indres, kidnapped by Leifs, had to rescue her friends from soldiers, escaped the Aurum court on Dean's vessel, found Matilde and Vera and finally having someone to train her with her magic. Only to have that all ripped away when Maelia had murdered the king and queen. To have Dean ripped away.

She winced and stepped away from Kael. She couldn't—no, she *wouldn't* think about Dean. Creator only knew what dark tunnel that would lead her to.

Kael seemed surprised that she'd backed down, but truthfully, she was exhausted. There was no escape from this place and certainly not in her condition. She was terrified to return home to Byern, but it made her wonder how Kael got away with it…with magic. Byern was sworn to eliminate all magic. There hadn't been any in two thousand years after Viktor Dremylon killed the love of his life, Domina Serafina. The Doma had fallen, and magic had been wiped out.

How had Kael kept it a secret?

"I see that you need to rest. We have a long journey ahead of us, Cyrene," he said with a small mock bow. "Perhaps I can answer all of those questions swirling in your eyes at another time."

She reached for the wall that kept intruders out of her mind and found she didn't have the strength for it. *Creator!*

She didn't know if Kael was able to enter her thoughts, but the way he had so easily held her before without her even feeling it worried her.

He laughed, as if he could indeed read her thoughts and found what she was considering amusing. "Don't worry. I have always been able to read your thoughts."

"Stay out of my head," she snapped.

"I never have to get in your head. If someone knows you well enough, Cyrene, as well as I do, they can see your thoughts clearly for themselves."

He grasped her hand. She tried to yank it back, but he wouldn't let her. She felt all the passion and desire and aching for him rush through her body, like she had that day on the docks. That zap and electricity that generated between them at a mere touch. The feeling she had gotten just from being near the ship he was on. It pulsed through her like a living, breathing dragon desperate to fly free.

"Stop using your magic on me," she spat.

He grinned then, slow and purposeful. "So, you do feel it then?"

Her head felt heavy, and she realized she was leaning toward him. "Feel what?"

"Good," he said, abruptly breaking the contact.

He turned and strode to the door, leaving her utterly clueless and a bit light-headed.

"What did you do to me?"

Kael had his hand on the door. "I will have a bath drawn for you."

And, with that, he left the room.

She picked up the nearest object—a small, circular candleholder—and flung it at the door. It shattered into a thousand pieces on the floor. Cyrene stared down at the broken shards of glass scattered across the floorboards. Broken and hopeless and never able to be put back together.

That was how she felt. She was the fragments of glass. Her fury was there, only to mask her grief, but reaching down and touching the pain within her that mourned the loss of her best friend—no. She would never go there. She would build a brick wall with a moat around that place and raise the drawbridge. She couldn't fall apart now.

Her very life depended on it.

Kael Dremylon saw that she was cracked. He could force her to do whatever he wanted to. And she needed to figure out how he was capable of it. Her magic was bleeding, but it was still there. When she had started the hurricane after making love to Dean and then used all her magic to stop it right after, against all odds, she hadn't burned out.

Anyone else would have.

Her magic might be in protest, but it was still there.

She would figure out a way to stop this.

Five

THE TUB

Cyrene didn't know how many soldiers it took to draw and heat a bath for her, but by the time it was finished, she really didn't care. A ship might not be the best place to take a long, luxurious bath, and she certainly wouldn't get to fully relax until she was back in Byern. As long as they didn't prosecute her for witchcraft. But this would do.

It was a large white claw-foot bathtub with the fresh scent of roses wafting from its depths. With all the grime and salt caked into her skin, she wasn't sure if she would ever feel clean again. But she would give it a good try.

She hastily stripped out of the ragged dress that she had been wearing and piled it onto a stool. Then, she dipped her toes into the steaming water to check the temperature before dropping her whole body into it. She sighed with pleasure. The first pleasure she'd had since that fateful day that changed everything. Ruined everything.

Her heart constricted, and she forced her eyes shut. Thinking about it all would only overwhelm her. Wondering why would only suffocate her.

Perhaps she would never know true luxury and pleasure again. It would always be marred by an open wound that would never heal. A crack in the facade that she could never patch.

With force, she grabbed the soap and scrubbed her body clean. Removing every last reminder of that dreadful day, every last recollection of what her body had endured, and every single last memory that would come back to crush her. When she was finished, her skin was as pink as a newborn baby.

She felt like a new woman.

A different woman.

She had walked into the Nit Decus castle in Byern almost a year ago with no other desire in her heart than to become an Affiliate and, ultimately, the Consort. Her goals had changed exponentially since then. Between the discovery of her magic and all the broken hearts, she felt like she had aged a decade rather than a single year.

With a sigh, she closed her eyes and sank back into the tub until her hair was completely covered. She sat there until the water turned lukewarm, verging on flat-out cold. Her teeth were chattering, and she wished she had her magic. She certainly hadn't mastered fire yet. Water was the only element she had any control over. She hesitantly reached for the powers just to see if they were there. The water heaved over the side of the tub and soaked the flooring.

She cursed noisily and sat up. She was never great at using magic without Avoca, but with her magic on the fritz, even attempting something so small, she messed up. All she wanted was for the water to heat up.

As soon as she had the thought, the surface of the water actually *froze* under her fingertips. On instinct, she screamed and jumped up out of the tub. Little crystalized pieces of ice fell off her bare shoulders and fell to the floor just as the door flew inward.

"Are you all right?" Kael asked at once. His eyes were wide, and his sword was out.

And Cyrene stood there, stark naked.

His sword arm dropped, and he stared. She was sure that this was the last thing he had expected.

She scrambled for a towel on the bench and wrapped it around her body. "What are you doing in here?"

"You screamed," Kael said. His eyes were still roaming her body, as if the vision of her naked figure would be forever branded on his retinas.

"Yes, because the water was cold! Not because I needed help."

"How was I to know the difference between your screams?"

"Well, you claim to know me! Figure out my screams."

His smile was wicked. "I'd like to."

She shook her head and huddled deeper into the towel. She was shaking slightly from the chill of it all. The cold had gone straight to her bones.

"Why must it always come back to this?" she asked in frustration. If she was going to have to be here with him for who knew how long before she got back to Byern, she wanted to get this sexually charged conversation out of the way.

"Because you're a beautiful woman who is attracted to me."

"I am not," she spat furiously.

Okay. Kind of a lie. Kael Dremylon was…gorgeous. Even with his more sinister, dark undertones, he was still shockingly attractive. But that didn't mean she wanted to be with him.

"Cyrene, you have been lying to yourself from the day you met me."

"The day I met you, you tried to force yourself upon me."

"Your version of history is amusing," he said.

"My *version?*"

"Indeed."

"What is that supposed to mean?"

Kael stared at her with a cocked eyebrow and a silent smirk. He made her feel as if she were somehow missing an inside joke in all of this. Then, he placed his hand on the tub. The ice thawed and melted, and suddenly, steam was billowing out of the tub once more.

"Let me know if there's anything else I can do for you."

Her eyes narrowed at the insinuation, even as her cheeks heated. Though she wanted to blame it on the steam, she knew it was because there was an inexplicable electricity between them.

Then, he disappeared back through the door from where he'd come.

There wasn't anything in the small bathroom to fling at his exposed back as he exited other than the towel wrapped hastily around her body. When he closed the door, she dropped it and immediately hopped back into the tub. She could enjoy the heat he had given her, even as she puzzled over what he had said and how he had heated the tub.

What version of history had he been referring to? She remembered perfectly well what had happened that night. She would make him tell her. Though… she didn't know how to do that at this point.

She hated to admit it, but Kael Dremylon had the upper hand.

It made her grit her teeth in frustration. No matter what her traitorous body felt in his presence, he was her enemy. After what had happened on the docks, how could she think otherwise? Not to mention, she knew all-too well what the cost of the magic he possessed was.

She shivered again, as if the water had iced over.

When she had been shipwrecked on the beach with Dean, another vision of Serafina had come to her. She had watched as Viktor Dremylon murdered his firstborn daughter and used a spell to gain dark blood magic. Then, he had bound himself to Serafina for all of eternity.

Cyrene's head spun as it all came back to her so quickly. *What kind of powers did it give someone to take magic from murder? How did it corrupt them? And was that how Kael had achieved his own powers?*

She might be relishing in his warm bath, but that didn't mean this was all okay. It was far from okay. Because, if what she had seen from her vision was correct, then Kael had murdered someone.

The thought chilled her completely, and she gave up on enjoying the rest of her bath. She hurried back out and wrapped herself in a fluffy towel. She found a comb resting on the counter and dragged it through her knotted hair. It took forever before it was in one long mass down her back. She pulled it all to one side and then plaited it simply. In dismay, her eyes turned to the dress she'd been wearing. She didn't have any other clothes.

With a huff, she left the bathing chamber and entered the thankfully empty living quarters. She rummaged through a wardrobe and found that Kael had actually accounted for her stay. She'd thought he'd have relished in the fact that she'd have had to be naked around him all the time.

Pulling a shift over her head, she climbed into the enormous bed stuffed full of the softest goose down. She tried to bring up some kind of shield to keep Kael out, but it was no hope. She didn't think she could hold a shield like that in her sleep even if she knew how to conjure it. And beyond that…Kael had more power than her at the present moment. If she put up resistance, he could probably slice through it like butter.

She was too tired to figure out an alternative option. As soon as her head sank back into the pillow, she promptly fell asleep.

Time was a wily beast.

It stole. It destroyed. It healed.

Constant and immovable.

And each day brought a new morning.

Time was dependable. And only time could move the world forward.

Time had slipped away from Cyrene. It was a thief in the night, scrubbing away the hours and leaving her disoriented.

At first, all she could feel was the soft bed beneath her body. For a moment, she thought of Dean. Lying against his chest, waking in the morning with his arms wrapped tightly around her, knowing that another night had passed. Another night closer to their wedding.

Then, another second ticked by, and that memory stabbed her in the chest. There would never be another morning like that. There would never be another dawn with Dean. There would never be another moment in Eleysia. For she was bound to Byern. And always would be.

Her eyes flew open, and she scrambled across the bed in horror. Her hand touched her mouth…and Kael Dremylon's eyes slowly opened with a lazy smile on his pretty face.

"Morning," he said, biting back a yawn.

"What in the Creator's name are you doing in *my* bed?" she all but shrieked.

"Sleeping."

"How dare you come into my quarters and share my bed with me! Do you think I have no honor? Do you think I have forgotten what you tried to do to me?"

She had woken up curled around Kael! Her leg wrapped around his. Her arm flung across his bare chest. His arms cradling her, as if he even knew what comfort was.

Now, he was staring at her as if she had gone completely insane. *How could he possibly think this was okay?*

"Do you know where we are?" Kael asked.

He sat up and leaned on one elbow. The sheet slipped off his body, revealing every rippling muscle. She snapped her gaze back up to his face.

"I don't see how that matters."

"We are on a Byern warship. This is the only room on the ship with quarters this nice. Otherwise, you can sleep below decks with the crew. Is that what you want?"

She shook her head. "Surely, there must be somewhere else. I can't be expected to sleep here. What will everyone think?"

He laughed a bitter, rough laugh. "Now, you are concerned about this?"

"If I am to be carted back to Byern, then I should have the luxuries of an Affiliate."

He held his hand out. "And you are afforded those luxuries."

Cyrene opened her mouth to argue, but he cut her off.

"This is a war vessel, not a pleasure ship. We are not on procession, like the last time you had the full attention of Byern royalty in your bed," he said viciously. "If you do not sleep with me, in my rooms, then you sleep below decks. With the crew."

Cyrene glowered at him. Of course, he would use every advantage that he had while he had her here. And, even though she had never slept with King Edric, it still prickled her to think that everyone, including Kael, believed that she had. But, if it irritated him to consider it, then she wouldn't contradict him.

"So, you expect me to sleep next to you the entire time I am trapped here?"

"Yes," he said simply. "Now, if you want to roll back over and lie on me again, I won't object."

She ground her teeth and turned away from him. She hated that she had done that. She hated that she couldn't control her body in her sleep. And, right now, she really hated Kael for making her do this.

Of course, she couldn't sleep below decks with the crew. She didn't have her magic to defend herself, and she didn't have any delusions that someone wouldn't take advantage of the fact that a pretty girl was all alone. Her fury built like a fire being stoked.

"What do you want from me?" she asked softly, staring down at her hands clasped together. It was the first time in a long time that she felt helpless, and she didn't like it. It made her want to fight harder.

"Why do I have to want something from you?"

"Because you're Kael Dremylon."

"Believe it or not, Cyrene," he said, his voice drawing nearer, "I have always wanted what is best for you."

"You're right. I don't believe it."

His hand went to the tie at the end of her plait. He slowly removed it and then trailed his fingers through the braid until her hair was loose once more. It fanned around her face and down her back. She could feel the way he practically breathed her in. And she had to remain ramrod straight and still the whole time. She didn't trust whatever passed between them when he touched her. And she couldn't trust him.

"You should," he whispered into her ear before disappearing completely.

Six

THE JOURNEY

Cyrene couldn't sleep after that.

No matter that Kael had left her all alone again. The thought that he could come back into his rooms at any moment set her on edge. She needed to figure out what he really wanted from her. And she wasn't set to believe him when he'd said he was looking out for her best interests.

Kael Dremylon looked out for one person and one person alone.

Himself.

A servant entered the room just then. A slight woman, not much older than Cyrene. She curtsied to her and placed a breakfast tray on the table across the room.

"I would like to take my breakfast on the deck," Cyrene said at once.

"I'm sorry, Affiliate," the servant said. "However, you have been confined to your rooms for the duration of your stay."

Cyrene gritted her teeth. "Confined."

The servant curtsied again in acquiescence and then left the chamber. When Cyrene peered through the door, she saw she had two armed guards outside. *Are they keeping me in or others out?* Either way, she had just traded one prison for another.

No matter how Kael dressed it up with a big, comfortable bed, a long, hot bath, and more Byern luxury than was ever necessary, she had moved into another dungeon. No drugs this time at least. Unless she counted Kael. And that was a real possibility.

She would have to figure out a way around it, but in the meantime, she was starved. Her stomach growled as she looked at the enormous breakfast that had been brought in. She didn't remember the last time she had eaten. She had been so tired last night, and sleep had been more important.

Now, she dug into the food, as if she hadn't eaten in weeks, which wasn't far off. She wasn't even ashamed to see the empty tray when the servant came back to collect it later. Cyrene knew the value of food. She had spent enough time traveling without much and having to steal to survive to take advantage when she could.

After she'd eaten, she took her time exploring every nook and cranny in Kael's rooms for clues. But, by the time he returned for lunch, she had found absolutely nothing of value. This might be where he slept, but he didn't work here. He had made sure all of his documents were gone, and there wasn't a weapon in sight. She could improvise if necessary, but trying to cooperate to get information seemed to make more sense.

"I see you've decided to grace me with your presence," Cyrene said, striding over to Kael after he entered the rooms for dinner. She sank into a seat at the table. The food was already making her mouth water.

His eyes traveled the bright red dress she had found in the wardrobe. He'd surely meant it for her. She was the only one in court who flaunted this color. She would oblige.

"Yes, well, I had matters to attend to."

"And you decided to leave me here in a guarded room?"

"For your own safety, of course."

Cyrene picked up a strawberry from the table. It was a real delicacy at the end of its season in Byern. Though still plenty in Eleysia, where it was more temperate.

She bit into it and contemplated her words before diving straight in. "Am I to be a prisoner?"

"No."

"Then, why have you traded my prison cell in Eleysia for one on your boat?" *Screw cooperating.*

Kael strode toward her. His figure towered over her, but she refused to get riled up. Still, she could feel their connection. Like a low buzz in her ear, telling her to just give in, to just say yes, to forget this argument. She closed her eyes and inhaled sharply. It was almost too much.

He lifted her chin and forced her to look up at him. Her body shivered at the touch.

"There are no bars. There are no barriers. The guards are there so that I can protect you. Court has changed since you left Byern, Cyrene. Not everyone agrees that you coming back is a good thing. If you thought it was dangerous before, you have no idea what you're walking into."

Cyrene swallowed and scooted back in her chair to avoid him. "Don't do that anymore."

"What?"

"Touch me."

He laughed and sank into the seat next to her. "I won't promise you that, Cyrene." He winked at her. "You might ask me to someday."

"Tell me about court," she said, ignoring his comment.

"Eat," he insisted instead. He plucked a piece of chicken from the plate and started eating himself.

She pursed her lips and waited for him to say more. "Tell me."

"You'll see soon enough."

"How can I be prepared?"

"You have me."

"Kael." His eyes went to her lips, and she knew he liked the way she had said his name. "Please."

"We are preparing for war, Cyrene," he told her finally.

"War?" she whispered. "But it's been…three hundred years since we've gone to war."

"Indeed. But my brother"—Kael gritted his teeth at the mention of King Edric, and he was not someone that Cyrene wanted to think about either—"believes that we should go to war with Eleysia. I have made plans to ensure that does not happen."

"Plans," she said stiffly. *With Dean.*

"Yes. And I'm bringing the fleet and a pretty little prize home," he said with an arched eyebrow as he popped a strawberry in his mouth. "Eat, Cyrene. You need to regain your strength. We need to make an impression when we return. We wouldn't want them to think anything is wrong, now would we?"

"Is that a threat?" she demanded.

"You and I both know that magic is forbidden in Byern," he said so softly, as if he didn't want the wind to catch the words.

"How did you know?" she finally asked the question that had been killing her this whole time.

That day on the docks, he had pulled her magic up to the surface from within her depths, as if he had known exactly where to look for it.

"I have always known." He picked up another piece of chicken and ate it. Then, he grabbed a roll and stood. "I have been saving you from the start, Cyrene. If it were not for me, you would have died the day of your Presenting."

Then, he left her seated at the table to contemplate how it could be possible.

She rushed toward him right before the door closed. "Please, let me out of here!" she yelled, banging on the closed door.

But it was no use. She was left here with nothing but her thoughts and a half-eaten meal.

And she spent ten *long* days that way.

Meals with Kael were half-chore and half-torture. She badgered him every way she could think to get him to tell her about court, what he had meant about keeping her safe, and more about his magic, but he wouldn't budge. And, sometimes, when he was so near her, her brain would shut off entirely, and she'd actually enjoy a meal with him in peace. The worst times were when her body was filled with electricity, and he was the power source.

Yet he was her only source of communication and interaction. On some level, she looked forward to when he would show up each afternoon for lunch and each night for dinner. She had wanted to resist the sleeping arrangements, but after constructing a pillow barrier between them, she'd felt confident enough that she wasn't going to roll back over toward him and trigger another breakdown. She still didn't like that they were going to walk into a court that she didn't recognize with her only known ally being…Kael Dremylon.

She knew he wanted it that way.

She remained hesitant. She wouldn't fall into his trap. Not when he was using his magic on her, and she was still defenseless.

The sustenance and rest had definitely helped her. She could feel her magic again. But it felt…wrong. Like darkness had clouded her powers, and touching them only made her control slip.

She didn't know if Kael had done something to her powers. That seemed the most logical explanation. They weren't suppressed…just coated in an inky, dark substance that made her feel like she was trudging through sludge.

Any other explanation was too painful to consider. Like thinking about Maelia or Dean or her friends. That was more like taking a fire poker to her bare skin. She couldn't go near it. She wouldn't go near it.

She shook her head and backed away from the well of magic at her core. The door to her chambers opened. *Creator, when did I start to think of them as my chambers?*

Cyrene had been meditating all morning in the center of the bed, trying to figure out the problem but to no avail. Now, she had a cold sweat, and she felt disoriented.

"Are you unwell?" Kael asked.

She didn't trust her voice in that moment.

"Cyrene?"

He strode to the bed and reached for her arm as she tried to slide to the edge and stand. Power jumped between them as he helped her to her feet. She actually leaned on him as her body steadied.

"I'm fine." She pulled away from him and repeated, "I'm fine."

"I thought to give you some fresh air today, but if you're ill, I won't chance it."

Cyrene's gaze darted to his face, and her mouth opened in shock. "You'll let me go above?"

He smiled. "If I'd known I'd get this response, I might have allowed it sooner."

"No, you wouldn't have."

"No, I wouldn't have," he agreed. "But I have something to show you."

Cyrene immediately straightened herself. All sense of vulnerability was obliterated from her mind. She might not be able to reach her magic, but she was still formidable in her own right. She had always been…long before she discovered her true potential. If she was to witness something Kael wanted her to see, then she would do it like an Affiliate of the realm.

She slid her Affiliate guise back on, like a second skin. "I'm ready."

Kael held his arm out to her, and with a deep breath, she placed her hand at the crook of his elbow. If she tried hard, she almost couldn't feel the point of contact or the rush that hit her. *Why in the Creator's name was it so much more powerful than it had been since I left?* Another answer Kael would not give her…or he did not know.

She eagerly followed him back up to the top of the deck. The taste of the salt on the air and the smell of the sea nearly brought her to tears. Living all those months in Eleysia and waking to this every morning had ingrained the ocean into her body. Water called to her even though she could not harness it.

If she were like Avoca, then she would have been able to replenish her magic from the elements around her. But Leif magic was not like Doma magic. Doma powers were internal. You burned from within. You healed from within. All it would take was time.

"What did you want to show me?" Cyrene whispered.

Kael slowly turned her around to face the other direction. Her hand flew to her mouth, and there, like a bird's song, she could hear her home calling to her.

"Enjoy," Kael said into her ear. He led her to the railing and spoke to his guards, "Do not leave her side." His hand touched hers. "I will be back at lunch. Do not do anything foolish."

She nodded. She didn't have a plan to do anything foolish. All she could do was stare at the city of Albion, which stood as a bastion on the coast. The White City glimmered from the distance. Krisana castle was the tallest among them, all made of whitewashed seashells.

She theorized now, in a way she never would have been able to before, that Krisana had been made by Doma. Magic had built the palace. And it could never be duplicated again. For that ability had been lost when her people were slaughtered two thousand years ago.

The happy memory of seeing her home for the first time in so long disintegrated. She was returning to a country that would kill her. She was returning to a home that had betrayed her bloodline. She was returning to a place that was anathema to her very existence.

Byern might call to her, but it was a lie.

And she would not forget it again.

Her mind was elsewhere when she heard the twang of a sword being removed from its sheath. Cyrene gasped as she realized that it had come from her own guard, and her gut told her to run. She ducked at the last second and heard a sword bang into the railing where her body had just been.

Cyrene rolled out of the way just as he righted his sword. She reached for her magic but had nothing. She was as helpless as she had ever been. And she was staring up a cold, hard killer. She couldn't possibly die like this.

She scrambled backward to get away from the guard.

"You will pay for your crimes!" the guard bellowed as he swiped his sword down toward her.

Cyrene flung herself away from him, but his blade caught her arm, slicing open her biceps. She screamed as the pain of the injury lanced through her. She fell face-first onto the wooden deck. Her arm hung uselessly next to her. She rolled over, determined to face her attacker if this was the end of it all.

He brought the sword down to her throat, and she breathed heavily as she glared at him.

"Do it, you coward," she spat. "You attack a defenseless woman with no battle training. You are spineless and worthless. You will certainly deserve your execution."

"Pray to your Creator," the man said. "Though she will not answer a witch's prayer."

Cyrene refused to close her eyes and give him the satisfaction of seeing her afraid. She was deaf and blind to everything else going on around her. All she saw was this one man. Her own executioner.

Then, a sword slammed straight through his chest from behind. Cyrene's face was splattered with the dying man's blood. Her mouth gaped open in shock. She couldn't even process what was happening. He was dead. She was alive. That was all that mattered.

Then, the sword was wrenched out of the man, and Kael shoved the guard to the side. She stared up at her savior, unable to fathom this turn of events. He looked horrified and terrified. Like the thought of losing her was unbearable.

Kael's eyes roamed her face for confirmation that she was okay. She nodded. Then, he landed at her side. He tilted her chin to inspect her throat and then down to inspect her arm. His hands were measured and calculated, yet she could see he was frantic beneath it all.

"You're injured," he said.

"I'm fine."

"We need to stop the bleeding."

Cyrene reached out with her other hand and gently placed it on his arm. "I heal fast."

Kael ignored her and hefted her into his arms, as if she weighed nothing. "Get rid of the body, and clean up the deck. If anyone has information, step forward at once. Let it be known that an act against Affiliate Cyrene is an act against the Dremylon royal family," he said to the astonished crew. "If there are other traitors in our midst, I will root them out. There will be no pardons for treason."

Cyrene didn't even argue with him when he carried her below decks and treated her wounds himself. Her brain was working overtime to try to process what had happened.

All she really knew for sure were two things—someone wanted her dead, and Kael Dremylon had saved her life.

Seven

THE MISTAKE
—AVOCA—

"I felt something," Avoca gasped.

She touched her chest, as if she couldn't believe what had just hit her. A small tug at her core that could only mean one thing.

"Cyrene?" Matilde asked.

Vera jumped to her feet. "You felt her?"

Avoca nodded. Relief flooded her bones. "I know where she is. We should leave at once."

Matilde and Vera didn't delay. Matilde threw on a midnight-black cloak and handed Vera a matching one. Vera tucked it under her arm and pocketed the golden coin they had been observing for the last couple of weeks but to no avail. They had filched it out of Maelia's things before the Eleysian guards had thrown out all of her possessions. Along with the mysterious coin, they had recovered the priceless Doma magic book that Cyrene had acquired. Nothing else seemed of any value. Either Maelia had truly been working independent of anyone else or she'd destroyed all correspondence because they were no closer to figuring out why she wanted to kill the Eleysian king and queen.

And, up until this moment, they'd had no idea where Cyrene had been kept prisoner. They had searched the dungeons with no luck, and any magical contact between Avoca and Cyrene had been like throwing herself up against a brick wall. Even that light tug had felt more like being dragged through mud. The three of them knew it meant something was wrong, and Avoca hated not having answers.

They left Matilde and Vera's home behind in the Swamp District and took a gondola out through the flooded lands. Vera flicked her hand and made them hurry along the empty waterways. Luckily, it was late, and no one would ask questions as to why the boat was gliding along without anyone pushing it. Avoca cared very little for human concerns at the moment.

She needed to find Cyrene. She was duty-bound to her. To her greatest shame, Cyrene had saved her life. When Avoca had offered her life to Cyrene to eliminate her humiliation for her fallen Six Team, Cyrene had refused. As payment for her life debt, they had been bound. Their magic would be tied together until the debt was repaid, or one of them perished.

Then, Cyrene had disappeared. Avoca had been with Matilde and Vera, working their magic together out of the capital city. Weather magic was unpredictable. Only Cyrene had any real affinity for it, and she was the first person in more than two thousand years who was capable of it. They could only manage the threads she had created for the hurricane and attempt to handle them in her absence. They had thought it was a brilliant plan to keep the Byern ships from sailing into Eleysian territory to collect Cyrene.

Only it had all backfired. Something had happened with Cyrene. Her magic had exploded, and the hurricane had hit with a ferocity that they had no chance of escaping or stopping. It'd destroyed a quarter of the capital city in one blow before dissipating nearly as fast as it had come. A burst of magic that had burned Avoca to her core from the impact. She hadn't been able to touch her magic, let alone the bond, for a week.

"Here," Avoca said. She stood from the seat of the gondola and swayed easily with the boat. "She was here. She went that way."

They followed Avoca's trail until they hit the open sea, and then Avoca sank back down with her mouth hanging open.

"Is that…"

"Yes," Vera whispered.

"By the gods," Matilde said.

More than a dozen Byern warships were poised to attack. They were floating like ducks in a row—not close enough to get through the rocky barrier between the ocean and the city, but far too close for comfort.

"And she's headed that way still?" Vera asked.

Avoca nodded her head once.

"Then, we wait," Matilde said. "For if she is headed that way…she is not alone."

Every muscle in Avoca's body told her to go after Cyrene. To climb onto that boat, use her ice-white Leif blade, and kill anyone who stood in her way. But logic dictated that she could not take on an entire army alone. A wicked grin split her face at the thought of it though. She would give them a fight.

They waited in the shadows as Cyrene's bond moved farther and farther away. And then, as the ships came to life before their eyes, another smaller boat began to drift back toward them with two men in it.

"There," Vera whispered.

"So disappointing," Matilde responded.

"Indeed."

Avoca sometimes felt like the two-thousand-year-old Doma sisters were speaking their own language in her presence. She knew they had been revered in their time and that they were more knowledgeable than nearly any Leif still alive today, but they were an odd pair. Wonderful but odd.

"What do you mean?" Avoca asked.

"Wait," Vera said.

"See," Matilde followed up.

So, Avoca did as she had been told. When she finally saw what Matilde and Vera must have realized all along, she nearly roared in fury. Coming toward them in the little boat were Prince Dean and his man Darmian.

"He didn't," Avoca growled.

"Let's find out," Matilde said.

She flicked her hand, and suddenly, his boat swerved off course, veering straight toward them. Both men looked up in confusion and shock as the boat moved of its own accord. Eleysian people might be more accepting of the idea of magic, but they had no idea what any of them were capable of.

Avoca stood then, holding her blade out to the side. The warrior side of her brain took over, and when they were at a good distance, she vaulted from the boat and into theirs. She landed with feline-like grace. Darmian moved to attack her, but he was big and bulky. He had none of the finesse or grace from years of training in the Leif city of Eldora.

She darted toward him, jabbing her hand into his throat, and then smacked him over the side of the head with the butt of her knife. He staggered back and nearly fell into the water. She gripped the front of his shirt, twisted him around, and then held the knife to his throat.

"Don't," she snarled at Dean.

He had risen, and his hand had gone to his sword. Though he looked more wary than ready to fight. He was an excellent warrior, but even he couldn't truly fight magic. He removed his hand from his sword and raised his hands in surrender. His boat knocked gently against Matilde and Vera's, who were still sitting serenely.

"Ah, Prince Dean," Matilde said. "What a late night for a boat ride."

"Where is she?" Avoca said, ignoring pleasantries.

"You don't need to hurt him. He will leave at my command," Dean informed Avoca. "Just…let him go. We can talk."

"You think it is time now to talk?" Avoca asked. "Where have you been for the last two weeks? And where is Cyrene?"

"I'll answer all of your questions as soon as you let Darmian go. He had nothing to do with this."

"As far as I heard, he turned Maelia in and had her executed," Avoca said. She protected what was her own. She felt shame that she had not been able to protect Cyrene's friend…Avoca's own friend. That they had been stranded and not even known what had happened at the beheading until late that evening.

"She murdered the king and queen," Darmian said. "No matter my affection for her, she was a murderer. She deserved her death."

Avoca slid the blade in tighter on his neck, and warm blood trickled from the spot. "Be careful what you say about my friends."

"Our quarrel is with the prince," Vera said amicably. "Let his man go."

Avoca shoved him forward, and he fell to his knees. "Go, you snake."

Darmian glanced back once at Avoca before speaking to Dean in a low voice and then disappearing. She was furious that she could enact no revenge for Cyrene. Blood deserved blood. Revenge might not bring peace, but sometimes, it did bring satisfaction.

"We let him go," Matilde said. "Now, tell us where Cyrene is before I let Avoca hunt him down and kill him for sport."

Dean's eyes shifted cautiously between the three women. "I let her go."

"Go where?" Vera asked.

"All we saw were Byern war vessels. Letting her go would mean she would have come to us, and frankly, we haven't seen her since she was last with you," Matilde said pointedly.

"I sent her home." He straightened his spine. "I handed her over to Prince Kael Dremylon of Byern in exchange for peace between our countries."

Avoca stared with hard, furious eyes. Maybe gutting him would make her feel better, but it would be less than he deserved.

"You did what?"

"Are you out of your mind?" Matilde demanded.

"Mati, I don't think he's aware of the dire consequences of his actions."

"What consequences?" he asked. "I know that she does not…trust her prince, but surely, it is better for her to be in Byern than Eleysia. She would have been tried for treason and executed here. The only way I could help her was to get her out of the city."

"You never thought to inform us?" Vera asked.

"And I thought you loved her," Avoca said with a laugh.

"I do," he said, rounding on her. "I do love her. Desperately, unequivocally, maddeningly so, considering what she has done to my family."

"You believe she participated in the slaughter of your parents?" Vera asked.

Matilde scoffed. "You can't truly believe that."

"Whether or not she was in on what happened, she'd brought Maelia here. She'd brought an assassin into my court, and my parents are dead because of that. Maelia was one of her closest friends. I did what I had to do to keep her safe," Dean said with deep regret on his face. "My sister would have seen her on trial right away, but I convinced her that she was too dangerous to do so. I bought time for her. I kept her away from harm. I kept her alive, and I believed sending her back to Byern was the only way to make sure she stayed that way."

"Fool!" Avoca sneered.

"You've made a grave mistake," Vera said.

"I did what I thought best."

"Perhaps," Vera conceded. "However, you have put her in mortal danger."

"You have no idea how long we have waited for Cyrene," Matilde said irritably. "She alone can fulfill the prophecy and break the curse on our people. If she dies because of your failure, the weight of the world will fall on your shoulders."

"Prophecy?" Dean asked, bewildered. "I have heard of this, but it is true? And Cyrene is the key?"

"At the very heart of it," Avoca said. "And you just sent her to the very people who would see her dead before letting it come to pass."

"Now, you will need to make it right," Vera said.

"How can I make it right?" Dean asked a bit wistfully.

"We need a way into Byern," Matilde said. "And you will give us one."

Eight

THE LETTER
—AHLVIE—

"I really hate this idea," Orden said again.

He'd said it at least two dozen times since they departed in haste from Eleysia at Cyrene's request. Ahlvie hated that they'd had to leave her behind. Even more that he had left without saying good-bye to Avoca. Without getting to tell her how he truly felt. It was a grave mistake, and walking up to the Byern castle was making it more and more apparent how idiotic it was.

"You hate all my ideas," Ahlvie said instead.

"With good reason."

Ahlvie shrugged and tried to put on the airs he had acquired in his time in this very city. He'd come a long way since he first came to Byern to become a

High Order. At the time, it had felt like a death sentence. But he had adapted. Not that anyone in the High Order knew what he did with his time when he wasn't required to be at court. He preferred it that way.

But, now, they were walking back into the very castle that had tried to convict him of murder. No matter that the deaths were because of a Braj that Cyrene had killed with her powers. He couldn't exactly tell that to anyone without being considered insane.

"Cheer up, old man," he said, trying for jovial. "I'm a High Order in this town."

"They suspect you of kidnapping and had you on trial for murder."

"There is that," he agreed. "But this is just a game, and I can play games."

"You cheat at games."

"Exactly."

Orden blew out a heavy breath. "You're going to get us killed."

Ahlvie clapped him on the back. "We need to buy Cyrene time. You and I both know that she is the key to everything."

"And you seem to be falling right into line," Orden said, staring directly into his eyes.

Ahlvie cut his gaze away from Orden. He didn't like when people looked in his eyes anymore. He never knew exactly what they were going to see. *Would it be me or the beast within?*

"How about we focus on what's coming next rather than a two-thousand-year-old prophecy?"

Orden shrugged, as if it didn't matter either way. But Ahlvie knew it did. The prophecy was everything. It was the reason he even knew Orden. It was the reason they were working together and trusted Cyrene to the ends of the earth. It was the reason they were on a fool's mission.

Luckily, he was a fool.

Ahlvie nodded his head at the gate to the Nit Decus castle. Just being in the city for the short time he had been, he could already tell things had changed since his departure with Cyrene. The weather was arid, and with summer just approaching, it was supposed to be blooming with life. There was a lot he had to learn about being back, but first, he needed to do something stupid.

"Hey, you," he said to the first guard he saw standing at attention.

The man observed his fine clothes, which admittedly he had stolen upon arrival, and narrowed his eyes. "What is your business here?"

"I need an audience with the king."

"You'll be getting no audience with the king unless you were invited to court. The king has made it clear that no one shall enter or leave the court without his permission, or did you not read his decree?"

Orden frowned at him. "Good sir, we have just arrived in the capital and were unaware of the change in protocol. But, if you could let an attendant know that we have news of Affiliate Cyrene, then I am certain we will get the requested audience."

"The king has sent a ship to collect the Affiliate. Your information is worthless," the guard spat at them.

"I'm certain that, if you just…"

"No," the guard said. His hand went to his sword. "Now, move along."

"Sir," Orden continued.

Ahlvie put his hand out and pressed Orden back. "I've got this."

Ahlvie didn't get a chance to see what Orden's face looked like as he stepped forward. He probably would have appreciated it as he slammed his fist into the face of the guard on duty. The man dropped like a sack of potatoes, and another guard was on him nearly at once.

"Arrest this man!" someone else yelled.

But Ahlvie was now engaged with a second guard. He was dancing on the balls of his feet, dodging swings and landing easy jabs on the amateurs who considered themselves soldiers. Then, he took a swift hit to the gut, and he stumbled back against the wall surrounding the castle. Another crack across his jaw, and he hit the ground.

He'd let that one happen at least, but, Creator, did it make his head pound. He rolled and avoided the next hit. Then, he swiped the man's legs out from under him. He landed in a heap on the ground, and Ahlvie vaulted on top of him, pummeling his face.

He was hauled off the now-unconscious soldier as three guards yanked him backward. He kicked and spit and tried to get them off of him.

Orden was standing there with his arms crossed, staring at him with an expression that was half, *Are you done?*, and half, *This is your idea of handling it?*

"You are under arrest for the assault of two Byern guardsmen. You will be moved to a jail cell at once," a man said, coming around to look at Ahlvie's bedraggled face. "Do you have anything to say for yourself?"

"Just one thing," Ahlvie said, looking at him with a mischievous grin.

"Well, spit it out."

"Your man assaulted a High Order of the realm."

The guard bit out a laugh. "And where is your proof?"

Ahlvie spit blood out of his mouth and then nodded to Orden. "Show them."

Orden sighed and shook his head in frustration. "Boy, you're as bad as she is."

He removed a pin that High Order would wear when traveling on official business. Most of their garments were embroidered with the High Order logo—the Dremylon *D* wrapped in flames—but Ahlvie hadn't forgotten this little piece.

"Where did you get that?" the guard demanded.

He reached for it, but Orden pulled it out of range.

"It's his." Orden nodded his head at Ahlvie.

The guard turned a horrified expression on Ahlvie. He scrutinized him up and down, as if he couldn't believe it possible that Ahlvie, of all people, would be a High Order. He was used to that treatment. Even he thought a backwoods kid from the tiny town of Fen, lost in the north Taken Mountains, wasn't much of a High Order. Not that he respected the title or anything.

"Release him at once," the guard demanded.

Ahlvie smirked as the guards stepped away from him, as if his skin had scalded them. He readjusted his stolen clothing and realized the sleeve was torn. Oh well, he preferred his clothing in some state of disarray. He ran a hand back through his dark hair.

"Now," Ahlvie said, taking the pin from Orden and securing it to his chest, "I said, I'd like an audience with the king."

The gates parted at once in front of a sea of mistrustful guardsmen. He was sure that some of them were worried about losing their jobs over this, but that wasn't why he was here. He thought the whole thing was funny.

Orden strode beside him and shook his head. "Couldn't we have just told them you were High Order from the beginning?"

"Sure, but then I wouldn't have gotten to see their faces when they realized the truth."

Orden shook his head. Ahlvie knew that he frustrated him at every turn, but what was life without a little fun?

They were walked in with an armed guard that Ahlvie was sure had more to do with the fight he had just gotten into than any ceremony. He was shocked to see how many *people* were in the castle. Nit Decus was an enormous castle built into the side of a mountain. It could house half the population of the entire capital city if need be. But he had never seen it even remotely close to capacity. By the look of the number of people passing through the entrance hall, it might be getting there now.

The guards at the entrance to the royal audience room saw his royal pin and opened the doors for him. Ahlvie was astounded by the sheer volume of people in the audience chamber. Typically, it was King Edric, Queen Kaliana, Consort Daufina, and perhaps Prince Kael along with some of their favorites. But the room was nearly full.

Orden gave him a grim look before gesturing for him to go first. Ahlvie strode forward, past the eyes full of curiosity and just as many with animosity. He didn't know how this audience was going to go, but he was gambling on a good outcome. And he usually bet well.

He stopped in front of the king's dais where he rested in a gilded throne for all to see. Ahlvie offered him a low bow of deference. "Your Majesty."

Orden did the same. "Majesty."

When Ahlvie straightened, it was the first time he looked into King Edric's face since he had accused him of murdering the Affiliates and High Order of the realm. Only with Cyrene's assistance had he been cleared of those charges, but he knew that he was not in favor at court, nor had he ever been. He had abandoned his post as High Order to leave with Cyrene.

Whatever they believed had happened, that would not go unpunished.

"Arrest them at once," King Edric said, jumping to his feet.

Guards hurried down the aisle toward them and apprehended them. Gasps and murmurs were heard all over the room as everyone tried to find out what was happening. But, even though Ahlvie was being restrained, he didn't back down.

"How dare you show your face here! You will be tried for treason. Take them away," King Edric cried.

"I have a message from Affiliate Cyrene," Ahlvie said calmly and clearly, as if the guards weren't trying to haul him down the aisle and take him to a dungeon.

"Wait," King Edric said. He held up his hand.

He stalked across the dais and down the steps to be level with Ahlvie. His eyes never left Ahlvie's.

"You mention her name in my presence? You and your companion," he said, sliding his gaze to Orden and back, "who stole her from me. You, who kidnapped her and brought her across the continent for a prize. Do you think me a fool?" the king asked. His tone was low and dangerous.

"A fool believes falsehoods when facts stare him in the face," Ahlvie retorted.

King Edric's eyes flickered with all the rage and fury of a man facing down the very people he had wanted to arrest for too long. Now, he had a decision. Ahlvie could see it in his eyes. Hear the message or get his revenge.

After a minute, he nodded his head to his guards to follow and walked back to his study. He gestured for Consort Daufina and some man that Ahlvie had never seen before in a black guard uniform to follow them. For the first time, Ahlvie realized that the queen wasn't even in the room. He wondered why. Kaliana would never relinquish a royal audience.

Ahlvie and Orden were escorted into a study and forced to stand before the king, who took a seat behind a large, ornate desk. Daufina stood at his side. The man in the black uniform came around to stand behind them.

"Tell me your message," King Edric said.

"Cyrene sent me as her messenger. She begs you not to make war with Eleysia and sent you a letter," Ahlvie informed him. Ahlvie held his hand up, so the black-suited guard could see, and then he retrieved the letter from a pouch. He passed it to the guard.

"I should test it for you, Majesty," the man said.

"That's enough, Merrick," King Edric said. He greedily held his hand out for the letter.

Edric split the envelope open and removed the letter. As he did so, a clink sounded against the desk, and everyone's eyes were drawn to the object lying there.

It was a delicate gold pin of Byern, climbing vines in a circle.

It was the symbol of the Affiliate.

Cyrene's Affiliate pin.

That meant only one thing. Cyrene was denouncing her title as an Affiliate and forsaking all of Byern.

Nine

THE DROUGHT

Cyrene might have clung to her ferocity, but deep down, she was dying.

Her heart was a black hole.

Her soul was a black hole.

Even her magic was a black hole.

Standing up and fighting Kael another day had been the only thing keeping her going. And, now, she didn't even have that. He had saved her life. He had protected her. She might hate him for things he had done in the past, but she couldn't seem to hate him now.

That brought her back to reality. And the reality was that she was constantly staring down the abyss.

This was her fault. All of this was her fault.

He had said that, and he was right. Maelia was dead because of her.

Dean had abandoned her because of what she had done. She had scattered her friends and lost them all because of her own hubris. Avoca hadn't even come for her.

Now, she was faced with the possibility of returning home to a place she worried she wouldn't even recognize. A world that wouldn't accept her.

They had docked a half hour ago, and still, Kael had not come for her. Still, there were guards at her door. Still, she was imprisoned.

She hadn't seen the light of day since the attack, except to switch from a warship to a speedier vessel for the ride up the Keylani River to the capital. Then, she'd been shocked to see the river so depleted. Usually, the snow from the Taken Mountains replenished the river every spring, but it was barren on both banks. The Fallen Desert was blowing into Albion, taking over the White City in Cyrene's absence.

She feared what she would see of Byern. She had grown up here, spent every waking minute exploring the city and then the castle. She couldn't imagine what could have happened when she hadn't even been gone a year. And, despite everything that had happened, she couldn't hate her home either.

Just when she was falling back into that black hole of despair, the door to her chambers opened. Kael Dremylon stood in the doorway, resplendent in all black dress attire with gold slashes across his chest and a Byern green cloak. He looked like a model image of the crown prince he was. She had chosen the red dress once more for her appearance in court and knew that they would appear as a matched set if they rode into the castle dressed as they were.

By the gleam in Kael's eyes at the sight of her, she knew that had been his plan all along.

He held his arm out. "After you, Affiliate."

She took a deep breath and then glided toward him. She could do this. She tilted her chin up and acted the part. No matter that she had denounced her title of Affiliate, that she had run from the king himself, that she was technically still betrothed to the prince of Eleysia…

Her hand burned at the ring still sitting heavy on her finger. Kael hadn't asked about it, but his eyes constantly drifted toward it. Just as they did right now.

"Are you going to wear that?" he asked before they exited the chamber.

She glared at him, hating that he was breaking their temporary truce on the subject.

"Okay," he said with a grin. "Touchy subject, I see."

"It isn't," she said.

Kael turned to face her, and she braced herself for that look in his eyes.

"Are you truly going to wear an engagement ring into the Byern castle?" She pursed her lips.

"An engagement ring to an Eleysian royal," he prodded further.

She gritted her teeth and ignored him, turning her face away. She did not want to discuss Dean. She did not want to discuss the ring. She didn't want to think about it. Yet she couldn't take it off.

"Cyrene, consider where you are going and that you will be watched like a hawk. Consider that my brother has been anticipating your return for a long time. Is wearing this really your best idea?"

"What would you have me do?" she snarled.

"I have no qualms with you wearing it," he said easily. "I suspect most people will believe that it belongs to me." He arched an eyebrow in question.

She snapped her head back to face him and glared harder. "You and I both know that you have not proposed to me, Kael."

"Not yet," he conceded with the boyish grin that she had not seen in so long. "But people will talk. Unless you want them to…"

He was fishing. And she let the hook dangle. She would not be caught. Marriage seemed like a far-fetched, foreign concept to her, and she couldn't fathom anyone ever proposing to her again. The first time had been one time too many, considering the circumstances.

However, if she was to play the part, walking in on Kael's arm while wearing an engagement ring was not the part she wanted to play.

"Why are you telling me this?" She knew he had an angle.

"When everyone thinks you are wearing my ring, it will be because I have proposed, and you *are* wearing my ring. I will not share you with anyone, Cyrene."

She knew he truly meant that, but it took every ounce of strength in her not to recoil at the way he had said it. The boyish grin had disappeared, and something deep and possessive had taken over him. A touch of darkness, a hint of madness, brimmed at the surface. She hadn't seen that from him since that night he *rescued* her from Eleysia.

What part of owning me brought him to the brink of insanity? And why did the thought frighten me so?

"We'll see," she finally said with a cool tone.

Deciding then that Kael had a point about the ring, she hurried back to the drawer and removed a long gold chain from a cabinet. She regretfully tugged the ring off her finger, slipped it onto the chain, and clasped it around her neck. Then, she tucked it down her dress and out of sight.

Kael seemed irritated that she hadn't simply gotten rid of the ring entirely, but he covered it immediately. "Good choice."

She sent him a dazzling smile at the praise and let him escort her above deck. The first glimpse of her home was unlike anything she had ever experienced. Until that moment, she hadn't realized how much Byern had been calling her. She knew that she was bound to the country and the Byern throne, but, even if that weren't the case, it would still sing in her veins.

The peaked mountains that grazed the horizon. The Nit Decus castle nestled in its depths, made of the same gray slate stones from the Taken Mountains. The capital city sprawled out toward the fading green hills in the distance. Her parents had a summer home out that way and would surely be taking Elea there for her last trip before her Presenting.

Cyrene's stomach twisted at the thought of Elea's Presenting. With everything else going on, she hadn't considered that her very sister might end up at the castle with her. Her oldest sister, Aralyn, was in Kell as an Ambassador, and her brother, Reeve, was a High Order. It seemed as if the Strohm family had been bred like horses for the highest positions of the land. And, for the first time, she feared that instead of relished in it.

Trying to clear her head, she took a deep breath and then walked off of the ship that had been her prison. A delegation for their arrival was waiting at the end of the dock, which meant that someone must have informed the court that they were on their way back.

Before they reached the end though, her steps began to quicken, and a true smile graced her face. "Creator," she whispered.

Kael's eyes landed on her, and he smiled. "I thought you would like to see them."

And then she couldn't hold back. She ignored all decorum and outpaced the crown prince, dashing to her family standing on the end of the deck. Her mother, Herlana, was bedecked in a soft pink dress and was glowing from head to toe. Her father, Hamidon, looked ever the part of an upstanding Byern lord. Having been part of the High Order, he now spent much of his time controlling the provinces surrounding the capital. Reeve stood resplendent in black High Order garb. His dark hair was pushed back, and his eyes shone with unshed tears at seeing her alive.

But it was Elea who had changed the most in the time Cyrene was away. In nearly a year since Cyrene had become an Affiliate, Elea had grown from a gangly teen into a gorgeous woman. She was taller than Cyrene now. Her dark hair was a mirror image of Cyrene's own—glossy and full. Her plum-purple dress was a good imitation of the style Cyrene herself had debuted at her first Affiliate ball. And she looked ravishing.

And it was in Elea's arms where Cyrene fell into first. "Oh Creator, Elle, I have missed you so much!"

"Cyrene, it's so good to see you," Elea said. "I cannot believe you're alive and that you have finally come home."

"We were so worried," her mother said. She joined her two daughters and pulled them both into a hug.

"I'm fine. Really," Cyrene insisted. It might not actually be true, but she was alive at least.

Cyrene released her mother and sister and fell into her father's arms. He held her like he had when she was a child. She might be an Affiliate, but she would always be his little girl.

"I'm so glad you're safe," he whispered against her hair.

Then, she moved to her brother, Reeve. He was the last member of her family she had seen before she left on procession to Albion…before she had run away. He hadn't approved of her relationship with King Edric, and they hadn't left on entirely amicable terms.

But the look in his eyes said that was all forgotten. He held his arms out, and she rushed him, squeezing him tight.

"Don't ever do that again."

Cyrene shook her head. "I won't."

That, she absolutely meant. She didn't know where her story was going. She didn't know what path she was on. She couldn't care less about some prophecy that was trying to lead her in whatever direction it wanted. Her future was her own from this day forth.

Then Kael reached them, and Reeve released her. Her family bowed and curtsied to their prince. Cyrene turned to face him again. He gave her that same warm smile. She hesitantly returned it.

"Thank you so much for saving our girl," her mother said with blatant gratitude on her face.

"It was my pleasure," Kael said. "I'm very glad that she is back and that her official delegation is so welcoming."

Cyrene felt Reeve's gaze on hers as she stared back at Kael. She knew he was probably wondering what had happened on the boat for the last two weeks while she was alone with Kael. Not that she was about to discuss that with anyone. Even if nothing had happened. She had been scrutinized in the Eleysian court, but it was nothing compared to Byern. Kael was right to say she needed to be on guard.

"If that is all, then we shall depart in the carriages," Hamidon said. He gestured to the row of carriages awaiting them off the docks.

Kael nodded, and her family stepped back to allow Kael to precede them.

Traditionally, royalty was first, and then it followed by position and rank, which meant her parents, Reeve, Cyrene, and then Elea. But Kael offered her his arm for her to walk with him at the head of the line.

"Are you ready?" he asked.

She took a deep breath and then stepped to his side. Appearances were everything, and she knew how this all appeared. Exactly how Kael had wanted it to. But she wouldn't snub him in this way. She knew there was a longer end game here with him, but she couldn't see the forest for the trees.

She placed her hand on his elbow and felt her magic stir for the first time. Her eyes widened in shock, and she glanced up at his face. He tilted his head, as if he also was surprised by the change. It was as if Byern itself was reawakening the powers that had lain dormant within her. As if coming home had loosened something in her chest.

Kael grinned, as if he knew a secret, and then they started walking off the dock and onto Byern soil. And it was as Avoca had always said it would be. The earth called to her. It wasn't even her first element, but the energy seemed to wrap around her feet and lighten her steps. The air was easier to breathe. The light brighter. The world better. Byern itself was more alive with Cyrene on the ground.

A guard opened the door for them, and Cyrene practically floated into her seat. All the elements felt more alive, more real, more welcoming. Like this very place knew her and her magic. Kael slid into the seat next to her, and then they were off.

"Something has changed," he said intuitively.

"Tell me about the Rose Garden Ceremony," she said, throwing him off guard. The ceremony was the only thing she could think that made sense.

If she was bound to the land and royalty, as she had been in the Rose Garden Ceremony a year ago, then surely, those things must work in the same way as how her magic connected with Avoca's. The land itself had an interest in her.

"As you know, we are not supposed to talk of such things," he said evasively.

"And who are you to follow the rules?"

The carriage jostled them into the city, and dust kicked up in the open windows. Kael slid them closed for this portion of the ride. She frowned at the sudden loss of seeing her homeland.

"It's just a ceremony, Cyrene."

"Is everyone bound?"

"What did you see?" he prodded.

She did not want to reveal her vision to him. Becoming Third Class, leaving the man she loved, giving up her baby, and Kael becoming king. They were visions, memories, past, and future. They could mean nothing…or everything.

"Nothing," she lied. "How does it work?"

"You know the rules," he said with an arched eyebrow.

"Magic can only be bound to magic," she whispered.

That was what troubled her the most. What had troubled Matilde and Vera as well.

What magic am I bound to here? The Dremylons themselves? A Dremylon like Kael with his own magic? The magical energy from the land of Byern itself? How could the spell be completed without magic to tie it together?

Her head was spinning with questions, but she saw that Kael was not going to answer about the Rose Garden Ceremony. And she refused to give him the information he'd inquired about. It felt too personal to let him know that she had seen him become king.

They bustled into the city on brick-paved roads that rattled them worse than the dirt roads. Kael wrenched back the curtains once more and showed her her city. And what she saw was…horrifying.

Her once clean and prosperous city looked beaten down and filthy. Desert sand coated the streets. Beggars stood on corners. Signs hung in taverns that read, *Water supply low*, with a number beneath it that she had to guess meant how much anyone could have at any given time.

"What's happened?" she whispered, aghast.

"It hasn't rained."

"In how long?"

"Not a day since you left."

Cyrene's head snapped back to Kael. "Not a drop of rain?"

"No rain. No snow. It was as if…you took the water with you," he said with a raised eyebrow.

She sat back in the carriage and let that thought sink into her. *Is it possible that I pulled the moisture from my homeland just by being away? Could it be that being bound to a place rather than a person could devastate an entire country in such a manner?*

That sinking depression hit her fresh anew. It was as if everything in this lifetime was her fault. Even the drought.

They clattered onto the castle grounds and to the front of the Nit Decus castle. Kael exited first and offered her his hand. She took it and stepped out to the place she had thought she would never see again.

Her eyes found Kael's for a brief minute. He seemed to sense both her excitement and caution. She took a steadying breath to try to regain her strength.

"The world is yours to take, Cyrene."

He bent down and placed a kiss on her hand where he had helped her out of the carriage. She watched him the entire time that he did it with that low buzz in her stomach from his touch. Then, she felt a great swell, as if her insides were sizzling, and she whipped her head toward the front entrance of the castle.

And there, standing in all his glory, was King Edric.

Ten

THE RAIN

Edric had changed in a million ways and yet not at all.

His dark hair was cut shorter than normal, and he was shaved smooth, making his cheekbones more chiseled. He stood with all the regal authority of a sovereign who had ruled since the tender age of fifteen. His figure took up the door, despite the milling crowd that appeared around him. Yet it was clear that he was the person of importance. He radiated with it.

And the bond between them crackled like firecrackers. Having both Kael and Edric in the same vicinity was almost overwhelming. She didn't know how to shut it off or turn it down. She wished she could eliminate it entirely because, at that moment, she felt inexplicably drawn to both men.

She feared Edric could sense it, too. For his eyes, those Dremylon blue-gray eyes, held dual flames of intensity. They were locked on the place where

Kael was touching her. Her hand in his. His lips on her. If Edric could have slain his brother with one look, that would have done it.

At the same time, the last year all seemed to dissolve between them. They were back in that same spot. Both the king and prince competing in their own for her favor. Her naïveté about the world and court shining like a beacon. The last time she had seen the king, he had invited her back to his chambers…and she never returned. She did not know where that put them now.

"Cyrene," King Edric said. His voice was a calling card, pulling her toward him.

Kael cleared his throat, and she came out of her trance. He walked her forward, knowing the image that they made before the king, before the man who had wanted to be her lover.

"Your Majesty," Cyrene murmured before dropping into a curtsy.

Kael gave a slight bow. "Brother."

Edric stepped down to her level, and a hush fell over the audience. Cyrene hardly recognized anyone other than Consort Daufina. And she and a man in a black guard's uniform both looked incredibly displeased.

"The entire court and all of Byern are incredibly relieved to see an Affiliate returned to her home," Edric said for the entire crowd to hear. "The throne welcomes you back to court. We all hope that you will feel safe once more behind these walls."

The audience applauded lightly for his short speech.

But Cyrene stood there, straight as a board, clutching her skirts. This feeling…it had to be the bond. What she had felt for him all along must be from the magic. *Because what else could explain the pull I feel, standing before him, when I knew in my heart that I did not love him while I was in Eleysia?*

How could I love someone who held so much power over me? Someone who had forced me to return to a place I did not want to be? How could I not blame him?

Yet she couldn't escape this feeling.

Edric took another step toward her and held out his hand. She reached out and placed hers within his.

"Welcome home."

Cyrene swallowed hard at the touch. He bent slightly at the waist and placed a kiss on her hand, as Kael had done. She gasped at the connection and could feel Kael tense next to her. Then, she felt Edric slip something into her hand.

Her eyes widened in confusion and then recognition. He had just given her her pin back. He'd read her letter. She breathed a sigh of relief. Ahlvie and Orden had made it. They were safe. She hadn't done everything wrong.

Edric straightened and smiled at her. That was when everything really seemed to hit her. Staring into Edric's eyes on Byern soil with other Affiliates and High Order, she really was *home.*

Home.

Emotions rippled through her, and then, as if a dam broke, a tear slid down her face. Just one tear.

That was all she would allow.

She had that moment of relief in a wasteland of grief.

And then thunder rolled in the distance.

Cyrene jolted. Edric and Kael jumped to attention. The entire crowd faded to silence and shock.

"Creator," she whispered.

She tilted her head up to the sky as clouds rolled overhead, and it began to sprinkle. The darkening clouds promised big, fat raindrops. More rain than they had gotten in months…since she left. And with her…came the rain.

"Rain bringer!" someone shouted from the crowd.

"Cyrene has brought the rain!" another person cried.

"It's a miracle!"

"She's blessed!"

The shouts became so numerous that she couldn't even make them all out. The crowd was cheering for her. They thought she had brought the rain with her return. But…that couldn't even be possible. She could hardly even use her magic, let alone control the weather in her condition.

Yet, as she reached down into her core, she found that she could touch her magic. That, if she dived down into the depths, she could be ablaze with power. It wasn't the same as before. The depths of her grief were deeper than the well of her magic, but being home had cracked through.

She laughed as more rain fell on her clothes. Perhaps she was the rain bringer. Perhaps she had been blessed by the Creator.

"Enough!" Daufina cried.

Cyrene stared at her in shock. Daufina never stepped out of line, especially not with Edric.

"No Affiliate can bring the rain. It is just a coincidence. She is not even one of us anymore after denouncing our very people!" Daufina strode forward and stared at Cyrene with venom in her gaze. "She is not an Affiliate. She is nothing to this country. She turned her back on us. We should not exult her for a coincidence. The rain was meant to come today one way or another. Just because she arrived today means nothing."

Daufina slashed her hand down in disgust. Rain droplets fell into her perfect dark hair and on the purple dress with its many tiers, changing the colors so that it was so dark, it was almost black. Fitting for her death speech.

Cyrene clutched the pin that Edric had given her tight in her hand. She could put it back on, walk into those halls, and continue her life as she had. Except that Daufina was right. She was no longer an Affiliate, based on the letter that she had sent to Edric. No matter that she had done it out of love for Dean. That she had desired to stay for him above everything else. A fool's notion to choose love over power.

She would be an Affiliate if she had to be.

But the rain itself spoke that she could not be thrown down. She was a force to be reckoned with. She would not allow Daufina to cast her aside.

"Edric, you cannot stand by and ignore the harm that she has caused," Daufina continued. "And how she has spat on your name by turning away from you."

"You're right," Edric said.

"Brother," Kael said, attempting to intercede.

"No, Daufina is right," Edric said. "Cyrene is no longer an Affiliate."

Cyrene swallowed at Edric's declaration. He was the king. He could make that decision. He could cast her down, just as she had seen in her vision. Throw her to Third Class and set her adrift.

It was possible. But she would not allow it. And it made no sense. *Why spend all that time attempting to get me back if he only wanted to humiliate me in front of the entire court?*

"My King," Cyrene said, keeping her voice steady. She was ready to plead her case.

She knew Kael would stand by her. Daufina could not be the only voice that mattered.

"Cyrene, the rain bringer, our own returned home, is no Affiliate," Edric said.

Edric turned back to face her. His eyes were alight, and he wore a smile.

But she could never have prepared herself for what came next.

"That is because she is to be our new consort."

Eleven

THE CONSORT

Cyrene's mouth hung open.

He wanted her to be…the consort.

To be *his* consort.

To replace Daufina.

She knew it was possible to replace the consort, but it was so rare. Usually, it happened as the result of a death. Very rarely did it happen because the king wanted a new advisor. The consort, much like the queen, was a life term.

Edric breaking from that tradition was unprecedented. And the shock on everyone's face said as much. The crowd was a mix of confusion and uncertainty. They didn't know how to respond to this news.

Kael looked livid. It was as if everything he had been planning, whatever he had been planning, had just been obliterated. It was the first time since she had gotten on that ship to return home that she could actually *feel* his dark magic brewing inside him, ready to release. She knew he had used his magic on her when she was vulnerable on board but not like this. Not this sinister.

But it was Daufina's face that said it all. She had not known about this. It seemed likely that no one had known about this…not even Edric. He had just decided on the spot when he saw her. Daufina would have murdered Cyrene then if she could. Cyrene gave her credit for holding on to her decorum though.

It was only Edric who looked happy about his decision.

The *only* person, including Cyrene.

She was not happy about this.

Becoming consort might have been her dream, but now, it felt like a death sentence. A way for Edric to keep her close even though he could not make her queen.

"Come," Edric said, offering Cyrene his hand. "We have much to discuss and an Investiture to plan."

Cyrene could do nothing but accept his hand with everyone looking on. *No* didn't seem to be an option.

He led her into the Nit Decus castle just as the skies completely opened up behind them. She could still sense Kael's presence and the darkness rolling off of him as he followed behind them, but she could pay no heed to him. She had to deal with this situation first.

The Investiture for the consort was essentially a coronation without a crown. The consort was the highest position in the land, save royalty. She was the king's greatest advisor, his strategist, his companion. Many past consorts had been the lover or mistress of the king. Some had borne him children.

Others had been best friends and closest confidants. The woman was to be brilliant, beautiful, and charming. She was everything you could want in the person standing at your side. While the king rarely was able to pick his queen, he chose his consort, and he chose well.

It was a great honor to have been chosen. Yet, with everything she had endured, everywhere she had traveled, all the kingdoms she had seen, Byern felt quite small, especially if she never had the opportunity to leave again.

"How was your trip?" Edric asked. "Pleasant enough, I hope, while on a warship."

Cyrene tilted her head. *Is he really going to ask basic pleasantries?* "Fine. The ship was fine."

"Did you spend much time with my brother?"

She measured the set of his jaw and the anxious tell in his eyes. He wanted the answer to be no.

"There was no one else of equal rank."

He nodded. Surely, he took that to mean yes. Though he could never know that she had spent the last couple of weeks in Kael's bed. Even if nothing had ever happened, she could see now that he would not take well to it. She was extra pleased that Kael had suggested removing her ring. Another thing Edric never needed to know.

"Now that you're back, we have much to discuss."

"Indeed, My King," she said.

"Cyrene, call me Edric."

"Of course." She took a deep breath and then continued, "Like you making me consort."

"It's brilliant," he said at once. "I should have considered it sooner."

"Edric, please, think about this. What about Daufina?"

"Don't worry about her. What's done is done. We will figure out the details at a later time. For now, I just want to relish in your return." He drew her out of the entrance hall and down a hallway. "It was dark days when you were gone."

The same darkness that came from Kael's magic seemed to lick at Edric when he mentioned her disappearance. Yet there was no magic on Edric. She couldn't sense a thing.

"I'm anxious to understand all the changes."

"Yes, much has changed since you left, but you will fit right into my inner circle. You will be at the center of everything from now on, Cyrene. Allow me to show you."

A guard opened a door to a chamber Cyrene had never seen before, and she followed Edric inside. The room was expansive with intricate molding circling the upper and middle of the room. A long, rectangular table ran down the center of the room, laden with maps and charts and an interactive display of much of the known world. It laid out all the stations for the military, where their ships were, and all potential enemy armies.

She could tell right away that this was a place that few had access to. Only Edric and his most trusted advisors were ever brought in here. The weight of the consort sank onto her shoulders, the further she stepped into the room.

"This is my war room," he told her.

"We have not been to war in three hundred years."

"Small skirmishes easily handled in that time, but you are correct, no full-blown wars. Nothing that could make the everyday person fear for their safety. However, this has been the same room through the generations. Viktor Dremylon himself stood at that table to wipe out the remaining Doma," Edric said, pointing to the head of the table.

Cyrene body would not move another inch. Her eyes were fixed on that spot. Right there, the man who had loved Domina Serafina and still murdered her for power had strategized how to slaughter her people. Cyrene's chest ached.

No matter what she had decided about her own mission, she had chosen to be Doma. Her magical powers were a part of who she was. They made her Doma. Yet Edric didn't even know about magic. He didn't know that Viktor had killed Doma because of their magic. He thought, as most citizens of Byern, that magic was a fairy tale, and Doma were unfair conquerors. But they were her ancestors. And, though she might not care that some ancient prophecy said she was important, she couldn't help but feel the pain of those who had been lost.

That, by working with a Dremylon in this room…she was betraying her own people.

Cyrene took a step back and then another. Edric was almost to the head of the table. He was still speaking, telling her about the history of the room. The importance of the room. Yet she couldn't hear a word he said.

Then, he was standing there. In the very spot she had imagined Viktor Dremylon—who, from her visions, she knew looked so much like Edric— and all she saw was betrayal. More betrayal. She couldn't handle that. She couldn't go through that again. She had nearly backed out through the door when he glanced up at her, as if he had finally realized that she hadn't spoken.

"Cyrene?" a voice said behind her.

She felt a light brush against her back, and she knew it was Kael.

"You're white as a ghost."

"Are you all right?" Edric asked at once. "Guard, bring her a chair."

Cyrene was pushed back into the Death Room and forced into a seat. Edric and Kael were arguing already. Cyrene wished she could block it out.

"She's had a long journey. She needs rest," Kael said.

"We have matters to discuss."

"You don't know what she's been like."

"Her health is my first priority, but we need information."

"You're putting her at risk."

"Stop," she said, looking up at them both.

"Cyrene," Kael said, "you need rest."

"I'm fine."

"We will be brief," Edric said.

Daufina and the man Cyrene had noticed in the black guard uniform both entered then. Daufina turned her nose up at Cyrene and marched to the opposite side of the room. The other man went straight to Edric and stood with his arms crossed in protest.

"You're not fine," Kael said.

"I was overwhelmed with everything that has happened. That is all." She narrowed her eyes, telling him without words to let it go.

Kael nodded, as if he understood, and backed off.

"First, introductions," Edric said. He turned to the man in the black uniform. "This is Captain Merrick. He is the head of my personal guard. All royalty has been assigned guards. You will be given a team at your disposal, and they will report to Merrick."

Cyrene hated him on sight. Everything about him from his inky-black hair slicked back off of his face to the curve of his nose and to the beady little eyes with a malicious glint in the irises said that he was her enemy. She did not want guards that Merrick would pick and who would report her every move to him. She would have to figure out a way around that.

"Very well," she said for now. "Pleasure to meet you."

"I have heard so much about you," Merrick said. "The pleasure is all mine."

He said it, but his eyes said he did not believe it. *How could Edric trust this man?*

Her gaze darted to Kael's, and he arched an eyebrow. She could tell that he felt the same way she did. At least he wasn't the only one who got a bad feeling from the man. And her gut was never wrong.

"On to the matter of your kidnapping and escape," Edric began.

"Actually," Cyrene said, standing to make her point clear, "I wanted to discuss Ahlvie and Orden. You must have gotten my letter." She flashed the Affiliate pin at him and watched Daufina's face sour. "I would like to see them at once."

Edric look to Merrick, who said, "They are being…detained."

"Detained," she repeated dryly.

"For now."

"Detained where? How? For what reason?"

"Imprisoned," Daufina spoke up with a whip in her voice. "They are imprisoned for treason."

"What?" Cyrene nearly shouted. "On what grounds?"

"Kidnapping, murder, impersonating a High Order, among other things," Merrick filled her in.

"None of those things are true," Cyrene said. "You must release them at once. They were helping me the entire time we were together. They did not kidnap me. I even said that in my letter."

"We were under the impression that the letter was coerced," Merrick said.

"I was not," Daufina said.

"We have more important matters to deal with right now," Edric said.

"No, we do not!" she said, whirling on him.

"Cyrene." Edric used the voice to try to calm her down, but she was furious.

Ahlvie and Orden were not criminals.

She turned to look at Kael for backup. She didn't know when that had happened. When she had become so comfortable with Kael that she expected him to be on her side against his brother, the king. But, still, it happened.

Kael tilted his head and gave her a look that said, *Choose your battles.*

She huffed but conceded.

"We will figure this out later though," she said.

Edric looked between Kael and Cyrene and seemed not to like what he saw. "Indeed, we will."

"What we should be discussing is the change in consort," Merrick said smoothly.

"Agreed," Daufina said with venom in her voice.

"We are not discussing that. It has been decided," Edric said. He waved his hand, as if he had a magic wand that would suddenly eliminate the concerns piling up around him.

"Your Majesty, you know that I have your best interests at heart," Merrick began. His eyes slid to Cyrene, and he sneered. "After the attempt on your life, you need to keep your friends close."

"Attempt on your life?" Kael asked at the same time as Cyrene asked, "What attempt on your life?"

"You know nothing," Daufina said. "This is a mistake. I have been with you since the beginning, Edric. And you just want to turn me aside?"

"Beyond that fact, Daufina is a strong ally. The people know and respect her. The Affiliates and High Order respond to her. They listen to her. You are about to embark on a war. You do not change horses midstream," Merrick reminded him.

"Brother, what attempt on your life?" Kael asked. "How was I not informed of this?"

"It was nothing," Edric growled. "I dealt with the man."

"It was two attempts," Merrick said. "Someone wants the king dead, and they are doing everything they can to get it done. The first, you were lucky to kill yourself. The second killed his taster by poison. We had only instated a taster three days before it happened. If I had not suggested it, you would be dead."

"It seems you have a common enemy with Cyrene then," Kael said. "She was nearly killed on our own ship on the way here."

Cyrene glared at him. She hadn't wanted that information known.

"What happened?" Edric asked. "Are you all right?"

"Fine," she said. It felt like that was all she was saying. Fine. Fine. She was fine. Nothing bothered her at all. Certainly not death, war, poison, murder attempts, prison.

"I killed the man," Kael informed him.

"Further proof that you need to be careful of your choices, sire," Merrick said. "They are already making attempts on her life. What will happen if she becomes consort? She will not always have a prince at her side."

"No, she will have *your* guards, Merrick," Edric said. "So, you do your job and let me do mine. I am the king." He strode to the desk and stood at the head of the table. "Must I remind you that I am king? I was born for this moment. Cyrene was born to be at my side."

Cyrene shrank back at the vehemence in his voice. The last thing she thought she was *born* for was to stand at a Dremylon's side.

Everyone remained silent at Edric's proclamation. They all knew he was king and that he held all the power. He could make Cyrene his consort with a snap of his fingers. Who wouldn't want the honor? His advisors might try to persuade him against it, but in the end, it was his decision.

"That is settled then. Daufina, you will begin to train Cyrene on her position henceforth."

"And what will you do with me after that, Your Majesty?" Daufina asked defiantly. She used his title like a whip.

"We will discuss it at a later time," Edric said dismissively. "Right now, I would like to understand the letter that my brother sent ahead from Albion. The king and queen of Eleysia are dead, and they executed one of our own Affiliates for the murder?"

Cyrene staggered back and put a hand to her heart. She had to close her eyes to block out the torment of the moment. Maelia. The crowd. The scaffold. Maelia's head rolling into the basket. Cyrene could have prevented it. She could have stopped it. If only she'd had a moment to think, she could have made it right. And, now, she was here, talking pleasantries with another royal court, when she should have been hanged in the other.

"Yes," Kael said. Though she could feel his eyes on her and not Edric.

"That is an act of war," Edric said.

"And I have negotiated peace." Kael removed another letter from his breast pocket and handed it to Edric.

"This is signed by the prince of Eleysia, not the new queen," Edric said. "This is a cease-fire in exchange for Cyrene's return. It is not binding. We *will* go to war."

The prince of Eleysia. Dean.

Her heart ached at the thought of him. He had given her up for peace. He had traded her so that his people would not die at the hands of the Byern warships sitting so near their capital. Whether or not he cared for her, she now understood why he had done it at least. She would not let Edric spit on that offer.

"No," Cyrene said. Her voice was strong and steady. She could not allow this.

"No?" Merrick asked in disgust.

"That's right. No. We will not go to war. Too many innocent lives will be lost if we do so. I was there. I know the heartbreak in the country. I know what they did to Maelia was wrong, but it would be insanity to take this a step further."

Edric shook his head and stared down at the map before him. "You do not grasp the whole situation just yet. I know you've had a trying trip. Perhaps my brother is right, and you need to rest."

"I've rested enough," Cyrene said. "What you are doing is morally abhorrent."

"I hate to say that I agree with Cyrene," Daufina said. "But I have been saying this for months. You have been looking for a fight since you marched our troops into Aurum. Now, you have found one that has a peace treaty staring you in the face, and you ignore it?"

"Enough!" Edric roared. "We are going to war. Get used to the idea. We must prepare. You are all dismissed."

Cyrene stared at Edric as he turned his back to the four people he listened to the most. It was clear he was taking no counsel. No one could sway him. Byern was going to war.

Twelve

THE GARDENS

"He's not going to go to war," Kael said as he followed Cyrene out of the war room.

Cyrene shook her head as she headed for the Vines, which were the quarters for the Queen and her Affiliates. Her old room was there, and no matter what she said about being fine, she suddenly felt overwhelmed and exhausted.

"I don't know what he'll do."

Kael touched her arm. "This way. They moved your rooms."

"How do you know everything?" she asked.

"They set them up before I left."

"Why is the castle full?"

"Edric called in all the Affiliates and High Order and bolstered court."

"He wants them to rally more soldiers for him," she said. "He does mean to go to war."

"He's not that stupid."

Cyrene shot him an apprehensive look. "Since when are you defending him?"

"We're in a different time, Cyrene. Surely, you know that much has changed. It was easier to act against my brother when our biggest differences were who our father loved more and you." He grinned. "If we go to war, I need to be at his side. The court needs to see us united."

Cyrene considered his point as they reached a room in a wing she had never visited before. "Where are we?"

"Your new rooms. Though I wonder if they will move you into the consort's rooms," Kael said.

He pushed the door open, and Cyrene strode inside.

Her jaw dropped. The space was even larger than the ornate rooms she had been given in the Krisana castle in Albion and the Lombardy palace in Eleysia. She had her own living area with space for at least fifty to comfortably sit, play music or cards, or read. Several adjoining rooms opened to her own bath chamber, a lush all white bedroom, a study, and her own patio with windows looking out across the castle grounds and the city.

"This is outrageous," she said.

"You're surprised?" Kael flopped down on the first available couch, as if he owned the place.

"I mean, making me consort."

"That…I was not expecting."

"Can I just say no?"

Kael's eyebrows rose. "Do you want to?"

Dear Creator, she was having a heart-to-heart with Kael Dremylon.

"What I want? Creator, what I want?" She splayed her hands out in frustration. "Does anyone even care what I want? I am a tool to be used. That's it. I am power and beauty, and that is all that matters. If anything else mattered, then I would have a choice in what I did with my life, but I have not had one since the day I stepped foot into this castle."

"And, if you had the choice"—he straightened; the energy radiated between them as he drew near her once more—"what would you choose?"

A month ago, it would have been the easiest answer. Magic. Dean. Friends. Prophecy. Her loyalties had been black and white. Her life had been ruled by destiny. Her plans had been set in motion by a chance encounter with a peddler and a book and a letter.

Now, she didn't know what she wanted. She felt adrift. Ruled by someone else's decisions. Edric's decisions. She hadn't even thought about what she wanted.

"I don't know," she said. "Freedom."

"That is not what you want. You are already free." Kael pushed a lock of her hair behind her ear. "What you want is vengeance. What you want is control. What you want is power."

She clenched her hands into fists to keep from touching him. His words sang to her broken heart. She did want those things. Hearing them out loud instead of the ideas echoing around her mind put everything into order. She was not the same person she had been when she left this castle. She had seen and done things that Edric couldn't even imagine. He might rule this kingdom, but he did not rule her.

"Yes," she said.

His fingers threaded through hers and pressed their palms together.

"This is what I can offer you."

His magic pressed into her body, filling her, drawing out her own magic. She gasped, but instead of wrenching back, as she had done on the docks when he invaded her, she met his power with her own. He did not have the control. They were both matched. What she had once thought was darkness and light was really just power. Raw energy. There for the taking.

It was not like linking with Avoca. This was like linking with wildfire—dangerous and uncontrollable.

"Here is your freedom."

His lips landed on her forehead, soft but inviting. She breathed him in as he came closer. Her attraction to him with their magic connected like this was uncontrollable. She was not sure she would be able to stop herself if he went further.

But he didn't.

Creator, he didn't.

He stepped back. He released her hand. He let his magic drop.

"Think on it, Cyrene."

He did a low bow, one reserved for royalty, and then departed her rooms.

Kael might be on her side now that it was clear what he wanted from her. But she knew, from seeing his energy, that she did not want him as an enemy.

Edric was a fool for underestimating him.

Now that Cyrene had finally been returned to a room with a bed to herself, she thought that she would want to go meander the corridors of the castle.

Maybe she could rediscover the home that she had lived in for such a short period of time when she first became an Affiliate. Yet her feet wouldn't carry her out of the room.

She was exhausted. Mentally, physically, and emotionally exhausted.

That brief connection with Kael had been more draining than the whole boat ride and everything with Edric combined. As much as she wanted out, she decided against it for the night. She had a target on her back, and she wasn't prepared for all the questions.

With a sigh, she flopped back into the oversize bed in the middle of the day and slept soundly. Not waking once, as she had the entire time she slept in Kael's bedchamber on the boat. Fear heightened her senses, and maybe she should have been on guard in the castle as well, but her body protested.

A tap on her door jolted her out of bed. She was shocked to see that it was still daylight out, if hardly. They were reaching the summer solstice when the summer sun stayed out long into the night. There was at least another half hour before the sun would set entirely, based on where it hung on the horizon.

Cyrene adjusted her hair and then hurried to the door. She wasn't expecting visitors.

When she pulled the door open, the king was standing there.

"Edric," she said in surprise.

"Hello, Cyrene. I had a maid come to fetch you for dinner, but she informed me that you were asleep, so I didn't wake you."

Cyrene shivered. Someone had come into her new room without her even noticing. She could have been dead by now. She would have to be more careful from now on. She needed a guard she trusted. Or perhaps just Ahlvie and Orden.

"That's quite all right. I'm not hungry."

"I was curious if you would accompany me for a walk this evening." His smile was eager, his eyes excited.

He had been waiting for this moment. His earlier erratic behavior aside, he seemed like the Edric she had left behind. All-too anxious to please her.

"Of course," she said smoothly. "I would be delighted."

She might have misgivings about Edric's rule, but she wanted to believe he was acting like this for the common good. And, if not, she wanted to know if she could change his mind about this war.

Cyrene walked with him until they reached outside. The hallways he used were mostly deserted. Though a few people stopped to bow to the king as they passed. Cyrene wondered if they were all about to run to Queen Kaliana to tell her what was going on.

Cyrene realized that she hadn't even noticed Kaliana's absence in all of this. It was odd that she hadn't been there when Cyrene first arrived or in the war room with Edric. Though, admittedly, she didn't think he liked Kaliana to be in plans with him for that sort of thing. It was still strange that she hadn't been around at all. The queen had made it her personal mission to make Cyrene's life miserable since her first day in the castle. Perhaps Edric hadn't wanted Kaliana's presence looming over him when he came to greet Cyrene. Perhaps—

But when they entered one of the gardens, she realized exactly where he had brought her. The very garden when he had first made his intentions toward her known. It was a stunning garden with roses blooming in a kaleidoscope of colors and a sea nymph fountain jutting water from her mouth. Cyrene had been stunned by Edric's advances at the time and terrified what Kaliana would do to her if she found out.

Now, she felt…nothing.

Being here with Edric was nostalgic. It made her wistful for the girl she had been. Ready to take on the world at a moment's notice with no knowledge of what that meant or the consequences.

"I saved the garden for you," Edric told her. "I knew you would come back."

"You saved it for me? What do you mean?"

"With the water shortage, we had to prioritize. The entrance to the grounds had to be preserved for state business, and I had this garden maintained through the drought. I knew that you, a gardener, would want to see it again in its glory."

Cyrene's head spun. It was a romantic gesture. She could see that was what he had meant it to be. A year ago, she would have swooned and fallen for him all over again. Now, she was confused.

"Why would you waste the water?" she asked.

"It was not a waste to see your face light up when you saw it once more."

Cyrene took a step into the garden and admired what he had done for her. For a moment, a glimmer of that girl she had been hit her, and she smiled. It *was* beautiful. It was also irresponsible.

"People don't have enough water in the city. You shouldn't have done this."

"I thought you'd be pleased."

Edric came up behind her, and she felt the tension of his presence. But she resisted that static between them. It did her no good. Not when she was trying not to be upset by what he had done.

He could have killed people in the city. He'd deprived people of water. He'd hurt families and businesses.

It would have been one thing if he had done it for court. The castle always had plenty, thanks to the underground water, but he hadn't kept extra water for the additional people he had invited. He had done it for plants. For a few roses that would wither and die by the summer solstice.

Cyrene turned around to face him. "How could this please me?"

Edric looked completely baffled by her statement. "I remember how much this meant to you."

"Yes, meant to me," she said stiffly. She remembered all the things she had seen on her journey. The homeless and starving and dirty. She had gone without. She knew the pain and would not wish it on anyone. "But a garden cannot mean more to me than the people of Byern."

"Court always has more," he said a bit defensively.

"It doesn't have to be this way."

Edric tilted his head, as if he were assessing her again for the first time. She didn't know what he saw when he looked at her. But she was certain he did not see the same girl who had first walked this garden with him.

"You're right," he conceded. "It was an idealistic notion. I'll divert the water to the city if it pleases you."

Cyrene nodded slightly and relaxed. "It would please me. Yes."

Edric stepped forward. There were mere inches between them, and her chest ached from staying still. These Dremylon men were going to kill her. Her heart jackhammered in her chest, and she willed him not to move forward. She could feel the want off of him, but even though her body was being pulled toward him, her mind and heart were not in it. She was still too angry at all of his rash decisions—sending an army to retrieve her in Aurum, having Kael follow her to the capital, demanding her return from Eleysia like a toy someone had stolen, making her consort, and now the garden.

"You will make a beautiful consort," Edric said, running his hand down her arm.

She shivered and then took a step back. "Thank you. But are you certain you want to make the change?"

"We don't need to talk about this again."

"Edric—"

"No, Cyrene," he spat. He bridged the distance between them. "You will be my consort. I have waited too long to get you back. I have been driven mad, waiting for you. That's the end of this."

Then, his hand came around to the back of her neck, and he crushed his lips down onto hers. His lips held none of the tenderness she had known from him. *How could he think this is what I want?*

He wrapped his arms around her waist and backed her into the side of the castle. She could have used her magic to get away from him, but she wasn't willing to show her hand for that just yet. Her hands were shaking, and she felt cold and numb. This was not what she had been expecting from this encounter. And it only made the darkness within her swell in recognition of the deceit.

"You were to come to my chambers that night," Edric reminded her.

He kissed down her neck, and she closed her eyes to try to pretend she was elsewhere. Creator, she needed to make this stop.

"Edric, please," she whispered, pushing against his chest. "It doesn't have to be this way either."

"I have waited all this time for you. You will come to my chambers tonight. We will finish what we started."

"Edric…no. You should respect what I want."

"I am the king. I take what I want," he told her.

Cyrene's eyes narrowed. "Perhaps, if you acted like a king, you wouldn't have to keep reminding people of the fact."

Edric straightened, as if she had slapped him across the face. Cyrene rearranged her dress and took a deep breath. Edric might have enjoyed her sharp tongue before, but she never would have dared to say such a thing. Now, he was acting like a child, and she would not go through with this. King or no king.

His hand came back up to her neck, and she held her breath for a second before he moved it down the chain of her necklace. She dared not move in case he looked too carefully at the chain.

"You speak very boldly."

"As ever, Majesty," she said, putting distance between them.

His hand dipped to the curve of her breast where the necklace set.

"Many things have changed here. You will learn to fit in here again."

She took that as the threat it was. Fit in or else.

Then, just as she was about to respond, he did the unthinkable. He pulled on the chain of her necklace, and the ring fell onto the top of her bodice. She sucked in a breath as he tilted his head in confusion and examined the ring.

"What is this?"

He stared at the oval-shaped diamond, precious and unbelievably expensive. When his eyes snapped back up to hers, she saw the recognition there. He knew. Why else would she wear a ring around her neck?

"Who gave you this?" he snapped.

She shook her head, refusing him the information.

"Who?" he roared, louder this time.

"It is not important."

Edric's eyes were murderous. If she had thought that he wanted to go to war before, it was nothing compared to the expression on his face now.

Without preamble, he fisted the gold chain and yanked it clear off her neck. She cried out in shock as it abraded her neck, but Edric didn't even seem to notice that he had hurt her.

"Whoever made you his whore will pay for this with his life," he snarled.

He flung the necklace and ring into the garden he had saved for her and then stormed from her sight. Cyrene took gasping deep breaths at his exit, unable to grasp how everything had gone so wrong.

Thirteen

THE PREPARATION

Cyrene plowed back into her room. She ripped out of her nice dress and flung it onto the bed she had been so grateful for. But, no, that was to be no more. It seemed everything was a prison cell. Everyone only wanted to use her or control her, and she'd had enough.

Edric had made a mistake. A grave mistake.

Just because he was her king did not give him the right to treat her in such a way. She would never be with anyone because they believed they had power over her. Nor would she give in to this ridiculous notion that she must be consort.

Consort might have been the one thing she had always wanted, but that was before her journey. Before magic. It seemed so inconsequential now.

Much like this ring.

She stared down at the diamond that Dean had given her only a short month ago.

She'd dug around in the gardens, using the moonlight to locate the glittering gemstone. She didn't know what had possessed her to look for it. Dean was nothing to her now. Thinking about him made her weary, and it was clear that they could never have a life together.

But, still, she had searched for it and dropped it back on her finger for safekeeping. It was the memory of a girl who had thought she would be able to have it all. Now, she knew better. Yet she couldn't get rid of the reminder.

Cyrene threw on an inconspicuous blue dress, pulled her long dark hair up and out of her face, and then left her beautiful rooms behind. Riches and luxury didn't woo her the way they once had. Funny thing about sleeping on the floor of a forest bed and running for her life, it put things into perspective.

When she stepped out of her room, she faltered only for a moment before leaving to find the one person she thought might help her. It was a gamble. But she had to roll the dice.

When she reached the room, she entered tentatively and breathed a sigh of relief upon finding it empty. She hurried across the enormous room and pressed her ear to the wooden door. It was silent on the other side. With a sigh, she knocked twice and then entered without waiting for an invitation.

Daufina was seated behind her round table with a bottle of wine and a half-empty glass before her. Her eyes were red-rimmed, and her body hunched forward. When she saw Cyrene, she righted instantly and sent her a venomous glare.

"What are you doing in my chambers?" she demanded.

"I've come to seek an audience with you."

Daufina raised her eyebrows. "I'm to train you in the morning. I don't think I want to see your face before then. Be gone."

"I want you to help me."

"And why would I help you with anything? You are my replacement." She snarled the last word, as if it had a disgusting aftertaste. "You're just an insolent little girl with a pretty face. Once Kaliana is out of confinement, he'll completely forget you."

Cyrene startled at that news. "The queen is in…confinement? She's *pregnant?*"

Daufina threw her head back and laughed into the heights of her chamber. "And you don't even know. Didn't that prince tell you anything about court?"

She opened her mouth and then closed it. This couldn't be. Queen Kaliana had had many miscarriages since she married the king. Many had given up hope that she would ever carry a baby to term. Yet she was confined, which must mean that she was in her last weeks and would soon give birth.

"When the king has a son to carry on his line, then he won't care so much about your pretty face," Daufina snapped. "And just think about the precedent it is setting. If he can get rid of me so easily, he could do the same to you."

"That's not why I'm here," she managed to get out.

Her head was buzzing with the new information. Not that there was a single thing she could do about it at the present. It could just be added to the list of things Kael had purposefully avoided informing her of.

"Of course not. You're here for a favor." Daufina slowly stood, towering over Cyrene. "I don't deal in favors, especially not with a little girl the king wants to take as his lover again."

"Again?" Cyrene countered. "I believe it is your turn to have your facts wrong."

Daufina quirked a half-smile. "I was on the barge with you on procession. I was there in Albion when he gave you the best rooms in the palace. I have known Edric far longer than you have. Forgive me if I don't believe you."

"Edric and I have never been together. In fact, only a short while ago, he came to my chambers to remind me of that very fact. Let me speak plainly," Cyrene said, setting her hand on the table. "I do not want to be the king's lover."

Daufina took a startled step backward. "You want the power then?"

"Do I look like the kind of person coming to *you* for power?"

"Insolent little—"

"I want out," Cyrene spat. "I don't want to be consort. I don't want any of this. You should keep your position and help me. Help me get out."

Daufina stared at her, silent for a minute. "This feels like a trick."

Cyrene huffed heavily. "Why else would I be here?"

"To gloat?"

"Am I gloating? I'm telling you that I want out of here. You know that I was not kidnapped. You read the letter that I had written to Edric. It was not coerced. What more do I have to do to prove it to you? If you help me, then I will be gone, out of the castle, and you can take over again."

Daufina pursed her lips and tapped her finger on her cheek. "I find this all hard to believe."

"Fine," Cyrene cried. "This was a waste of my time then. I took a chance. I'll figure out another way."

She turned on her heel, feeling supremely ridiculous. She knew that she shouldn't have taken the risk. She should have found her own way to the dungeons and blasted her way out of the place with Ahlvie and Orden. It wasn't like she didn't already know there was an alternative exit through the stables. She had figured that out on her first day when she was trapped in one of the underground water chambers on a prank from the other Affiliates and High Order.

Her hand touched the door when Daufina spoke, "Wait."

Cyrene stilled.

"You truly want to get away from here?"

"Yes," she said softly.

She couldn't give Edric what he wanted. She couldn't process her feelings around Kael. This whole land made her magic sing. She needed to get away to somewhere with no expectations, no obligations, and no prophecies. If that place even existed.

"I will help you."

"Why?" she asked as she turned around.

"You seem desperate, and it's in my own interest."

"Great. Let's go tonight."

Daufina held up her hand. "It will take me a few days to get things ready."

"I don't have a few days," she ground out.

"I'll do what I can, but I can't promise to be able to smuggle you out sooner."

"We have to get Ahlvie and Orden as well."

Daufina sighed. "Why am I not surprised?"

"Can you do it?"

"Yes, but I don't see how it helps me to let the prisoners go."

"Because I will not leave without them."

"Fine," Daufina said. "I can handle it. If anyone inquires about this meeting, we'll have to say that we came to terms with one another. I'll begin your training, as if nothing has changed. It would be best for both of us to be more…compliant."

Cyrene shot her a cheeky smile. "I can do that."

"Somehow, I highly doubt compliant is in your repertoire."

"You'd be surprised," Cyrene said, remembering how much easier it was to give in to Kael on the ship than to fight him on every little thing. However, there were some things she would never give in to, and what Edric was asking from her was one of them.

With that, Cyrene turned on her heel and left Daufina's chambers. She thought that had gone better than anticipated. Reaching out to Daufina could backfire. She could tell Edric about it as proof of Cyrene's insolence and try to get her kicked out of the consort position. But Daufina was practical. It would be easier to get rid of her than change Edric's mind when it was made.

And this whole thing with Kaliana. She still couldn't believe that the queen was pregnant. It explained why she hadn't been seen since Cyrene arrived. There was no way that Kaliana would have let Cyrene become consort without pitching a fit about the whole thing otherwise.

Cyrene was so wrapped up in her thoughts that she didn't realize she was being tailed at first. She slowed her steps as her heart ratcheted up. Even though she had her magic back, she didn't truly know how to defend herself. She was about to take off when a man lunged at her with a knife. His hand rammed into her cheek, sending fireworks exploding in her eyes.

She cried out and barely managed to dodge his next thrust. He was wicked fast, and it was only the adrenaline of the moment that saved her. She reached for that place in the pit of her stomach that called her. The part that was tinged with black and aching to lash out at the world. She thrust her hands out at the man, and he was thrown back like a rag doll against the wall.

Cyrene leaned over, breathing hard, as she regained her balance. The man was looking at her with wild, wide eyes, but still, he held his flimsy piece of metal. He was battered from her toss but not down for the count. She hadn't released her magic, and she let it fill her. Let the anger consume her.

"Come on then," she spat. "Aren't you going to try to kill me? A weak, defenseless girl?"

The man clearly didn't like the taunt and rushed her again. She was ready for him this time. She threw her magic at him, hauling him up into the air and squeezing her hand to constrict his airflow. He gasped and sputtered before her.

"Who sent you?"

He coughed as his face turned blue.

"Tell me," she demanded, releasing him enough to let him speak.

"I...I don't know."

"Wrong answer."

She clenched her hand again, snapping his wrist as easily as tearing paper. His screams carried down the empty hall. Her anger fueled her forward. She knew she should stop. A little buzzing in her ear said this was wrong, that this wasn't the way. But her rage finally had a source. She could finally control something in her Creator-forsaken life.

"Who?" she repeated.

"Merrick."

That one word, and her anger disappeared. She let the man drop like a husk. Merrick. The captain of the royal guard wanted her dead. Of course. That made perfect sense. Using a stranger who could do it quick and clean while she was alone. Blame it on assassins or truly anyone at this point.

"Who else knows this?" she asked the man.

"Just…just me."

"Well, that's wonderful to hear," Kael said, appearing practically out of thin air at the other end of the hallway.

"What are you doing here?" Cyrene asked.

"I came to find you. I heard you had an…altercation this evening. And, now, it seems I'm glad to have found you."

"Why?"

"Because I can handle this for you," he said, gesturing to the cretin crumpled on the floor.

"Handle it? I'll hand him over to Edric and get Merrick executed."

Kael smiled. His black cloak billowed behind him as he moved toward Cyrene. He cupped her cheek with his hand and inspected the bruise forming on her cheek. His eyes darkened in the candlelight. He looked murderous. "He did this?"

"That's not important right now."

Kael tightened his grip on her jaw. "Did he do this?"

"Yes."

Kael nodded. Just once. Then, he faced the man, withdrew his sword, and plunged it into the man's chest.

"Kael!" she gasped. "He was our witness."

"He saw you use magic. He was a death sentence, not a witness. Now, he got what he deserved."

"Are you mad?"

He withdrew his sword with a sickening sound. "You are still thinking short-term, Cyrene. I am thinking about the future. Merrick is not your only enemy. This castle breeds enemies for your kind."

"My kind?" she whispered.

His eyes slid to her. "You know."

"If I am what you say," she said, hedging on using the term *Doma* in the Nit Decus castle where they had all been slaughtered, "then why am I not already dead?"

"Because I am protecting you," he said simply. "As I have tried to do since the day you arrived. Don't you remember me telling you not to leave the castle walls? When I walked with you through Albion?"

"And how are you capable of protecting me like that?"

He grinned devilishly. "In time, I will share everything with you. For now, know that, as long as you're with me, no harm will ever come to you."

Cyrene shook her head, unable to fathom how that was possible. But she did remember Kael's warning not to leave all those months ago. And how furious he had been when she had. How terrified he had been for her when she returned to the castle in Albion. *Had he been looking out for me all this time?*

"What are you going to do with the body?" she whispered.

"I'll handle it. You should get some rest. And, Cyrene," he said as she turned to go, "tomorrow, we should talk."

"About?"

"Everything."

THE FITTING

Standing in front of a giant trifold mirror as Lady Cauthorn fitted Cyrene for an Investiture dress felt as if it were happening to another person in another lifetime. Lady Cauthorn had created her dress for the ball when she became an Affiliate. She had made the gorgeous thing in one night and taken nothing in payment, except for a favor when she asked for it.

If she had known then what she knew now, she never would have traded in favors so easily.

"Stop fidgeting, girl! Has nothing changed with you?" Lady Cauthorn asked, purposefully poking her with her needle.

"Poke me one more time with that needle, and you'll regret it," Cyrene muttered under her breath.

Lady Cauthorn laughed. "Same spunk at least."

Cyrene didn't even have the heart to banter further. Her mind was on other things. Like how to escape this castle with her friends and what she would do with her new life once she did.

And Kael. The bloody prince who always appeared at exactly the right time with his wise words and uncertain promises. The ease with which he had driven his blade into the assassin's chest. How her heart had ached at the thought of Maelia doing the same thing, suffering a similar fate.

And her magic. That was even more baffling than Kael Dremylon. At least he was constant. Her magic was a wild thing, and it had never been easier to use than last night. She had no idea how she had been able to control herself so completely. Even when she had been learning her powers from Matilde and Vera, she had only had real success when working with Avoca. Yet, last night, she had wielded her powers with ease.

"Are you even paying attention?" Lady Cauthorn asked.

Cyrene sighed. "I'm sorry. What did you say?"

Lady Cauthorn stepped back and appraised her. "I asked whether you were going to let Ahlvie and Orden suffer in prison or do something about it?"

Cyrene's eyes widened. "How do you…"

"*How* is the wrong question, dear. The more important one is, how will I help you?"

"You know Ahlvie and Orden?"

"People who are invested in the heir are all connected," she said with a wicked grin.

"The…heir?"

"Come now, girl. Don't play. We have very little time before Daufina returns, or we're interrupted. I can't imagine that it's been easy for you to be alone with the Dremylons these last couple of weeks. All things considered." She winked at Cyrene. "Now, who do I need to contact outside of the castle walls? Write me a letter quick. We can spare the time. I know your measurements well enough already. Though…you have lost some weight. Are they not feeding you? No, it must be stress."

Cyrene's mouth dropped open in shock and confusion. Everything that Lady Cauthorn was saying was going in one ear and out another. She couldn't comprehend where this was all coming from.

"Have you gone deaf, girl? I am trying to help you."

"I don't understand."

"Snap out of it. You know what they do to people like you if you stay."

"You…know what I am?" Cyrene whispered.

She glanced around the dressing room even though she knew they were alone. Her heart galloped ahead of her.

Is this really happening? Is Lady Cauthorn actually offering me help? Does she know about my magic? How?

"I just said I did, didn't I? Now, if you want my help, you need to write that letter. We aren't safe, talking here, for much longer."

Cyrene jumped into action. She didn't know why she trusted Lady Cauthorn, especially since she still owed her a favor. Now, Cyrene would be further in her debt. But she couldn't just wager on Daufina. It was always better to have multiple pieces on the board.

She had finished sketching out a hasty letter to Avoca when a knock at the door made both of them jump. Cyrene stuffed the letter into Lady Cauthorn's hands. She had no idea how Lady Cauthorn was going to get it to Avoca or how she would even find her, but Cyrene didn't ask questions.

Lady Cauthorn stuffed the note in her bodice and shooed Cyrene back onto the pedestal.

When the door swung open, Cyrene was trying to appear calm and collected rather than as flustered as she felt.

"There you are, Cyrene!" Elea said, traipsing into the room. She curtsied to Lady Cauthorn. "Good to see you again."

Cyrene breathed a sigh of relief. "Elea!"

"Aren't you the spitting image of your mother?" Lady Cauthorn said.

"And everyone was worried that I'd never fill out." Elea twirled in a circle. "And here I am, wearing one of your gowns."

"Indeed, girl. Do you have a reason for interrupting my work?"

Elea colored up to the tips of her ears. "I came to see my sister. It's been a year since I've seen her, you know!"

"A day," Lady Cauthorn corrected.

Cyrene laughed softly. "It's fine. We were almost done for the day, weren't we?"

Lady Cauthorn arched an eyebrow. "Of course. It'll take me a while to work on an acceptable dress for you anyway."

She hoped not too long.

Not that it would matter if she was able to get out of here with Daufina's help.

Cyrene turned her attention back to her sister. She couldn't believe how much Elea had changed in a year. She was always tall, but now, she carried herself with grace instead of awkwardness. They could have been twins at first glance if it weren't for the height difference. But Cyrene could still see the slightly elongated face, thinner pink lips, and long, nimble fingers that had endeared her to the piano forte.

Despite all of her plans to leave as soon as she possibly could, Cyrene couldn't help but revel in her sister. She stepped off the pedestal and wrapped her arms around Elea.

"I've missed you," Cyrene whispered. "It's been so long."

"And I thought it would be bad when you made Affiliate," Elea said, stepping back and sending her an easy smile. "I didn't imagine what it would be like with a kidnapping attached to that."

"Right," Cyrene said. She turned her head away from Elea.

No one here knew that she hadn't been kidnapped. She hated lying to Elea and even more that she was going to play the same ruse again.

Elea linked their arms as they exited the fitting room. "Now, tell me all about your adventures."

"Adventures?" Cyrene hedged.

"Come now, Cyrene. I'm your sister, and besides Rhea, your closest friend, I know that you've dreamed of adventure your entire life. Maybe even more than the thought of becoming consort. And, now, you get both!"

Cyrene kept her shoulders straight and tried not to betray herself. "Well, adventure isn't all it's cracked up to be."

"I'd assume not," Elea said prudently. "I don't need your kind of adventures. I just want to become an Affiliate next month and join the rest of my family."

"Yes. That would be Mother and Father's dream come true. A full family in the First Class."

What Cyrene didn't say was that it was her greatest fear. She wished that Elea could escape all of this in a way that Cyrene knew she never would.

Elea would be caught, too, if she stayed here. But Cyrene didn't know how to get her to come away with her. She didn't know if Elea would even leave with her. Rhea hadn't.

"Cyrene?" Elea asked.

"Yes?"

"Are you truly all right? I can't imagine how you are handling all of this."

All right.

All right?

Her best friend had been murdered. She had lost the man she loved. All of her friends were dispersed. And her magic was only responding to Kael Dremylon.

She was the furthest thing from all right.

"No, of course you're not," Elea said immediately. "What am I even thinking? I've spent the last several months imagining all sorts of atrocities that must have been happening to you. You seem to be in one piece, but I can see that, mentally, you're still not here."

"Truly," Cyrene agreed.

Her mind was still on a scaffold in Eleysia.

But she couldn't talk about that. Not with Elea. Not with anybody.

She was locking it all back up and concentrating on what she could control. That most certainly had nothing to do with Eleysia. Not a damn thing.

With a heavy heart, Cyrene pressed forward, eager to change the subject.

"I do wish that I had been able to see Rhea in Albion. However, we docked and immediately left again. There was no chance to get word to her."

Elea abruptly stopped, jerking both of them to a halt.

"What…"

"Did no one tell you?" Elea asked.

Cyrene raised her eyebrows. "Tell me what?"

"Rhea is here!"

"Here? But why?"

The last time she had seen her oldest friend, Rhea Gramm, she had been in Albion, working for her Receiver—Master Caro Barca, a mad inventor, who made Bursts for holiday events each year. When Cyrene had invited her to come along, Rhea had declined, deciding to stay behind in Albion to study the prophecy they had discovered. She had no idea what Rhea could be doing in the capital city.

"She was assisting in your investigation back in Albion. King Edric remained in the city for months, searching for you. He only returned at the Eos holiday when all else had given up hope of ever finding you. But, when everyone returned to court, her Receiver, Master Caro Barca, moved to the capital. She's been here, in the castle, ever since."

Cyrene's mind buzzed with all the new information. Edric had waited for her for *months* in Albion. No wonder he was mad with obsession. It seemed he had thought of nothing else since her disappearance. Not that she allowed that to excuse his behavior.

She wondered how Rhea must have felt, assisting in a kidnapping investigation when she had helped Cyrene escape. Or how she felt about being back in Byern when she had just adjusted to her new position in Albion. One that she had enjoyed and flourished in.

Only one way to find out.

"Take me to her."

Elea navigated the corridors better than Cyrene ever had. Soon, they were in a part of the castle Cyrene had never even known existed. The hallways were enormous. As tall and as wide as a house. No paintings or tapestries. Not even the expensive Aurumian rugs that Cyrene had become accustomed to. Everything was bare and dreary in the belly of the castle where the only light came from bracketed candles at indeterminate intervals.

"Where are we?" Cyrene whispered.

Elea shrugged one lithe shoulder. "It's an abandoned part of the castle. There was a cave-in at some point, and no one lives over here anymore. I'm not sure why it's so cavernous though."

"How do you know this much about the castle?" Cyrene asked suspiciously. "You only moved into the castle a couple weeks ago when the King brought all the major families into court."

Elea ducked her chin to her chest, and her cheeks heated. "I, uh…made a friend."

"Oh Creator! What's his name?"

"I…uh…um…"

"Elea?" Cyrene asked, suddenly nervous.

"Well, don't tell Mother…Prince Kael."

Cyrene sighed heavily and closed her eyes. "You've become *friends* with the prince?"

"Yes. We're…we're just friends though," Elea rushed on. "I was shocked that he'd even noticed me. Since I'm not an Affiliate yet, I can't participate in much of the court proceedings. Not even feast days." She pouted, as if being kept from a dance was her biggest concern. "But he saw me in the gardens once and startled me. He said he thought I was someone else."

Cyrene's heart raced ahead of her as she realized exactly what had happened. *Hadn't I just been thinking that Elea and I could be twins, if not for the subtle differences between us?*

"Me," she whispered. "He thought you were me."

"Yes." She nodded.

"And he's been your…friend since then? Only your friend?"

Elea nodded again with a grin that said that the last thing she wanted was for the prince to be *only* her friend. "He was the one who told me that Rhea was down here."

"I see," Cyrene said, chewing on her bottom lip.

That settled it. She had to bring Elea with her. There was no way that she could leave her sister here. She might be in a truce with Kael at the moment. A temporary thing that they were both prodding at gently to see where the edges frayed. But she didn't trust him enough with her sister to wait to see if—no, *when* it would all unravel.

"You've suddenly gone pale," Elea observed.

"Yes."

"You don't approve."

"Hardly," Cyrene said with a scoff.

"Well, I just don't think that you truly know him."

"Oh, dear Creator, you're enamored."

"Well, how could I not be?" Elea asked. "He is the crown prince!"

Cyrene looked into Elea's dark blue eyes, so like her own, and saw the innocence and naïveté that Cyrene had left behind all those months before.

She remembered being ensnared in Kael's web when she had not known what he truly was. And still ensnared now even when she knew better.

"Be careful," Cyrene warned, clutching her sister's hand.

"I will."

What else could I say? Cyrene certainly wouldn't have listened to advice to stay away from him. She still didn't listen to her own advice. Strohm women were stubborn, and it would just backfire on her and send Elea straight to Kael, which was the last thing she wanted.

Now, she was more determined than ever to figure out how to get Elea to go with her. So much depended on it.

Fifteen

THE BOMB

As Cyrene raised her arm to knock on the door, an explosion rocked the ground all around them. Elea was helplessly tossed back. A rip could be heard as she fell, catching her dress. Cyrene clutched on to the doorframe. Her knees were wobbly, and she banged her elbow against the wall but managed to stay on her feet.

She let go of the door with shaky hands as the aftermath of the event passed. She stepped over to Elea and held her hand out.

"What in the Creator's name was that?" Cyrene asked with a shake of her head.

Elea's eyes were wide, and her dress was torn down the seam, revealing her creamy white leg beneath. "I have no idea! But it ruined my new dress. Mother is going to kill me."

"Let's deal with that after we figure out what happened."

Cyrene turned back to face the door where the explosion had just come from...where Rhea was supposed to be. Then, with a determination she had for most things in her life, she strode through the door without knocking. What she found made her pause only a few feet into the room.

"Rhea?" she gasped.

The room was cavernous. It dwarfed the hallways that they had come from with a glass circular opening far above, shining light into the dark room. And there was Rhea, huddled in a corner, shaking. She was dressed in a man's breeches and had some protective goggles hanging around her neck.

Her head snapped up at Cyrene's voice. Her eyes widened. "Cyrene?"

"It's me," she said with a smile. "What in the Creator's name are you doing in here?"

Cyrene tentatively moved into the room with Elea on her heels. As she approached Rhea, she noticed black soot on her clothes and hands.

Rhea shook her head and seemed disoriented. "Working."

"There was an explosion of some sort. Are you injured?"

Rhea laughed manically and shook her head. "Hardly."

She rose to her feet and sighed, running a hand back through her bright red hair, which was stark against her pale cheeks. She chewed on her pink lips and smudged some soot onto her forehead.

"When did you get back? How did you get back?" Rhea asked.

"No one told you?" Cyrene asked. Her appearance had been news for the whole kingdom. She was shocked to find someone in the castle who wasn't aware.

"I don't really venture out. I mostly stick to my work."

"And what work would that be?"

Rhea glanced absentmindedly to a table with a bunch of powders and apparatuses on it. "Are you even going to hug me? We haven't seen each other in months."

Elea laughed. "And ruin her dress?"

Rhea's eyes drifted to Elea. "It seems she wouldn't be the only one."

"It was your explosion that did it!"

"It's fine," Cyrene interjected.

She pulled Rhea into a hug. The last thing she cared about was her dress.

"You're going to need to change before Consort—" Elea coughed slightly. "Apologies. Before Daufina finds you."

Rhea's eyebrows rose. "Why did you apologize?"

"I'm to be consort," Cyrene told her, point-blank.

"What?" Rhea gasped. "How? Why?"

"All excellent questions."

"Why are you even surprised?" Elea asked. "And shouldn't you be happy for her?"

"I'm…just…" Rhea shook her head. "I didn't expect this."

"No one did," Cyrene confirmed. "Least of all, me."

"It's so wonderful. Lady Cauthorn is making her a new gown. Daufina is training her to take over her position. The king is ecstatic with her return. The castle is celebrating!"

Cyrene and Rhea shot each other meaningful looks. She knew what her friend was thinking without her having to say it. They had much to discuss. That was clear.

"What is wrong with you two?" Elea asked. "Don't act as if I don't know the two of you. I'm missing something. What details am I missing?"

"Nothing," Cyrene said at once. "I'm just overwhelmed, being back and immediately being thrust into court life. I'm unaccustomed to it. Out of practice. I just want a minute alone with Rhea, if that's all right? You could try to catch Lady Cauthorn to fix your dress before she leaves. Then, Mother would never know."

Elea straightened slightly, and Cyrene could tell that her request had hurt her sister. She hated doing it, but she wasn't prepared to tell Elea everything that had occurred in the last year.

"Fine," she said, turning on her heel.

"Elea," Cyrene called.

"Just let her go," Rhea said. "She's been strutting around the castle with adolescent torment. I love her, but she always was the baby. I think she believes it's only a matter of time before she falls into line here and can be treated like an adult."

Cyrene stared after Elea's retreating back. There was nothing she could do about it, but having Elea upset with her wouldn't help with getting her out of the castle.

"Cyrene, what is going on?" Rhea asked.

She whirled back around to face her friend. "Everything has gone wrong, Rhea. I wish we had more time. I was brought back from Eleysia before I could complete my training, and Edric has made me consort against my wishes."

"So then, you found what you were looking for?" Rhea asked.

Cyrene nodded. "I did."

"That's incredible."

Cyrene opened her mouth to tell her that the price for discovering her powers was not worth it. That she wished it had never happened to her at all.

That she wished she still had Elea's innocence about everything. Finding out that she had been lied to her entire life—that magic existed; Affiliates were sneered at around the rest of the world; and maybe, just maybe, men and women weren't even as equal as she had thought. So much change, so fast.

"I need to leave," Cyrene told Rhea instead.

"Already?"

"It's not safe for me here. I had an assassination attempt on the boat on the way here and another one last night on my way to my room. If I remain, I will die."

Rhea bit her lip, and her green eyes widened. "What are you going to do? How can I help?"

Cyrene shook her head. "I don't want it connected to you. Daufina has a plan to smuggle me, Ahlvie, and Orden out of the castle."

"Daufina? You trust her? Didn't you take her job?"

"And wouldn't it behoove her to see me gone?"

"True. I worry."

"Rhea, come with me," Cyrene said, taking her hands. "Think about it. I can get you away from here. Out from under the thumb of the Class system and to a place where you can really use your talents."

Cyrene had never thought those words would come out of her mouth.

Byern was set up with three classes. First Class was the ruling class—Affiliates and High Order. They received a higher education and oversaw the other classes. In other places she had ventured, she had found them to be called lords and ladies. The Second Class was the military and all the new royal guard. While Third Class was all mercantile, farming, and service positions. Each person at the age of seventeen was brought before the court, and the class fate was determined. She had always dreaded the thought of joining a lower class, as Rhea had done when she was moved to Second and into Master Barca's care. Now, she was beginning to believe that these people had more freedom than she ever would…if not, as much opportunity.

"Cyrene, you know that I cannot," Rhea said softly.

"But why not? With what I know now, I know that we could survive on our own."

Rhea shook her head. "I'm sorry. I have…work here to do."

"What? Slave away for Master Barca and deliver things for the king on his whim? That is no life."

"Cyrene, stop. Do not come into my workplace and judge me," Rhea said defensively. "I love you. I understand why you have to leave. I understand why you left before. I always knew that you were meant for more. Do not ask me to be like you. I am not."

Cyrene took a step back and glanced away. Of course. Of course, Rhea would stay. Cyrene had begged the last time, but Rhea had stayed behind. She couldn't get her best friend back. Just replace the hole in her heart where Maelia had been.

"Cyrene…"

"No, you're right," Cyrene said. "But…I need your help."

"Anything."

"I need Elea to come with me." Cyrene's eyes landed back on Rhea's table full of tricks. "And I need one of your explosions for a distraction."

The next few days dragged.

Cyrene didn't see either of the Dremylon boys in all her time training with Daufina. She tried to think of it as a positive, but she had gotten used to feeling that spark fly between them. It was unnerving, how much she missed it.

Not that she wanted to run into Edric after what had happened between them. She assumed that he was keeping his distance after her rejection, but it didn't explain Kael. He'd claimed that he was going to come see her after the attack. However, he never showed up, and she had no idea what he was doing.

And she hated how that made her feel. That she felt anything at all in his absence.

Worse…she hated that she could walk back into the Nit Decus castle and fall seamlessly into the fold. She had been gone for months, and after only a few days, it was as if she had never left. In fact, it was even better than before she had been gone. With the queen on bedrest, she wasn't there to harass Cyrene at every turn.

The training she was receiving from Daufina was legitimate, too. Even though they were planning to leave the castle, she couldn't completely ignore their training, or someone would get suspicious. So, sun up to sun down, Cyrene would sit with Daufina and learn the tricks of the trade.

The more she explained the job, the more exhausted Cyrene got at the prospect. The consort did *everything*. Daily tasks with her select Affiliates and High Order, managing court, strategy meetings, any and everything the king wished, Presentings, all holiday events, and the list went on. Cyrene couldn't imagine how Daufina did it all. Where she found the time.

Cyrene was lounging backward on a chaise as Daufina described a typical day.

Cyrene groaned. "When do you sleep?"

Daufina smirked at her. "When the king permits it."

"You have all this power, and you're still subject to a man," Cyrene muttered.

"Bite your tongue, girl," Daufina growled.

"Just think about it," Cyrene continued.

Daufina hadn't had experience outside of these walls, as Cyrene had. She couldn't possibly see how absurd the entire notion was.

"You have the highest position in court that isn't royal. Yet you, above everyone, are subject to the whim of one man. You work harder and do more to keep this country afloat, and what do you get as thanks? Sleepless nights?"

"Some consorts enjoy their sleepless nights," Daufina said with a grin.

Cyrene wasn't surprised that she wouldn't comment on the rest of her statement. "And have *you* ever enjoyed your sleepless nights?"

"A lady never kisses and tells," Daufina said with a coy smile that said yes.

She and Edric had most certainly been intimate. Though Cyrene suspected they weren't currently, or perhaps Edric never would have replaced her.

"Have there been others?"

Daufina glanced down and shook her head. "Edric is a loyal and faithful man. Even to his detriment."

"And I am his detriment," Cyrene guessed.

"You are his weakness, and if I had known then what I know now, I would have listened to Kaliana."

Cyrene took it for the slap that it was and sat back hard. It was Daufina who had spoken up in her favor to be made Affiliate. Kaliana had opposed the choice from the beginning. She wondered if her fate would still have been the same if they had moved her to Third Class and gotten rid of her.

She returned to her rooms with the thought heavy on her mind. She had only just reached her door when the ground rumbled under her feet. With wide eyes, she latched on to the doorframe for support until it passed. Then, she darted out of her corridor and to the rapidly filling hallways beyond.

Everyone was speaking at once, no one knowing what the noise was. Many people had been pulled out of their beds from an early night, concerned that the castle was under attack. Cyrene blended into the crowd, keeping her head down and hoping that no one looked at her too closely.

Her heart was hammering in her chest, and her veins were filled with adrenaline as the lust for escape took over. It was finally time. After all of those days, she didn't have to wait any longer. She usually jumped at every opportunity to put her plans into place as soon as possible, but she had believed Daufina when she said she needed time to do it right. Plus, she hadn't heard anything more from Lady Cauthorn. And the distance was too great to reach Avoca. Cyrene knew where she was, generally speaking, but she couldn't call to her. Cyrene was truly on her own.

She darted down another hall and into the alcove where she had agreed to meet Daufina. But she wasn't there. Cyrene tensed, wondering if Daufina would betray her. Try to use her to prove her point that Cyrene shouldn't be consort. It seemed like such a risk for her though. She paced back and forth in the small alcove in frustration until a face appeared.

She jumped backward with her hand on her heart. "You frightened me," Cyrene told Daufina, who looked as serene and unconcerned as ever.

"We must move. Your friend's distraction will only last a short time."

Cyrene nodded and hastened after Daufina down the deserted hallway. Cyrene prayed to the Creator that their luck would hold out.

They spiraled ever downward as they approached the dungeons. The guard on duty was fast asleep at his post. Cyrene nudged him, but he didn't waken.

"What did you do to him?" Cyrene asked with a newfound appreciation for Daufina's brilliance.

"Sleeping draught. He'll be out for a while."

Cyrene shuddered. The thought of being knocked out made her physically ill. She would suffer anything to avoid that again.

Daufina removed the keys from a bag at her waist and hurried down to the last cell on the right. "Oh, dear."

"What?" Cyrene asked. She jogged to meet Daufina and stared into the cell where her friends were supposed to be. "It's empty!"

Sixteen

THE ACCUSATION

"Where could they have possibly gone?" Daufina asked.

"I…I don't know. I haven't been down to see them."

"We can't stay here, Cyrene. Someone will be looking for us soon. If we're going to get you out of the castle, we have to do it now."

"But…I won't leave without them."

"It seems they will leave without you though"

Cyrene didn't have a minute to think. She could already hear voices moving about above them. Their distraction had ended. Whatever had helped them get out would soon completely be lost.

"Show me the way."

Daufina nodded once and darted back down the hallway. Cyrene didn't feel right about this. Yes, she needed to get out of the castle, but at what cost?

She didn't know if Ahlvie and Orden were safe, let alone alive. *Who would have taken them out of their cell tonight of all nights? Had they been moved, or had they escaped? What was their fate? What did that mean for my escape? And what would I do to get them back?*

She gritted her teeth and dashed after Daufina. First and foremost, she needed to get away however she could. She would not be consort. Not to Edric. Not to anyone.

Her future was her own, and she would fight for it tooth and nail.

Spiraling down through the catacombs of the castle gave Cyrene the distinct feeling of a rat trapped in a cage. The deeper they went, the harder it was for her to breathe. Apparently, having hundreds of tons of rocks over her head made her uncomfortable. Probably a new side effect of being knocked out, drugged, and held in a dark, dank prison cell. Her nerves fluttered about obtrusively, and she pressed her fingers into the rock they passed to try to calm down.

"Where are we?"

Daufina had a small candle to guide their way, but anything more could mark their presence. Though Cyrene didn't know who would venture down below the castle like this.

"Almost there. Quiet," Daufina said sharply.

Cyrene clamped her mouth shut. A gust of wind carried down the stairs behind her, shoving both of the girls at the same time. Cyrene gasped and stumbled a few steps before regaining her composure. Cyrene only knew that Daufina did the same because she cursed under her breath.

However, the flame that had been their guide guttered out.

Daufina stepped back up to Cyrene and clasped her hand. "Don't let go."

Cyrene steeled herself for the rest of the way downward and then followed Daufina. They reached a bend, and she maneuvered around the empty corridor and then down another empty corridor. Truly, much of the castle was not in use. Cyrene couldn't imagine what it must have looked like when it was full of Doma. Then, she sighed and focused on the task ahead. Dwelling on a two-thousand-year-old court of magical people would do no good for her here. Truthfully, they had only brought her trouble.

They were almost to another set of stairs when Cyrene saw a candle approaching them. Daufina halted in her place, and Cyrene barreled into her.

"What do we do?" Cyrene gasped.

Daufina stood frozen, as if she were paralyzed.

Cyrene could not allow this to happen. Perhaps Daufina couldn't take control of the situation, but Cyrene was not powerless. She took a deep breath and felt her magic from the tips of her toes to the top of her head. She didn't listen to any of the months of training that she had acquired from Matilde and Vera. She just reached for that moment in the corridor when the assassin had come for her. She grasped on to the anger and fear and desperation…to the power that flooded her veins.

Then, she flicked her wrist, and the candle went out.

Just like that.

No thought process. No deep concentrating. No agonizingly slow method that exhausted her.

Power and control.

Air magic, which she had never touched before a day in her life. And it felt like second nature.

She pushed her palms out, sending whoever the person was sprawling backward, off their feet.

Then, Cyrene grabbed on to Daufina and tugged her. "Which way?"

"What…what did you do?" Daufina asked. Her voice was shaky and her body even more so.

"I have no idea what you're talking about, but we need to move. Now."

"You…you're a witch!"

"Daufina!" Cyrene snapped. "Do you want to leave or not?"

"You've entrapped me. Edric. All of us," Daufina said, stumbling back a step in the meager light. "It explains everything. You've possessed his mind. That's why he wants to replace me."

"You're not talking sense! I am not a witch, nor have I done anything of the like."

"Why else would you be so desperate to get away? He's offered you everything. What kind of person turns away from that? You know what you've done, and now, you're trying to escape consequence."

"You're mad. You know why I'm running? Because I. Don't. Want. This!" Cyrene shouted at her. "I want my own life. I do not want to be ruled by anyone. Certainly not a man born into this position. Someone who never had to earn anything. Thinking me a witch just eases your mind. It's not the truth."

"Break the curse!" Daufina cried. "Do it now, and get out of here. I want you out of his castle. I want you out of our lives. And I never want to see you again."

"Halt! Don't move!" a voice called, approaching from the corridor she had just thrown the person.

"Daufina, please, tell me how to get out of here!" Cyrene pleaded.

"You are on your own. I will expose you for what you are. Mark my words."

Cyrene turned to flee, only to find more soldiers at their back. She ran a shaky hand through her hair as light poured into the corridor they were in. A familiar face appeared.

Cyrene's mouth fell open. "Eren?"

She had met High Order Eren on procession to Albion so long ago. He had been investigating the death of his brother, Zorian. Of course, he never did learn that a Braj had murdered Zorian. More death and destruction were on her conscience. Perhaps her ledger would always bleed red.

"Cyrene," Eren said with a nod in her direction, "you need to come with me."

"Yes, apprehend her at once," Daufina said.

"Both of you," Eren said.

He tilted his sword at the pair of them, and the guards moved forward and seized them.

"What is the meaning of this?" Daufina cried.

Cyrene didn't even move as her hands were pulled behind her back. She stared Eren down, unable to believe that she was thwarted by one of her own friends.

"You are under arrest."

"Arrest!" Daufina's shriek could probably be heard by the rest of the castle.

"Indeed," Eren said without providing further information. Then, he motioned for them to be brought behind him.

Daufina didn't go quietly. She was furious and being most unladylike. Cyrene didn't see the point. She could probably…maybe take out the group of soldiers. But she didn't know at what cost. Anytime she had used that much magic in the past, she had passed out and been incapacitated for hours. She couldn't afford that if she couldn't get away. It was another moment where she desperately missed her friends.

Eren and the guards shuffled them back up the endless stairways until Cyrene was so turned around, she couldn't have found her way out of a paper bag. Daufina shouted at them the entire way. By the time they reached levels with more human activity, she looked a wreck—hair falling out of its perfect coif, dress askew, eyes wide and feral.

The next level up, Cyrene could sense the direction they were walking. The constant tether that drew her to the Dremylons practically ached, the closer she got. It must be both Kael and Edric because it was never this strong with just one of them. Now, it was almost painful.

She took a deep breath to steady herself before answering the call and walking into the war room.

Edric was standing at the head of his long, rectangular table. Older men and women that Cyrene had never seen before, plus her mother and father, were standing around in elegant clothing in an attempt to match the king.

But it was Kael that drew her eyes. He was the only person seated. He lounged with one arm draped across the back of a chair with his leg crossed at the ankle. He put on airs, as if he couldn't care less about the entire thing, but she saw the truth in his eyes.

She and Daufina were stopped in front of the king, and Cyrene dropped into a regal curtsy. Daufina, however, didn't move. Something she might have been able to get away with while she was consort, but since she had been stripped of her position, Cyrene could tell, just by the tense atmosphere, that it would not be okay this time. Cyrene could feel it—the anger and bloodlust. It clouded everything, nearly choking her.

"Daufina," Edric said, his voice cutting like a razor, "you will curtsy to your king."

"Edric, I stand before you as your one true consort." She bowed her head slightly, only slightly. A deference between equal rulers.

"Bow, or I will make you."

Daufina lifted her chin higher. Cyrene made no move to assist her. Stepping out of line was not in her best interest.

Then, the Captain of the Royal Guard, Merrick, materialized out of nowhere and pushed Daufina's legs out from under her. She gasped and fell forward, hard, onto both knees. She caught herself with her hands, and Cyrene could see her face burning with humiliation and insult.

"That is not how you treat your—"

"Enough," Edric spat. He gestured to Daufina on the floor. "This is better. I approve of you addressing me from this position." He leaned forward, resting his hand on the table and staring down at her. "And you have no right to use my name without the proper honorific."

Daufina openly glared up at Edric. "Of course, My King," she said with venom in her voice. "However, your soon-to-be consort is a witch!"

She hurled the accusation at Cyrene, and Cyrene pushed her shoulders back and let the words fall off of her. She couldn't react. Certainly not to that. She couldn't even look at Kael. Though she could feel his eyes on her like a brand.

"That is quite an accusation," Edric said, holding his hand up to silence his court around him. "What proof do you have of this?"

"Down in the corridors, she used magic to blow out the candle of a soldier and then pushed him back down the hall without touching him. She did it with a flick of her hands! My King, she has been casting enchantments on the castle. She has cast one on you!"

Edric straightened, and his nostrils flared. "What makes you believe that

I am under such an enchantment?"

Daufina should have seen it as the warning that it was, but she barreled on, desperate to prove her point. "The way you have been acting the last year. You are enthralled with the girl. You would do anything for her—send troops into foreign territories, threaten foreign dignitaries, even go to war. You are mad with love for her, and she has made it so!"

Everyone was stark silent now. A pin dropping in the room could have been heard. Cyrene wasn't even sure if anyone breathed at that moment. Her own cheeks were hot with the words that Daufina had spoken. Declaring that the king, a married man, was not only infatuated, but also madly in love with another woman was an accusation never to be said in present company. But to say that he felt that way simply because he had been beguiled by witchcraft…that was beyond insulting.

"Interesting," Edric said. His voice was clipped, his eyes boring into Daufina. "Interesting that you would make such a ludicrous claim when I brought you here on account of treason."

"Treason?" Daufina said, struggling to form coherent words. "For…for what?"

"We were tipped off this very evening that you were going to stage an escape for the prisoners in the dungeon and try to force Cyrene out of the castle so that you could get your position back."

Cyrene's head snapped to Daufina. She knew that there was always a chance that Daufina would turn on her, but *she* had released Ahlvie and Orden? *What had become of them? Had they made it out? Or had the guards stopped them?*

Daufina looked like a fish out of water. "Who would make such a charge? I should be able to look my accuser in the face."

Edric raised an eyebrow and then motioned to Eren. A girl stumbled into the room. A small, slight girl with wild strawberry-blonde hair that Cyrene would recognize anywhere. Adelas. An Affiliate lackey of the queen's who had fallen in with a bad crowd of Affiliates with Jardana as their leader. Jardana was another person Cyrene had been fortunate not to see.

"Adelas?" Daufina asked in shock. "One of my own?"

Adelas dipped into a curtsy. "My apologies," she said, her voice wavering. "I couldn't let you get away with it."

"Thank you, Affiliate," Edric said. "You did the right thing."

"I did nothing of the sort," Daufina said. "Cyrene planned this whole thing. She wanted to escape. She told me herself."

"In fact, we have a firsthand account of High Order Eren hearing you tell Cyrene to leave and never come back," Edric said. "Or is his testimony a lie as well?"

"I…I…I didn't," Daufina said. "Cyrene, say something!"

Cyrene arched an eyebrow. Speak up for a woman who had accused her of witchcraft, who had been willing to throw her to the sharks on the hope of saving her own skin? No, she would be happy to offer her the same courtesy.

She faced the front of the room and could hear Daufina whimper next to her. But she couldn't look at her. It was Kael's eyes she found. His hands were steepled in front of him, and he leaned forward in earnest. At her glance, his smile widened, as if she had walked directly into his trap. She didn't know what it meant, but for the first time, she didn't even mind.

"Daufina, you are charged with treason and conspiring against the crown," Edric said. "I have seen all relevant evidence. You will be executed at sun up in three days' time. In the meantime, make your peace with the Creator."

Seventeen

THE NIGHT
—AHLVIE—

Ahlvie's ribs were on fire, and his chest ached. His legs were burning. His breathing was ragged but not completely uncontrollable. Even though he had just run for what felt like leagues, he knew that he could continue on for as long as he needed. And he felt suddenly... free at the prospect.

Of course, he had almost left Orden behind on more than one occasion. The man was a dozen years his senior and as thick as a tree trunk. Running was not exactly his forte.

But they were out.

Out of that insufferable prison.

No longer underground, no longer behind bars, no longer in that dank, dark cell.

Creator!

He could breathe. He could finally breathe again.

Never again would he let himself be locked up like that. He couldn't do it. It went against his very nature. Everything he had been and everything he had become in the last couple of months.

"Can you not slow down even a step?" Orden growled. "We're off castle grounds. No one is chasing after us."

Ahlvie's eyes shot to the castle on the horizon. Orden was right, of course. They had outmaneuvered the guards who had been moving them to a new cell on King Edric's orders. An explosion had rocked the castle, and they'd used it to their advantage. Ahlvie had wanted to use the opportunity to find Cyrene, but Orden had been practical. They needed to get free, regroup, and come up with a real plan. Wandering the halls of the castle would only end with them both back in prison.

Ahlvie slowed his loping stride and returned to Orden. "Where to, old man?"

"Your death if you call me that again, boy," Orden bit out.

His laughter bubbled out of him. "Fair."

"We'll have to reconvene with Rita."

"You want to go back into the city?" Ahlvie asked dubiously. "And, really…Rita?"

"Lady Cauthorn to you. Don't let her hear you say it." Orden grinned from ear to ear at the mention of Lady Cauthorn.

Ahlvie always thought that they were sweet on each other. Though, he usually pushed any female attention away.

"All right. We'll have to sneak back in at nightfall," Ahlvie said.

The pair found a place to make camp in a small cave on the edge of the Taken Mountains. They'd been fed regularly but in small quantities of tasteless mush and stale bread. Still, he'd scarfed it down to give him the energy to keep his mind and body intact. He'd need them both by the end of this. When they'd gotten the jump on those guards, no one had ever suspected they were capable of it.

When the sun finally set, Ahlvie's ears perked up. He stopped Orden with a hand.

"What is it?" Orden asked.

His now yellow eyes peered through the dark night, seeing much more than he knew he should be able to. The wide, barrel-chested bodies and stalking grace of a predator.

"Indres." The word ripped from him.

Evil wolflike creatures. Pack hunters. Warriors. Razor-sharp fangs. Yellow-eyed demons.

A bite.

A kill.

An alpha.

Losing control.

That night in the gardens in Aurum came back to him like a punch to the gut. He shuddered from head to toe. His body vibrated at the pulse beckoning him forward. Like calling to like.

"Boy," Orden said, "remember who you are."

Ahlvie clenched his jaw and took measured breaths. *Remember who you are. Remember who you are. Remember who you are.*

Orden placed a reassuring hand on his shoulder. "Let's get out of here. I wouldn't like to meet those beasts, unprepared."

Ahlvie agreed. He wouldn't like to meet them ever again.

They swept through the empty streets of Byern, sticking to the shadows and avoiding the castle guard. Lady Cauthorn's residence was in a house off of the Laelish Market, which was thankfully closed at this hour. They slunk around the edge of the building and to the back door.

Orden was about to knock when the door swung open. They both stopped as a man stepped out of the door, clutching a piece of paper in his hand.

"You bastard!" Ahlvie cried, launching himself at Dean in the doorway.

Dean's eyes rounded, and he wrenched backward as Ahlvie came at him. Ahlvie slammed his fist into Dean's face. The crunching sound was incredibly satisfying. But Dean blocked his next attack and used the small doorway to his advantage. They sprawled on the floor as Dean tried to hold him off.

"Ahlvie, stop!" Dean yelled into his face.

"You betrayed her!" Ahlvie yelled again.

"Is this truly necessary?" Lady Cauthorn demanded from the doorway.

"Apologies, my lady," Orden said, stepping on both of them as he strode into her house. Ahlvie and Dean both grunted as they took the brunt of Orden's weight. "Get inside, you fools, before someone hears you."

Ahlvie shoved Dean away from him and hopped back to his feet.

Dean stood, gingerly touched his nose, and frowned. "I think you broke my nose."

"You deserved it," Ahlvie muttered. He bumped his shoulder into Dean's as he passed into the house.

"You, too, young man," Lady Cauthorn snapped at Dean.

He took a deep breath and then followed them back inside.

"What in the Creator's name is he doing here?" Ahlvie asked, his blood boiling over.

He didn't know the whole story, but the guards had gossiped enough for him to piece together that the prince of Eleysia had given up Cyrene for a peace treaty after Maelia killed his parents. That meant, Dean was a traitor—to their group and to Cyrene—which meant he was their enemy.

"Prince Ellison is here as the emissary of the Doma Court," Lady Cauthorn said smoothly.

Ahlvie stilled completely. "The Doma Court?"

"The Master Domas he traveled cross-country with cannot enter Byern without their magic being detected There is a magical shield of some sort up around the country only those who are aware of it can sense. Thus, Dean has been kind enough to be the messenger for them."

"But how would you even know?" Ahlvie asked. Then, he shook his head. "The Network."

"Yes. So, as you see, Dean is here as my guest, and you have broken his nose."

"He betrayed Cyrene!" Ahlvie cried out again.

"Perhaps. Perhaps not," Lady Cauthorn said in that haughty way of hers. "He is here for her. Maybe all is not how it appears."

Ahlvie glared at Dean. *Yeah, right.*

"And, you," she said, turning to Orden, "I heard you were in a dungeon. How are you at my doorstep?"

"Ahlvie and his incredible knowledge of the inner workings of the castle mostly. We would have been caught otherwise. We are here to beg assistance from you."

"I think your assistance lies with Prince Ellison," Lady Cauthorn said.

"Housing or aiding known fugitives would not help me or the Network at all."

"What *is* this Network?" Dean asked.

Lady Cauthorn appraised him. "An ancient community dedicated to the return of magic."

"And you all have been working together for some time?" he asked, looking at Ahlvie, Orden, and Lady Cauthorn.

"We are more prolific than you know," Orden said. "But that matters not. What matters is, getting out of here once more so that Lady Cauthorn is not disturbed and then finding a suitable place to rest for the night."

"Prince Ellison will see to your accommodations. I will have access to Cyrene up until her Investiture. She seems different," Lady Cauthorn confessed.

"Different how?" Ahlvie asked.

"Depressed and hopeless. Her trials and tribulations have left a mark on her. You will have to really help her see the good once more."

Ahlvie processed that as Lady Cauthorn ushered them out of her house. Cyrene didn't break easily. If she truly was hopeless, then she must be really lost. He thought about that the entire way as Orden took charge over both of them, and they followed Dean's directions back out of the city and up into the mountains.

Ahlvie suppressed the call that was scratching to take root.

Come, brother.

Come.

Kill.

Feast.

No. He wouldn't.

You belong with us.

You are one of us.

Our leader.

Ahlvie ground his teeth together and fought to block it out. He was not one of them. He would never be one of them. That was not the life he had ever wanted, and he would never give in.

They entered the mouth of a cave after an arduous climb up the mountainside. And what he saw when he entered knocked the wind out of him.

"Avoca," he gasped like a prayer.

She turned in all her ethereal glory. Tall, sleek gold hair, round, innocent eyes that bore more than a hundred years of wisdom. Gorgeous. Feral.

Mine.

Ahlvie didn't think twice. He barreled past Dean and Orden and scooped Avoca up into his arms. He held her as light as a doll as he kissed her senseless.

He had gotten on that ship and left her behind to deliver Cyrene's letter. Avoca hadn't even seen him off.

All he wanted in that moment was to take her to the nearest bed and show her exactly how much he had missed her. Taking his time and letting the message sink in, in excruciating detail.

"Ahlvie," she said with a soft laugh. A laugh he would kill for. "You…you made it out!"

"What happened to your nose?" Matilde asked with her own stifled laugh as she beheld Dean.

Dean cocked his thumb at Ahlvie. "I picked up some strays."

"Good. Then, we're all back together," Vera said, coming to face Dean. "I think you look very handsome as it is, but I will set it, if you like, so it heals straight."

"Get it over with," Dean said.

Vera touched her hand to his nose, and a crack rang out in the cavernous cave.

Dean winced. "Thanks," he muttered halfheartedly.

"Ahlvie, are you ever going to put Avoca down, so we might have a meeting?" Matilde asked impatiently.

"No," Ahlvie murmured against Avoca's lips.

She kissed him once more and then slid out of his arms. "I'm glad you are well."

He knew that was a lot, coming from her. Her people, Leifs, weren't one for big displays of emotion. But, when they loved, they loved endlessly, and he was damn sure going to be around when that happened.

"We must get Cyrene out of the castle. Untold damage could be done to her mentally in the time that she remains within those walls, surrounded by Dremylons," Vera said.

"Worse, she could be killed," Matilde added.

"All right," Ahlvie said, "how are we going to get her out?"

Dean handed Avoca the scrap of paper he had been holding. "Lady Cauthorn received this from Cyrene."

Avoca snapped it out of his hand. Ahlvie noticed that she had as much venom for Dean that he did. She read it quickly and then fumed.

"Cyrene is...not herself," she said, tucking the paper away. "We need to move as quickly as possible. Dremylons are circling like vultures, and she's to be made consort as soon as the king sees fit."

Dean snarled something vulgar and paced away from the group.

Ahlvie didn't much like it either. He'd heard talk of it from the guards. Then, a light seemed to blind him with recognition.

"I have an idea," he said. "You might actually like this one."

Avoca tensed next to him. "With the risks you take, I doubt it."

"Me, too," he said with a toothy grin.

Eighteen

THE ACCUSATION

Twin guards flanked the entrance to Edric's room. Cyrene wasn't barred from entering, but she also was not here by invitation. In fact, it was ridiculously early in the morning, two days after the meeting where Daufina's execution had been planned.

Edric hadn't said a word to her since then. No one had. Cyrene hadn't complained about the seclusion. It had helped clear her thoughts. Given her confidence in her actions moving forward.

Cyrene took a steady breath before knocking twice on Edric's door. She could do this.

After a minute of waiting impatiently, the door opened, and of all people, Merrick appeared before her. Cyrene took a step back. Something about Merrick felt…wrong. Inherently, viscerally wrong.

"Can I help you?" Merrick straightened to his considerable height and adjusted the front of his black guard uniform.

"What are you doing here?" she asked instead.

He arched an eyebrow. "Not that it is any of your business, but as the Captain of His Majesty's Royal Guard, I sleep in his quarters with him to be of assistance in case of an attack."

Cyrene's mind whirled. *Edric allowed this man to sleep in the same quarters as him?* She shuddered as the thought hit her.

"Now, what are *you* doing here, Miss Strohm?"

Cyrene bristled at the tone and refusal to call her Affiliate. "I need an audience with the king."

"He is sleeping."

"Then, wake him," she commanded.

Merrick shot her a condescending look. "Unless it is a matter of state business, I do not presume to wake the king before he is ready to rise. You might be consort soon, but you do not yet command such respect."

"I understand," she said, taking a small step backward. "I believed that the king rose early and hoped to catch him before he broke his morning fast. My apologies. I'll come back later."

She turned to leave, but Merrick caught her arm.

"Wait." He sounded irritated that he even had to say it. "The king will have my head if you came by and I did not allow you entrance. Come in and hurry."

Cyrene managed a victorious smile before returning to a state of calm as she entered Edric's private quarters. She had never been here before and was shocked with the simplicity. Much of the castle was ostentatious to a fault. She had gotten so accustomed to the overdone drapes, enormous tapestries,

Aurumian rug after Aurumian rug layered on the cold floors, ornate furniture draped in silks, and crystal goblets with all silver flatware. Decadence upon decadence.

Leather-bound books were on the wooden bookshelves, and the desk was cluttered with paperwork. A table and chairs were set up for when he dined in his rooms, and a sitting area was cloaked in neutral shades. Not much to look at, but perhaps he enjoyed it that way.

Cyrene was wrapped up in disentangling the state of the room from the man she was about to meet. When she had first met him, he had been loving, caring, interested in her beyond the physical, and while she had always been hesitant about his power, he had never used it to his advantage. It was in sharp contrast to the man she was seeing today. Her absence had driven him insane. His actions were erratic at best, deadly at worst. Whatever connection there had been between them had turned rotten to the core. Perhaps she shouldn't blame herself, but she was sure it was her fault.

"Cyrene," Edric said, dismissing Merrick with a wave of his hand.

Merrick glared at Cyrene before striding from the room.

"Excuse Merrick. He doesn't like visitors after the last assassination attempt."

Edric wore an easy smile. His clothes were askew, as if he had thrown them on at the mention of her name. He still looked gorgeous in loose-fit black pants and a white button-up shirt, half-undone at the neck. Cyrene could keenly feel their connection in the space between them. She wondered if it felt the same to him. If her king was still there under it all.

"I was curious if you would come to me."

"Yes, My King."

He sighed. "Please, Cyrene. Edric. I will always just be Edric to you."

She wanted to say that was what Daufina had thought as well, but look at how that had turned out. However, she was still here for diplomacy. It could win this out as long as she kept her temper under wraps.

"Of course…Edric."

"Why has it taken you so long?"

"For what?"

"To come to me." He paced across the room, as if the thought of waiting for her to come to him had been pure torture. "It has been a week since I called on you. I thought you would have come sooner. Much sooner."

His blue-gray eyes found her in the distance, and she shivered. He thought she had come for much more than the real reason for her being here.

"You waited for me to come to you?"

"Yes. After our last…encounter," he said, snarling out the last word, "I thought it would be best for you to remember who you were dealing with. For you to remember and come for me. And you have."

Cyrene opened and then closed her mouth. He believed that, if he gave her time to cool off after their incident in the gardens, she would get over it and come back to him. He thought she should feel honored by his intentions…no matter how dishonorable. Her skin crawled.

If anything, she had been glad that he gave her the time to think. To put her life back together. But not enough to come running back to him. *How delusional must he be to think that I would do that? Or had he been in a place of power so long that he couldn't fathom someone not wanting him?*

Edric bridged the space between them, and Cyrene pulled back from the tension.

"I have missed you so much."

He brushed back a loose dark curl around her face and smiled. And, in that moment, he was her Edric. It would be so easy to get lost. To be that innocent girl once more. The one who had been so willing to give up everything for this man.

She closed her eyes and stepped back, letting his hand hang between them.

That girl was dead.

"I'm here for Daufina," Cyrene said instead.

"For Daufina." His voice was cold, and he straightened, as if realizing this wasn't that kind of house call.

"You cannot execute her, Edric."

"I see." He crossed his arms over his chest. "And why not?"

"Because she is innocent."

"She freed the prisoners and attempted to smuggle you out of the castle. Then, she accused you of witchcraft. I would think you, of all people, would want her gone."

"Wait…she freed the prisoners? Ahlvie and Orden are gone?"

"We had already discovered her plot. So, we were moving the prisoners to a different cell. We had them in chains, and they were escorted by half a dozen guards. Yet, somehow, they managed to get free of their restraints and overpower six of my most highly trained guards to flee the castle. That sounds to me as if they had help. Does it not?"

Cyrene shook her head. No, it sounded like…Ahlvie. "I wouldn't put it past them."

"No two men could do such a thing."

"No two ordinary men perhaps. They are not ordinary. I do not think Daufina had any part in it. You have known her longer than I have. Do you truly believe that she has committed treason? If anything, her fault is that she loves you too much."

Edric turned away from her. "If she loved me, as you say, then she would not have conspired against me."

"Do not be paranoid. You are a strong leader. You do not have to resort to this! Your people love you. Would you prefer they fear you? Because that is the line you are walking."

"And what do you know of it?" He whirled around, his eyes hard. "You are no ruler. You are just a girl. Not born or bred for the throne."

"Maybe," she snapped, "but I know leadership. I know fierce and loyal followers. I know that, if they fear you, they will hate you, too. And love might mean nothing to you…or me, but it can win wars without lifting a single weapon." Cyrene took a deep breath, trying to calm the feral anger deep within her chest. "And I am *not* just a girl."

"You say all of this in defense of a woman who would have you hanged as a witch?" Edric asked, ignoring her last statement.

"Yes!"

"You are not talking sense."

"Edric, please, you can't do this."

"I do not have to defend my actions to you, Cyrene. If you are not here to see me, then you are dismissed. I am a very busy man." He turned his back on her and stepped toward his bedroom.

Cyrene ground her teeth at the dismissal. As if he could get rid of her so easily. "If you do this, I will never be your consort. Never. I could never be yours."

She hated dangling that nugget out there, but she had to go for the jugular. Hit him where it hurt. Or else he would never listen to her.

He whirled around. "Do not threaten me."

"Then, make peace. Please," she begged, rushing back toward him. She took his hands in her own and stared up at him with all the pleading she could muster for this.

Daufina was in this position because of her. No matter that she had turned Cyrene in for her magic. She couldn't let her hang for this.

"That is all I ask."

"And what of your…engagement?"

"I am here. Does it look as if I am engaged?"

She swallowed hard, hating the part that she was playing but reminded herself that this was the right thing to do. Daufina would not suffer Maelia's fate. Not on her watch.

Edric's face loosened, and he linked their fingers, drawing her closer. "All right. If you want peace, then I will grant you peace."

"You will?" Cyrene breathed.

"Indeed, my dear." He brought her fingers to his lips and placed a soft kiss on her hand.

Cyrene sighed softly, ignoring the way her skin ignited at the barest brush of his lips. "Thank you."

"I am happy to please you, Cyrene."

Diplomacy. Diplomacy could work. She just needed to remind herself of that. She could get out of the castle and out of whatever tacit agreement she had just entered in with Edric another way.

She slowly extracted her hands from his with an easy smile.

"Wonderful. I'm glad we could come to an agreement. I'll just…go to my fitting this morning then."

"This early?" he asked, edging closer.

"Yes. Bright and early."

Then, she smiled coyly and all but fled from Edric's bedroom.

Creator! What am I going to do? She couldn't go through that again. Being near him was hard enough with the way her body reacted to him. It was unfair to play with his emotions. Yet she couldn't seem to get through to him any other way.

As soon as Cyrene was out of his rooms, she dashed down the hallways, thankful that she had come at such an early hour. No one was out and about, except the help, and she could move freely.

She hadn't been completely idle since her failed attempt to escape. She had just made it appear that way. In her spare time, she had found out where Daufina was being held. Though she hadn't dared to ask anyone about Ahlvie or Orden. She hadn't wanted that to get back to Edric. At least they were somewhere safe.

Cyrene found a guard standing outside of the tower quarters Daufina had been given for her final days. The man bowed when he saw her and allowed her to enter.

"Daufina?" Cyrene called into the room.

The consort appeared in a simple purple dress. The plainest garment Cyrene had ever seen her in. Her hair was down and loose around her face. She seemed resigned to what had happened.

"Leave me!" Daufina snapped.

"Daufina, I've come with news."

Daufina trained angry eyes on Cyrene. Her expression was one of deep loathing. "Be gone, witch. Are you here to cast a spell on me? Well, you already did so, and it worked. You have my position, my king, my life. What else could you possibly want from me?"

"I want none of that."

"You are a liar."

"We knew that trying to get me out of the castle came with risks. But in no way did I believe that it would result in this, Daufina. You must believe me."

"I believe that you set me up and left me to drown."

"I went to Edric to ask for a pardon for you," Cyrene told her.

"You did what?"

"He has granted my pardon. You will be safe."

"No, he wouldn't."

"He did. I just saw him."

"But…why would you do that for me?"

Cyrene's heart hardened at the thought. "Because I could not do it for someone else, and she didn't deserve her fate either."

Nineteen

THE PARDON
—DAUFINA—

The girl gave her hope.

Daufina had seen Edric's face when he ordered her execution. She had known that he was serious. She knew him well enough to know when he was set on a course. And this declaration was a crash waiting to happen. Nothing could steer him away from his decision.

But Cyrene.

Somehow, Cyrene.

Daufina had known that she was a wild card from the start. When she had agreed to make her an Affiliate against Kaliana's wishes, she had thought that she would have a pawn, a trump card that she could play in her favor. And, for a time, Daufina had believed that Cyrene truly was that player in her deck of cards.

She had pushed her onto Edric's barge for procession. Daufina had been tired. So tired. Her physical relationship with Edric had diminished when her love for the crown and power overtook her intimate affection for the man himself. Daufina knew she would never have a bastard child with the king, like so many previous consorts. She had taken measures to ensure that would never happen.

And Kaliana drove him mad. It seemed, for so long, that he would never have a child with her.

Daufina had known that she had to foist Edric off on somebody else. He was a loyal man, but she was certain she would be able to find someone to catch his eye.

When Cyrene had come about, it had seemed obvious. Edric was interested in the girl. Cyrene was young, naive, and willing. Putting the plan into motion should have been easy. Then, the girl had gone and disappeared in the middle of the night and ruined everything.

Now, Kaliana was pregnant, and Edric wasn't the father. A fact no one but herself and Kaliana knew. A fact she would take to her grave if need be.

With Cyrene's interference in the matter of her execution, she didn't want to hope that Cyrene had such control over Edric's actions. But how could she not? After seeing the way Cyrene seduced him…possibly even controlled him with her magic, she was capable of changing his mind. Daufina hated the idea of being indebted to a witch, but she would accept that if it meant she got to live.

All she had to do was wait and see what would happen.

Life or death.

When the guards came for her at dawn, she was ready.

Her hair was brushed, and her face was clean. She had on a new dress. It was as black as her midnight hair and simply adorned. Her hands were red from wringing them through her anxiety. Her cheeks were pale with dark smudges underneath, revealing how little sleep she had gotten the last three nights.

She was unshackled and allowed to keep her dignity. She was thankful for this kindness. As small as it was.

She held her head high and walked with grace. Part of her wished that Kaliana would be there to make a scene, as she always did. Then, at least she could count on someone coming to her defense.

Though a part of her heart was praying that Cyrene was right. She wanted to believe that with all her heart.

Her slippered feet carried her down the last staircase and out toward the open courtyard outside of the castle walls. A scaffold had been erected from remnants of one from the forgotten parts of the castle. A noose hung loose from the bar at the top. A crowd of Affiliates and High Order gathered for the spectacle. No common folk. Nothing but the best for a consort stripped of her title.

Edric was seated on a raised dais, opposite of the scaffold. Merrick stood at his back, but no one else was beside him. Not his queen, not his new consort, not even his brother. He was judge, jury, and executioner in one with no need for guidance. Ultimate power in the form of one little boy who had been thwarted by his father in his last minutes. A sad excuse for a king. So much potential thrown away.

Daufina shivered as she climbed the stairs up to the top of the scaffold. A guard ushered her to the center of the wooden platform. Her feet tripped across the trap door, and she shivered, despite the June summer weather. No heat rolled off of the Fallen Desert this early morning. It was just a breeze from the mountains, wet and chilled.

The brisk wind caught her hair as the noose was secured around her neck and tightened. She swallowed as tears threatened to spill from her eyes. She couldn't believe she was here. Standing right here.

After all that she had done for Edric, after everything she had done to keep Byern afloat in those years when Edric thwarted allies and advisors and insisted on ruling how he saw fit. In those years when Kaliana hadn't even known how to do anything but act like a spoiled princess, let alone how to rule Affiliates. Or the days when she had been the only one worried about all of the minor things that Edric had neglected.

She had been the backbone of Byern, and this was what it had gotten her.

A thick rope and a six-foot drop.

Merrick stepped up next to Edric to address the crowd, but Edric stood and pushed him backward.

Daufina's heart was pounding. This was the moment. This was it. He would tell everyone this was a mistake. He was a showman. He wanted everyone to know that no one was safe. Not even his favorites.

He was standing before them, letting them know that he had a zero-tolerance policy. Next time, he would go through with it. He would do anything for the kingdom.

But her pardon was coming.

That was what Cyrene had said. And, above everything, he wanted

Cyrene. To his detriment. If he had given her a pardon, then surely, it would be coming any minute.

"Thank you for coming," Edric said. "Today, we are here for an execution with the crimes of conspiracy and treason. How do you plead?"

Daufina felt sick to her stomach. She was going to throw up. She couldn't make it through this. She just wanted him to say it. Her eyes were wide with panic. *Please, just say it.*

"Not guilty, Your Majesty," Daufina said, her voice strong and carrying.

"Yet the evidence is overwhelming. You helped prisoners escape, drugged guards on duty, and attempted to remove the future consort from the castle. No doubt you would have had her killed to get her out of your way. You have conspired against the crown and have been found guilty."

The crowd was silent as her crimes were listed by the man she loved, her very best friend.

She reached out for Edric. "Please, My King."

It was time. Now or never. He was supposed to give her the pardon. Cyrene had said.

Edric turned his thumb over, giving the signal, and shock rocked through her body. The last thing she saw was Cyrene and Kael rushing through the crowd to try to reach Edric. She was screaming something that Daufina couldn't decipher as she fell through the door and disappeared forever.

Twenty

THE LINE

Cyrene screamed.

Her hands reached for the scaffold. Her body convulsed at the atrocity. Her eyes widened with disbelief. Her heart lodged in her throat. Her magic burrowed down deep.

"No."

It was the only word she could utter before she saw Daufina's legs swing.

"No."

She couldn't pull away.

Not again.

"No."

Her fault.

All her fault.

"No."

And then anger.

Pain.

Suffering.

Death.

"Cyrene, please," Kael muttered behind her.

His arms were around her waist. He was pulling her backward. Trying to keep her under control. He, and only he, knew what this meant to her.

But she couldn't comprehend whatever else he was saying. It was white noise through the haze in her mind. She had been here before. She had seen Maelia's beautiful head of blonde hair drop into a basket. She had looked into dark eyes and felt the unexpected bite of betrayal as the sword crashed her into oblivion.

This time…she only saw blue-gray.

And the same treachery.

But not the same motive.

Dean had been in shock over the death of his parents. An idiot and a coward. He had done everything wrong in that one moment when he could have done everything right.

But Edric. Oh, Edric.

This was not shock. This was not panic. This was not trying to save Cyrene's life in whatever way he could.

No, he had *lied* to her. Directly to her face. He had offered her exactly what she wanted to hear. All those lies delivered on a platter for her taking, and she had bought it. The falsehoods were painted on his skin in black ink.

Deceiver. Destroyer. Fraud. Hack. Cheat. Liar.

A child king playing dress-up.

And she would not stand for it any longer.

"Let me go," Cyrene said.

She pushed her hands out, and Kael released her. Silence fell as the crowd parted for her and the prince. She walked like royalty up the stairs to where Edric was still standing before the crowd of Affiliates and High Order. No one had made a move to get Daufina down. No one even breathed.

Merrick moved first to try to block Cyrene's path. "Stand down."

"Out of my way," Cyrene barked.

"You will not make a scene," he ground out.

Kael stepped up next to her and quirked an eyebrow. She shook her head. She wasn't ready for everyone to know of their magic. It still felt like a precious jewel, a hand to play when she had no other options. With Edric, she had one more.

Cyrene instead ignored Merrick as she shouldered past him and moved to stand before the king. Not her king. No longer.

"What have you done?" she asked, her voice clear and strong.

"What needed to be done," Edric answered simply.

"You think this makes you strong?" She threw her hand out at Daufina's lifeless body.

"I would watch what you say, Cyrene."

"The time for that has come and gone. So has this," she said, wrenching her Affiliate pin off and flinging it into his chair. "You knew the consequences. You did it anyway. I do not serve a deceitful king."

A gasp rippled through the crowd. She was making a show. She wanted people to know what Edric had done. For she had been like them once. So swept up in who he was—the title, the crown, the good looks—that she hadn't seen there was a murderer down beneath. That he would look her in the eyes and tell her he loved her, he wanted her, she could trust him, he would give her what she wanted…only to turn his back and kill a woman he had known, loved, and relied on for years.

A muscle twitched in Edric's jaw.

She could see he was fighting with himself not to make an example out of her. With the anger burning through her veins, she almost couldn't even feel their connection. But it was still there. Despite it all.

He rose with a jerk, the pin in his hand. He held it tight in his hand until blood seeped from his skin where the needle bit into him. "This pin is a symbol of something greater than you," he spat. His eyes moved from Cyrene's to the crowd. "Greater than all of you! It is a symbol of our people, of the sacrifice that we had to make all those years ago. And the fortune that has been heaped on us since. My decision here today was not made lightly. But I do not condone someone who has worn this pin to commit treason against the Dremylon name and against all of you. I do this for Byern!" He raised his bloody fist into the air. "For Byern."

And, like little parrots, the crowd roared its approval. "For Byern!"

Cyrene was disgusted. He had turned her display around so easily. Yet this was not the end of it. She knew it in her heart. She couldn't stay here one more minute. She'd walk out the front doors, tear them down brick by brick if she had to.

"I'm leaving," she spat in Edric's face.

He reached out and gripped her wrist. "Cyrene…"

"You *lied* to me, Edric. Give me one good reason not to walk out right now."

"Because I have your family."

Her blood ran cold. "Is that a threat?"

He straightened to his considerable height and then offered Cyrene his arm. He didn't say another word. Just gave her a look that said, *Come with me and find out.*

It was the last thing she wanted to do. But she had never considered her family to be in any danger. Not once in her entire life. They were a formidable bunch. Strong, smart, and resilient. Nothing could harm them. Except the king…

Cyrene gritted her teeth and placed her hand on Edric's sleeve. To everyone else watching, save Kael and Merrick, she and Edric were united once more. All was right with the world. Yet it was so far from the truth.

The truth. She nearly laughed manically at the very thought. *What is the truth anyway?* The more she learned of it, the more she didn't believe that she had ever heard it correctly. She had been lied to her entire life. A beautiful lie passed down from generation to generation. It wasn't until she'd left Byern and found out the ugly truth about her Doma heritage that she realized how much her entire existence had been false. She might be some heir to some destiny, but right now, she was just a girl who would do anything to save her family.

Cyrene could feel her magic pulsing in her core as she followed Edric down the steps and back to the entrance to the courtyard. An answering rumble to her anger thundered in the distance. She hadn't even intentionally called a storm, but her powers seemed to intensify with the feelings beating through her body.

She could taste rain approaching and prayed to the Creator that it was something that would wash away this stain on her soul. This ache that told her to forget everything in her existence and give in to this grief. For a split second, she wanted nothing more than to take off Edric's head. Like the day on the boat during the hurricane when Dean had slain Robard, and blood magic had called to her like a beacon.

She wanted to go back to a time when her biggest threat had been Kaliana, and her biggest fear had been whether or not she would get the right educational path at court. Carrying this weight was heavy and draining, and she wanted to collapse under it all. But she couldn't. She wouldn't. Not when more innocent lives were at stake.

When Edric dragged her into the first empty room he could find, he slammed the door behind himself before Kael and Merrick could even follow. Then, he whirled around and shoved her into the wall with manic eyes and unsteady breathing.

"I could have had you on that scaffold next to Daufina for what you just did!" he yelled into her face.

"Then, why didn't you?"

"Because I'm in love with you! Don't you see that?"

"This is love to you?" Cyrene asked in a rage. "Bullying and threats and hangings?"

"I found Daufina guilty in front of a room of my top advisors. How would I have looked if I had set her free?"

"Merciful!"

"Mercy is weakness!"

"And so you would rather lie to my face? That instills trust and strength in others, does it?"

"I never lied to you. I said that I would make peace, not that I would issue a pardon. You heard what you wanted from me," he said, slamming his fist into his open palm. "You ask too much and give too little."

"Fine. You didn't lie. You openly deceived me. You had me believe you would pardon Daufina and then murdered her anyway. There was a line, Edric, and you crossed it."

"Enough!" Edric roared. "That is enough. I am not a murderer. I did not have her murdered. I found her guilty of treason, and the price of that is execution by hanging. Why will you not see that I am doing this all for your sake, Cyrene? Have you changed so much in your time away that you no longer see me as the man I am? A man who loves and adores you?"

The answer was yes. She had changed beyond measure. Heart, body, mind, and soul. Edric no longer held sway on a single part of her...except that thread that seemed to connect them.

That...thread.

There was something familiar about it.

Something she hadn't considered before.

That thread...

Cyrene's eyes glazed over, and suddenly, she wasn't in the room. She wasn't with Edric. She wasn't even in the castle.

She was back in her vision of Viktor and Serafina, reliving the memory she had seen of them after she passed out in Eleysia from trying to stop the hurricane.

Viktor stood with the blade between him and Serafina, his firstborn babe in his arms. Serafina was reading from a book, an old blackened book with a spell. She had said that she would find a way for them to be together...always. That they could make it happen. That magic would no longer be a barrier.

Then, Viktor slit his infant child's throat and used the intense bond between father and child to generate his own deep, dark blood magic. His magic fused with Serafina's, and together, they were bound.

Much the same way that she and Avoca had.

Cyrene hadn't thought too hard about it before. But something in that moment clicked with her.

Together. For all time.

A Doma and a Dremylon.

It couldn't be. *Creator! It couldn't possibly be true.*

She had known that, after the Rose Garden Ceremony following her Presenting, she was bound in some way to Byern—the throne and the land itself. But she hadn't considered that her vision was showing her the present.

That perhaps…that thread she felt, the electric energy she couldn't escape from either Dremylon boy…meant she was bound to them. That a Doma and a Dremylon had been bound…so they could be together forever. And it extended beyond the grave.

She supposed anything was possible after bending the laws of magic. No one could be bound who didn't have magic. Going against nature and stealing magic had to have consequences. *Could this be a consequence of something Viktor and Serafina had done for their love all those years ago?*

Her body shivered as she came out of her trance. Someone was shaking her. She was on the ground.

"Cyrene? Cyrene, are you all right?" Edric asked. He was on one knee, trying to rouse her.

"What happened?"

"You fainted."

"I…fainted?" she whispered.

"Yes. Out of nowhere. Must have been the strain of the day."

Cyrene tried to clear her head. She had gone so deep into her own mind, trying to put the pieces together, that she had completely passed out from the effort. And she didn't even know if she was right. But it felt right. It felt as if it all made perfect sense. In a way that she couldn't explain.

"Let me help you up. I can take you to your room," he said, gently lifting her.

She shuddered, taking a step away from him.

Did I only ever feel something for him because of some two-thousand-year-old curse? And what about Kael? Did this apply to him as well?

It was too much all at once.

"Are you still upset with me?" Edric asked, taking her distance personally.

She blankly stared at him. She was beyond upset with him. She wanted out. She wanted to get away from all this. She didn't want to be a pawn piece in anyone's game.

"I'm leaving," she told him, point-blank.

His eyes narrowed. "We already discussed this."

"Yes. I said that I could no longer stay here."

"You will learn to love me again."

"Edric," she said, shaking her head at his delusions.

"Or your family will pay the price."

She stilled again. She couldn't believe he would issue the threat not once, but twice.

"Your sister has a Presenting soon. I'd hate to see her moved down a class and have to leave her family."

"That is *not* how Presentings are supposed to work," she spat.

"Your family only serves a purpose in my court so long as you fall into line, Cyrene," he said, bridging that distance one more time. "So let me speak plainly. You are my consort. You will stay here and play the part. If you do as you're told, your family will be rewarded. If you attempt to defy me again, as you did in the courtyard, or even think about leaving my side, I will end them. Their lives are now in your hands, Cyrene."

Cyrene opened her mouth to tear him apart limb from limb, but a figure burst into the room.

"Your Majesty!" a woman said, dipping into a low curtsy.

"Yes? What is it?" Edric asked impatiently.

"The queen! She's in labor!"

Twenty One

THE ALLIANCE

Edric rushed out of the room without a backward glance at Cyrene. She should probably hurry out after him. Falling into line and protecting her family and all that, but she wasn't ready to do as she had been told. She couldn't leave. That much, Edric had just solidified. She would never do something to knowingly harm her family. If that meant staying here and playing house with Edric, she could do that. For a while.

But it didn't mean that was her only option.

And it didn't mean she had to enjoy it.

A calm settled over her. Her anger had taken up residence in the place she always associated with her magic and was sizzling around in there, getting acquainted with its new home. But it wasn't the cold fury she had felt before that drove her to desperately ask for Daufina's help.

This was something else.

As if a plan had magically materialized in her mind. It felt as if it had always been there. Like she had somehow known it would come to this. Now that it was here, she wasn't even frightened. She was prepared.

Cyrene straightened her dress and then left the room Edric had abandoned her in. She was glad that he had Kaliana to distract him. She needed him out of the way.

She closed her eyes for a minute before deciding on her way. She felt that tug, that thread that she always associated with Avoca. She had thought it was unique. But she had never before considered that she could be bound to more than one person. In fact, up until this moment, she had believed it to be impossible. The idea that she had been somehow bound to the country itself had terrified Matilde and Vera. No wonder she was so unstable if she were also connected to the Dremylon boys.

If she searched calmly, knowing exactly what she was looking for, she could feel all three threads deep within her. Avoca's was strongest. That was the one she had willingly walked into. She tried not to think about Avoca and why she wasn't here. If Avoca had answered her call all those weeks ago, why hadn't she come for her? That was like falling down a rabbit hole.

Cyrene quickly schooled her features and followed the paths of the other two threads. Faint but there. Edric and Kael. Both of them there. One leading off toward the queen's confinement chambers. The other in the stables.

Her feet automatically carried her toward the stables. She knew what she would find. But she was nervous to discover that her magic was true and that she would finally, *finally*, have an explanation for something in her life.

Kael had his hand on a midnight-black stallion. The beast wasn't cooperating, but it was clear that Kael knew how to handle him. He didn't ask for assistance. He just firmly showed the horse who was in charge. He placed the bit in the horse's mouth and then secured the bridle. After that, he went about fastening the saddle into place. Then, he led him out of his stall and stopped when he saw Cyrene standing at the door.

"Going somewhere?" Cyrene asked.

"A ride helps to clear my head," Kael informed her. "Care to join me?"

"Sure."

He tied up his steed and prepared another horse for her.

"How did you find me?" he asked, passing her the reins to a chestnut horse.

"Lucky guess," she lied.

Kael offered to help her onto the horse, but she put her foot in the stirrup and hopped into her spot, as if she had been made to be on the back of a horse. He quirked a smile at her and mounted the midnight stallion. He guided them out of the stables and toward the tree line.

Once they were on a well-worn trail, Kael turned his attention back to her. "Tell me what happened."

"What happened?" Cyrene laughed humorlessly.

"What else happened," he clarified. "You seem…different."

"I'm ready."

"For?"

"That conversation. You said you would tell me everything. That we needed to talk and you would explain. Then, you avoided me at all costs. I am ready now."

"Cyrene—"

"No," she said, her voice harsh. "If you are trying to play nice with Edric, I'd advise against it. I no longer think a united front is a smart play."

"How so?"

"Kael, just stop it," Cyrene commanded.

She came to a halt, and he pulled up next to her.

"He threatened my family. He said he would kill them if I tried to leave."

Kael's face was impassive. She didn't know what he was thinking or feeling about the incident.

"He has lost his mind. I don't know what has changed with him, but he is no longer the person I knew. And, frankly, I don't want to know him. I will not be threatened, but I won't put my family in danger either."

"What is it that you want from me, Cyrene?" Kael asked with that devilish smile.

"You told me that you were protecting me, that you knew how to control it, that we could be so much more if we were unified," Cyrene baldly told him.

"True."

"Then, show me how. Train me. If we're better together, then I want what you're offering. I am tired of always being a step behind and always being used. I want the power. I want to rule."

Finally, a true smile broke on Kael's face. "You realize that is treason you are speaking, my dear."

"I know exactly what I'm saying."

"Good." His eyes swept over her body. "This suits you."

Cyrene tilted her chin up. "Well, will you teach me?"

"Of course," he said, reaching his hand out toward her. "All you had to do was ask."

She placed her hand in his, and a tingle ran up her arm. She tried to shake off the feeling that she had just made a deal with the devil. But it lingered like a fever.

Kael gestured for her to follow him, and she edged her horse into a trot. He finally came to a stop in a small clearing that reminded her of the place where she had met Dean. Her heart constricted, and she buried the feeling. It was just a meadow. That was all.

Cyrene dismounted, and Kael tied up their horses nearby. Her eyes roamed the clearing, trying to ascertain why he had brought her here. The grass was short and yellowing from the drought of the past year. But it was already coming back to life from the last storm. With dark clouds rolling in from her earlier temper, she knew the ground would once more be soaked. She didn't know how long she and Kael could even be out here with the storm brewing so near.

"Stand here," Kael directed her.

She moved to the center of the field and expectantly faced him. Everything she had learned from Avoca and then Matilde and Vera flittered through her brain, and she prepared herself for what was to come. Long hours of meditation, communing with the elements, readying her mind to accept magic, and working methodically to improve bit by tiny bit. For she had never had trouble with excess magic; it was always the little things that she couldn't master. And, without each step along the way, she never could become a master.

She took a deep breath and closed her eyes.

"Whatever are you doing?" he asked.

Her eyes snapped open. "Preparing?"

"Forget everything you know, Cyrene."

"What do you know about what I know anyway?"

His grin was quick and merciless. "That you have more potential than you know what to do with and no idea how to wield it."

"That's not—"

"Don't lie to me. You asked for my help. I'm giving it. You need to stop hindering yourself. Stop fumbling for control that you already possess."

"But I don't—"

"You do."

He snapped his fingers, and she staggered forward a step into him. He tilted her chin up so that their lips were almost touching. She tried to pull away from him, but he held her in place with a glance. She glared at him in response.

"Give in to your emotions, Cyrene."

"Let me go."

"Make me."

She ground her teeth together, struggled unsuccessfully to free herself, and stared back, defiant. "What emotions?"

"All of them. All of the buried anger and fury and jealousy and lust and wrath. Let go of your fears, and give in to that raw power you're hiding away."

"You're not making any sense."

He trailed a finger down her cheek. Her heart accelerated, and she swallowed. She didn't know how far he would take this. How much he would push her. She was immobilized, and he had barely blinked. He could have done this to her at any point on the boat while they were in the same bed… yet he hadn't.

This was part of the lesson.

"Do you remember that time I came to your rooms?" Kael asked.

He paced a lazy circle around her, and she hastily tracked him with her eyes.

"You believe I took advantage of you."

"How exactly could I forget that night?" she spat. "It was after my Presenting ball."

"What did you feel that night?"

"Like I was going to rip you apart limb from limb for being so presumptuous."

He laughed, as if she had made a joke. "Your history is so interesting. But, nonetheless, take that feeling, rip it out of you. Let it guide you, and take a step."

"I don't see—"

Kael was standing in front of her in a second, his eyes darkening and his mood shifting. "Don't waste my time, Cyrene. I gave you a command. There are a lot of better ways that I could be spending my time with you." His eyes flickered up and down her body. "You stopped that assassin from killing you with no thought whatsoever, except anger fueling your body. When you submit to that, I won't be able to do this unless you want me to."

His hands moved to her shoulders and down her arms. Then, they spread to her hips and up her waist to run along her rib cage. She closed her eyes and remembered exactly how she had felt that night when he tried to do this without her permission. How she had felt when that assassin attempted to murder her. The anger burned through her. Her magic came to her on instinct, and without breaking a sweat, she pulled her arms up and sent Kael sprawling backward into the dirt.

"Do not touch me without my permission." She seethed.

But Kael just smiled. "Well done. Now, do it again."

This time, when she was immobilized, she didn't even blink before breaking out of his entrapment, as if she were tearing through cotton.

Kael stood and dusted off his pants. "You know, the funny thing about memories."

"What's that?" she asked, heady on the feel of her powers actually working for once.

"Sometimes, they're false."

"How could my own memories be false?"

"You remember me trying to take advantage of you. You wield that night like a weapon. You push that distance between us because of it."

"With good reason."

"I never tried to take advantage of you, Cyrene."

He took that last step toward her and intertwined their fingers. Her magic hungrily fed off of his, and their powers sparked and hissed with the connection.

"I felt *this*. The moment you walked into that room, you were like a beacon in the night. I couldn't have walked away if I tried. When I escorted you back to your room that night, I believed that you felt as I did. This."

Cyrene swallowed. "And you acted like a pompous, entitled jerk when you were wrong."

"That's who I am, love."

Cyrene shook her head and stepped back from Kael. She felt like an idiot for working with him.

Even if he had felt their connection from the moment I met him, did it really change anything between them? She had too many questions and not enough answers.

"Why does my magic react to anger?" she asked to change the subject.

She wasn't sure if she wanted all of her questions answered yet. She might come to regret her own decisions, but for now, she needed the power.

"Because your magic comes from within you. When your emotions are high, you are in more control. You need to reach that place within you that lets you feel most acutely, and then there are no limits."

It seemed so counterintuitive. So backward to how she had been taught. Yet she knew he was right. She flicked her wrist, and water from the nearby stream pooled into her palm. She circled it between her fingers like waves and then made a halo around Kael's head before drawing it back to her hands. Water always was her main element. The easiest, even when she had fumbled for control. But, now…it felt like breathing.

"You have the world at your fingertips, Cyrene. All I want is to be at your side as we take it over."

Her magic faltered, and the water dropped helplessly onto the ground. Her hands were wet and she sighed. So much for control.

She knew the path she had entered on would have consequences. Yet she couldn't help second-guessing every choice that she had made to get here. And she needed to stop.

She had power. She was not going to let it go to waste any longer.

"And how exactly will we do that?"

"In my experience, it's best to do it from the inside. Then, no one will see it coming."

Twenty Two

THE BABY

Falling into the role of the soon-to-be consort was effortless when Cyrene had a mission to work toward. She had her family to consider, and though falling into line had never been her strong suit, she was determined to keep them safe. It helped that Edric was preoccupied with the birth of his first child, and Cyrene could go about getting ready for her Investiture without any more of his wild interference.

It was three days after her blowup with Edric when she was called to the queen's rooms. She had no idea why Kaliana would possibly want to see her. They were rivals at best, bitter enemies at worst. But she did as was expected of her.

The queen's rooms were still set for confinement. Dark curtains covered all but one window, and only a handful of candles otherwise brightened the room. Kaliana was lying in a massive bed set low to the ground. Her hair had been pulled back off her face, but she looked gaunt and drawn, as if the birth had not been easy. As if she was only a few steps from the grave.

"You wanted to see me," Cyrene said, stepping into Kaliana's room and curtsying. It was barely a curtsy though. More of a short bob between equals. A deference to her throne but not to her power over Cyrene. For the best thing of all of this was that the queen no longer had any power over her at all.

"Cyrene," she spat the word like a curse. "Yes, come in."

Cyrene stepped into the room just as a small coo came from a nursemaid in the corner. Cyrene's eyes swept to the woman and saw she was holding the tiny infant.

A girl.

That was as much as Cyrene knew. As anyone knew.

The baby's name wouldn't be announced until tonight. When Cyrene glanced once more at Kaliana, she could see the disappointment etched into every line. All of that work…for a girl.

"She's beautiful," Cyrene offered.

"She's a girl."

"Yes. And a beautiful woman she will become."

"To be married off to some prince for an alliance."

"Strong," Cyrene continued. "Like her father."

Kaliana flinched. "Worthless."

Cyrene felt as if she understood Kaliana in that moment. Just a young princess sent from her home to be with a man she had never met. Then, to not even be able to produce a male heir after all she had suffered. If she wasn't such a wretched human being because of it all, Cyrene might have sympathized with her more. *What is my world coming to that I'm aligning with Kael and identifying with Kaliana?*

"Have you decided what to call her?"

"Alessia Salina."

"Perfect." Cyrene stepped up to the baby and saw her little tuft of hair peeking out of her swaddle. "Little Alessia Salina Dremylon."

"Davila," Kaliana said sharply, "take Alessia into the nursery."

The nursemaid hopped up at once and scurried into the next room over.

"We need to talk," Kaliana said as soon as they were alone.

Cyrene turned to face the queen and arched an eyebrow. Kaliana looked sickly, even more run-down than when Cyrene had first entered her rooms.

"Do we?"

"Don't play games with me. You're still my Affiliate until you have your Investiture. You will listen to me."

Cyrene laughed in Kaliana's face. "When did I ever listen to you?"

"You were always trouble. Seducing my husband, walking around as if you were royalty, as if you owned the kingdom. So young. So naive. So idiotic," Kaliana spat at her.

"I did not come here to be insulted," Cyrene said. "If you cannot control your sharp tongue, then I have no qualms in leaving you here to rot."

"Is that a threat?"

"Hardly. But I am no longer that girl you remember, Kaliana, and I will not tolerate your insolence."

"My insolence," Kaliana said on a gasp. "You wretched girl."

"Creator, I don't know why I expected anything else from you." Cyrene whirled around and headed for the door.

She hadn't come here to be insulted. She certainly hadn't come here to have to deal with Kaliana, as she had a year earlier. She might not want to become consort, but she wasn't about to turn down the privilege of holding that over Kaliana's head. The queen frankly had no hold on her any longer.

"Wait," Kaliana said, stopping Cyrene at the door.

Cyrene stilled, but she didn't turn around.

"I didn't ask you here to argue."

"Really?" she asked, whirling around. "It appears that way to me."

"You won. Is that what you'd like to hear?"

"Not at all. It was never a competition. You were the only one who saw it that way."

Kaliana waved her hand in the air, dismissing Cyrene's words. "I'm sick, Cyrene."

Cyrene paced back toward Kaliana's bedside. "How sick?"

Kaliana's watery blue eyes said enough. Very sick. Deathly sick.

"I'm not worried about me anymore. I knew this was always a possibility with my…previous pregnancies."

Kaliana had had a number of miscarriages before, and Cyrene, as many others, had thought she might never have a child.

"What matters now," Kaliana continued, "is Alessia. Protect her. Care for her. She is a royal princess, and I don't want her to be pushed aside. I want her to grow up as she should."

"Kaliana," Cyrene said softly, "I don't know what you expect from me."

"Edric will remarry. You. I am sure of it," Kaliana said with a grimace.

"She will be your stepchild. All I ask is that you care for her as I would. As if she were your own child."

Cyrene felt dizzy. Her head was spinning. It was all too much at once. If Kaliana died, Edric *would* remarry. He would never be satisfied with Cyrene as his consort if he could have her as his wife.

And another vision hit her fresh. One she had not thought about in some time. In the Rose Garden ceremony, when she had been bound to her home and the Dremylon line, she had had a vision of Kaliana taking Cyrene's child, insisting that it was the last heir of the Dremylon line. It had been an illusion, a possible past, present, or future. Or just a dream. She still didn't know. But the idea of taking Alessia into her arms, of even considering taking her away, seemed too close for comfort.

"Kaliana, I cannot," she finally said.

"Haven't you done enough harm to this kingdom? Must you be so selfish that you cannot even be tasked with saving an innocent's life?"

Cyrene closed her eyes and ground her teeth together. She was responsible for the troubles in the kingdom, but she would not be Edric's wife. And, if she would not marry him, then the baby would never be her responsibility.

"All right," Cyrene relented, "I will care for her."

Tears welled in Kaliana's eyes. Tears of gratitude. "I can go in peace now."

"But you will get well, Kaliana. I am a contingency plan. You will make it."

"It matters not."

Cyrene sighed and wondered what kind of promise she had just given. For whatever she had done, Kaliana did seem at peace.

Just then, the door burst open. Cyrene jumped back from Kaliana's bed, and her magic came to the tips of her fingers without thought. She braced herself for an attack, but only Edric stepped into the room. He stumbled forward a step at seeing them together.

"Cyrene," he said like a vow. Then, his eyes swept to his dying wife. "Kaliana."

"Edric," Kaliana said crisply.

"How is our daughter?"

"She's nursing."

"I'm going to…" Cyrene gestured to the door.

She slipped out the door and sighed in relief at having escaped. She needed to see Kael. She needed to train more. Her magic was coming to her easily, but she wanted more. Every time she used it, it felt as if her core was draining of power. She had never had that sensation before without using unimaginable quantities of power. She'd been eating twice as much as before to try to sustain at the level she was working at. And, worse yet, sleep hadn't been coming readily. When it did, her dreams were plagued with nightmares—sinking ships, monsters, death. Always death.

Still, she didn't want to stop. She couldn't stop. No matter how hard she was working and how much easier it came, she was still behind Kael. He pushed and prodded at her boundaries, and she would fight back, but he'd had so much more time than her to practice.

She was on her way to find him when Edric popped back out of Kaliana's room. Cyrene grit her teeth in frustration. But, as he approached her, she saw that he was glowing and buoyant. Not the crazed tyrant that she had been dealing with these past weeks. It was as if she had gone back in time, and she now saw the Edric she could have fallen in love with.

"Cyrene, may I have a word?" Edric asked with a bounce in his step.

"Of course."

She followed him through the winding hallways until they reached an empty office that she had never entered before. It was full of scrolls, from floor to ceiling, in no discernible order. It smelled like fresh parchment and ink, and Cyrene loved the place on sight. It was like stepping into the library, knowing the worlds she could venture into were limitless.

Edric closed the door behind them and faced her. "I want to apologize for my actions the other day."

"For the hanging or for threatening my family?" she bit out.

Okay, so her anger was still rampant. If anything, her training with Kael had only intensified her displeasure.

"Cyrene, please, I have been on edge with war preparations, your imminent Investiture, and Kaliana's pregnancy. You are to be consort. I should treat you as such."

"Does that mean, you are no longer threatening my family?"

Edric shot her a merciless glance. "Do you still wish to leave my side?"

"No," she told him. She wished to take his place.

His smile was radiant. "Then, your family is safe."

That wasn't the answer she had been looking for. It was still a threat. But she was playing a part, so she let it pass. Soon, hopefully, it wouldn't matter.

"We have much more to discuss. You will officially be named consort in four days' time, but that is the easy part. We will immediately have to begin the preparations for your sister's Presenting ceremony the week henceforth."

"Elea's?" Cyrene asked, momentarily stunned. She had forgotten that her little sister's birthday was so soon.

"Yes, of course. This is a large duty of the consort, and I am pleased that

Elea will be the first we work with together."

Edric reached out and took her hand. She didn't jump at the connection this time. She had known it was coming and what it meant. But his touch still made her skin tingle.

"And then what?" she asked.

"Then, you begin your work with the Affiliates and High Order of your choosing."

"And what of this war?" Cyrene pressed.

Edric sighed, lazily running his thumb over her hand. "I am waiting on word from the Eleysian Queen Brigette. I have chosen to extend a hand of diplomacy if she will agree, but I have troops already deployed to Albion in the event that she refuses."

"I am pleased." Cyrene offered him a rare smile. "As much as I am upset by what happened to Maelia, I would not want to see such bloodshed for either country."

"I would like to make someone suffer for what they did to our own, but I would be glad to have more troops in the city after the troubling news that came in this afternoon."

"What news?"

"Wolves."

"Wolves?" Cyrene asked, suddenly going still.

"Enormous wolves have been rampaging the countryside. Villagers are flocking into the city to escape the relentless creatures. I have a report of ten dead and many more wounded. And the wolves are getting closer and closer to the city each day."

Cyrene frowned. Wolves didn't act like that. They certainly didn't attack villages, unprovoked. But Cyrene knew of a wolflike creature that did.

Indres.

Could it be that they had begun killing innocents?

Cyrene had been attacked with her friends in the Hidden Forest on her way through Aurum. It was how she had met Avoca in the first place. But the legendary creatures attacked on command and with purpose. They were intelligent and incredibly dangerous.

If they were in Byern, then that meant something was coming.

Something horrible.

Twenty Three

THE GUEST

Cyrene reached for her magic and felt it respond to her summons like a caress. She drew from her core with barely a thought, a fireball appeared in her hand. Matilde and Vera had said that fire was the hardest natural element, and she had effectively mastered all four in a week. *Take that, Master Domas!*

She launched the fireball at Kael's smirking face. He waved his hand, and water from the basin on the ground between them shot straight up, blocking the path of the fire.

Her heart thudded as she swept a blast of air through the water. The fire, though diminished, continued on its trajectory. And she sent a second one careening toward him through the open hole.

He elaborately twirled his fingers, and all of a sudden, a cyclone of earth and air sucked the first fireball out of sight. He clasped his hands together, and all three of the elements fell to pieces in his hands. For a second, she thought he hadn't seen the second fireball. Then, he caught it in his open palm and tossed it up and down, as if it were a toy. He closed his fingers around it, and the whole thing went up in smoke.

"Not bad," Kael said with as much appreciation as he'd ever dished out.

"Not bad? A week ago, I could barely move a speck of water without intense concentration. That's a miracle."

"Hardly. It's what you were made for. What I was made for. It comes easy because it is easy."

He didn't bother crossing the distance between them. He just lifted Cyrene off the ground with a gentle touch of the air and brought her directly in front of him. She would have been angry with him for doing so, but the feel of flying was too exquisite to yell at him.

When her feet touched the floor, she took a nearby seat and placed her hand over her heart. It was galloping ahead, as if it were about to burst out of her chest. She bent forward slightly and closed her eyes as another headache intensified.

"Headache again?" he asked.

"It'll pass."

"It'd better. You have a big day ahead of you."

Cyrene straightened as the pain began to diminish. She reached into her pocket for a slice of bread that she had grabbed earlier and scarfed the whole thing down faster than she had ever thought humanly possible. It should help with the side effects. She wasn't sure why they were there, but they weren't as bad as passing out, so she wasn't about to complain.

"I really don't want to talk about today."

"You're not ready?"

"To become consort?" Cyrene asked. "Are you kidding?"

"I have a feeling it's going to be…eventful."

"It's going to be miserable."

"You'll look stunning," he said.

His eyes captured hers, and the air heated between them. She didn't know if that was their magic reacting to their nearness or just their connection.

"Irrelevant."

Kael held his hand out to her, and she allowed him to pull her back to her feet. His eyes were expectant. She swallowed and glanced away.

"One more round?" she asked.

He shook his head. "No. Get to your fitting. Conserve your energy."

"All right."

"And, Cyrene," he said once she was already walking away from him, "save me the first dance."

Cyrene smiled. "As if you deserve it, you scoundrel."

His eyes were dark. "I'll take what's mine anyway."

She laughed but knew by his expression that he wasn't joking. "I'd like to see you try."

His answering grin was vicious. She could see that he had taken her words as a challenge, and he never backed down from a challenge.

With a heavy heart and an anxious mind, she disappeared from the room she had found to train with Kael. It was one of many empty sitting rooms.

They had rearranged the furniture so that it was open for their purposes. It was easier to get to than the woods. Lugging water and earth in for the practices hadn't been her favorite thing either. Plus, a part of her missed the direct connection to the elements. Not that she had felt a connection since training with Kael. It was her and only her. And, already, she was famished again.

She hurried down the empty corridor with her magic at the ready in case of an attack but made it to her fitting room without incident. She pushed the door open and was surprised to find Lady Cauthorn already present.

"Lady Cauthorn!"

"There you are, girl. Don't you know what day it is? We have much to do and little time. It would help if you weren't late."

"Late?" she asked, glancing at the three other helpers the seamstress had brought with her. "But I'm early."

"Enough of that. Onto the block. Let me get a good look at you."

Cyrene ran her hands down her hips and stepped up for inspection. Lady Cauthorn tsked and sighed and impatiently swatted at her.

"What have you been doing, child? I believed you were skin and bones when you arrived, but this?" She poked Cyrene's side. "You don't have to waste away to nothing in this place."

Cyrene held her head high. She knew why she was losing weight. And it had nothing to do with this place.

"Into the dressing room with you. Quickly now," Lady Cauthorn said. "Let's see how it fits, and I'll bring it in to match your new…figure."

Cyrene's eyebrows bunched together. *Into the fitting room to put on my dress myself?* Normally, she stripped down to her shift, and the assistants fitted her into the dress. Especially since her gown had this horrid corseting.

"Myself?" Cyrene asked.

Lady Cauthorn sent her a withering glare. "Do as you're told."

"All right," Cyrene said uncertainly.

She stepped through the curtain and into the attached changing room. Her dress hung from a hook against the wall, and she found it hard to even admire the thing, knowing it was more like a death trap. Just as she went to reach for it, a hand appeared out of nowhere and grasped her wrist.

She didn't scream; she just reacted.

Her magic came to her fingertips on command. She whipped the person away from her and slammed their body into the wall with a crunch. The man wheezed from the impact.

"Who are you?" she snapped.

Then, Cyrene got a good look into the man's face. She gasped and released him. "Ahlvie?"

"Nice to see you, too, Cyrene," Ahlvie said. He tenderly touched his ribs and shot her a rueful smile. "What in the Creator's name did you just do to me?"

"Nothing. Forget it. Why are you here?"

"Nothing? That was nothing? My ribs would say otherwise," Ahlvie said with a choked laugh. "Holy Creator!"

"Ahlvie, what are you doing here? How did you get in? Why aren't you free, as you should be?"

Ahlvie ran a hand back through his hair and gave her that mischievous smile that she knew meant trouble. She'd seen it when he tried to sell her to the owner of a gambling hall over a game of dice and countless times since then.

"Oh no," she muttered.

"I'm here to rescue you."

"You're here to rescue me?" Cyrene asked slowly.

"Lady Cauthorn got me in so that I could sneak you out with me."

Cyrene shook her head in disbelief. "Today?"

"You're about to be forced to be the consort. I thought today made perfect sense. Come on. I have a game to get back to." He winked and opened up a panel in the back of the room.

"Ahlvie, wait," she said, reaching for him.

"Through here. I know all the passageways. Now that I'm not in chains, I can get us in and out."

"You're insane. How did you get out in the first place?"

"We really have a narrow window. I can tell you everything when we get back. Move your cute butt through the hole, and let's get out of here. Orden is waiting for us in case of trouble."

"You really came to rescue me?"

She had felt so alone for so long. Trapped and lost and missing her friends. Missing having anyone to confide in.

Rhea was trapped in her rooms with her strange explosions. She had been confined to her rooms since aiding in Cyrene's failed attempt to escape. Cyrene was lucky that she hadn't been put up on the scaffold with Daufina since it was clear that she had helped.

Cyrene couldn't talk to her family. They didn't understand, and they were so sickly proud of her.

There was only Kael. And she didn't know how she felt about that at all.

"Who do you think I am?" Ahlvie asked. He made a flourishing movement with his arms that she had seen him make as an entertaining mendicant in Eleysia. "I'm a cheat, but I'm loyal."

A smile spread on Cyrene's face. This was it. She could get out. She could start over. No one would need to get hurt for her escape this time.

She took one step toward Ahlvie and then stopped. Except that wasn't true. Someone would get hurt. Her family was in perilous danger. All because of Edric's obsession with her. He'd claimed that her family was safe, but she had once taken him at face value, and that had gotten Daufina killed.

He clearly still meant that her family would be safe so long as she stayed by his side and did as she was told. The thought made the anger and fury rise in her chest. Darkness settled in her heart, and she felt the distinct stirrings of shadows curling around her sleeves. She would right these wrongs. But she could only do it from within.

"No," she said softly.

"No?"

"I cannot go with you."

"Cyrene, what are you talking about?"

"You don't understand. You must leave me here and not come back."

Ahlvie narrowed his eyes as they swept her body. "What's wrong with you?"

"Nothing is wrong with me," she insisted. "But I'm needed here."

"Needed? You're not needed here," he spat. "You hate this place. This place will *kill* you. It is already changing you. How can you want to stay with these people when your friends are waiting for you on the outside? You are special, Cyrene. You are needed. Don't throw that all away."

"I don't want to be special or needed," she told him. "And I'm not throwing anything away. I'm protecting what's mine."

Ahlvie put his head in his hands. "Creator, Cyrene! What kind of mess are you in now?"

"Edric threatened my family, Ahlvie. If I leave, he'll kill them."

Ahlvie cursed obscenely. "He won't do it."

"In case you didn't hear, he killed Daufina. I would put nothing past him. He wants me at whatever cost. I won't risk them."

He cast a string of curses that would make a sailor blush. "Fine. Fine. Fine."

"Just go. I'm safe here for now."

His eyes searched Cyrene's, and he shook his head. "You're about as far from safe as I've ever seen you, and we've been through a lot together. Promise me something."

"I don't have any more promises to give."

"Just say, from one con artist to another…you'll still be you when I finally get you out of here."

She glanced down at her hands and then clenched them into fists. *How can I promise that when I don't even know who I am? When I feel like my very existence is slipping away from me?*

She was becoming what she needed to be. And she would settle for nothing less.

Cyrene pushed him back into the tunnel with her magic. His eyes were round with concern.

She placed her hand on the sliding panel before she said, "Don't come back for me, Ahlvie, and you'll never have to find out."

THE INVESTITURE

B reathe.

Just breathe.

Cyrene stood before the closed doors on the very ballroom where she had had her own Presenting ceremony a year prior. At the time, she had entered from a side room with her heart in her throat and all her dreams swirling through her mind.

Now, her thoughts were empty.

Her heart was empty.

Her life was empty.

This moment should have been the best of her entire life. Yet it was the one she dreaded above all else. She would trade anything to avoid being shackled further to the Dremylons. To avoid having to parade around at Edric's side and give him counsel that he would not listen to and provide entertainment that would bring her no joy.

She was doing this for her family.

For a wide-eyed Elea, who had been permitted to hold her train as Cyrene entered the vestibule.

For Reeve, whose High Order duties always kept him furiously busy.

For her mother and father, who she knew were enjoying their lives back at court after so long away.

She didn't want to tear any of them from their simple lives. Least of all, tear any of them from this world. She would persist as she had done until she could take no more. Until she was ready to actually do something about this injustice. To stand up and fight for what she believed in.

Guards stepped forward and opened the doors, and Cyrene took one more deep breath before stepping through them. Her gown was heavy and tight. Boning cut into her ribs and held her waist into an even more miniscule size than she was. She was bedecked in the traditional Dremylon gold from head to toe with a slight shimmer to the fabric, so she shone like sunlight. The sleeves swept off of her shoulders, revealing her pale collarbones and the ruby necklace that Edric had brought for her at the last moment. It was a weight at her throat, but she knew he meant well. It had belonged to his mother. And it was a consolation for not getting to wear a red dress as she pleased. She hadn't even gotten to wear a comfortable pair of slippers. Instead, she was in heeled shoes that made her take tiny steps forward and pinched her toes. But at least she looked stunning. The shock and awe on all the attendees' faces said as much.

It felt as if it took an hour to walk down the aisle as a string quartet played a holy song to the Creator. Finally, she made it front and center before the dais. Edric was seated alone with Kael standing off to the side. Kaliana's place was unoccupied, as she was still too sick to attend the ceremony. Daufina's place was noticeably empty. A place she was to fill. A place that never should have been vacant.

Cyrene pushed away her fears of the moment and approached the officiant, stopping just before the raised platform. She kept her eyes forward through the entire ordeal. Affiliates and High Order watched her from all sides. And she felt judged from the solid wood doors, past the sweeping jade and mother of pearl columns, all the way to the gilded throne. No one believed she deserved this. An Affiliate only a year into her residency. Someone who had not even been with them the full time. No matter the circumstances of her *kidnapping*.

Yet she held her head high. She ignored their stares and had walked in, as if she were queen.

The crowd sank into their seats as the officiant raised his hands.

When silence fell once more, he addressed the crowd before him, "It is with great pleasure that I stand before you in honor of the great Creator and benefactor of her glory to invite a new host into such an esteemed position with the Byern court."

He bent his head and intoned a long prayer to bless the ceremony and her commitment to the throne. All Cyrene could think about was how much her feet hurt.

Finally, the officiant ended his prayer, collected a circular talisman that she knew she had to hold in her left hand, and a green cloak with the sign of the Dremylon royalty hand-embroidered into the cloth. It had belonged to the very first consort in existence for Viktor Dremylon himself. As soon as it touched her shoulders, she felt nauseated.

She didn't know if it was cursed or if the thought of all she knew of Viktor Dremylon made her physically ill. This was wrong.

It was her turn to move up to the top of the dais and claim her place before the entire court. Yet she was frozen in place.

Edric leaned forward in his seat and was staring hopefully in her direction. She couldn't even look at him, or she might empty her stomach all over the throne room floor. This couldn't possibly be right. Her eyes turned to the long glass windows that took up the far wall. It was a beautiful sunny day. Not a cloud in the sky. And she couldn't possibly understand why.

How could the storm have answered my call and my fears on the day of my Presenting? How could my magic respond to the start of my adult life yet absolutely nothing was happening when I was about to do the unthinkable?

She wanted a storm. She wanted to be vindicated. She wanted to know that this was the right choice, despite her gut telling her it was not.

"Come along, my dear," the officiant said, gesturing for her to take her place of honor.

With a deep sense of foreboding, she willed her feet to move up the steps. She shot one uneasy look in Kael's direction and found him a blank slate. Whatever he was feeling, he masked from her. And she could sense reluctantly that Edric was upset with her for even seeking out his brother.

She turned in place, letting the folds of her dress swirl in the most alluring fashion to face the crowd. There, before her, was a sea of strangers.

She only recognized her family in the front row. All of her friends and the people she loved, even Rhea, were not present here.

The officiant cleared his throat and addressed Cyrene, "Are you willing to take the oath?"

Another oath. *How many more ways could I bind myself to this country?*

"I am willing," she found herself saying.

"Will you solemnly promise to do your duty to your country and your people? To stand with the king of Byern henceforth, forevermore, until your time at his behest has concluded? To do all within your power to uphold the law, justice, and mercy before the eyes of the Creator and to do so with your best judgment in all things?"

"I will." Her voice was strong. Though she did not feel the vow in her heart. She felt it like the noose that had slithered around Daufina's throat at the behest of His Majesty.

"I present to you, Consort Cyrene!"

The crowd applauded her confirmation just as the first window shattered.

Black-hooded figures leaped into the room, silent and deadly. The cheers instantly erupted into screams. Chairs were overturned, feet were stamping on the ground, and everyone was in a panic at once.

And then the slaughter began.

Swords drawn and faces obscured by masks, it was impossible to tell who had managed to invade the castle so seamlessly. But Cyrene knew the skill involved with the creatures' stealth, and she had seen firsthand what those wicked curved blades could do to flesh.

Braj.

Unholy creatures of the night. Assassins who wore the mutilated faces of their victims. Deadly killers who would never stop coming until they felled their prey.

Cyrene didn't have it in her to scream. She wasn't even mad that they'd interrupted her Investiture ceremony. She just wished they'd come a little earlier. Saved her the trouble.

Magic came to her fingertips at will, and within a second, Kael was standing at her side, sword in hand. She could practically breathe in the amount of magic he was pulling in. So vast a depth, she felt dizzy. Her own magic was heady but no longer bottomless. Not when she had been drawing so deeply every single day in training. Not when her anger burned it so effortlessly. But she could hold her own against a Braj. It wouldn't be the first she had killed.

"Cyrene, get out of here," Edric called, rushing to her. "We must go. We must get you safe."

She brushed him aside. "I will not run while my brothers and sisters are being slaughtered by assassins."

"You are not safe here! You must protect yourself."

"I am not a maiden in need of defending. I will stand for what is right. Now, draw your sword, and help us!" she spat at him. Then, she stretched her hand out. "And, if you will not, then give it to me, for I know how to use it."

Edric looked as if he wanted to argue, but already, Kael was rushing into the melee. Cyrene didn't wait to see what Edric would do. She frankly didn't care. She dropped the precious consort cloak, tossed the talisman to the cowering officiant, kicked off her heels, and dashed toward the fight.

She didn't care that facing off with half a dozen Braj was suicidal. Or that using magic at all in front of Byern citizens was certain to draw attention. Or that she probably looked ridiculous in a dress and corset while rushing into battle.

All that mattered was that adrenaline pumped through her veins, and she felt useful. Important.

This asinine consort ceremony had made her feel like a spectacle. She was a pawn, a doll, a prop. Here, in this moment, she was so much more. It was what she had felt all those months as she discovered her magic and found her way to Eleysia to train with Matilde and Vera. Her heart sang, and for the first time since Maelia's death, she let it.

More guards rained into the room to help the guards who had already been in attendance for the festivities. To take the place of the fallen soldiers who had done their duty to their country.

Soon, the tang of blood filled the air, and sweat beaded her brow as she threaded into the fight behind Kael. She didn't have a weapon, and she hastily scooped one up from a fallen soldier. It wasn't as heavy as the one she had practiced with Orden, and she found that was to her advantage now. She had never been great with a sword, but she infused her magic through the blade and let it guide her.

Then, with a huff, she nearly face-planted over her dress. With Kael preoccupied with a Braj, Cyrene sliced into her dress, letting the many layers tumble to the ground, freeing her legs. She couldn't do much about her corset, so she measured her breathing and then moved deeper into the battle.

She found her first Braj after it sliced off a guard's head. Its eyes found her, and if it could smile, then she was certain he would have.

"Heir," it growled. "You slaughtered my brothers."

She paced in a circle with the creature. Her pulse beat a tattoo against her temple, and her hands sweat in their grip on the sword.

"They would have killed me just as easily."

"As I will do."

It came at her with lightning speed, but she had been practicing with Kael all week. Her instincts were sharp and crisp. Her motions fluid as a dance. She stepped out of his path and met its sword with a twang of her own as they burst against each other. She felt the first faint touch of its mind against hers and she laughed aloud.

She exploded into his mind, blasting it out of her own and unraveling whatever it had been attempting. "Not such an easy target." She sneered.

Then, they stepped through a series of clashes. Sword meeting sword. Offense. Defense. One step forward, two steps back. A game, a riddle, a synchronization. She didn't give any further, and then, without warning, she blasted it backward off his feet with her wind magic. She heaved over at the exertion and felt a headache blossoming in her skull. She pushed it away, kicked the Braj's sword from his hand, and pressed the tip of her blade to its neck.

"Who sent you?" she cried amid the remaining sounds of warfare.

The Braj simply laughed tonelessly. "I came for the heir, but your soul is no longer true."

"Don't speak in riddles to me. I don't care of your heirs and your darkness and your meaningless words. Tell me who sent you!"

She pushed the blade against its throat, hard enough to draw blood. It was black as ink and came from its neck as a sludge. It choked and sent her a venomous glare.

"Pure as snow. Light as starlight. Radiant as the sun. Tides will turn, and the prophecy is now."

Cyrene nearly screamed at its obtuse words. But, before she could ask it anything further, it wrenched his body forward, pushing itself onto her blade and committing suicide. Then, she did scream. Her body full of rage. Wholly unable to believe that she had had it and lost it without any answers.

She wrenched her sword from the Braj with a squelch and moved to help with the rest of the battle. Only one more remained, and it was squared off against six guards. She could feel the pulse of its magic binding their minds together.

Her anger sliced through the magic like a knife, and the guards recovered in a daze. Then, Kael was there, out of breath, and he hacked off the head of the last Braj, the black blood covering himself.

The silence that followed was deafening.

A destroyed throne room.

A pile of dead bodies.

A missing king.

Twenty Five

THE AFTERMATH

"Where is Edric?" Cyrene asked in the stillness.

Panic seized her. Despite all he had done, she did not wish him dead or, worse, captured. Her eyes roamed the bodies and found the six dead Braj. There had been no more than that when they crashed through the windows. She was sure of it. She tried not to see the devastation they had wrought. At least three dozen guards and a few unfortunate Affiliates and High Order who had been too close to the windows all lay scattered across the once-white marble floors.

She heard someone wretch nearby. Cyrene's sword clattered to the ground, and she covered her mouth in horror.

Kael was by her side in an instant, pulling her against his chest. She clung to him like a lifeline.

So much death.

So much unnecessary death.

Her fault again.

"Where is he?" she whispered into his blood-splattered dress clothes.

"We'll find him, Cyrene. Breathe and release."

She hadn't even realized that she had still been holding on to her magic, but with a sigh, she let it go. Her body felt as if it had been trampled by a horse and carriage. Her headache whipped across her skull, and her knees would have given out beneath her had Kael not been holding her up.

"Why am I so weak?"

"You will get stronger," he told her, his breath a prayer against her ear. "Just feel all the power around you. Drink it in."

She closed her eyes and tried to sense what he was saying. But all she could feel was death. Death and destruction. Blood. Blood everywhere.

Then, that feeling of longing locked into her heart, and she remembered that time she had wanted to pull in magic from Robard's blood. How inviting it had been. How much it had sung to her.

That was what she could sense. Not the magic she had been using all along. Not the elements feeding her body, communing with nature. But forbidden magic. The life force of others calling out to her. She closed her eyes against the torrent, as it all seemed to hit her fresh. But she didn't grab on. She didn't take it.

She had seen what had happened when Viktor killed his own child. How it had perverted the binding spell between him and Serafina.

What would it do to me if I give in to it? How would it affect someone who already had Doma magic deep in their veins? Would my soul even be able to handle it?

At once, her eyes flew open, and she shoved Kael away. "You!"

His eyebrows rose in a question. "Cyrene, you've had quite an eventful day. Perhaps we should get you some food and have you sit down."

"This was what you wanted?"

Energy radiated from him. Darkness deepened his sharp features. Inky-black tendrils practically crawled from his sleeves toward her.

"How could I want this, Cyrene?"

"You said today would be…eventful," she accused.

His eyes were so black, the blue practically vanished. "It was, but I never expected this."

"Yet you revel in it."

"Don't you have a king to find?"

She glared at him. "This isn't over."

"Oh, I look forward to it."

Cyrene stormed away from Kael. Her magic stuttered and spat, even as her anger intensified. She had nothing to draw from. Nothing to replenish. And Edric was missing. She had lost him in the battle. In fact, she didn't even know if he had followed her. She was barefoot, covered in blood, with an aching headache. She wanted a bath and a good night's sleep. But she couldn't rest until she knew what had happened to him. Her instincts told her to press on.

Her eyes roamed the room and found it almost completely empty, save the remaining soldiers and the dead. She picked up the tatters of her skirt and ran toward the office door where she knew his first line of defense was. She was halfway through when Merrick appeared.

"Do you have Edric?" she gasped.

He shook his head once. "He went after you."

"And you didn't follow him?"

"I was…detained."

Cyrene nearly shrieked in his face. She didn't even know why she cared so much. For all intents and purposes, Edric's disappearance would be a relief for her. But she couldn't stop the panic that seized her heart. He had to be here.

Then, she froze. She knew how to find him. She closed her eyes and reached into her center, past the thread for Avoca, away from the mess of a thread for Kael, and to that flickering light. She tugged on the binding that connected them and hurried in the direction that pulled her. She didn't want to think about how she would explain this later. Right now, her priority was Edric.

She dashed down the aisle and through the tossed open double doors. Her feet carried her down the foyer, to the entrance of the castle. She skidded to a halt. Her hand flew to her chest as she stared at more bloodbath.

There hadn't been six Braj.

There had been seven.

Her mother was already on the ground, bleeding out of a wound in her stomach. Tears streaked her gorgeous face. Her father held her hand, even in death. His eyes were closed. A flimsy weapon discarded at his side.

Her mother and father were dead.

Herlana and Hamidon Strohm were no more.

The words felt…wrong. Foreign in her mouth. In her mind.

How?

How could they be dead?

She had done everything she could to protect them. Everything she could to be the daughter they deserved. She had even become consort for their lives. And, the minute her back was turned, they had been slain by an unholy creature.

The rest of the scene came into focus before her. Reeve and Edric with swords aloft, holding back the Braj. Elea was paralyzed with fright behind them but not backing down. A Strohm girl through and through. A young man, whom Cyrene had never seen before, stood beside her with his eyes focused on the battle.

Cyrene wanted to sink to the floor and hold her parents in their final moments. She wanted to cry and scream for the atrocity of them being taken from her too soon. But she hadn't gotten to do it for Maelia. She wouldn't do it now.

She would grieve when the battle was won.

The clash of swords reminded her that this was not over. She had no weapon. Nothing to use against the Braj, save her magic. And, if she had to reveal that to Edric and her siblings, she would use it.

"Hey!" she shouted.

Edric's and Reeve's heads snapped up at the same time.

"Cyrene, no!" Reeve shouted.

"Stay back!" Edric cried.

Elea's hand flew to her mouth. Whatever she said was drowned out over the roar of the Braj.

"You," it said.

It turned, slicing at her mind in a surprise attack, but she was ready. She held it off with sheer force of will.

It moved away from her family to stride toward her with its curved blade. "The heir has finally come to face her death."

Edric and Reeve used its momentary distraction to rush the Braj. It turned around with anger and darted out at them. Reeve dodged the blade, but Edric was not so lucky.

"No!" Cyrene screamed, knowing full well that a Braj blade held a horrible venom. She had only survived her own cut because of her magic and herbs from a healer in Albion.

Edric had neither.

He collapsed to the ground at once, an inhumane shout reverberating through the entrance hall. The poison had taken mere minutes to pass through her blood system. What would it do to Edric?

Elea knelt at his side, but surely, she had no idea how to help him. Cyrene needed to get to him.

"Little King," the Braj said in disgust, "the Destroyer will take you all in the end."

Cyrene reached out for the very essence of the Braj. She didn't know what she was doing, just that it had to be done. These creatures…this darkness could not take everything that mattered in her life. It was not capable of destroying her any further. She might see the end one day, but she refused to let it be today.

She tightened her hand into a fist, feeling her powers weaken, even as she grasped for more. If it was the last thing she did, she would not let this Braj survive another day.

It grunted as she held it in place, squeezing the very life force from its body. She would have finished him off just like that, but Reeve took the opportunity to run his blade through the creature.

Cyrene released her powers with a gasp and fell to one knee. Empty. She was totally empty. Holding the Braj for that long had felt like fire running through her body, leaving behind blinding white-hot coals.

Reeve released his sword, and the Braj slipped onto the marble floor. His blood leaked out of him, staining the white tiles black.

"Cyrene," Elea called. Tears ran tracks down her cheeks.

Not done.

She still wasn't done.

Edric.

She hoisted herself off the ground, despite all protests to the contrary. Her eyes found Reeve's. They were wide and disbelieving. He had trained his whole life for a fight that he never believed he would have to face. Death was not an easy thing to have on your hands even if it was a creature who would take yours with glee.

"Find Kael," she told Reeve. "Now!"

He bolted into action, disappearing from view at a sprint.

Cyrene rushed to Edric's side. She ripped open the side of his shirt where the blade had gone into his chest. Already, the wound was hot to the touch, green, and festering. He didn't have long.

"Elea, we need a healer. Anyone who is proficient. The king will die without one." Cyrene turned to the boy with her. "I need supplies—boiling water, clean bandages, herbs. Hurry!"

"Cyrene," Elea said, reaching for her.

"Do you want your king to die?" Cyrene asked.

She feebly shook her head.

"Then, go!"

As both of them dashed away, Cyrene set to her real work. There was nothing a healer could do if the poison couldn't be drawn out of his system. This wasn't like a normal poison. She had felt it through her veins. She had felt the sear of it eating her alive. This was otherworldly and menacing.

For a moment, she pulled back and looked up into Edric's waxy face. That beautiful face that she had admired for so long was now pale, sweaty, and near to death. His blue-gray eyes were closed. He must have passed out from the pain.

And, for a moment, just a moment, she sat back on her heels and wondered…

Would it be so bad to allow Edric to pass?

She felt horrible for contemplating it. No one else deserved to die. Not on her watch.

But, if Edric were gone, she would no longer be consort. She would be free. Her family would be safe. Her life could go on without this chain tightened around her neck.

It would be so easy to allow him to fade. An honorable death for a king to die in battle. For his bravery and steadfastness, he would be revered high above any king since Viktor Dremylon.

She stared at that disgusting puckered wound and knew that, despite all of that, despite knowing that she could get away from this, Edric didn't deserve this. And she refused to be the kind of person who would allow this.

"No," she whispered. "I will save you, Edric. I will."

She placed her hands on the open wound and closed her eyes. Drawing on her powers, she reached into his body with her mind. She sought out how far the poison had gotten into his system, and the pain Edric was feeling lanced through her in response. It was everywhere. Spreading so fast. Impossible to remove without magic. That was clear from inspection.

But, as quickly as she had found it, her powers stuttered and flickered out. She didn't have enough. She needed more. She had depleted everything, going up against the Braj.

She needed Kael.

Her eyes flew down the corridor to where she had sent Reeve. If Kael arrived, then they could link and work together to save his brother. They had to do this.

She kept working, trying to use whatever tiny reservoirs came up as her body replenished. But, without food or water or anything, she was tapped out.

"No," she cried, pushing harder against the wound to try to do what she knew she was capable of.

Tears collected in her lashes as she worked. Tiny amounts of the poison were being removed but not enough. Not nearly enough.

"Where is he?" Cyrene groaned.

She checked for Kael again, but he wasn't there. He had abandoned her to this and abandoned his brother to his fate.

Edric's body seized, and he shook uncontrollably under her touch.

"No, no, no," she cried desperately.

She closed her eyes and tried with all her might to make things work. She had put her faith in her magic. That her heightened emotions—anger, grief, fury, lust, pain—would drive her home. It had been so easy. So impossibly easy.

And, when she really needed it, it was failing her.

She cast out for any magic, any at all, to save him.

But she was too late.

His body stilled beneath her fingers.

Twenty Six

THE AWAKENING

When it all hit Cyrene, it came with silence.

No!

She couldn't.

She wouldn't accept this.

Not failure. Not death. Not anymore!

Cyrene cast a wide net. Anything to save Edric.

But he was gone.

Her desperate pleas had not been heard.

Her parents' bodies lay only a short distance away from her. Their blood pooled on the floor. Their life force ebbing out of them.

Already dead.

Never coming back.

She knew that she shouldn't.

But she had good intentions. No matter that the road to hell was paved with them.

A life for a life.

She grasped on to the sickly-sweet feel that radiated toward her. She knew what it was—unholy, perverted, wrong—but she had no other choice. She imbued herself with their essence, taking it all, filling herself to the brim.

Blood magic infused her body. It struck directly into her hardened heart, cracked through her bones, bit at every nerve, sang through her mind. It filled and filled. A death song and a life song. A connected circle. Then, as soon as she gave in to that feeling of rightness, the slime followed, and wrongness settled into her system.

It was a rush unlike anything she had ever experienced. Her head felt light. Her body felt energized. Her mind felt as if she were capable of taking on the world and winning. No matter the film that seemed to coat everything. She might be breathing in tar, but, Creator, did she feel good!

Unstoppable.

She thrust her hands back down on Edric's open wound and cleared the poison from his system, hardly taking a breath. It was there, and then it was gone. She focused more intently, as if she were seeing everything in Technicolor, working beyond what she had ever thought she was capable of. She pumped his heart and knit the wound back together until it was almost perfect. Her mind working in the background reminded her that she had to give the healer something to do.

She was working so fast in overdrive, she didn't even hear the footsteps. Or see the people who came to surround her. To them, she had her hand on his wound, tears streaking her face. To them, she was doing nothing but grieving. But she would not give up.

"Cyrene, step back. Let the healer work," someone said behind her.

Hands touched her shoulders, and she eased away from them.

No. She wasn't ready. She wouldn't give up.

He couldn't die.

He couldn't.

Not when she could save him.

Two more beats. Three. Four. She could make this happen.

Then, miraculously, it did. The next beat was his own. And the next.

Edric came to, coughing and wheezing.

Cyrene sat back on her heels, stunned. Blood coated her hands. Edric's blood. More blood. She could sense it, taste it, touch it. She could drown in it. She could bathe in it. She could fill her soul with it. Never hit the bottom of her magic again.

Life force.

Whole.

Filled.

Her mind started rocking in on itself. Knocking against the walls, trying to see who was home.

"Come in," she said.

"Cyrene! Cyrene!" someone shouted over her.

How did I end up on the floor?

"Who is it?" she cooed.

Everything was fuzzy. Blinding on the edges. Bright lights swirled into colors. So many colors on the ceiling. She reached out to try to touch them and giggled as the paint smeared. A finger painting. All the colors mushing together.

"What's wrong with her?"

"What even happened to her?"

The voices sounded so far away.

Lost in the colors and light.

She bit down on her lip until it bled. Not once feeling the pain.

This was what heaven felt like.

Or was it hell?

"May the Creator bless you," she whispered.

Then, darkness swept over her.

Cyrene landed in a familiar body in an unfamiliar place.

She was standing on a bridge overlooking a great river surrounded on either side by tall buildings. She looked out through the great Domina Serafina's eyes, but everything seemed blurry. Faded. As if she was half-there and half-not.

Serafina craned her neck out across the bridge, as if she was waiting on someone, expecting someone. Cyrene tried to clear away the muddy feeling of the vision, but nothing helped. She had no control here. She saw and felt only what Serafina did.

But the more she looked around, the more Cyrene realized she *did* know where she was. The deep channel beneath her feet, the tangy scent in the air, the close-cropped buildings.

Eleysia.

Cyrene's heart twanged at the loss of this country where she had been prepared to become their princess. But she couldn't mourn long. Suddenly, the ground seemed to shift under her feet.

Cyrene tried to grasp on to something, but she couldn't do it. Nothing was there. No one was there.

Then, she was in a dark tunnel. Black as night. She couldn't see or feel a thing. But she was herself.

She had never been herself in a dream before.

She took a hesitant step forward and back.

Where am I? How have I been here? What ripped me from Serafina?

"Hello?"

Surely…a dream couldn't hurt her.

A cackle weaved through the darkness, reverberating through the walls, knocking into her chest. Cyrene stumbled backward and nearly fell to the floor. She caught herself on instinct.

The air wavered and broke all around her. This place felt…wrong. It had a faint feeling of something crawling up her spine. That prickling sensation of fear and adrenaline and panic.

Cyrene took a steadying breath and reached for her magic to cast a light about the room. But, when she plunged into those depths, there was nothing. Not like she couldn't access her magic. Like her magic never existed.

Real horror seized her. *How could there be a place where I don't have magic?*

"That won't work here." A feminine voice slithered out from the stillness and echoed across the chamber. "You don't work here."

"Who's there?" Cyrene demanded.

"We'll meet soon enough."

"What do you want with me?" Cyrene tried to take a step forward but was frozen in place. Her arms were bolted to her sides, and she was completely immobilized.

Then, the ground shifted again.

"No!" the voice shrieked as she disappeared.

She landed once more on the bridge in Eleysia. Everything was worse than normal. Her tunnel vision was so bad that she couldn't even see the buildings around her, only the bridge and the water and a handsome man standing before her. His eyes were dark as midnight, and they held such longing in them. Cyrene had never seen him before in her life.

"This can never be," Serafina said. "Never."

"But our love is stronger than your country! Please, stay. Be with me! As you have been!"

"I cannot. You know I cannot. You know what I am destined for."

"I know what they will use you for," the man said. "But I love you and your magic. You do not have to be torn in half because of me."

"Jon, stop, just stop! Byern is my home. My duty is to the Doma. I was sent here to train with the Masters, and I have done so. You cannot ask more of me."

"I know there is someone else, Sera."

Serafina didn't flinch, but she straightened. "What do you know?"

Cyrene leaned in, anxious to hear what this man would say. Serafina had had another lover? Other than Viktor Dremylon?

But, before she could hear, her body moved.

She pooled back onto the floor of the dark chamber. Her body felt torn in two, as if she needed time to piece it all back together.

She tried to get to her feet, swayed, and sank back down to the ground.

"I wouldn't try that again." The woman's voice echoed through the room.

Her vision flickered, and she tried to hold on to consciousness. "Who-who are you? What do you…do you want with me?" Cyrene asked, trying to gain control again. Her mouth felt like she had swallowed cotton balls. "An-answer me!"

"The correct question is, what do you want with me?"

"Nothing! I don't know who or what you are or even why I'm here."

"You have a gift. You are squandering it."

"What gift?" Cyrene gasped.

"Come to me when you discover it. You will know what to do."

Her feet began to shift again. "Please!" she cried out. "Tell me something, anything!"

"I'm in the forgotten place. A place of awakening. You can find me—"

She landed back on the bridge once more. She could have screamed. The man was gone. All she could see were Serafina's hands. She was staring at them, as if in horror at what she had done. But Cyrene didn't know what that was. Or why it even mattered.

She just wanted answers. She wanted to know what was going on and why she was having these visions and how any of it could help her. Because, right now, all these dreams were doing was making her life more complicated. All they had ever done was make her life miserable. From the moment they had told her to find Matilde and Vera in Eleysia, she'd had nothing but pain and heartache.

She just wanted *out*.

With a great wrenching feeling, her body seemed to rip in half. She gasped, and when the noise came…it was from her own mouth.

She looked up as her vision cleared, and she saw Serafina for the first time.

Her mouth fell open, and she stuttered back a step. "Creator!" she breathed.

No wonder Matilde and Vera had confused her for Serafina at their first meeting. They looked…identical. Well, not completely so but close enough for question. They most certainly could have been sisters at the very least.

"Cyrene," Serafina said with a sigh. A smile split her features. "I have waited so long for this."

Then, against all logic, the Domina—the highest-powered Doma of all time, the once creature of her nightmares and evil fairy-tale monster of Byern legend—hugged her.

"Um…" Cyrene muttered.

Her hands were at her sides, and then she reached up and awkwardly patted Serafina on the back. Serafina laughed lightly and then stepped back.

"What are you? How are you? What? Why? I mean…*how*? How is this possible? You're dead."

Serafina gave her a look that Cyrene had always given to her parents. "Magic never really dies, now does it?"

Cyrene shook her head. *What a nonanswer.* "Why am I here? How have I been seeing these visions? Just explain things."

"I'll do the best I can," she said, glancing up at the sky in worry. "We don't have a lot of time, and I must share with you something important before you leave me once more."

"What? What is so important that you keep drawing me in?"

"Because, if you do not know the past, then you are destined to repeat it."

"To repeat what?"

"Everything I have done wrong. I tried to reach you once your magic awakened, but I was spurned from reaching you, except at your weakest moments when the gate between our worlds fell. It is only now, when you are blindingly bright with power, that I could get you to sever your connection and give in to your spirit powers."

"When I learn to control spirit, I can talk to you?" Cyrene gasped.

"Possibly. But that's not why I'm here. What you need to know, Cyrene, is that you must trust your friends."

"What? That's it?"

"They're more important than you could ever know. Trust them. Believe in yourself."

The ground started shaking, and the buildings all around them began to crumble, falling into the water and shattering their momentary sanctuary.

"Tell me more. Quickly!"

"Use the coin. Find the lost ones. Learn the truth. Let the past be your guide to remake the future."

"I don't know what any of that means," Cyrene cried as the bridge they were standing on began to collapse.

"You will know. They will help you. Don't give in to this blindness. There are bigger factors at play, trying to draw you in and away from me, and I want you to be safe. Guard your mind and open your heart."

"What factors? Who is trying to draw me in?"

Serafina shook her head and rounded her eyes. "I dare not speak her name."

Cyrene trembled with fear. There was someone even Serafina was afraid of?

"Cyrene," Serafina said, tugging her close once more.

Cyrene wrapped her arms tight around Serafina, knowing they were both going to their doom.

"I will come for you again as soon as I am able."

"Don't go! I need to know more."

Serafina touched Cyrene's temple. "I am always with you."

And then she vanished.

The bridge collapsed.

Cyrene tumbled into the water to drown.

Cyrene awoke with water filling her lungs, choking the life out of her. She coughed and coughed, spilling the water onto the floor and bed. Then, she lay back, panting. Her hand was on her heart, and she took another deep breath.

She wasn't dead.

She hadn't drowned.

It was a dream.

Just a dream.

Except…if it had been a dream, where had the water come from?

She glanced around the room and found Elea asleep in a chair next to her bed. She was the only one in the room. Cyrene breathed a sigh of relief. No one had paid witness to what had just happened.

"Elea," she said, then louder, "Elea!"

Her sister started and then jumped up when she saw Cyrene was awake. "Cyrene! Oh my Creator! You're okay!"

"Yes. I'm…I'm okay."

Understatement of the century.

She had just had an actual conversation with Serafina and almost drowned while in bed. Not to mention, that second voice. The one that Serafina said she dare not even speak her name. She shuddered, just remembering it.

"You're soaked!" Elea said. "You must have sweat through the sheets. Let me get you something else."

Elea dashed out of the room, and a servant came in and stripped the bed. Cyrene peeled off her soaked shift and changed into a clean one. But she was weak and could hardly stand. Yet, at the same time, she had never felt better. Magic still sang through her veins. She could have remade the world with all the power brimming in her.

"How long was I out?"

"All day. It's nearly midnight."

"And…and Edric?"

"He's recovering. His wound…it, well, it didn't look as bad as when I remember you opening his shirt. I think I was just too lost to the battle and the…the death," she said again. Her eyes filled with tears, and she glanced away. "The healer says he'll make a quick recovery."

"Mother and Father?"

"Gone," Elea spat out. "That assassin killed them in cold blood. Reeve is sending word to Aralyn for her to return, but I don't think she'll make it in time."

"And Reeve?"

Elea shrugged. "He's Reeve."

Cyrene nodded. Her brother was a fighter. He wouldn't let anything stop him or slow him down. He would grieve in his own way, in his own time.

"I'm more worried about Aubron."

"Aubron?" Cyrene asked in confusion.

"The High Order who was with Reeve and me. The one you sent to fetch supplies. He's only been here six months. He's from really far in the north. Some small village. Fen, I think."

"He didn't take well to the bloodshed?"

Elea shot her an exasperated look. "None of us did, but he will have to deal with Reeve."

"Why?"

"Cyrene, honestly, do you not pay attention?"

Clearly not.

"They're together," Elea told her. "Love at first sight."

"Oh!" Cyrene gasped.

Her brother was in love! And she had missed it. So self-absorbed.

Dealing with her own problems. Didn't see anything at all.

"Don't be a prude."

Cyrene almost laughed, but she realized there was nothing funny about the situation. Nothing at all. Her mother and father were dead. She and her siblings were orphans. Edric had nearly died. And she...she had accepted blood magic.

She needed to make a choice—stay or go.

She couldn't let her life guide her any longer. Look at how well that had gone for her. Her life had been thrown into shambles all because she stayed. There was no right answer. Only the answer that her gut told her was true.

"And, now, they're telling me that my Presenting has to be postponed." Elea pouted.

"Postponed?"

"With all the bloodshed, they're concerned about having another big ceremony so soon."

Cyrene frowned. "They can't do that."

"Well, it seems that they can."

"Last I checked, I'm consort," Cyrene told her. "And I say that they can't."

Even though it was the last thing she wanted. Postponing Elea's Presenting should have been welcome. But with everything else going on, she couldn't leave Elea like this. Without their parents, what else did Elea have?

"You think you'll be able to convince the king otherwise?" Elea asked, hope returning to her voice.

"I think I have some leverage."

Like saving his life.

"Cyrene, please, please, please. I would be indebted to you forever. I have waited for this my entire life. I can't have one more thing taken away."

She knew how that felt all too well.

"I'll work on it." A plan was forming in her mind. Serafina's words echoed through her head. She knew what she needed to do. "Elea, you said Aubron was from…Fen?"

"Yes, I believe so."

If she needed to trust her friends, then she would trust her friends.

"Can you bring him to me?"

Twenty Seven

THE PLAN
—AHLVIE—

"We can't just do nothing!" Ahlvie argued again. "I knew that something was going on with all those attacks in the country. I should have knocked Cyrene out and dragged her back with me."

Matilde and Vera pursed their lips in mirror images of each other.

"From what you tell me, her magic has grown much more powerful than when we last worked with her. I think you stood no chance," Matilde said.

"Thanks for the confidence," Ahlvie spat.

"Ahlvie," Avoca said, "it's not about confidence. It's about keeping everyone alive. Something is wrong with Cyrene. I've been scouting the palace and our bond. You all know that something is not right. I should be able to reach her. Yet I've been blocked."

"Warding." Vera mused. "Yes, it would explain much. Likely keeping her in as much as us out."

"Another obstacle." Orden fretted. "We'll have to bring those wards down if we hope to succeed."

Ahlvie swore loudly and ignored the frustrated looks from the twins. He didn't see how it could possibly get any easier than Lady Cauthorn sneaking him into the castle and then sneaking Cyrene back out. Anything else they planned would be futile. If she wasn't going to come with them, then they needed to use something else to get her out.

"Hey, lover boy," Ahlvie spat at Dean.

He was sitting in the corner and hadn't said a word since the meeting began. Dean lifted his head to look at Ahlvie and raised an eyebrow in question.

"You have anything important to add, or are you here to mope?"

"He's here to mope," Avoca said savagely as she turned her back on Dean.

No one was particularly happy to have Dean with them. Not that he was a bad guy. He was fine. Ahlvie had even sort of liked him for a time. He'd liked that he made Cyrene smile, made her live for a bit. Live for something other than her mission. But, now, all he saw was red when he looked at Dean.

"I can get us in whenever you'd like," Dean said, leaning back against the rock wall.

"That's what you keep saying," Ahlvie bit out.

"I'm here to make things right, but I don't know enough about magic to take down wards or stop a Doma from wielding air magic on me," Dean said. "And, if Cyrene is as powerful as you claim, then I don't think she would hesitate if she saw me."

"Yeah, she's not the only one."

"Stop fighting!" Matilde shouted. "You two are always at each other's throats, and if I have to hear any more of it—"

"She'll likely box your ears," Vera finished.

Ahlvie pinched the bridge of his nose and walked further away from the group. Their crew was splintered without Cyrene to hold them together. That much was certain. He didn't know how much longer he could keep this up. It was bad enough with the Indres in the countryside. Bad enough that he had to deal with…that…while trying to figure out what to do about Cyrene.

"Let's just…take a break," Ahlvie said, waving them off. "Reconvene in the morning."

He retreated deeper into the cave network, trying to get his thoughts in order. Avoca was at his side in a second, as silent as ever. She placed her hand on his back, and he turned into her, pushing her into the wall and capturing her lips. She released a sigh and opened her mouth to him. He slipped his tongue inside and devoured her.

He could never have enough of this woman. Not ever.

No matter that she was a Leif, nearly a hundred years older than him, and had magic that he could never comprehend.

She was the only woman who he had ever felt matched him. And she did in every way. Wits, intelligence, bravery, charm, looks. She had it all, and she constantly kept him on his toes. The time they had been apart was torture. She hadn't come to see him off, and he'd never gotten to tell her how he felt.

He still hadn't actually.

The words kept slipping on his tongue.

He knew it was dumb to hold the words in. While he had been stuck in that dungeon, he had thought of how stupid he was not to tell her. Knowing that he might never see her again and had wasted his chance. Yet, now that they were together—his hands on her fair skin, her mouth against his, their bodies melding into one—the words were lost.

"Ahlvie," she murmured his name like a prayer.

Then, she stiffened.

"What is it?"

"Alarm tripped," she said.

Then, they were both running down the tunnel, back to the others. Avoca had her ice-white blade in her hand before she even reached the entrance. Orden and Dean had both drawn their swords and were striding after her. Matilde and Vera had their hands linked and were chanting some unheard words.

He was rushing after them to the entrance, praying they hadn't been found, when he stumbled to a stop. Avoca had a young High Order locked against her. Her blade at his throat.

"Who sent you?" she snarled.

"It's okay," Ahlvie said. "It's okay."

"Okay?"

"Ahlvie," the boy cried, fear blatant in his eyes.

"Release him. He's my brother," Ahlvie said, plunging forward.

"Your…brother?" Avoca asked.

"Aubron."

She released Aubron at once, and the boy tumbled into Ahlvie's arms. They embraced.

It had been years since he had seen his younger brother. Years since he had left Fen behind to become a High Order. He hadn't known that Aubron had followed in his footsteps and become a High Order himself. He would never have wished that for him. Aubron had been everything that Ahlvie wasn't. Soft, where Ahlvie was hard. Kind, where Ahlvie would cheat. Caring, where Ahlvie was callous.

And, now, he was…here. In the bloody lion's den.

"How did you find us?" Avoca asked harshly. "He could be a spy sent to root us out."

"I went to find Lady Cauthorn. She told me how to find you after she read what I had," Aubron explained. He produced a piece of paper from his pocket. "The consort sent me."

"The…consort," Ahlvie said, taking the paper. "Cyrene?"

"Yes!"

"We should get farther inside," Avoca warned. Her eyes cut across the horizon, like the sentinel she was.

Orden and Dean sheathed their swords now that the danger had passed. The group hurried Aubron deeper into their lair. Orden quickly explained to Matilde and Vera who Aubron was and how he had come upon them. They instantly took to the boy and busied about making him comfortable.

Ahlvie knew that he should stop thinking of him as a boy. But it was nearly impossible not to think about the thirteen-year-old boy he had left behind. Plus, he was still so small. It was hard not to see him as younger than his seventeen years.

"Now, tell us, why is it that Cyrene sent you?" Vera said calmly.

"I brought news from the consort," Aubron said. "From…Cyrene."

Ahlvie held up the paper Aubron had offered him and then hastily read through it.

He shook his head. *Cyrene. Welcome back.*

He handed the piece of paper around, and once everyone read it, he could see that finally, *finally*, they had a plan in place.

"Well," Avoca said with a toothy grin, "let's do it."

"But, first," Ahlvie said, turning to Aubron with wide eyes, "what is this about you having a boyfriend?"

Aubron's cheeks heated pink. "What? He's not my first."

The entire party laughed, and the tension they had been holding all these weeks vanished. They were a team once more.

Twenty Eight

THE PRESENTING

Cyrene paced back and forth in front of the wooden door. It was the night before Elea's Presenting, nearly a week since the attack at her Investiture, and as consort, she was completing her final duty before the ceremony. Though she technically didn't have to be standing here at this door in the castle at this precise moment, she was too anxious not to.

She held in her hand a folded piece of paper that she'd had on her person since her own Presenting ceremony a year ago. Her eyes narrowed on the riddle.

What you seek lies where you cannot seek it.

What you find cannot be found.

The thing you desire above all else risks all else.

The thing you fight for cannot be won.

When all seems lost, what was lost can be found.

When all bend, you cannot be as you were.

Nonsense. She still believed it to be so. Even though she knew the Circadian Prophecy existed and that this was somehow part of that prophecy. She suspected the first two lines were about her magic. The second two lines, she hated to believe were about love. But the last two lines, she had no clue. Still, a year later, she knew nothing. Didn't even know if her ideas regarding it were right.

And, as the door swung open, she took a deep breath. Today, she wanted answers.

A stooped and withered old man stood in the doorway. His hair was shot through with white, and he leaned on a cane. "Can I help you?" the man asked her.

"Yes," she said, recovering her voice. "My name is Cyrene. I am the new consort. I have come to collect the Presenting letter."

The man's bushy eyebrows moved together. "I usually dispatch it to a guard."

"I understand. Since I'm new to the role, I wanted to come meet you in person. What is your name?"

The man looked at her, flabbergasted, as he handed over the letter. "Owel is my name, miss. I hope you don't mind me saying, but I have been writing these letters for a long time, and I've never had anyone try to meet me."

Cyrene tucked the letter into the pocket of her gown. "I know this might not be typical, but I wanted to meet you. I've wanted to meet you for a long time."

"I...don't understand."

"About my Presenting letter."

Owel's features deepened further. "I just write the letters, miss."

"Yes, but mine is…well, it's unusual." She thrust the piece of paper out toward him.

He took it in shaky hands and opened it. He read it through and shook his head, his eyes bulging. "Where did you get this?"

"Like I said, it's from my Presenting."

"I see here that it's my handwriting. So, I must have written it, but I can't recall ever writing it."

Cyrene's heart deflated. "Truly?"

He passed it back to her. "You're the consort. You know that the letters prepare you for your Presenting and help you decide what you want to accomplish in your time in residency. Miss, this letter doesn't tell you any of that. If I've done wrong, I apologize."

"No, no," Cyrene said quickly, stuffing the letter out of the way. "You've done nothing wrong. It was clearly a misunderstanding."

Cyrene hurried off. Her heart was hammering, her magic sparking under her fingertips. All of that time, she had put so much stock in the writer of this prophecy…these silly words. But the man didn't even remember writing them. If he were a seer, then he certainly didn't know it. That had been a waste of time. Another stupid dead end.

She was in such a hurry that she ran smack into Kael as she rounded the corner. Their magic collided with a fury, shaking the floor and sending them both toppling to the ground. Cyrene tried to rein it in, but this new magic, this blood magic, fought her, as if it had a mind of its own. Kael touched her again, and she cried out, as it felt like an earthquake was about to hit the castle.

Cyrene scrambled away from him. She held her hands out in front of her. "Don't touch me."

Kael appeared wounded for a moment and then schooled his features. "What are you doing out in these parts?"

"I could ask you the same thing."

"I didn't come here to fight with you again," Kael said, rising to his feet.

He held out his hand to help her up, but she ignored it.

Cyrene bared her teeth at him and stood on her own.

When Kael had come to visit her as she was recovering this week, she had completely blown a gasket. She had needed him when she was at her most vulnerable, and he hadn't been there. No one had. Alone. Again. She hadn't wanted to hear his excuses and had nearly shoved him through several feet of stone wall to get him away from her. He hadn't approached her since.

"Then, leave me be."

"I can't," Kael said, his voice almost pleading with her. "You know I can't."

"You had no problem abandoning me when your brother was dying."

"I was righting the throne room. I had no idea that you were in harm's way. I had no idea that Edric had even ventured into the battle. Your safety is and has always been my first priority."

Cyrene hated how hurt she felt that she didn't believe him. No matter that he had been her enemy for so long, something had shifted between them in the past couple of weeks. Their last week of training together, they had almost seemed like…friends. She had almost let him crack open her black heart to see what it could be like to feel again.

"I don't know that. I don't know anything about you, Kael. How you got your magic, how you access it, how you are so good at it, what your true feelings are for me—"

"Don't," he ground out, taking the first step toward her.

Cyrene matched him, pacing backward. "What you want from me, what you expect out of all of this, what your end game is—"

"You are merely fooling yourself if you don't know the answers to your questions."

He took another step and boxed her back against the stone wall. Her magic hummed uncontrollably through her veins. Their connection intensified, like a lightning bolt sizzling through everything it touched.

"You tell me nothing."

"My end game is you. I want you. I have always wanted you." He tilted her chin up to meet his smoldering gaze. "Tell me you want me, too."

"I…no, I…" Cyrene said, hardly able to breathe with him touching her.

"Tell me I am not completely misguided."

Her heart cracked wide open at the blatant devotion in his eyes. At that feeling of being wanted, needed, for exactly who she was at that very moment. Despite the death and chaos and constant consequences of all of her actions…despite the blood magic, he was still here, asking her to give him her heart.

"You're not," she whispered. She was finally admitting to that darkened piece of herself that connected to him, that yearned for him.

He responded by pressing his lips to her mouth. For a second, she fought him. She didn't know if she was ready for this. This step. But then her fingers were clutching on to the front of his shirt, dragging him closer. A shock wave seemed to explode out of them at the mere brush of his lips on hers. She had no idea what the repercussion of that magic would be, but her mind settled into blissful silence.

His hands slipped around her waist, practiced and fluid, splaying them flat and caressing up the curve of her dress. His thumbs traced her ribs, lightly touching under her breasts. His body pressed tight against hers.

It was like bursts exploding in the night sky on a holiday. Chocolate and pretty dresses and adventure, all rolled up into one perfect kiss. One kiss that had been building and growing endlessly.

She didn't know if it was her magic responding to his or just this solitary feeling that she couldn't escape, as if she had been lost and was suddenly being found.

By someone who knew her better than she possibly even knew herself.

Who didn't step back from her magic but embraced it. Pushed it to its limits. Ached for more.

Her fingers threaded up into his hair as she opened her mouth to him. Their tongues pressed against one another. The heated passion in the moment was unbroken by the knowledge that there was so much wrong about this. Yet she wanted it. Some part of her desperately wanted this.

It was only steps coming down the hallway that finally made Cyrene break away. She looked up into Kael's flushed and hungry face, only to turn and see Elea's shocked face staring back at them. Her eyes were wide, and she stared between Cyrene and Kael with stark horror. Then, without a word, she turned and sprinted away from them.

"Elea!" Cyrene called.

She stepped forward to try to go after her, but Kael caught her hand.

"Don't."

"She's my sister."

"She needs some time," Kael explained.

"No, she needs to know the truth."

"Which is what?" He pulled her back toward him and brushed the dark curls from her face. "What she saw was the truth."

"I…I don't…" Cyrene had no idea what to say. She had seen Elea's shock and the look of betrayal on her face. "She has a crush on you."

"A little thing born out of a bit of kindness. She'll be fine."

Cyrene sighed. She wanted him to be right, but a nagging part of her told her it was not fine. And Elea would not be all right.

The feeling followed her all through the next day as she prepared for her first official Presenting. Elea hadn't spoken to her since she saw her kissing Kael.

Creator, I kissed Kael.

But that was beside the point!

Today was her little sister's Presenting, and though Cyrene didn't care for the ceremony any longer because of the significance it held to the destruction of the Doma, she understood why it was important to Elea. She wanted to be there for her, but Elea had rebuffed any of her attempts to talk to her. Three days ago, they had buried their parents, and Elea would not speak a word to her because of one kiss. Now, the ceremony was about to begin, and she hadn't even been able to wish her good luck. Let alone give her a birthday present.

Consort duties held her in the receiving chamber outside the largest ballroom. Repairs still needed to be made to the throne room, so they'd had to move the Presenting. Edric and Kaliana were both waiting impatiently with her. Childbirth had been strenuous and difficult for Kaliana's delicate frame after all her miscarriages, and though she looked pale and ghastly, she was no longer on her deathbed. Cyrene wondered what she thought about the conversation they'd had. If she regretted it.

Edric anxiously paced the room. He clutched at his side every now and again, as if he could sense the wound underneath. His injuries weren't healing quite as well as everyone had hoped but well enough for him to prowl the chamber like a caged animal. Though he remembered nothing of her saving his life. It was likely better for everyone that those memories were safely tucked away.

"Where is he?" Edric growled in frustration.

Cyrene didn't respond. She busied herself, adjusting the new red dress she'd had commissioned for the occasion. Edric's ruby-red necklace hung at her throat, and even though the servants had wanted to pin her hair up, she'd insisted on leaving it down in tendrils. She certainly looked the stark contrast to Kaliana with her severe blonde bun.

"He'll be here," Kaliana said. Her eyes darted to Cyrene as if to say, *This is your job.*

"Yes, he will. He won't miss this," Cyrene said.

And then he did arrive. Late, of course, but still here.

Cyrene took a breath at Kael's entrance. He looked refined in his all black attire. His back straight, shoulders back, ready and willing to take on the world.

She hadn't seen him since last night when Elea found them together. He'd wanted them to retreat to his rooms, but she'd insisted that she needed a good night's sleep. When he caught her attention, his smoldering eyes said he had been thinking of nothing but that kiss since they parted.

She hitched a hasty breath and averted her gaze.

This was the first time that she had been in a room with both Dremylon boys since her Investiture, and with a gasp, she realized that she felt nothing from her bond with Edric. She actually tried to push aside the blazing magic that poured from Kael to her and could sense nothing. Not a thing.

It was as if the bond itself was…broken.

Her head swam. That wasn't even possible.

Nothing could break a binding spell.

Matilde and Vera had told her as much.

They themselves had been trying to do it for near on two thousand years and had been unsuccessful.

How could I have possibly done something like that? Unknowingly!

"What?" Kael asked, at her side at once. "What is it?"

"It's…nothing," she said. She shook her head and swallowed hard.

Kael gave her a questioning look, but it was Edric's narrowed eyes at Kael's hand on her lower back that made her falter. She stepped out of Kael's touch with her head held high.

But Cyrene had no time to think on what it could mean that she no longer felt anything for Edric. The Presenting had begun. She proceeded into the ballroom where she took her place at Edric's side as consort for the first time. It was hard to believe, only a week ago, she had been named consort in truth. This moment felt utterly surreal.

Her sister swept into the room like a vision in Dremylon green. A bold choice to be sure, to wear a royal color for the ceremony. But green always was her color, and it suited her. She looked so much older than Cyrene could even imagine. Seventeen today, and Cyrene hadn't even been able to give her a birthday present.

Elea breezed through the program much faster than Cyrene had. Cyrene had stumbled and teased Edric and done everything wrong. She should have been cast aside for her failure, yet she was sitting before everyone today in the highest station that was not royal. And she wished she could give it all up.

Edric announced that they had to deliberate, and Elea retreated back down the aisle. Her time had come and gone so quickly. It felt like hardly a moment had passed, and already, they were back in the receiving room, staring down at all the paperwork they had collected about Elea. Years of tutor notes, proficiency tests, signed forms for etiquette training, and more. All this work, and her parents couldn't even be here today to see Elea in her final achievement.

They'd buried them three days prior. Her oldest sister, Aralyn, hadn't made it back from Kell where she was an Ambassador. Cyrene knew that Elea must have been disappointed that Aralyn couldn't come to her Presenting either. Especially with all the loss in their lives.

"Well, we all know what Cyrene is going to say," Kaliana said with bite in her voice.

"Move her," Cyrene said.

"What?" Kaliana snapped.

"I think court would eat her alive."

"You're actually suggesting not making your sister First Class?" Edric asked in disbelief.

Cyrene swallowed hard and made the argument she had settled on while planning. She hated doing it, but it had to be done. "Yes. She's emotional and unreasonable. With the death of our parents, I believe she is spiraling into depression. I know that more of the same would stabilize her, but we have to think of court. Only the best are made Affiliates."

"You don't want your family to be kept safe here in the castle?" Edric asked.

She nearly scoffed. He meant trapped.

"I want what is best for the kingdom. After all, that is the point of the Class system."

Edric blankly stared back at her. Kaliana looked disturbed. She clearly didn't believe her. Cyrene didn't care. As long as she could get Edric on her side.

"All right," he said, pushing the papers together, "if that's what you think. You know your sister best."

Cyrene breathed a sigh of relief. "I do."

They sauntered back out to the room. Kael shot her an inquisitive look, as if he could sense her unease through their bond. She grinned at him and then hastily took her seat. Elea returned to the front of the room. Cyrene could tell that Elea had her stomach in her throat and was shot through with nerves. She hated that she was about to dash Elea's dreams. After Elea seeing Cyrene with Kael, she knew that she should have done something to brighten her sister's spirits. She just couldn't let her suffer in this life, too. She wasn't safe here. No matter what Edric had said.

Edric moved before Elea, and Cyrene took a breath.

"It has been decided that you will be selected into the Guardian First Class."

Cyrene's jaw dropped. *What?*

Her head snapped to Kaliana, who looked smug.

The queen's eyes said, *You should have known better.*

Cyrene wanted to demand answers, but clearly, now was not the time.

"Your Receiver will be Queen Kaliana," Edric continued. "And, from this day forth, you shall be known as the queen's Affiliate."

THE PRINCE

No, no, no, no!

This couldn't be. They had decided against it.

Edric had agreed with her and then gone back on their agreement. Again!

Her ears rang through the applause as her frustration ate away at her. Her magic sparked in her blood, and she had to close her eyes to control the raging tempest. Her anger felt vile. Like a living thing. A deadly creature willing to do anything to sate its hunger.

But she couldn't feel this.

Not right now.

Still, she couldn't stop.

Thunder cracked in the distance. She could practically feel the lightning bolt shattering into the open field beyond. Though she could not see it as the ballroom was entirely enclosed, save a door leading to the gardens. She knew it had happened. She could feel the pulse of its energy, and for a moment, she believed that she could capture its power in her body.

No one else was paying attention to her inner turmoil. Though she could feel Kael's eyes on her. He couldn't suspect that she had wanted a different outcome.

Cyrene opened her eyes long enough to see Edric place the coveted Affiliate pin in Elea's hand as he announced, "In your palm, I place the queen's symbol, a circular pin of Byern climbing vines. So long as you have this with you, you will have a piece of your land, our land, and you will be known throughout the world as one of our own."

"Thank you, Your Majesty," Elea gasped.

Edric addressed the crowd with his arms opened wide, "Thank you all for attending the Presenting for our newest Affiliate Elea. As always, there will be a ball in her honor here tonight."

With that dismissal, everyone in attendance began to mingle around the room. Kaliana stood on shaky legs and shot her a look full of pity.

"What?" Cyrene asked.

"You will learn, with Edric, if you're lucky, you'll only ever get half of what you want."

"Duly noted." Her voice was sharper than intended.

Edric had just ruined all of her plans. But she had to remain calm...to even be excited for Elea. When it was the last thing she wanted to do.

She forced herself past Edric without a word, down the dais, and before

Reeve and Elea.

"Congratulations!" Cyrene gushed.

Elea turned the first real smile on Cyrene. "Oh Creator, I can't believe it!" She threw her arms around Cyrene.

"Well deserved. All four of us in First Class," Cyrene said.

A death sentence.

"Well-bred horses," Elea joked.

It was what Cyrene had said a year ago.

Horses sent to slaughter.

"Indeed."

"And a full ball in your honor," Reeve said. "What do you think about that, kiddo?"

"Reeve!" Elea groaned. "You can't call me kiddo anymore. I'm seventeen. I'm a woman now."

Reeve laughed. "Of course you are."

"I wish Mother and Father could have been here," Elea whispered.

"Me, too," she said. "They would have wanted to be here. To see how lovely you look."

"They would have been proud," Reeve said, pulling his sisters in for a hug.

Despite being the consort, Cyrene was granted a few hours' leave to be with her family on this occasion. She was glad of it even though Elea still hadn't completely forgiven her. That much was clear at every turn. Reeve even seemed confused by the way that Elea was treating her, but Cyrene couldn't exactly explain why Elea was mad at her. Reeve had always been a protector. She didn't doubt that he would go after Kael for it.

"Elea, are you going to talk to me?" Cyrene asked in the short break that she had while Reeve had gone to change.

"About what, Cyrene?" Elea asked, her voice tight.

"You know what."

"What?" Elea came out of the dressing room in her Presenting ball gown. It was a tight fit to her upper thighs and then fanned out like a mermaid's tail at the bottom in the most stunning shade of emerald green.

"You look unbelievable."

Elea turned to face the mirror and smiled. "It's the most incredible dress I've ever worn."

"Yes, it is."

"So, stop trying to mess it all up by talking to me about last night."

"Your crush on Prince Kael," Cyrene started.

Elea laughed at her. "Crush? *Crush?*"

"I'm sorry. What else should I call it?"

"We're in *love*, Cyrene! And you ruined it."

Cyrene took a step back. "Excuse me?"

"He confessed his love to me before he went to collect you, and now that you're here, it's as if I don't exist."

"Has something…happened between you two?"

"What did I just say?"

"Physically," she amended.

Elea colored. "No, of course not! What kind of woman do you think I am? *I* don't go throwing myself at anyone who will look at me."

Cyrene took the jab for what it was. Jealousy. She doubted that whatever had transpired was exactly what Elea believed it to be. Kael was a scoundrel, and maybe Cyrene was blind, but she didn't think he would set himself on a minor.

"I'm sorry, Elea. I don't know what else to tell you."

"Don't bother, Cyrene. You have always gotten exactly what you wanted. It only makes sense that the king would be in love with you, and you would desire his brother instead, stealing both of their royal hearts."

Cyrene winced. She wished she could explain how complicated everything was, but she didn't even know where to begin.

Is it better for Elea to believe me a harlot or a witch?

A whore or a prophesized Heir of the Light?

A thief or a Doma?

"I won't apologize for my heart, but I do wish that I hadn't hurt yours."

Elea waved her off. "Leave me be, Cyrene."

And, though that was the last thing Cyrene wanted with the evening they were walking into, she kissed her sister's cheek and left the room.

Rhea was waiting in Cyrene's chambers when she went to change for the ball. "Are you out of your mind?"

Cyrene arched an eyebrow and drew her best friend into her arms. "It is so good to see you."

"I don't know what you did to get me out of those rooms, but I'm grateful." Rhea squeezed and released her. "That does not excuse your insanity."

"It never has."

"This is not a joke." She threw the scrap of paper at Cyrene.

"No. I wasn't joking."

"I can't just leave my work."

"They will use you to get me back. They know that I love you. They know that I would do anything to see you safe. I cannot risk your safety, Rhea," Cyrene said.

"They. They. They. Tell me who *they* is."

"Edric," Cyrene whispered. She glanced at the door. "I won't risk your life. I want you safe."

"You don't know what I'm capable of."

"What are you doing in those massive dungeon-like rooms that is so important?"

Rhea shrugged. "You wouldn't understand."

"Help me to." Cyrene took her hands. "It was not so long ago that you and I were like sisters. Much has changed in a year, but surely, Master Barca can continue his work without your aid."

"I am…working alone," Rhea finally admitted.

"Alone?"

"He doesn't exactly approve of the work I'm doing."

Cyrene's eyes widened. "What exactly are you doing?"

"You've seen the explosions…the bombs," Rhea said softly. "It started for the wrong reasons. Eren—do you remember Eren?"

"Yes," Cyrene said, recalling the High Order who was currently deeply involved in Edric's military. He had been the one who had stopped she and Daufina.

"I did it for him. We were placed together for your investigation, and the time we were together, I fell for him."

"Oh, Rhea! That's incredible."

"But…he was in love with Maelia."

"Oh." Cyrene's face fell. She had forgotten that Eren had been sweet on Maelia all those months ago when they were on the same boat for procession.

"And, when the news came back that she had been killed, he took it hard. He stopped seeing me entirely. I thought, by making these bombs work, he could use them in the upcoming war. That it would give us an edge in battle. I've been stockpiling an arsenal."

Cyrene's jaw dropped. "Against Eleysia?"

Rhea nodded. "Yes, if war comes."

"And you believe this will win him back? That is why you wish to remain?"

Rhea's cheeks heated. Her bright red hair fell into her face, and she hastily pushed it aside. "I do not presume to think that a High Order could want to marry a Second."

"Don't talk like that," Cyrene said, cursing the Class system.

"It's true! But…I have to hope. And, as long as I have hope, then I'll stay."

"I don't want you to stay here."

"You cannot protect everyone," Rhea told her. "And you are not my only ally. I am a survivor, Cyrene. Count on it."

"I will." Cyrene nodded as tears pricked her eyes.

She felt like she was always walking away from Rhea. One step out the door.

They embraced like sisters once more, and then Rhea laughed softly. "Let me help you into this dress."

As Rhea was buttoning the hundreds of tiny buttons on the back of

Cyrene's dress, she took a deep breath and made a confession of her own. "You are right about the prophecies."

Rhea's fingers stilled and then continued. "It has the sense of truth."

"I just wish…it weren't about me."

"Perhaps it's not."

"You don't believe that."

"No, I don't," Rhea said.

"I went to see the letter writer for our Presentings."

"Did he tell you what you were looking for?"

Cyrene shook her head. "He was just a man. He had no clue. Another dead end."

"Cyrene," Rhea said, finishing the last button and coming around to face her.

Cyrene's heart was jackhammering in her chest. Her magic felt brittle and unpredictable, as if she were able to use it to attack the nearest person to her. She folded her hands behind her.

"A prophecy is never certain. What you know about it is a riddle. Unless you have more information than what I read a year ago, you should know that…you can make your own destiny. Your life is not predetermined."

Cyrene pulled Rhea in for another hug. She hoped against all hope that what Rhea had said was true.

If only every person and creature in all of Emporia didn't believe her to be this destined Heir.

Belief was powerful.

It had the ability to make things come true.

Cyrene heard a knock at her door as she finished the last touch of rouge on her cheeks. She tightened her leash on her spitting magic.

"Who is it?" she called even though she could feel the matching pulse of her magic behind the door.

"Who do you think, love?"

Cyrene wrenched the door open and came face-to-face with Kael Dremylon. "What are you doing here?"

He grinned that wicked grin that she had grown so accustomed to and bowed slightly at the waist. "To escort you to the ball, of course."

"And how will that look?"

His eyes said it all. He didn't care. "Forget appearances tonight. Just be with me."

Cyrene chewed on her bottom lip. "Edric might kill you."

"I'd like to see him try." Kael tugged her forward with the force of his magic and dropped a kiss on her lips.

"Kael," she admonished halfheartedly.

He tipped the door to her room closed behind him. "Say it again."

"What?"

"My name. I adore the sound of it on your tongue."

"Kael," she repeated.

"Perfection."

His hands slipped into hers, lacing their fingers together. He drew her hand up to his mouth and kissed each knuckle. She braced herself for the magic that sputtered out of her at their nearness.

"Don't you see?"

"See what?" she asked.

"You and I. We're a matched set."

"Are we?" she breathed as his tongue darted out to caress her thumb.

"Together, no one can stand in our way."

Cyrene took a breath and then pulled away. As much as her body…her magic ached to give in to what Kael was saying, she had not forgotten her promise in that cell back in Eleysia. She could give in to lust and no more than that, and she was sure that Kael would take that, but he would not be satisfied. It was easier to keep things simple. And, tomorrow, it might not even matter.

"Don't we have a ball to get to?" Cyrene asked instead.

"Indeed." He didn't seem fazed by her nonanswer.

He extended his arm and whisked her back out the door. Perhaps he was used to her ignoring his advances. Maybe not answering him felt more like a victory to him than a straight refusal.

The ball was in full swing when they arrived. And they did make an appearance. Cyrene would have been happy to walk in from a side entrance and disappear into the crowd. But the consort didn't disappear and certainly not on the arm of the crown prince.

The crowd quieted, and hundreds of pairs of eyes turned to gape at them together. Kael was dressed in the all black regalia he'd taken to wearing, and Cyrene was in a full blood-red dress. And, in that moment, Kael was right; they *were* a matched set. Blood magic infused her very bones, creaking and clawing at her insides to expel some of her energy, and the essence of their mingled magic radiated around them.

It was Edric's eyes she found first. They were narrowed and irritated across the ballroom. He stood with Kaliana—a weakened, injured pair. A sharp contrast to she and Kael, and the shift in the room seemed to recognize the tides turning, as if this were their court.

Cyrene ventured deeper into the room with Kael. The sea parted for them as they drew toward the dance floor. Her mouth went dry when she saw the stunning woman in green standing before her.

Elea's lips pursed, but she held her head high. She couldn't rightly be offended that the consort outshone her at her own Presenting ball…but she was. Even if she could never voice that opinion. Or that she wanted Kael for herself.

"Dance with me?" Kael asked Cyrene, taking her hand.

"I believe the new Affiliate should receive her first dance," Cyrene said instead.

Elea's eyebrows rose as Cyrene stepped back.

Kael had the decency not to say a word about the tense interaction. He held out his hand to Elea. "May I?"

Elea's entire face burned bright as crimson. "Of…of course."

The music began, and Kael had moved Elea through her first pass of the intricate steps when a rumble went through the crowd. Cyrene looked up at the commotion and found a man at the front of the room.

A man with light hair, an easy smile, and cunning eyes.

A man in the finest dress attire available, which only accentuated his muscular frame from hours upon hours of training and military drills.

A man who had shattered her heart into a million pieces and thrown it into the ocean on a whim.

Dean.

Thirty

THE DIVIDE

"**D**id someone say there was a party?" Dean asked with a self-indulgent smile on his face.

Cyrene was frozen. Completely immobilized.

This could not be happening.

This is impossible.

Dean had dumped her and walked away.

She had spent all of this time trying to forget him. To forget the diamond engagement ring that he had slid on her finger or the feel of his body on top of her as they'd made love or the way one smile could lighten her very soul.

She remembered the way the tangy scent of the sea seemed to cling to him. The light in his eyes the first time they'd met and how she had scolded him for killing a deer. The feel of his fingers through her hair. Every little defense he'd made for her against his family. And innumerable other instances when he had set her on fire.

Now, he was here. In Byern, of all places.

What is he doing here?

What did he want?

Her first thought was that she needed to get him out of here. She took two hasty steps forward and then stopped. No, she couldn't do that. She couldn't acknowledge him. People would know. It would complicate things.

Creator! What am I supposed to do?

Her heart raced as she swung around to find Edric striding toward Dean. She chewed on her bottom lip, knowing she had to make a decision. Either she fled the ballroom now before anyone could put two and two together or she faced Dean like the consort she was…and gave him the greeting he deserved.

One heartbeat.

Two.

She cursed violently, took a deep breath, and then forced herself into a role she was not looking forward to playing. She plastered on a soft smile and moved through the crowd to the front of the room.

Edric beat her there by only a few seconds. He looked disturbed to find Dean standing before him.

"What do we have here?" Cyrene asked. Her chin was held high, and she dared not show an ounce of recognition.

"An emissary from Eleysia," Edric said tightly. "Why the prince is here though, I have not gotten that answer."

Dean raised an eyebrow and cocked a smile. "In my country, we entertain our guests before interrogating them."

No, you don't.

"Well, we're not in Eleysia," Edric spat. "And we're not on good terms as it is."

"I don't wish to speak of the unpleasantness of my parents' deaths. Come," Dean said, maneuvering Edric away from the door, "let's have a drink and dance. Tomorrow, we will discuss the diplomatic measures my sister has sent me for."

Edric grumbled in frustration. "So, she accepts the offer?"

"Tomorrow," Dean said with an easy smile.

He hadn't once looked at Cyrene, and she was grateful. She didn't know what one look would betray.

It was clear Edric did not want to wait another day, but he was a good host. Dean was royal after all. Not some subordinate messenger that Queen Brigette had sent. Respect was due between the men.

"Of course," Edric said finally. "Allow me to introduce you to my consort, Cyrene."

Cyrene saw a muscle twitch in Dean's jaw before he finally flicked his brown eyes toward her. Her heart constricted, and a thousand emotions churned through her all at once. First and foremost was anger, but others competed for the crown—pain, heartache, love, betrayal, lust, hope.

"Pleasure to meet you," Dean said, taking her hand and placing a kiss on it.

She didn't trust herself to speak. She just nodded and then removed her hand from his.

"Come. I will introduce you to my wife as well," Edric said.

He curiously glanced at Cyrene and then offered her his arm. She took it without looking at Dean once and then walked with him toward Kaliana.

"What is your read on him?" Edric whispered into her ear.

"Foolish," she said and meant it.

"Indeed."

He has no idea.

Edric introduced Dean to Kaliana, but Cyrene heard none of their conversation. She only saw exactly what he was portraying to everyone. An engaging party boy, who drank deeply and flirted shamelessly with Kaliana, who brightened like a blooming rose from the attention. Whatever the reason that Dean was here…it was about more than her.

Perhaps he didn't even want to see her.

Perhaps he didn't even care.

She swallowed hard at that thought.

All this time, trying not to think about him and move on with her life, and then he was just here. Invading her space and…ignoring her!

And he knew she couldn't do a damn thing about it if she didn't want to reveal her relationship to the king…which she didn't.

But it wasn't Edric she was worried about. There was one person in this entire court who knew exactly who Prince Dean Ellison of Eleysia was…and what he had meant to Cyrene. And he was dancing with her sister.

Kael hadn't looked up at her or Dean since he took Elea's hand. Her sister looked entranced by her dance partner, and Cyrene knew it had been the right move to offer this dance as a truce. But she was not looking forward to when it would be over, and Kael would notice that Dean was here. She didn't know what he would do or what their entire bargain had been.

As the song was drawing near the end, she moved to the edge of the dancers. She wanted to claim Kael's next dance before he could do anything stupid. Dean was occupied with Kaliana. Surely, he wouldn't even notice—

"Consort." Dean's crisp voice cut through Cyrene's concentration.

She turned back to him, trying to mask her horror.

"Would you do me the honor of the next dance?"

Cyrene opened her mouth and then closed it. She could see Kaliana's pinched face in her periphery. At another time in her life, Kaliana's irritation would have been enough for Cyrene to jump into Dean's arms.

"The next one was already requested by Prince Kael," she said deftly.

Flames ignited in Dean's eyes at her words.

"Nonsense," Edric said. "Prince Dean is our guest."

Anything to keep her from Kael. Though, Edric never did recognize the real threats.

"Of course," she said, trying to appear demure. Instead of like a wolf in sheep's clothing.

Dean offered her his arm, and with noticeable hesitation, she placed her hand on his sleeve. He escorted her out onto the dance floor just as Kael passed them. Kael's head whipped around at the intrusion. He took one menacing step toward Dean with his teeth bared before realizing exactly where they were. Then, his royal mask snapped back into place. His expression said everything. If he had his way, he would kill Dean by the end of the night.

As soon as the music started up, Cyrene snapped at Dean, "What in the Creator's name are you doing here? You dropped me on that boat. You do not get to come to my home at your whim. You should take this dance and then *leave*."

Dean didn't respond at first. He took her hand in his, placed his other hand on her waist, and tugged her closer. Then, he swung them into the waltz step.

"I'm here to get you out," he said under his breath. "We received your message. Others are waiting on the outside. I made a mistake, Cyrene. I will never make it again."

"A mistake?" she snarled. "A mistake!"

She knew she sounded hysterical. *How could he think what he did to me could be dismissed so easily?*

His eyes were pained and honest. Eyes she had trusted and now could hardly look into. "I said I would always find you. Here I am, trying to right that wrong."

"I don't want to hear it. Tell me the plan, and never speak of this to me again."

Dean was about to answer her question when a roar from the other side of the room silenced the chatter, the musicians, and all the dancers. Dean and Cyrene whipped their heads toward the noise and found Edric charging toward them. He had his sword in his hand and was pointing it directly at Dean's chest.

"You," Edric spat.

"Your Majesty," Dean said with a rueful smile.

"You dare come into my kingdom, my castle, and lay hands on her after what you did." Edric looked maniacal, like he had that day when he ordered Daufina's execution.

"Oh no," Cyrene whispered.

Dean stood tall and broad. He was at least an inch taller than Edric and seemed to fill up the space when confronted. He must have been expecting it.

"What offense do you speak of?" Dean asked.

Edric couldn't say what he wanted to say. She could see him sputtering to find the words to say that she had been sullied by him. Virginity wasn't a prize in marriage, as it was in some of the northern countries, like Kell and Mastira, but it was never appropriate to speak of.

"You courted her," Edric spat.

The crowd tittered at the revelation.

"That is a crime?" Dean asked.

"You assisted in her kidnap, knowing full well that we desired her safe return, and held her in Eleysia for months without notifying the kingdom. You are a liar and a scoundrel. And I formally challenge your honor."

"No!" Cyrene cried, jumping between the two men.

"I accept," Dean said with glee.

"Stop it, both of you!"

"Clear the ballroom ten paces," Edric said.

"This is absurd. Please, you cannot do this."

"It is a matter of honor, Cyrene," Edric told her. "And he has none."

"We'll see," Dean said. He strode several paces away from her and withdrew his sword as the room was cleared for a duel.

But Cyrene didn't move. She stood in the middle, between men she had thought she loved. The men who would now fight to the death.

Her hand was over her heart, her mouth open. This was not about honor. This was about her. About who could win her over.

She was not a prize. No duel would ever change that.

And where is Kael Dremylon in all of this?

Smirking like a fool across the room.

She stalked toward him. Her anger was a lit fuse, ready to burst at any moment.

"What have you done?" she demanded.

"Careful, Cyrene," Kael said. "You do not want to get in the middle of this."

"Why did you tell Edric? You are going to get your brother killed!"

"I didn't tell him anything."

"Liar!"

He arched an eyebrow. "You think it wasn't obvious the moment he pulled you away from Edric? He knew. He didn't even need my confirmation."

"Though you gave it, I'm sure."

"Now, do you think I'm the kind of person who would like to see you suffer?" His hand reached for hers.

She yanked it away. "Perhaps you enjoy suffering. You could stop this, yet you are doing nothing."

"Nothing can stop this. It was inevitable."

"Well, I am not going to stand on the sidelines and watch."

Kael grabbed her hand. "You are the consort. For the time being, that is exactly what you will do."

"Do not test me, Kael."

"That is all I plan to do." He leaned forward and brushed his mouth against her ear. "If you want to stop them from going through with this, do it. Coerce them."

She jolted back. "I'm not going to do that."

"Then, you will play the victim. Again."

Cyrene glared at him—more because he was right than he was wrong. She wanted him to be wrong. But both Edric and Dean were hotheaded. Both trained warriors. Both infatuated with her.

If she wanted to stop them, then she had to make it happen. But mental coercion felt…wrong. On so many levels.

"Have you done it to me?" she asked.

"Once since the docks."

"And when was that?"

"When you were starving, filthy, and spent on my ship, and all you wanted to do was argue with me. I needed to take care of you first, and you wouldn't let me. You were so beaten by that prison," he said softly.

Cyrene tensed at his words. She hated thinking about that prison and the shell of a person she had been when she got out of it.

"I would do anything to be the man ripping out Dean's throat for hurting you. No one should ever make you feel like less than you are."

Cyrene swallowed and closed her eyes as Dean and Edric turned to face one another, swords out. She had seen the way Dean fought. She knew Edric was trained, but she didn't know his skill. She wanted neither of them dead—particularly because she had just done something utterly horrible to save Edric's life.

Slipping into Edric's mind was like burying her feet in soil—grounded and teeming with possibility. Her powers released with a sigh, as if she had been made to do this. She sifted through memories, getting a sense of exactly who Edric was—proud, fair, erratic. There was something almost wrong with the way his mind was working. She couldn't exactly place it.

The crowd gasped, and she opened her eyes, losing that grasp on his mind. This was not the time to be learning a new skill.

"Help me," she begged of Kael.

"You can do this. Tell them to stop, if that is what you truly desire."

She ground her teeth and blindly reached back. This time, she sank into Dean's mind. It was like dipping her hand in cool water—effortless and refreshing. The water called to him. Though he had a soldier's mind, his thoughts were like reading poetry. Refined, flowing, and charismatic, but with a precision she couldn't possibly explain. Order and disorder, all in one.

The men circled each other as she went to work, trying to find a way to tell them to stop. Yelling it into their mind did nothing. This seemed more intricate work than brute force. And brute force was always her specialty.

Swords clanged. Teeth bared. Choreographed footwork maneuvered in circles. Dean struck quick and true, slicing across Edric's arm. Edric growled and retaliated, reaching for Dean's exposed shoulder. He nicked him, but Dean danced out of the way. The next attack from Dean showed how much he had loosened up. He was exquisite. Cyrene had seen him fight for his captain's position back in Eleysia. Fierce and deadly. In fact, now that she looked more closely, it appeared that Dean was toying with Edric. He could have ended it at anytime.

"He's messing with Edric," Cyrene whispered.

"You've just noticed? Your captain appears to have been practicing since we last fought," Kael said with a bite in his voice.

She reached out for Dean one last time to try to will him to stop this. She read the shift in his intentions at the precise moment he decided to go for the killing blow.

"No!" Cyrene reached her hand and commanded him to stop.

And he did.

It was like trying to stop a galloping horse with her bare hand, but she did it.

"Very good," Kael said.

What was not so good was that she couldn't possibly hold Edric at the same time. He charged Dean and opened a long gash through his arm. The pain lashed through Dean, and she released him with a gasp.

She held her own arm, as if Edric had sliced through it, but there was no blood. Only remnants of the pain Dean felt.

"Aren't you going to do more?" Kael taunted.

But she could do no more.

Within seconds, Dean batted Edric's sword from his hand and knocked him to the ground. Dean stood over him, the clear victor, as he held his sword to Edric's throat.

Thirty One

THE DEBT

"**D**ean, please," Cyrene cried into the silence.

No one could believe what had just happened. Their king had dueled and…lost? It seemed impossible.

Cyrene knew that Dean was a fool for coming, but Edric was the fool for underestimating his opponent. She had thought that Dean would win but hadn't wanted to consider what would happen for either of them.

The terms of duels were simple. A fight to the death.

That meant that Dean could take this killing strike in front of all of the highest-ranking officials in Byern and walk away scot-free. For Edric had initiated the duel, and law stated that no man could be punished for the death. Not even of the king.

"Please," she whispered, fighting to contain her magic as rage pulsed through her.

All of this over what?

She uncoiled the magic from her center and set it free to build in her hands. She would stop this madness. Dean would not do this.

Her head held high, she stepped into the empty circle. "Do not kill him."

Dean didn't break his concentration from Edric, who was clutching his injured side and breathing heavily. "I'll offer you a trade."

"I've no interest in negotiating with you," Edric spat.

"A life for a life," Dean said. "Your honor intact."

"I'll never give her to you. I'd rather die."

"I know that feeling well."

Cyrene came to stand before Dean. "No one can give me to anyone. I pick and choose where I go. I will not be bound to anyone ever again," she said firmly. "Let him go, Dean."

"He will lose all honor if I do so. He will owe me a debt for the rest of his life."

"Then, take me with you," Cyrene offered, appearing like a martyr before her people.

"Cyrene, no," Edric cried.

"It is the only way."

She offered Dean her hand with promise of vengeance in her eyes. If he thought for a second that he could hurt Edric while she was here, she would prove otherwise. He had thought her magic made her dangerous before… but he had no idea what she was capable of now.

With a wince at the look on her face, Dean sheathed his sword and took her hand.

"The debt is paid," she said simply.

"Cyrene, please!" Elea cried from the corner. "Don't go!"

She faced her sister with grief on her face. "I love you. I always have, and I always will." She looked around the ballroom for her brother but didn't see him. "Tell Reeve and Rhea the same."

Elea nodded with tears streaming down her face. No matter that they had quarreled, her love was true.

Then, Cyrene took a deep breath and prepared to leave Byern again once and for all. Not a kidnapped innocent but a martyr.

Dean sighed next to her, as if he couldn't believe that his ruse had worked. They walked toward the door, and the sea of Affiliates and High Order parted before them. Not a word was spoken. Every set of eyes was one of deep pity, compassion, and gratitude. This was how it was supposed to be. Now, she could leave and never look back. She could be at peace.

But then she felt it.

A tug on her bond.

A slight shift in the air.

A fury that rivaled her own.

She wheeled around at the last possible moment and threw up a shield as a ball of swirling darkness shot toward them. It harmlessly bounced off the shield and disintegrated. Cyrene knew exactly whose magic that belonged to.

Kael Dremylon stepped off the sidelines and into the ring. "You will *not* take her anywhere."

He was holding another ball of darkness, as if he were holding an apple, and the silence from the crowd turned into screams. Pandemonium ignited in the room as everyone realized exactly what they had seen.

Magic.

In a world where magic did not exist.

Or so they'd thought.

"Try to take her away from me again," Dean growled, removing his sword.

"I should have killed you when I had the chance," Kael told him.

"The feeling is mutual."

Kael lobbed the darkness at Dean with a quickness that was unrivaled. Cyrene barely got her shield up in time to protect Dean.

Her eyes darted around the room. No one was leaving. *Why is no one leaving?*

Then, she felt it. Kael had enclosed the room. No one could leave. They all had to bear witness to what was about to happen. He wanted an audience.

If he wanted a show, then Cyrene would give him one. She stepped in front of Dean and faced off with Kael.

Here he was…finally showing his hand. Darkness, chaotic destruction, and madness filled the room as his power intensified before her.

Darkness and light.

Heirs.

A matched set.

He couldn't have been more right about that. Drawn to each other like magnets.

Good and evil.

Perhaps the prophesy had simplified it all down to that, but she knew that she was not wholly good, and he was not wholly evil. But, as she squared off with him, everything seemed to click into place. This was the showdown of a lifetime.

Forget all the buildup to the end and all the added revelations the prophecy promised to her. She was here and he was living death. She wasn't ready, but she knew she never would be against Kael.

"You protect him?" Kael snarled. "After all he did to you?"

"I protect the innocent."

"He is hardly innocent."

"He does not deserve death for his idiocy."

"Come back to me, Cyrene," he pleaded. He held out his hand. "Rule the world at my side."

"Who did you sacrifice for it?"

His eyes darkened at her question.

"What did you do to attain it?"

He lashed out at her shield, shattering it into a million pieces. Then, he clawed at her mind, but she was prepared. She had up a mental barrier that she had learned while battling the Braj. Nothing was getting through that she didn't allow. Not while she was brimming with blood magic.

"Do you even mourn them?"

"You don't know what you speak of."

"Oh, I think I, of all people, know exactly what I speak of," Cyrene said. She drew wind to her and threw it at him like a knife.

He batted it away, as if it were a fly. "Try harder, love."

The ground beneath them shook as she shoved the tiled floor toward him, trying to knock him off-balance. He used the air to haul himself off the ground and landed, unharmed, not five feet from her.

"This isn't practice. If you want to get out of here, you're going to have to do more than that."

"I don't want to hurt you," she told him.

Kael laughed. "You're not capable of it."

Cyrene gritted her teeth and took the taunt for what it was. Because she knew, deep down, that the only reason he had walked into that circle was because he was hurt. Her taking Dean's hand had hurt him. A betrayal in his eyes. One he could not, would not, forget.

"Cyrene, let's just go," Dean begged behind her.

"I wouldn't be so sure she *wants* to go with you," Kael ground out. "She's spent all this time with me, trying to forget you."

Kael shot a bolt of lightning at Dean. He threw himself into a dive roll to avoid it. The crowd screamed and scrambled away from the magic. The bolt hit the wall with a sizzling smash, leaving a crack from floor to ceiling. Cyrene could hear the women weeping at the explosion.

Her eyes landed on the one woman who hadn't gotten away. A young redhead with alabaster skin and wide-sightless blue eyes. She hadn't gotten away fast enough. A name drifted up to her from the depths—Affiliate Robin. And now she was dead…at Kael's hand. An affiliate.

Dean reached for Cyrene's hand, trying to tug her out of the ballroom, but she knew she couldn't leave it like this. Not with Kael's shield up. She would have to finish this before she could leave.

"Kael," Cyrene said, "please, stop this. You don't have to be this person."

"I'm afraid I do," he said, his hands crackling as he readied himself for another attack.

"I knew that you had these powers. I…suspected where they had come from," she said, inching toward him. She held her protective shield up…

wondering if it would be enough to stop him. "But I didn't believe that you… or anyone could take blood magic."

"*You* did it," Kael told her.

"My parents were already dead! And I did it to save Edric's life," Cyrene said.

A murmured gasp came from the crowd. Cyrene's eyes darted to Edric's, who was behind a wall of guardsmen.

"It doesn't seem to matter," Kael said.

And, in her split second of distraction, Kael shot forward, air circling her and yanking her off her feet. She was lifted ten feet off the ground before she could find a way to break through the air with a sword made of flames. She dropped like a stone in the sea but landed gracefully on her feet in a crouch. Then, she stood, whipping her dark hair out of her face and holding her flaming blade aloft.

"Impressive," Kael said with a grin.

"Let these people go. They are blameless."

"No one is entirely innocent, Cyrene. You taught me that."

"Tell me what happened, Kael. How did it happen for you? Who did you kill?"

"You know, I can't seem to remember them all."

Cyrene let the horror show on her face.

"But Jardana was the most powerful. The greater the connection, the more magic."

"Jardana?" Cyrene muttered. She had hated the queen's lackey and Kael's lover at one point, but she had never wanted this to happen to her. "How could you do it?"

"Oh, you'll feel it soon enough."

"Feel what?" she asked. She stepped forward, clearing the remaining distance between them, and angled the sword toward his chest.

He looked at it as if it were a toy. Not a deadly weapon.

"The hunger. The need. When the magic runs low, you crave it. You're sitting at the top of a full well. Wait until you reach the bottom."

"You said yourself, we could do anything together," she said, pushing the sword against his chest. She singed his black button-up and left a small mark over his heart. "Then, end this now."

"Have you ever thought that maybe I don't want to?" Kael asked.

She saw the swell of magic in his eyes. She felt the raw power that emanated from him, and it filled the room.

"I want the power, and so do you."

"Not like this!" she cried.

"Yet you sank into his mind so easily."

"To keep them from killing each other!"

Kael laughed and snapped his fingers. Her sword went up in a cloud of black smoke. She was left holding her empty hand out toward him. Kael latched on to her wrist and tugged her forward. Their faces were only an inch apart. He could kill her as easily as he could kiss her. And, with the magic brimming through him and the intensification of her own at his touch, she had no idea which it would be.

"Good intentions mean nothing with blood magic, love," he whispered like a prayer. "Once this is gone and the power disappears…you'll kill. You'll try to justify it, but I'll know. You'll know."

"I won't."

"When have I ever been wrong?"

"I'm sorry," she said. She shed only one tear and pressed a soft kiss to his lips.

It was all she needed to divert him. She reached deep in her powers and sent a shock wave against him. He released her and shot thirty feet across the ballroom, slamming back against the far wall with a crunch.

His shield dropped at once, and the crowds he had held back dashed through the exits in a hurry. But she just stood there. Her magic stuttering and sizzling against her skin. The force she'd had to use to tear down his shield and stop him from harming anyone was tremendous. Not quite like stopping a hurricane, but Kael was more powerful than she had ever dreamed. If she hadn't had that edge, she didn't know if she ever would have stopped him.

"Cyrene," Dean said, gently touching her elbow.

She jolted away. She couldn't tear her eyes from Kael.

It had all gone so wrong.

She had thought that they would be able to make it.

That he wouldn't choose this.

That he wouldn't choose power.

That he would see that all he had to do was choose her.

But it had been a game.

And she had been tangled in his web.

She had been so lost after Maelia's death that she clung to the first person who showed her any kindness. And perhaps he loved her, but how much of it was her, and how much of it was her magic? How much of it was the bond?

"I am sorry," she whispered to Kael before she finally let Dean drag her away from his lifeless body.

Thirty Two

THE BARRIER

The run out of the castle was a blur.

Dean kept talking through the whole thing, but Cyrene didn't hear any of it. She was sure he was trying to use it as a distraction. If she was overwhelmed with everything that had happened, she didn't doubt that Dean was, too. That everyone who had been in that room was.

Magic was out.

No longer a fairy tale.

The entire Byern court had seen that she and Kael had it. One or two people could have tried to push the thought away as a hallucination but not hundreds of people. This changed the fabric of their world. She was sure there would be repercussions, but she didn't want to be here to find out.

"Cyrene, this way!" Dean said as he nearly slammed into a body.

"Took you long enough," Ahlvie said. "Hello again."

Cyrene grinned. "I told you not to come back."

"Then, you sent my brother. Decided to ignore your first request and listen to your second."

"Of course you did."

"Weren't you supposed to wait for us on the perimeter?" Dean asked Ahlvie.

Ahlvie shot him a disbelieving look. "You think I'm going to trust you?"

Dean breathed heavily out through his nose. "I was taking all the risks. You could have at least given me the benefit of the doubt."

"Not a chance."

"Stop. Both of you," Cyrene snapped. "I don't want to hear it."

Ahlvie and Dean fell silent and hurried along. They burst out a side entrance and sprinted through darkened gardens.

"This way," Ahlvie said, running ahead through the maze, as if he could see the twists and turns perfectly in the dark.

She was panting as she tried to keep up. And then, out of nowhere, they rushed out of the hedges and ran straight toward an open gate. The handful of guards lay like knocked over dominoes as they passed. Cyrene felt a tug as she stepped through the exit. It was as if she were passing through an invisible barrier that didn't want to release her. She pressed forward, and it let her go with a pop.

"Creator!" she breathed, leaning over with her hands on her knees. "What was that?"

"That's whatever has been keeping you from your bond with Avoca,"

Ahlvie said.

Cyrene's mouth fell open. "She's here?"

"We all are, but we should hurry."

No wonder she could never sense Avoca. She could feel the bond, but she had assumed Avoca was too far away, still in Eleysia, and that Cyrene couldn't pinpoint where Avoca was because of that. But no. She reached down within herself and felt that bond snap back into place.

She gasped as the familiar sense radiated through her body.

Avoca.

She tugged on that bond and immediately felt a response. She placed a hand on her heart and was near to tears. After all this time of feeling so abandoned, it had been this invisible barrier blocking her from Avoca. Her friend had been here, waiting for her.

"Enough crying over some barrier thing," Ahlvie said with a laugh. "You'll get to see her in a minute."

"Yes, of course. You're right."

"Oh, I love the way those words sound out of your mouth."

She smacked him on the shoulder as she passed, moving in Avoca's direction. "Don't count on hearing it again."

Their trek was longer than she'd anticipated. Up, up, up they went through the Taken Mountains until she thought her legs were going to fall off. Her energy was waning. She could feel the last dregs of adrenaline leaving her body, and all that she had to hold her up was sheer force of will. But, when they came to the mouth of a cave, it was all worth it.

Avoca stood at the entrance, dressed for battle in fighting leathers. Her long blonde hair waved in the mountain breeze. Her features angular and pensive.

Her ice-white blade held loosely in her hand. Her body tensed for a fight.

"Ava," Cyrene whispered.

Avoca's blue eyes slanted to her, and then a smile ripped across her stunning face. She dashed down the rest of the mountain and pulled Cyrene into her. "Do not ever leave my side again."

"I won't," she promised.

"How can I protect you when you are away? When I cannot even feel you?"

"I missed you, too."

"I know."

Cyrene laughed, the first soft and buoyant thing she'd had in so long.

"I see you've finally decided to join us," Matilde said from the doorway. "Do you think we could do the hugging inside? We're in a bit of a hurry."

Cyrene's eyes rounded. "You're here! You…you came from Eleysia?"

"No, I'm still in the southern islands, and you're imagining things. Step one, two, girl. Let's get this moving."

Avoca and Cyrene released each other and hurried into the mountain cave. She gaped at the high ceilings and spacious living area. This must have been here a long time to accommodate so many people.

"What she means to say is, welcome back," Vera said as she appeared around a bend, carrying two oversize packs.

"What is this place?"

"A remnant from a time long past," Vera told her. "An old Doma retreat. The entrance was still sealed off to us, so we knew that no one had been here. We'll do the same when we leave."

"Which is now," Matilde told her.

"Yes," Vera agreed. "Please take a pack, all of you. The remaining supplies are down with the horses."

"We're leaving now?" Cyrene asked.

"In quite a bit of a hurry," Vera said with an easy smile as she handed her a bag. "You might want to change. I think your ball gown might be recognizable."

Cyrene had completely forgotten that she was even wearing it. Another gorgeous dress in tatters. Just like her life.

Vera stepped forward and placed a warm and comforting hand on her shoulder. "We'll explain everything once we're on our way."

She nodded, grateful that her hesitation was understood. Avoca led her to a room in the back. There were straw mats on the ground and little else. Cyrene attempted to undo all the tiny buttons that Rhea had done up earlier.

"Let me," Avoca said.

She took her blade and sliced up the back of the dress. It fell away in pieces.

"Well, that's one way to do it."

Cyrene balked at the matching fighting leathers that she pulled from her pack. "Someone expects me to wear these?"

"There will be a time for gowns once more. That time is not now."

She felt ridiculous once she had them on. They hugged her frame in all the right places. Her butt in particular was on full display. Her legs were thin but muscular—a fact she never noticed in her dresses. All in all, she felt exposed.

"You'll get used to it," Avoca said with a wave of her hand.

Cyrene added the precious Dremylon red ruby necklace into her bag, and then she was trailing the others down a different path through the mountain. From her vantage point, she could see the Nit Decus castle below. She wondered what was going on in there and if they would recover from what she had done.

Soon, they reached the base of the mountain on the Keylani River and found a pack of horses clustered together in an alcove. Cyrene's eyes darted between the people in attendance—Orden, Reeve, and Aubron.

Her heart sank.

"Where is Elea?" she asked frantically.

Reeve glanced up at her with panic on his face. "I thought she was with you."

Cyrene shook her head. "No, no, no. We have to go back for her. That was the deal. My entire family out."

"You cannot go back there," Dean said in anguish.

"Do not tell me what I can and cannot do."

"Dean is right," Avoca said, as if it pained her. "We cannot risk you."

"The king said that he would kill my family if I tried to leave. If I leave, I'm signing Elea's death warrant."

"An empty threat," Reeve said.

"You did not see his face when he said it."

"I think they have some recovering to do before they think of hurting anyone else," Dean added.

"What happened in there that you are not telling us?" Ahlvie asked.

"Nothing," she said at once. Her eyes cut to Dean to tell him not to reveal a thing. "I won't leave her."

"I'll go with you," Reeve said at once.

"No," Aubron said. He put his hand on Reeve's sleeve. "They'll kill you, too."

"Who was responsible for her?" Cyrene demanded.

Everyone glanced around. No one wanted to assume responsibility, but then Aubron stepped forward. His head was tilted up, and though he was small in comparison to the rest of her party, she saw he had fire in him.

"I attempted to corral her out of the party, but she wouldn't listen to me. Then, I asked her to meet us in the gardens. She refused. When I went to collect her, I was barred from access to the ballroom."

Cyrene sighed. Kael's barrier. Of course. Not Aubron's fault.

"She likely wouldn't have come with me anyway. Not when…" She trailed off and glanced down at her hands.

"I understand that you fear for her," Vera said very quietly, "but if we are to save all of our lives, we must go."

Cyrene nodded. Sacrifice one for the many. Just like they had with Maelia. Her heart constricted, and she sent up a prayer to the Creator to keep her sister safe.

Their party hastened to the horses. All of her friends were together again. It felt too good to be true…except that she'd kept losing people along the way. First Rhea, then Maelia, and now Elea.

Dean placed a hand on her sleeve. "Come with me."

She snatched her hand away and sent him a venomous glare. "Don't touch me."

He held his hands up in defense. "My apologies. I wanted to show you to your horse."

"I can do it myself."

"Cyrene, please," he muttered. "I was wrong. Everything that I did after my parents' deaths was wrong."

"Yes, well, I know exactly how that feels, and I didn't go off and try to ruin someone's life."

"But you teamed up with your enemy," he countered.

"An enemy you threw me at," she hissed.

"I'm trying to make things right."

She shoved her finger in his chest. "Start by keeping your mouth shut about everything you saw in that ballroom."

"If that's what you wish."

Orden appeared then with her horse. "Here you are. I think she'll remember you."

Cyrene's mouth dropped open as her prized dapple, Ceffy, appeared before her. "Oh Creator! How? How is this possible?"

"I had her brought back for you," Dean said softly. His eyes were open and unguarded. "I knew what she meant to you."

"You brought my horse back, all the way from Eleysia?"

"I thought it was the least I could do."

She averted her gaze at the heat coming from him and attached her pack to the saddle. "Thank you."

"Of course," he said.

Then, as if realizing that was all she was going to give, he went to hop on his own horse.

She patted Ceffy twice and hugged her before hauling herself up into her saddle and departing, leaving the rest of her life behind her.

Thirty Three

THE ATTACK

Traveling was no more fun than Cyrene remembered it being. Saddle aches and pains returned with a vengeance, and after her huge drain of power, there wasn't enough food to sate her. Not to mention, they had to ride a whole league out of the way to get to a bridge to cross the Keylani River. And, with a party as large as theirs, it was hardly inconspicuous.

She still couldn't believe that there were nine of them leaving the city. Though…it should have been ten. She tried not to think about Elea. What she had seen. What she must be thinking. If Edric was in fact going to kill her. Cyrene had abandoned her sister, and she felt personally responsible.

Though everyone assured her she wasn't.

The bridge itself was on the official dividing line between Byern and Carhara, their militaristic neighbor. Lucky for them, the soldiers guarding either side of the bridge were too busy arguing with each other to notice a shift in their surroundings. Matilde and Vera managed to cloak their entire group across the bridge without either military being any the wiser.

"How did you do that?" Cyrene asked Vera once they were across.

"I'll teach you once we're safe again."

Cyrene's expression must have shown exactly what she thought about that.

"I promise, I will. It's an incredible drain on powers especially for a party this size. For now, I think you need some time away from your powers."

"Why?" she breathed.

Vera raised her eyebrows. "I can feel that much has happened since we were last together. I am not trying to stop you from learning whatever you wish. Nor will Matilde. However, I would like to ensure you are being trained properly."

The key word, *properly*.

For no matter that she had gained considerable control back in Byern, she hadn't done it the right way. The painstakingly slow, obnoxious way that she detested.

"Patience," Vera said with a kind smile. "You will get it. I believe in you."

Cyrene didn't say another thing, just trudged forward.

For six days.

Six agonizing days of no magic. After training so regularly, it felt like torture. And, worse, though she was desperately happy to be with her friends, she felt as if she didn't fit in the same way that she had before. Then, she had been an ambitious, reckless girl but a leader. Now, she was withdrawn and distant. Dean was the only one who had seen what she did, and she wasn't about to confide in him. Nor was she ready to confide in anyone else.

But they all looked at her, as if they expected her to take the lead, to be the leader she had once been, but she didn't.

She didn't ask where they were going.

She didn't try to take charge and order people around.

She didn't even try to cajole Matilde and Vera to work on her magic with her.

She just…existed.

And she tried to forget the burning feeling of blood magic racing through her system. The connection between her and Kael that called to her with desperation. The tug of a bond she was trying to ignore. The darkness that crept up through her.

She had information to share about going forward. All the things that Serafina had said that she hadn't dare let herself think about, beyond getting out of the castle.

"Use the coin."

What coin?

"Find the lost ones."

Who were the lost ones?

"Learn the truth."

Which truth?

"Let the past be your guide to remake the future."

Whose past? How would she remake the future?

"Don't give in to this blindness."

Had she been blind?

"*There are bigger factors at play, trying to draw you in and away from me, and I want you to be safe. Guard your mind and open your heart.*"

That was not very encouraging. She already thought that there were too big of factors at play in this fight.

"*I dare not speak her name.*"

Who was this mysterious woman? And how could she possibly frighten Serafina that much. If she was that terrifying then Cyrene was doomed.

But she didn't share her fears.

They made camp on the banks of the Taken Mountains about a mile outside of Levin—a northern Byern city ruled by a regent, Duke Wynn Reagles, whose brother, Duke Halston Reagles, was regent of Albion. Cyrene actually liked Duke Halston and his wife, Duchess Elida, who had been pregnant when she last saw her. Though she dearly hoped she would not meet Duke Wynn.

"I'm going into the city to get supplies," Orden told them only a few minutes after they set up camp.

"I'll come with you," Ahlvie said at once.

Reeve jumped up as well. "I will go too."

"No offense," Ahlvie said, "but I don't think you can exactly fit in as Third Class."

Reeve looked offended at the comment, but Aubron held his hand out.

"He's right. I'll go."

Cyrene took her time brushing down Ceffy before stepping back into the circle of people and taking a seat. Orden, Ahlvie, and Aubron had already departed. Avoca had taken one look at the camp and said she was going to set up traps in the woods. Dean had offered to go with her, but she had snarled at him so violently that he sat down and started up a dicing game with Reeve. She was glad that Ahlvie was not here to cheat them out of what little money they had brought with them. It made her heart ache to see Dean and Reeve together like that. She quickly looked away and focused instead on Matilde and Vera.

"Can I ask a question?"

"You just did, child," Matilde said.

Cyrene gave her a halfhearted smile. "How can you be here if the magical barrier is still up in Byern?"

"The barrier is down," Matilde told her.

"What?"

"Yes, it is a strange thing. You probably cannot feel it, but to those of us who know what we're looking for, a magical barrier such as the one constructed two thousand years ago by Viktor Dremylon has a consistency to it. Like running your hand through water."

She understood that. She had felt something similar when leaving the castle. "And now that it is gone?"

"The night before we got you out of the castle, we were planning on how to move up through the mountains to avoid magical detection. Then, out of nowhere, it was as if a shock wave went through the mountains. Matilde, Avoca, and I all instantly felt it."

Cyrene felt sick to her stomach. "This brought down the magical barrier that had been there for two thousand years?"

"Yes. It must have been something very powerful."

Cyrene turned away. She knew exactly what had happened the night before Elea's Presenting and had felt the very shock wave Matilde and Vera spoke of.

It had happened when she kissed Kael.

It was almost dark when Cyrene first felt that something was wrong.

"Shouldn't they be back by now?" Cyrene asked. She paced a line in the grass as she waited anxiously.

"Indeed," Vera said.

"They'll get here when they get here," Matilde said.

"No, something is wrong." Cyrene shook her head. "This isn't right."

"Cyrene, the trek to Levin and back with supplies could take a considerable amount of time," Reeve said, adding his two cents.

"Are you sure?" Dean asked instead.

She glared at him. "I trust my gut."

Though she knew that she shouldn't. It had been wrong before. It had been wrong about Dean.

"I'm going out to look for them," she said, pulling her hair back into a ponytail and setting off.

"Wait, wait, wait," Dean and Reeve said at the same time. "You can't go alone."

Cyrene ignored them. "I'll be back in ten minutes. One of you, go check on Avoca. But, if you mess up her traps, you'll pay for it."

Matilde and Vera didn't even argue with her. They were back in their silent conversation. What about, she didn't know. But she could see the blatant worry on their faces when they looked at her.

Yeah, she didn't look like a savior so much anymore. She didn't feel like one either.

Cyrene moved out of the narrow mountain pass where their glen was secretly concealed when she heard footsteps behind her. She rolled her eyes.

Of course Dean is going to follow me.

"I don't want to talk to you. So, run back up to camp. I'll be there in ten minutes," she spat without looking over her shoulder.

The footsteps drew nearer, and she huffed out in exasperation. Seriously, she wanted to be alone.

"I cannot believe—"

A hand clamped over her mouth, and a blade was being held at her throat.

"Don't say a word," it breathed into her ear.

She froze as still as a board. Whatever was touching her was not of this world. If it had been a man, she could have sunk into its mind and commanded it to release her or blast the person away from her.

But this was no man.

This was…evil incarnate.

The touch of the blade at her throat and the hand on her mouth made her insides squirm and her mind want to pull away. But fear held her steady. She needed her wits about her to figure out what she was going to do.

"I will be happy to gut you from throat to navel, but my master desires your safe return," it said. The voice slipped and slithered over and all around her. "Lucky for you, I do love the taste of magic. It feeds my bones, and it has been far too long since I tasted one such as yourself."

Cyrene shivered. "What are you?"

The blade cut deeper. "I said…don't say a word."

Cyrene closed her eyes. She could smell decaying flesh and rotten eggs. She wanted to gag , but she swallowed and tried to focus. Though the hand on her felt sturdy, it seemed to be made of smoke, as if, at anytime, she could break through the form and find it not to be corporeal.

"What are you waiting for? Take me back to your *master*," she spat the word out.

A forked tongue glided out of its mouth and came to lick up her cheek. She shuddered.

"I think I would like to taste this one before we go."

Not a good sign.

"Does Doma flesh still taste like sucking the juices out of a pig? Succulent and brimming with energy?" The thing cackled. "I think I'd like to find out."

Cyrene couldn't wait another moment. She shot a blast of energy in a burst of power. The thing released her, and she abruptly stumbled forward. She whirled around to face her attacker with her hands up, ready to fight. But there was nothing and no one there. Just mountains.

Her heart was racing, and her skin was hot and clammy, as if she had a fever. She reached down for her magic, that overflowing well, and found next to nothing.

Holy Creator!

The energy she had used to throw Kael across the room was tremendous, but she'd still had plenty. He'd said that blood magic from someone you were close with would give you more powers. She had assumed that meant she would have gotten a lot from her parents. *How could I possibly be running low when all I did was cast aside that strange creature?*

She took two steps back up to camp before her legs gave out. She collapsed down onto one knee and raised her hand to her forehead. *Have I been poisoned? Is its blade like the Braj? Whatever it was…*

She touched her hand to the spot where the blade had been, but there wasn't any blood. Not even a nick. It had been holding her in place, not trying to hurt her. Well, not yet anyway.

Her thoughts stalled as hurried footsteps sounded from the trail below her. She turned her head to see what the commotion was and found Ahlvie, Orden, and Aubron sprinting toward her with at least a dozen guardsmen on horseback following a clip behind them.

What now?

"The fun never ends," she bit out as she rose shakily to her feet.

"Cyrene, out of the way. Get going!" Ahlvie cried once he was within range.

But she held her ground and reached for the magic she still had harnessed at her core. She could do this. She could make this all right. The truth was that they could not be followed. She would *not* be captured and taken back to the capital to face Kael and Edric. She was finally free, and she was damn well determined to stay that way.

"Go," she spat as all three men formed up around her. "Go warn the others."

"Aubron, do it," Ahlvie commanded.

His brother nodded once and then scampered up the mountain pass. Orden and Ahlvie dropped their supply packs and traded them out for swords.

"They're mine," she told them.

"Cyrene, you look near to death," Ahlvie told her.

"What a compliment from a scoundrel."

He grinned ferociously at her. Something in his eyes shifted from brown to hazel to gold, his features more angular, his teeth bared.

"Ahlvie is right," Orden said. "Allow us."

"None of us are getting out of these mountains if you do not get out of my way and let me work."

Then, she took a step forward, drew her powers into her, and let them loose on the guardsmen barreling toward them. The ground shook with the force of an earthquake. Their horses skittered across the rocky ground, tossing their riders and falling into a crack she had created in the earth. The rumble lasted for what felt like an eternity before ceasing.

But, still…more came forward. One or two had managed to remain on their horses and a handful more with swords drawn, warily approaching where she stood. She raked her hand to the side, knocking the two remaining riders off their steeds, and then spiraled all the men up in a wave of air, constricting their airways and keeping them from breathing.

"Cyrene," Orden whispered softly.

"Cyrene, please," Ahlvie said, "drop them."

She did as he'd said. Fifteen feet down they went without any of the feline grace that she had.

Crunch.

And, it wasn't enough. She stalked forward, a predator advancing on her prey. She reached for the men still living and tasted the blood on their bodies. Tasted the hint of magic emanating from the dead. So much power. So much right here for the taking. All she had to do was—

No.

No, she wouldn't. Couldn't.

But if she did…

She seized all the broken bits of guardsmen and dragged them toward her with a flick of her wrist. Then, she lined them up in a pretty row and dropped into their minds like wet sand.

"You did not see us here. You will forget our faces and everything you saw and heard. You came out to investigate the earthquake. You found nothing unusual. You will ride back to Levin and not report anything out of the ordinary to your commander."

She precariously held them. Her magic waned. And, in all of it, all she felt was the ache. It crawled at her. Begged her. Coaxed her.

Who are these men and women?

They would have killed her or collected her with no conscience. No hesitation. She would have been halfway back to Byern, her friends slaughtered.

Why didn't they deserve the same thing?

A life for a life after all.

She reached for it. Ready to drain the life force from these men to refill her well. Because, if Kael was right, then she would need it. And, right now… she did. She desperately did.

"Don't!" Ahlvie said, jumping in front of her. "They have families, Cyrene! Wives and husbands and children. They were following orders. Let them go home."

"They wouldn't have done the same for us."

"I know I might not look it, Cyrene, but you and I, we're the good guys."

"What does that even mean?" she shouted. "What is good and evil in this world? There is only power. Who has it and who doesn't and how far you are willing to go to take it."

"You don't believe that," Ahlvie pleaded with her. He stepped forward, and with no fear in his eyes, he took her trembling hand. "You are good. So, maybe we all have a little darkness in us, but we are not murderers. We do not silence voices of dissent. We listen and help change the world. And, those men, Cyrene, they want more than you are going to give them. Let them find that new world with us."

"How can you be so sure?" she asked, her voice wavering. Her grasp on her magic slipping.

"Because there was a time when you believed in me when no one else would. When you had no reason to. When I could have been that killer. And I believe in you just as much as you did in me."

Cyrene looked up into Ahlvie's shining eyes, and with a gasp, she dropped her hand. All of the guards crumpled onto the ground. Confused to be sure when they woke up but alive.

"Thank you," she muttered. "Thank you."

"Come on," he said. He put his arm around her frail frame. "Let's get out of here."

"I don't know that I can…"

She was lucky that he held her because she took two more steps before collapsing as thoroughly as the guards.

Thirty Four

THE OFFER

—RHEA—

Rhea groaned noisily as she came to. Her hand went to her head, and she felt the nasty lump where Captain Merrick had dropped his sword against her skull.

What an idiot she'd been to think that she'd be safe when Cyrene left. To think that they wouldn't come for her. Sure, she might have been doing good work for the kingdom, but that didn't mean anything now.

She sat up in the dungeon cell and let her eyes adjust to the dim lighting. The stone cell itself was tiny with nothing more than a pot to do her business. Iron bars took up the one other wall, and she rattled them until her shoulders ached but to no avail.

Finally, she sat back on her heels and waited. Surely, someone would come back for her. Right?

It wasn't until a few more hours of utter solitude when she heard crying from the cell next to her.

"Hello?" Rhea called. "Who is there?"

"I'm…I'm not alone?" the voice said.

Rhea grinned when she recognized the voice and then immediately frowned. "Elea?"

"Rhea?" she whimpered.

"What are you doing down here?"

"Cyrene, Cyrene…she…she did horrible things," Elea whispered. "And, now, we're to be punished for it."

Rhea frowned. "What kind of horrible things?"

"You won't believe me."

"Try me."

Elea peeked her head against the bars, and Rhea could barely make out her face.

"She…she used some kind of magic to fight Prince Kael. They both have the curse. They blocked off the ballroom of my Presenting ball, so no one could get out. Cyrene threw Kael thirty feet into the wall before we could all get away."

Rhea sighed. She had known it would only be a matter of time before everyone knew that magic existed. She had come to terms with it a year ago when Cyrene told her. But performing it in front of the entire ballroom? That was suicide.

"What happened to Cyrene?"

Elea shook her head and sniffled. "I don't know. It all happened so fast."

Rhea breathed a sigh of relief. That meant that Cyrene could have gotten away after all. There was still hope.

"How long do you think they'll keep us down here?" Elea asked, her voice trembling.

Rhea took a deep breath. She didn't want to give Elea false hope. "A while. Long enough."

"But I didn't *do* anything!"

Rhea shrugged even though she knew that Elea couldn't see it. "Doesn't seem to matter."

Elea grew quiet from then on. Rhea didn't know what she was thinking, but she could hear her soft sobs from the other side of the wall. She understood how Elea felt. They had been close before she went through her own Presenting. And, now, the day she was to become an Affiliate, everything had been ripped from her. Worse than what Rhea had felt when she was placed into Second Class. Elea was imprisoned just for being related to Cyrene. She'd lost her parents, her sister, her status, and her freedom, all in one week.

It was a long couple of hours before anyone else ventured down to the dungeons. Elea must have fallen asleep somehow because Rhea hadn't heard a peep from her in some time. Not even any of her muffled tears.

Rough footsteps scraping on the floor made Rhea jump to attention. She stuck her head out to see who was approaching, but the light from the lantern blinded her in the darkness. She had to blink spots from her vision before she was able to see that it was not one but four people.

They stopped before Elea's cell, and a gruff voice said, "Get up, girl."

Rhea heard that voice in her nightmares. She shuddered as he came into view.

Merrick.

The king's Captain of the Royal Guard.

His interest in her work had been…unstoppable.

In fact, he'd had interest in more than just her work. If she hadn't had Kael as her ally, she wasn't sure where exactly she would be. Not that she was exactly singing Kael's praises at this moment. He had manipulated her as thoroughly as anyone to get what he wanted—bombs of his very own. But at least he hadn't tried to put his hands on her. Not like Merrick.

"I said, get up," he snarled.

Elea sniveled, and then Rhea heard her easing onto her feet.

"What…what do you want with me?"

"We need information."

"What kind of information?"

"On Cyrene. Everything she told you before she left. Everything she might have hinted at. We need you to recall every little detail. Did she seem off? Did she seem distant? Had she been planning anything?"

"I…I don't know." Elea hedged. "We got into an argument. I didn't really talk to her."

"But did she say anything about planning something?"

"You mean, about the magic?"

Merrick shot his hand through the bars and grabbed Elea by the neck. "Do not use that word in this kingdom!"

Elea broke down into sobs, and Rhea couldn't take it.

"Leave her alone!"

Merrick's eyes shot to her, and he dropped Elea. "Hello, Rhea."

She took a step back at that voice. "She doesn't know anything."

"How would you know that?"

"Because Cyrene isolated herself completely while here. I only saw her twice, and from what I gathered, she was with Prince Kael the entire time. Maybe you should question him," she told him.

"We intend to," a second voice added.

Rhea startled when she saw King Edric step into view. "Your Majesty."

Elea blubbered from the other side of the wall as their attention turned to Rhea. "Please, please, let me out of here. I didn't do anything! I didn't know my sister had magic. I didn't know she was going to go insane! Please, I'm not at fault here. I'm an Affiliate. You gave me my pin. I shouldn't be treated like this."

Edric turned back to face Elea. His expression was dark and haunted. "You say you know nothing. Yet your brother has disappeared from the premises as well."

"Reeve?"

"That means you must have all been plotting together."

"But I'm still here! I didn't try to run! I came back to my rooms. I was in fear for my life after what I saw. Please, I will do anything. Anything you ask."

"Shut up, Elea," Rhea snapped.

Merrick hadn't taken his focus off of Rhea through Elea's tirade. "I think we'll have better luck with this one. The young girl seems to be clueless."

"Still," King Edric said with a shrug, as if he didn't much care if Elea rotted down here, "she might know something."

"I don't! I don't!" Elea cried.

"Tell us what you know," Merrick said to Rhea. "Or I can make this very unpleasant."

Rhea glared back at him and remained silent. Elea might dissolve into a sniveling idiot at the first provocation, but Rhea wasn't about to divulge what she knew. And she knew a lot more than Elea ever did.

"Open her door," Merrick snapped at the other guards who were guarding the king. "I will take great pleasure in peeling off each of your fingernails. To start. We'll see how long you last."

She raised her chin. The horrors that awaited her were hers to bear. She would not give up her information about Cyrene without a fight. If Merrick wanted to have one, then she would steel herself for the challenge.

"Do you think these bars can hold me?" came a voice from the cell to Rhea's right.

All heads whipped to the side as a maniacal laugh came from the dungeon. Rhea shivered at the sound. No one moved.

"Bars can't hold me. Nothing can hold me."

Rhea gasped as she realized who was in the next cell.

"Brother," King Edric said, stepping past Rhea.

"Well met," Prince Kael said. He leaned into the bars with his arms dangling forward.

"I didn't think the bars could hold you."

"Yet I am behind them."

"I wanted to know where you would be if…when you awoke," the king said. He hadn't stepped within reach of the prince though. He was smart enough for that.

"And here I am," Prince Kael said with arms spreading wide.

"You have been keeping a many good things from me, it seems."

"Only as many secrets as I could."

"We have a lot to discuss."

"Do we?" Prince Kael asked.

Rhea could see his sharp grin at the king's arrogance.

"I believe we can work together," the king offered, dangling the carrot before him.

Rhea thought he would laugh it off. *After all, if he did have magic, what use would the king be to him?*

"What's in it for me?" Prince Kael asked instead.

King Edric smiled, but it was bitter and angry around the edges. "I never thought you had any interest in ruling."

"And now that I do?"

Rhea couldn't believe he had said that. *What he'd said was treason!*

"I believe we can do this together. We'll get her back and break everyone who has ever stood in our way," King Edric said with vehemence in his voice.

"I'm listening," the prince crooned.

"I want to start with the backstabbing murderers…Eleysia."

"What did you have in mind?"

King Edric grinned like a madman. "I want to raze them to the ground."

Thirty Five

THE ARRIVAL

Cyrene landed in darkness.

All kinds of shapes and shadows seemed to move all around her. Touch her, taste her, know her. As if the very air she breathed physically knew her. The wind roared around her, whipping her hair into a frenzy and stinging her eyes.

"The time is now," a female voice called.

Cyrene didn't bother responding. Her voice would surely be caught by the breeze and carried away from her. She felt trapped, as if she were in a box, being pushed in on all sides.

"Come to me, Cyrene. Come to me."

She ducked down and put her hands over her head. Her ears were pounding. Her vision was blurry. She was torn and tight and twisted. Constricted and beaten and lost. There was only the air and the wind and the nothingness. Only lost hope and death.

No air. No sound. No breath. Nothing.

Then, it all stopped.

As if something had reached out into the heavens and stilled the world.

She glanced up from where she was crouched, only to see a hooded figure standing before her. The shadows seemed to bend and swirl around the woman. And Cyrene knew intuitively that this was a thing of nightmares. Was this the woman Serafina feared?

"Who are you?"

"Your salvation." A soft and feminine hand reached out from the deep sleeve and touched her chin. The hand was cold as ice and made of marble. "Come to me."

"What…what are you? What do you want from me?" Cyrene whispered.

"Do not be afraid," she said, smooth as a siren's call from the cowl of the hood. "I will temper you like steel. Forge you into something more. Make you who you were always meant to be."

"What if I don't want any of it?"

"You will need answers. I have the answers." The disembodied hand reached for Cyrene's hand. She flipped it over, exposing her palm, and placed something there. She closed Cyrene's fingers around it. "You will come to me. Use it."

When Cyrene uncurled her fingers, she gasped. She was holding a gold coin.

When she looked back to demand answers, the figure was gone.

And she was entrapped back in the shadows once more.

"Try to keep her steady," Matilde bit through her dream. "If she doesn't stop shaking, this could kill her."

"I'm doing the best I can!" Avoca shouted back at her.

Cyrene felt pressure on her legs. Something hard pressed into her shoulders.

"She's waking up, Mati!" Vera cried. "You're doing it."

Cyrene's eyes opened to a room full of people. Her eyes hurt. Her body hurt. Everything hurt.

Then, she couldn't keep her eyes open any longer. They dropped closed, and she shook violently. Her teeth clattered together. Her skin was hot and heavy on her body. As if, at any minute, the heat would burn through so quick, it would rip her skin and leave her muscles and bones exposed.

A hand touched her center, and a wave of cool pressure suffused her. As if someone had stuck water under the surface to cool the fire. It was wonderful. Calmed her for a whole minute before her teeth started up again.

Then, she was freezing.

And then screaming.

On and on.

Endless.

Screaming.

"You try!"

Another wave hit her, and she felt free. Free as a bird. Soaring away high into the skies.

And then it was gone. Gone. Gone. Gone.

She ripped her arm away from the pressure on her shoulders and vomited up everything in her stomach. When she finished with that, she dry-heaved until all she had left were tears and coughing and choking and stomach acid.

Another hit of the energy poured through her veins.

Sweet reprieve. Sweet, sweet bliss.

Her jaw was pried open, and water was poured into her mouth. She sputtered around the water before finally getting it down. Another mouthful and another.

Where it all ended up on the floor once more.

The shaking intensified, as if she could rattle the earth. As if she could shake so hard, she could force the stars out of the sky.

But there were no stars. There was only pitch black night. And the hell she was in.

She fell down a rabbit hole as the people around her tried to yell in disembodied voices. But she couldn't reach them.

And then they were gone.

"Creator! I got you," Serafina said.

They were standing outside of a manor home on the foothills of a mountain with the Nit Decus castle in the distance.

Cyrene flinched when Serafina moved to touch her. "Why am I here? What do you want with me?"

"I am trying to protect you."

"Then, tell me the truth. Tell me everything I need to know. I am blind to what is going on out there. No one even knew that you and Viktor were together!"

It was Serafina's turn to flinch at the name. "I have been trying. You do not know how difficult it has been to relive these memories with you. The happiest times of my life were tainted by what followed."

"And what did follow?"

"Viktor destroyed me to rid the world of magic," Serafina said. "That part of the story is true."

"But magic still exists. I am proof of that."

"Yes." Serafina took her hand. "Yes. It has been passed down to you through the ages. The blood that runs through your veins could have manifested generations before you, but now that we're here, I see, it had to be you."

"Why?" Cyrene asked desperately. "Why me?"

"It is the mark of the chosen to question the Creator's judgment. I constantly asked the same thing," Serafina said with a sad smile. "In times of hardship, the world needs a dreamer with their gaze cast to the stars to right the wrongs of this limited existence."

Serafina flickered before her, as if she were an image that Cyrene could pass her hand through.

"What's going on?"

"You're waking up. Or someone is drawing you away from me again."

"By who? Who is the shadow in the darkness?"

Serafina shook her head, but then she disappeared again. Cyrene was still standing before the manor house. Suddenly, all alone.

No answers. Just riddles. Again!

Then, Serafina reappeared. Her face was pale, and she looked exhausted. "The reason," she gasped out. Her knees buckled, and she went to the ground.

"Oh Creator, are you all right?" Cyrene asked, reaching for her.

"Listen to me, Cyrene. I know you want answers. I will tell you everything I can when you are able to reach me, but the things that we say here are not always safe. Others might be listening."

"Who could be listening?"

Serafina frowned. "An evil. I will shield you from her the best that I can. Right now, she is contained. So what matters is that you know you are on the right path. And I know…I know that it is hard. But I have faith in you because the reason you have magic…"

Her skin started flickering again. She shook her head and tried to grab Cyrene's hand. But she went straight through Cyrene, as if she were made of air.

"Sera, please," she gasped.

"The reason you have magic," Serafina rasped out, "is because…I had a child."

Then, she disappeared once more in a flash. Cyrene glanced around, trying to process what she had just heard.

Serafina had had a child?

That must mean…Cyrene…was descended from that ancient Doma line.

Her thoughts became muddy, and then the scene before her disappeared entirely.

Cyrene gasped and shot straight up in bed.

It was nighttime, and the room was empty.

She opened her hand, only to find it empty. No coin.

"Just a dream. Just a dream," she whispered.

A twinge in the pit of her stomach said she'd not eaten in a while. She took stock of her surroundings—small wooden room with one pallet bed, a chair, and a water pitcher. She eased out of bed and then nearly fell to her knees. Reaching for the chair, she hoisted herself back to her unsteady feet and poured herself a glass of water.

After drinking a full glass, she forced herself to stop. The last thing she wanted was to get sick. She was weak and ached all over, but she was clearheaded. That was a first in a long time.

Cyrene eased open the door to the room she was staying in and found herself in a tiny log cabin. The large living space had a clean stone floor, crackling fireplace, and a small kitchen. An old woman Cyrene had never seen before was seated in a rocking chair, fast asleep.

But no one else.

Not her friends.

Not her family.

Nothing to indicate where she was or what she was doing here.

Alone. All alone again.

THE VILLAGE

Cyrene bit her lip and then decided it was better to get out of there than to ask questions. She edged past the woman and out the front door with no trouble at all, breathing a sigh of relief when the door shut behind her.

But what she was looking at was as foreign as could possibly be. Maybe more foreign than anywhere else she had ever traveled. She wasn't in a city or on the water or at court or really any of those things.

She was in a…village.

A small, small village.

The setting sun revealed mountains off to her right. The scant log cabins were clustered off the edge of a forest. The air had a bite to it that made her think she was in the north, but otherwise, she couldn't have placed herself on a map.

Cyrene suddenly heard laughter from not too far off. She marked the cabin she had woken up in and then slunk through the shadows, down the lane, until she finally came upon a bonfire blazing high. And it was surrounded on all sides by people…dancing, drinking, laughing.

Happy people.

She hung back and observed the festivities. Bare-chested boys younger than her picked girls in flower crowns out of the crowd. They danced in circles, swinging their flowing skirts to the up-tempo beat. Men and women alike were circling around barrels of spirits and drinking merrily. Food was spread out on a long wooden table nearby. But of her friends, she saw nothing.

As the song ended, an old woman moved forward. Her limbs were stiff, her shoulders hunched. A youth helped her onto a stage. She brushed her waist-length braided hair off her shoulder and raised her hands.

A hush fell over the crowd, and Cyrene felt a brush of magic touch her skin. She jolted in shock.

"Come closer," she said, her old voice so frail yet somehow amplified beyond the stretch of her vocal cords. "Old Mana wants to tell you a story."

As if under a spell, Cyrene felt her feet moving. She came out of her hiding spot and stood among the people of this strange village. But no one seemed to notice her. Everyone's eyes were caught on Mana and the tale she was about to weave.

"Long ago, at a time before our people, there was a lone wolf. His pack had abandoned him in the dark mountains to starve. They had found him nearing the human settlements, risking them all, and he had been cast aside to fend for himself. Without his pack, the lone wolf was lost, broken, and desperate."

Mana waved her hand in the air, and the dark sky shimmered with an image of the wolf. Cyrene's eyes were glued to the display.

"He ventured deeper into the mountains. Farther and farther, he went. He was determined to find people of his own sort. Ones who knew the value of knowledge, the taste of freedom, and had the heart of a believer."

She cast her hand forward in a sweeping motion. This time, three objects floated in the air before her—a book, an arrow, and a heart.

"Alone on that mountain, he spent one week searching for a way out and a way to begin anew. When he climbed out of that mountain pass and found this land, he knew he had found his salvation. A new way of life and a deepened belief in who he was."

She raised her hand, and stars ignited over the heads of the bare-chested boys. "Lone wolves, assemble."

The boys moved to stand before her. Not a one of them was older than fifteen. Some, it seemed, were much younger. And then, out of nowhere, a girl scrambled into the fold. She wore nothing but a scrap to cover her breasts and the tight-fitted pants the other boys were wearing.

Mana gave her an outraged look but seemed to decide to berate the girl at a later date.

"Lone wolves, you honor your people and your heritage today by venturing back into those mountains to find whether or not you have the heart of a believer."

"Aye!" they all cheered as one.

"You have one week in the mountains. You may take nothing with you, save one book, one arrow, and your own beating heart. May you return with all of them," she said rather ominously.

"Aye!" they shouted again.

"Good luck."

The crowd erupted into applause and cheers. As one, the boys trotted off into the darkness, toward the mountains beyond. The spell was broken as Mana grabbed the girl by the shoulder to stop her from following after them. Cyrene shook her head as everyone began to move again.

Cyrene was trying to get her bearings on the situation as the party started up around her again. There were enough people that she could blend into the crowd but not enough that they wouldn't notice an outsider. Her feet moved out of the circle and away from the group, but when she heard what the people near her were saying, she slowed.

"It is too bad that we have to send them this week," someone said behind Cyrene. "I don't feel safe, having Barton out with all the attacks."

Attacks?

What attacks?

"I agree. We should have followed the wraiths farther into the forest and taken back our land. We give up more and more of the trees every day."

"The more we chase, the more of us that die. If we leave them alone, they only—"

"Take one of us a month?" someone else shouted. "That is not acceptable. Not with our numbers so low since those southern Byern bastards keep stealing our best and brightest."

Cyrene's head was reeling. She must be in another kingdom for them to think of Byern so poorly.

A cold northern kingdom perhaps.

Carhara?

Mastira?

Cyrene heard the next comment as she slunk away, only because the man was shouting in his inebriation.

"What we need is to mount an attack. Send men into the woods to stop this. Then, we can actually pull up the harvest. Because, if we do not work soon, snow will be upon us, and then we'll go hungry all winter!"

Cyrene had been about to turn around to demand answers to all of her burning questions when Ahlvie exploded through the group. She gasped at the sight of him, and then he pulled Cyrene into a bone-crushing hug.

"You're alive!"

"Yes, I'm alive," she choked out.

Ahlvie was squeezing the life out of her.

"But, if you keep hugging me, I might not make it."

"Oh, right," he said, abruptly releasing her. His eyes stared deep into her own. "And you're…you're really okay?"

"Weak and hungry, but, yeah, otherwise okay."

He shook his head in disbelief. "Wow."

"What?" she asked.

But she was promptly cut off by Avoca slamming into her. "Do not *ever* do that again!"

"Okay," Cyrene gasped.

"You're crushing her," Ahlvie observed.

Avoca reluctantly let her go. They both stared back into her eyes, as if they were seeing a ghost.

"Seriously, what is up with you two? And where are we? Some Doma magic was used by an old woman, and they sent kids up into the mountains, alone, with just an arrow. Not even a bow! I'm wondering if we should go after them. Plus, they wouldn't let the girl go with them! How backward is that? Women can do anything men can do."

And then Ahlvie was doubled over on his knees, laughing hysterically. Avoca clapped him on the back twice. Maybe a little too hard.

He straightened and held up his hand, as if he couldn't keep it together. He wiped his eyes. "Phew! That was…wow. I've missed you."

"I don't…what did I say?"

"Cyrene," Ahlvie said, gesturing to the bonfire, the people, and all the tiny cabins, "welcome to Fen."

"Fen," she whispered.

He grinned like a lone wolf himself. "This is my home."

Cyrene's cheeks heated. *Foot, meet mouth.* "Ahlvie, I'm…I'm sorry. I didn't mean to sound so—"

"Condescending?" he offered. "Entitled? Arrogant?"

She clamped her mouth shut and nodded.

"I'll forgive it since I'm all of those things as well. And that backward ceremony you were talking about is our most sacred ceremony. I went out when I was fourteen, and I turned out just fine."

Avoca snorted next to him.

"I feel horrible. I should have learned by now that, just because I don't understand, it doesn't mean it's wrong."

"Well, you were raised from the dead. I would think it'd make you cranky."

"Raised from the dead?" she gasped.

"We have a lot to discuss," Avoca said. "We should go back to Avniella's."

"Avniella?"

Ahlvie grinned and slung an arm over her shoulders. "Ready to meet my mom?"

"Your…your mom?" she sputtered.

"Yep. You get to meet the person who I learned all my annoying habits from."

Avoca raised her eyebrows. "Avniella is not a drunk, nor a cheat."

"But she sure has a way with words," Ahlvie said. "Plus…you haven't seen her drink. She can drink grown men under the table."

"Sorry to interrupt, but…how exactly did we get here?" Cyrene asked.

"By horse," Avoca said, as if that ended the discussion. Then, she bustled Cyrene along back to the cabin she had woken up in.

When they entered, she found it full of people. In fact, there were so many people in the small room, it felt claustrophobic. Cyrene shrank back as all eyes stared at her.

"I found her," Avoca said as way of an introduction.

"Actually, I found her," Ahlvie interrupted.

Her eyes flickered to the three people in the room that she didn't know. An older woman, who Cyrene realized was the person who had fallen asleep by the fireplace when she escaped; a woman in her middling years; and a man of indeterminate age, who was as thick as a tree trunk.

The younger woman stepped forward, silencing Ahlvie. "We're so glad to see you on your feet, Cyrene. I'm sure you are very confused. I am Avniella, mother to your traveling companions, Ahlvie and Aubron. This is my brother, Ryon, and my mother, Lace."

"Pleasure to meet you," she said, manners kicking in.

"Pleasure is all ours," Avniella said. Her honey hair fell in a thick braid over her shoulder, and when she smiled, laugh lines creased her eyes and mouth. She seemed the type to laugh a lot. "We're so pleased to see you well."

"Yes. Well, thank you for your hospitality and everything you did when I was ill," Cyrene said.

Her eyes darted around the room, finding first Matilde, then Vera, then Orden, then Reeve and Aubron, and finally Dean. He stared back with a hollow expression and sad eyes.

Cyrene cut back to Avniella. "How long was that exactly?"

Everyone shuffled their feet, as if they didn't want to talk about what had happened.

"Two months," Orden finally barked out.

Cyrene swayed on her feet, and Avoca put a steadying hand on her.

"That long?"

Vera stepped forward with a grim look on her face. "Everyone here knows the grave danger that you were in, so I will not spare you what happened. You took blood magic, Cyrene."

She swallowed and nodded.

"There are only three ways in which you can access magic—birth, earned, and stolen. Blood magic is a…curse. It's stolen magic. It uses you up instead of you using it, and when you run out, it eats away at not just your body… but also your soul."

Cyrene placed her hand on her heart. "Did…did…"

She couldn't bring her mouth to shape the words. *Did I lose part of my soul? My whole soul?*

"No one has ever recovered from the corruption without taking more blood magic, and that has its own price."

"But then…how am I living?"

"We infused you with magic. Matilde, Avoca, and I. It was so draining that even some of the local healers and their ancient ones assisted where they could," Vera said, nodding at Lace in thanks. "We weren't sure it would work. We only hoped for the best."

"Thank you," Cyrene said around a suddenly tight throat. "You…you did all of this for me, not knowing whether or not I would even live?"

"We're not entirely sure how you *are* alive," Matilde said. "Or the state of your mind now that you are fully awake."

"I don't feel like myself," she told them.

The room tensed at those words.

"But I don't feel like the thing I was before either. It's as if I'm something entirely new."

"I believe you are, dear child," Lace said. "I can feel it in my bones. Nothing in this world has ever seen the likes of you."

Cyrene wasn't sure how she felt about being something new. At the same time, she finally felt like herself again. As if the foolish girl who had been so anxious to prove herself were a dream. As if that person she had been back in Byern, surrounded by the Dremylons and court and expectations, was a nightmare. This…this was her reality.

"What happens now?" Reeve finally asked from the corner.

He had his arm slung around Aubron's waist, and they looked content.

"You are all more than welcome to stay in Fen for as long as you need," Avniella said.

"I fear we must be on our way," Matilde said.

"No," Cyrene spoke up.

All eyes snapped back to her.

"No?" Avoca asked in confusion.

"These people housed me for two months at my darkest hour. I owe them a life debt," Cyrene said.

Avoca's eyes rounded. She understood the importance of that statement. She had surrendered her own life to Cyrene once and bound them together for it.

"It's not necessary," Avniella said, waving her off.

Cyrene stepped forward. "There is a threat to this village, hunting and killing your people."

Ryon nodded. "The wraiths."

"Don't listen to his silly ghost stories," Lace said, swatting at her son. "Focus on your mission. We can handle ourselves here."

"I would like to end this threat to your village."

"Cyrene, you can hardly stand up," Ahlvie noted. "How are you going to stop these wraiths?"

She smiled and touched his hand. "The way we always have. Together."

THE WRAITHS

Cyrene spent the next four days regaining her strength, generally avoiding more important conversations, and learning everything she needed to know about these wraiths. Truth be told, there wasn't much to glean from the villagers' accounts. No one had ever actually faced one. The village was secluded in the curve of the Taken Mountains and the start of the forest. If attacks were coming, it was purposeful.

No one tried to deter her from her decision after her announcement of her life debt, but she knew more than one person was anxious for her. If all Matilde and Vera had said was true, then she should not be alive.

More worrisome, she might have lost part of her soul. A fact that frightened her so much, she had to block it out of her mind.

One task at a time.

Find the wraith.

Kill the wraith.

Save Ahlvie's people.

At midday, she caught a break. Not the kind she wanted, but the one she expected. A wraith attacked, but its victim managed to escape.

Cyrene hurried over to find out what had happened. She was unsurprised to see the girl from the lone wolf ceremony standing with her arms over her chest, looking defiant.

"You were sneaking out to try to join the boys again?" her mother shrieked at her. "Can't you accept that you are a girl? Not a boy?"

"I accept that I can do *everything* they do and more. I accept that I have Nana Mana's gifts. I accept that I am old enough to make my own choices."

"You are fourteen years old, Caldreva Anamarya!" her mother cried. "While you live under my roof, you'll follow my rules. Now, get inside, and change out of those clothes!"

"Excuse me. Sorry to interrupt," Cyrene said.

The woman went pale. "Bloodbreaker," she whispered.

Cyrene startled at that name. "May I speak with Caldreva, please?"

"You can call me Cal," the girl said, shooting past her mom and toward Cyrene. "All my friends do."

"Creator above!" Her mother cursed before stomping inside.

"Cal, nice to meet you. I'm Cyrene."

"I know who you are. My nana helped you during your blood curse."

"That was very kind of her."

"Do you want to know about the wraith that attacked me?" Cal asked.

Her bright green eyes were wide with excitement. Her hair was the color of wheat and fell past her shoulders. And, though Cyrene could see she was slight, she had definition in her arms and legs that came from intense labor. She didn't doubt every word that Cal had said to her mother. In another village, another world, she would have been a skilled warrior by fourteen.

"Yes," Cyrene said. "You can show me, can't you?"

"Absolutely! Let me get my bow!"

Cyrene laughed. Her enthusiasm was infectious.

Cyrene had tugged on her bond with Avoca, and by the time Cal was back outside, Avoca appeared with Ahlvie and, to Cyrene's dismay, Dean in tow. He nodded at her as he stood by her side, and she cut her eyes away from him.

"Ahlvie!" Cal cried, breaking the tension.

"Hey, squirt," he said, nudging her. "Still getting in trouble?"

"Trouble? You were the one who taught me how to fight, how to ride, how to shoot! You're the troublemaker."

"Well, I enjoyed watching you outshine Aubron."

"He's still awful with a bow," Cal said, scrunching her nose.

"It's already nearly midday," Cyrene interrupted. "I'd like to track the wraith that attacked Cal and see if we can find its lair. If we don't find anything, we'll circle back before last light and regroup with the others."

"Excellent," Cal said with a wide smile.

"Cal, after you."

She trotted forward with enthusiasm.

"You've released a monster," Ahlvie muttered in her ear.

"With pleasure."

Cyrene wasn't a natural tracker. She had learned much of her skills from getting lost in the Hidden Forest in Aurum while on their way to Eleysia. Now, after seeing Ahlvie's home, she understood why he was always good at it. Avoca was self-explanatory. This was her life. But Dean…she didn't know why he'd ever had the need to track, but even he seemed to have more skill at it than her.

But it didn't matter to her. She followed in Cal's graceful footsteps and kept her eyes open for whatever this wraith was. She knew that it was a distraction from her real problems, but she needed to do something to prove useful once more. And this problem seemed like such a small thing she could do for them. Something she could actually fix.

"It's probably about two miles ahead," Cal said. "I ran like the wind when it tried to grab me. I know they say, if it touches you, you're done."

"What did this wraith look like?" Cyrene asked. "All of the accounts I've gotten have been…well, ghost stories."

"That's because you don't see them until they touch you."

"But you said—"

"I didn't see the thing. I felt it."

Cyrene frowned. "Okay. What did it feel like?"

Cal stopped for a second and then nodded her head to the right. "Cold and wrong. I don't know. Like, you know, when you're completely alone, and then you feel eyes on you even though it's impossible?"

"Yeah."

"It's like that but worse. You'll know it when you feel it. Just don't let it touch you."

"Got it. No touching. Think you can handle that, Ahlvie?" Cyrene asked with a raised eyebrow.

"Did you just make a joke, Bloodbreaker?" he teased.

Cyrene stuck her tongue out at him. Something about this place and these woods and Cal made her feel younger than she had in so long.

"So, Ahlvie, who are your friends?" Cal asked, eyeing Avoca and Dean. "Is this your girlfriend?"

Avoca raised her eyebrow at Ahlvie. "Be careful how you answer that."

Ahlvie actually choked. "She's my…she's…well, she's more than that."

"Are you married?" Cal gasped.

Ahlvie's eyes rounded. "No. Nope. Not that I'm…opposed. I mean… well, we have a lot going on."

"I'm bound to Cyrene," Avoca clarified.

"Oh," Cal said, as if she understood what that meant. Then, she nodded at Dean. "And who are you?"

"Dean."

"How do you fit in? Are you bound to Cyrene, too?"

Dean glanced over at Cyrene, and a small frown touched his lips. "Something like that."

"Well, cool," Cal said, "I like you lot."

Cyrene laughed softly. She wanted to keep Cal talking. She found that she felt lighter with the casual conversation rather than all the heavy silences. "What happened with the lone wolves? I saw you stand up with the boys."

Cal ground her teeth. "Nana wouldn't let me go."

"Hmm…that doesn't seem right. What is it exactly? Ahlvie said it was a ceremony."

"It is," she announced.

"It's our rite of passage," Ahlvie explained.

"I can tell it," Cal muttered.

"Then, tell it, squirt."

"Look, we're not actually descended from wolves," Cal said with an eye roll. "It's just a story explaining that our people were abandoned, and they found this land. And they made it here through the dead of winter with nothing but a book and their last arrow. So, every fall, a week before the harvest, all of the boys go out into the mountains as—like Ahlvie said—a rite of passage. If they can survive, then they become men." She rolled her eyes again.

"And you wanted to do it to prove what?" Cyrene asked.

"That I can do anything! I can go into those mountains, blindfolded, without a stupid book or arrow and come out stronger and better than any of those lone wolves."

"Take it from me," Dean said, "no matter what you do and how much you try to be better to prove your worth to your family, it will never be enough. Accept who you are in your heart, and you'll learn that is what matters."

"Yes," Avoca said with a rare smile for Dean, "that is true. You can only truly prove your worth to yourself."

"Yeah, well, in the meantime, it sucks," Cal muttered. Then, she froze. "I…I think we're here."

"Fan out," Avoca said, taking the lead. She had been a sort of general in the Leif army before she gave her life over to Cyrene. She knew what she was doing.

Cyrene, however, did not. So, she just tried to stay out of the way. That essentially meant wandering around the woods and trying not to step on anything. Plans were her thing. Action was her thing. Wandering around in the woods, not so much.

"I was right here," Cal said with a sigh. "I think…maybe there's no trail."

Cyrene stepped over to her and glanced at the ground. It didn't seem any different than anywhere else. Then, she took two steps behind Cal and froze. "Do you feel that?"

Cal's green eyes widened, and she moved into the exact location Cyrene had been a second ago. "Yeah," she said with a shiver. "That's it."

Dean moved next to them and shook his head. "I don't feel anything."

Ahlvie tried, too. "Nope. Avoca?"

"It's faint but there. Do you have magic?" Avoca asked Cal.

"Oh my God, I knew it!" Cal cried, pounding her fist into her hand. "I knew I had Nana's gifts, but she said I wouldn't know until I was seventeen."

"Looks like you have some innate ability," Avoca confirmed. "Because, whatever we're dealing with, it reeks of magic."

"That's encouraging," Ahlvie grumbled.

"So, what do we do?" Dean asked. "Head back and try to figure out what kind of wraith has magic?"

Avoca shook her head. "No, the trail will be lost by then. We should follow it and see where it leads us. Form up, and stay sharp. We have the advantage here. We do not want to lose it."

Avoca took the lead with Cal on her heels. Cyrene and Dean followed behind her with Ahlvie taking up the rear. Whatever magic was emanating from this wraith, it was definitely cold and wrong. Cyrene could sense its otherworldliness. And, for a second, she felt as if she had known this feeling before, but she didn't know where or when.

So, they soldiered on. And on.

When they came to a small stream, Avoca feared that it was the end of the trail, but once she was across, it took her only about fifteen minutes to find where it had gotten out of the water.

Avoca waved them on. Cyrene was glad that she had taken a drink from the stream while they had had a small break because this was turning into an endeavor she had not anticipated. She'd thought they'd find the clearing and then reconvene later to discuss what to do. But she knew that this was the right move.

Cyrene's eyes veered to the horizon where she saw the sun sinking lower and lower. They had already been gone for hours. If they didn't turn back soon, then they would have to camp out here with next to no supplies and these wraiths in the woods.

Abruptly, Avoca came to a halt. "No," she breathed.

"What's going on?" Cal asked.

She skirted around her, but Avoca reached out and grabbed her shirt.

"Hey, let me go," Cal said.

"Do not take another step forward," Avoca warned.

Cyrene moved to stand beside Avoca. "What is it?"

"We're at the edge of the forest," Ahlvie told them. "You know where we are, Avoca."

Avoca's eyes twinkled in the light. "Truly?"

He nodded. "I wasn't sure we were going in that direction, but it makes sense that the wraiths would use it as their home base."

"Can someone fill us in?" Cyrene asked.

Avoca took a deep breath and nodded. Then, she pulled back a branch that had obscured the valley. Below them was a giant pile of rubble and the blackened and charred tree that still stood as tall as the eye could see.

"Whoa!" Cal said. "What is this place?"

"Aonia," Avoca said. "The home of my northern kin."

Thirty Eight

THE RUINS

"Your northern kin must not be doing that well," Cal said with a frown.

"They were slaughtered like animals," Avoca said.

"*This* is what happened to Ceis'f's people?" Cyrene asked.

Avoca nodded grimly. "Twenty years ago, Ceis'f was on a diplomatic mission for his people, and he came back to this. He wouldn't speak of it. Not even to me. He was the only survivor."

Cyrene hadn't thought about Ceis'f since he abandoned them in Eleysia. He had been so determined to take Avoca home to Eldora, marry her, and make her queen. He hadn't seen that she was falling for Ahlvie. Things had gone south quickly.

"No wonder he hates humans," Ahlvie said.

It was a rare day when Ahlvie could defend Ceis'f, but looking out across the ruins, Cyrene could see why. His people hadn't just been slaughtered; his home had been destroyed, burned, and desecrated. What had once surely been a beautiful home was now a wasteland.

"And, now…wraiths are living here?" Cyrene asked.

"It appears that way." Avoca turned her head away from the view. "The trail leads straight into Aonia."

"Well, at least we have the whereabouts now," Cyrene said. She touched Avoca's arm. "We can head back, mount a larger party, and then come back to clear this all out."

"I hate to be insensitive," Dean said, "but we just hiked leagues through those woods. What if these wraiths can sense your magic as easily as you can sense theirs? Then, the wraiths will move camp, and we will have lost the trail."

"If Avoca isn't ready to go in there, I will not force her," Cyrene said, glaring at Dean for the suggestion even though she knew it was valid.

"He has a point," Cal chimed in. "I mean, we've been tracking these things for months, but we never sent out an ancient one. We might never have this opportunity again."

"Ahlvie?" Cyrene pleaded.

"It's up to Avoca," Ahlvie said.

"I'm fine," Avoca said, shaking off Cyrene's concern. "Let's slaughter these beasts and be gone from here. It makes my skin crawl."

Then, she burst from the tree line and out toward the ruins of Aonia.

Cyrene had to agree. The closer they got to the lost Leif city, the more disturbed she became. Whatever had happened here was not any ordinary attack. Humans alone could not have done something this horrible… something this wrong.

Cal slung her bow over her shoulder and shivered. "This place gives me the creeps."

"The creeps?" Cyrene asked with a half-smile.

"Yeah." Then, Cal ran her hands up and down her arms and shook from head to toe. "The creeps."

"Yes. There is something not right about this place."

"Don't wander off," Avoca snapped at Dean as he began to open up crumbling doors to peer into caved-in rooms and empty buildings.

Their ragtag group formed up and followed Avoca deeper into the crumbling city.

Cal's eyes were wide with wonder. "How did I never know about this place?" she asked.

Ahlvie nudged her shoulder. "This place is forbidden."

"As it should be," Avoca snapped.

"But it's not that far away. I should have at least heard about it."

"Most kids aren't told about it until after they pass their lone wolf test," Ahlvie told her.

"I'm not a kid!"

"Not you, of course. Your mother would have my head if she knew I'd brought you out here."

"Have you been before?"

Ahlvie sharply glanced at Avoca and then nodded. "Once. A group of us came out here the night before I was to leave for my Presenting in Byern.

Trekked through the snow and got rip-roaring drunk."

Cal laughed, and it sounded so out of place.

"Not much of a story," Cyrene said. "Don't you get drunk everywhere?"

"Quiet!" Avoca snapped. "Have some respect for the dead."

After that, all conversation ceased. It wasn't easy to forget that they were on the site of hundreds of dead Leifs. The feeling emanated from the very stones they walked on and leeched into the dead grass and poisoned what little what remained.

Avoca stopped before what appeared to have once been an enormous building. Possibly a castle of some sort in its former glory. Inside was the blackened tree.

"The trail is gone," Avoca said. "Or it's everywhere. The wraiths have definitely been here. All over the city if I had to guess. They seem to have taken over the ruins themselves. I can feel it in the stones and the very air. I can't even take in air magic here. It feels…tainted."

"Well, we can't search every building here," Ahlvie said. "The city is sprawling. We'd have to split up."

"No," Avoca said at once.

"Which I don't think we should do," Ahlvie added.

Avoca shook her head. "Let's search the site of the sacred tree and then head back. If they're not here any longer, then we've lost them."

Avoca pushed open the door to a crumbling ballroom.

"Why is the tree sacred?" Cal asked as they entered.

"Because, thousands of years ago, it was brought over from my ancestors' world to symbolize the magic and life force of our people. When they discovered this land, they picked three sites to build new homes for their children and their children's children. One took a sapling to the Hidden Forest, where my kin still live in Eldora; another took one to Isola in Kell, where civil war destroyed their people long before I was born; and one was brought here to Aonia. As you can see, whoever destroyed this city, they did a thorough job."

"A little too thorough," Cal muttered under her breath.

They meandered across the ballroom, up a half-dozen stairs, and into a round chamber with many doors. At the center was the sacred tree. No matter that it had been burned and blackened, even in death, it was still magnificent.

"Someone has definitely been here," Dean observed.

Ahlvie frowned. "Yes. There isn't a hint of rubble here."

Cal dropped her hand to the ground and drew a finger across a marble stone. "Has someone swept? Have the wraiths been taking care of the sacred tree?"

Avoca moved her eyes around the room. "It doesn't make any sense. What kind of creatures would try to steal people from your village but take care of the sacred tree?"

"You know," Ahlvie said, "now that I think about it, the last time I was here, this room was walled off. We tried to get to the tree, and there was no way inside. Not even by climbing to the roof. We tried."

Avoca shot him a dirty look.

He held his hands up, as if to say, *What? I was a stupid kid!*

"Well, whoever has been here even cleaned this mirror," Dean called from the other side of the room. "It almost looks like a window."

"No!" Avoca cried, startling everyone. "Don't look in it."

Dean jumped back, as if she had hit him. "Why not?"

"Creator! You almost looked into the Mirror of Truth."

"The what of what?" Cal asked as she rushed to the other side of the room.

"Surely, someone would have shattered a mirror in here," Ahlvie said. "Like the people who did this?"

"It's unbreakable. I would have thought it had been moved, but perhaps it wasn't possible." Avoca trailed her hand down the intricate carvings on the side of the floor-length mirror. "See here? It looks like someone tried to pry it off the wall. Whatever spell keeps it here might keep it here until the end of time."

"What does it do?" Cyrene asked.

Avoca shook her head. "It shows you the truth. Not the truth you want to see, but the truth you need to see. Past, present, and future. In Emporia, it's told that anyone who looks into the Mirror to see the future is never the same. I was told that a Leif foresaw the breaking of magic back before the Battle of the Light and promptly went mad."

"It's just a mirror," Cal said. "How could it make you go mad?"

Avoca put her arm on Cal's shoulder and turned her away from the mirror. "Let's never find out, okay?"

"I have a few truths I'd like to know," Ahlvie muttered.

"Not this way."

"If Avoca says it can harm you, Ahlvie, then we'd better not," Cyrene said. "Come on. This isn't why we're here anyway."

Cyrene was halfway around the dead tree before realizing that not everyone was with them. Her head swung back toward the mirror, and she gasped. "Dean, no!"

But it was too late.

Dean had fully faced the Mirror of Truth and was gazing headlong into its depths.

"Avoca!" Cyrene called before sprinting after Dean.

Cyrene grabbed his arm and tried to bodily pull him away from in front of the mirror. But he was locked on, as if whatever powerful magic was in that mirror held him on a leash.

"Please, please!" she cried. "What truth do you need so desperately?"

Dean's eyes were as big as saucers, and his pupils blasted out. "No," he gasped. "No, please! No!"

Tears streamed down his face, and Cyrene was helpless, standing there, watching him uncover whatever he'd had to know. Avoca reached for her, but she pushed her away.

"This is his burden to bear, Cyrene," Avoca said.

"You said he could go mad!" Cyrene cried.

"He can. He knew the risk and did it anyway. It is usually that way for those who are desperate to know."

"And he is," Ahlvie whispered.

"What? Why?"

"They're dead," Dean moaned. "All dead. All of them."

"Who?" Cyrene asked.

"We didn't know how to tell you," Avoca said gently. "While you were unconscious, Byern led an attack against Eleysia. All reports suggest that the capital city was burned to the ground."

Cyrene's hand flew to her mouth. "No! How could they do that? Eleysia has the best navy in the world."

Ahlvie shook his head. "No one knows. Not much reaches Fen, but if it's big enough, it does. This…was."

"What does that matter?" Cal asked in confusion.

"He's from there," Avoca told her.

Cyrene shook her head and turned back to Dean. No matter their differences or what had transpired between them, she had never wanted him to suffer something like this.

It had been bad enough when Cyrene endured Maelia's death. Then, Daufina. Then, her parents. Her heart had broken and hardened with each new blow.

But to lose everyone you know and love. Your home. Your whole world. She couldn't imagine what that must be like.

"I'll do it," Dean said. "I will."

Then, he collapsed in a heap on the floor.

Cyrene threw herself on top of him. "Dean! Dean, wake up." She slapped him across the face. "You do not get to go stark raving mad. You do not get to leave this world. I am still too mad at you to allow you to do that! Get up! Get up now!"

"Cyrene," Avoca said, pulling her back.

"No! No, I have lost too much. He cannot be gone, too. He's a fool, but he stayed. He knew his family was dead, and he could have gone to his home to pick up the pieces. But he stayed, Avoca," Cyrene said, tears now falling from her own eyes. "He stayed for me. So, you'd better help me bring him back! Or so help me Creator!"

Avoca frowned. "There isn't a cure, Cyrene."

"There wasn't a cure for me either!"

"Um…guys," Cal said, turning back to face the front of the room and drawing her bow and arrow.

Everyone's eyes shot to the same place. Ahlvie pulled his sword from its sheath. Avoca suddenly had her ice-white blade in her hand. Cyrene reached for her magic, ready to face the wraith.

Only, when the creature stepped forward into the light, Cyrene gasped. Avoca's blade clattered to the ground. Ahlvie took a step forward to block Avoca.

It was only Cal who was ready. She let her arrow fly. It soared through the air, true to its mark. But, at the last second, with a flick of his wrist, the arrow flew harmlessly wide.

"What the…" Cal asked.

And then he stepped fully into view.

"Hello, Ava," Ceis'f said.

Thirty Nine

THE TRUTH

"Well, this is a surprise," Ahlvie muttered.

"You come to my city and are surprised to find me in it?" Ceis'f asked. His eyes roamed over the faces of their party before landing hungrily on Avoca's face.

"We had no idea where you went," Cyrene said when Avoca remained silent.

"Perhaps I didn't want to be found."

Everyone shifted on their feet, except Cal, whose eyes were darting between Ceis'f and Cyrene. "What's going on?"

Avoca breathed softly. "Just an old friend we weren't expecting to see."

Cyrene sighed. "Look, we're not here for any trouble."

Her eyes darted to Dean, who was still lying unconscious on the floor. She had not anticipated a reunion with Ceis'f in this plan. She'd thought it would be easy. A get-in, get-out kind of job. But, of course, nothing was ever easy in her life.

"Humans never are," Ceis'f spat. "Somehow, they always seem to cause it."

"Did you clear out the temple?" Avoca asked.

Ceis'f nodded. "Seemed like the right thing to do since I have nowhere else to go."

Avoca's hands flexed and tightened at her sides. "You know you are always welcome in Eldora."

"Don't," Ceis'f ground out. "That is not home, and with you gone, it is nothing at all."

"I understand," Avoca said.

Ceis'f grumbled something under his breath. "What are you all doing here anyway?"

"We've been staying at a local village, and it has been attacked the last couple of months by wraiths," Avoca said. "Cal here is from the village, and she was helping us track them. It led us here. You wouldn't happen to know anything about that, would you?"

"Wraiths?" he asked with a disgruntled snort. "Try a Nokkin, Ava."

Avoca stumbled forward. Ahlvie reached for her to steady her.

Cyrene sighed. "What is a Nokkin?"

"That's what I want to know," Cal said.

"A creature of legend," Ceis'f told them.

"They were once Doma, one of the first families in ancient times. They were extremely powerful and obsessed with dark magic. They were so determined to gain power that the power they gathered took over their bodies. It stripped their souls and made them something else. Something more sinister. They're humanlike, but they can become a shadow at will. They feed off magic and suck the life from people until there's nothing left of them, or so the stories go."

Cyrene swayed on her feet. Suck magic from bodies. Turn into shadow. Reek of dark magic.

Creator! She had faced one before. Perhaps the same Nokkin that had been terrorizing Fen. Perhaps it had come here because of her. She hadn't remembered that encounter in the mountains until now. She had thought that she had killed that thing by blasting it with her magic, but maybe she was wrong.

"But they're all dead," Avoca said. "Mother said they were all killed in the war."

Ceis'f shrugged as he circled around the tree. "Guess she was wrong."

"How do you kill them?" Ahlvie asked practically.

"If I knew, don't you think I would have done it by now?" Ceis'f spat. "I've been trying to get rid of the damn thing since I got here. So, good luck with that."

"We'll need to consult with Matilde and Vera," Avoca said, picking up her blade and concealing it once more. "They might be the only people still alive who have faced a Nokkin, and they will have some insight into how to defeat it."

"Can we speak alone for a moment?" Ceis'f asked, reaching out for Avoca's elbow.

Ahlvie crossed his arms and glared back at Ceis'f. Cyrene hoped the trio didn't ignite and burn the whole place down a second time.

"I'll handle this," Avoca told Ahlvie before disappearing with Ceis'f.

"Well, he's a real treat," Cal muttered when he was gone.

"You can say that again," Ahlvie grumbled. "I'm going to go spy on them."

"Can I come, too?" Cal asked excitedly.

Cyrene was about to tell them both off when she heard a loud groan behind her. "Dean?"

She fell to his side and tried to help him sit up as he seemed to come to. Cal abandoned Ahlvie's pursuit of Avoca to help Cyrene lift him.

"Is he going to be okay?" she asked.

Cyrene bit her lip. "I don't know. I don't know enough about that mirror to be sure."

Dean groaned again and then leaned forward, pushing his hands into his head. "Ugh!"

"Dean, are you okay? Can you hear what I am saying? Can you see me? Do you remember who I am?"

She pushed her face right before his, and he cracked open an eye.

"Cyrene?" he muttered. "You look beautiful."

"I look like I trekked hours through the forest and need a good meal and hot bath."

"Just like the day I met you," he said, winding a lock of her hair around his finger.

She abruptly pulled back. She hadn't meant to make that so personal. She had been worried that she would lose someone else. Not that she entirely forgave Dean for what had happened, but she could tell he had been trying to prove himself to her.

"Well, at least you remember that much," she said. "Do you remember anything you saw in the Mirror?"

He frowned, and his pupils dilated. "Pieces. Bits and pieces. Things that I didn't want to see. And…a path. A way to earn it."

"Earn what?"

He shook his head and glanced off. "What did I say?"

Cyrene sighed. He was too out of it to remember anything yet. Avoca was right. They needed to get back to Fen and figure all of this out with Matilde and Vera. Maybe Avoca could even convince Ceis'f to come with them. If he was from here, he had to know something about the Mirror of Truth. She'd be happy to have as much information as she could at this point.

Cyrene and Cal eventually hoisted Dean up between the two of them. Not an easy feat, considering he was a huge military captain and they were two relatively small women. Cyrene would have liked to use her magic to help him walk, but she hadn't used any since she detoxed from her blood magic. She wasn't about to start unless they ran into trouble.

By the time that they got Dean out of the room with the sacred tree and down the steps into the ballroom, Avoca and Ahlvie were storming back up toward them.

"What happened?" Cyrene asked.

"Ceis'f is being himself," Avoca spat.

"Bastard," Ahlvie growled as he went to take Cal's place holding up Dean.

"No, I've got him. Cyrene is smaller. No offense," Cal said with a grimace.

"None taken. I am."

Ahlvie ducked his head under Dean's arm, and Cyrene took a breath of relief. She didn't mind that she was smaller, weaker, or more vulnerable than the others. She was always feminine and dainty but fierce and wild in personality. Her magic matched her personality at least.

"So, he won't help us?" Cyrene asked.

"He won't leave," Avoca said. "And he won't talk further about the Nokkin. He wants us all out of his city by nightfall."

"Great," Cyrene said. "We should probably go back then."

Avoca crisply nodded once. Her eyes said she was ready to go find Ceis'f and beat him to a bloody pulp. But she held herself back and tugged on her bond with Cyrene.

Cyrene responded with a soft touch, as if to say, *I understand.*

"Did he at least give any more useful information?" Cyrene asked as they exited the building.

Dean had his legs under him, but he was stumbling and still slightly incoherent. She didn't know how they were going to make it all the way through the forest with him like this.

"If you consider taunting and thinly veiled threats useful," Ahlvie said.

"He did say that the Nokkin has no interest in him," Avoca said. "Though why, I have no idea. He has as much magic as the rest of us."

"Did he say why he's actually here?" Cyrene asked. "You know it's not because he isn't welcome in Eldora."

Avoca tensed. "He said he came to look in the Mirror."

"What?" Cyrene asked. "He seemed fine!"

"He said that Dean is lucky that it drove him insane," Avoca muttered, glancing back at Dean. "Because, when Ceis'f looked to his future in the Mirror, he saw nothing."

Cyrene clamped her mouth shut at that. She could feel the pain through the bond. Avoca wasn't usually the one of them who blasted her emotions so wildly. But, if Ceis'f looked into the Mirror of Truth and saw nothing, it likely meant…he had no future to behold.

"Why does this feel *so* much farther than the way there?" Cal asked.

"Because we're hauling dead weight," Ahlvie groaned. "Creator, I have to stop. I need a break."

The sun had already gone down long ago, and it was nearly pitch-black in the trees. Thankfully, Avoca had created some torches for them to see in the darkness, but the whole situation was blinding. They would never have made it back had Ahlvie and Cal not known the area so well.

"We'll stop right up ahead. I can feel the stream," Avoca told them.

And she was right. Only a dozen feet ahead of them, the stream they had crossed earlier that day was finally visible. Ahlvie and Cal dropped Dean onto the ground where he moaned and leaned forward.

"I am sorry about this," Dean said. "You don't have to keep helping me. I can walk."

"Thank the Creator!" Ahlvie said.

"Are you sure?" Cyrene asked.

Dean nodded. "I feel disoriented, like I have vertigo."

"It'll pass," Cyrene assured him. Though she had no clue if that was true.

"It'd better have been worth it," Ahlvie said, nudging Dean. "Carrying you around is not my idea of a good time."

"You should have known better," Avoca chided.

"I did," Dean said. "But I had to know."

"And?" Ahlvie pushed.

"The capital city of Eleysia is gone," Dean told them. "I saw...I saw Byern battleships traveling through our reefs and rocks as effortlessly as our own naval captains. It should have been impossible, but they did it. Then, I saw fire and explosions. The entire island was burned to the ground, and it's all my fault."

Everyone shifted uncomfortably in the wan light. The only person who knew exactly what Dean was feeling right now had refused to come back to Fen with them. It was impossible to feel the depth of Dean's grief in his words.

"I believe I can share some of that blame," Cyrene said in horror.

"I spared Edric's life, and he did this," Dean said with a shake of his head. "He used Kael's magic as a weapon and bombed my entire home."

"He was working with Kael?" Cyrene gasped.

Dean looked up at her with hollow eyes. "Yes."

"Creator..."

"We've rested long enough," Avoca said softly. "Perhaps we should keep moving."

Dean had just risen to his feet when Cyrene felt it.

"Nokkin," she gasped.

Instantly, everyone was on high alert.

"Cyrene, to me!" Avoca cried. "Link up, and trust me. Trust yourself."

Cyrene gulped and then nodded, feeling the brush of Avoca's magic for the first time in months. It was cool and refreshing. Nothing like the fire and darkness that she had felt when linking with Kael.

Dean and Ahlvie removed their swords while Cyrene hastily pushed Cal and her strung bow and arrow into the middle of their circle. She was not going to risk the life of a fourteen-year-old girl for this monster. She had become much too fond of her already.

The Nokkin blended into the darkness, like shadow and smoke, swooping into their group and trying to reach out for them. The feeling of wrongness…of a contamination reverberated through the group. It was so intense that Cyrene could practically feel its forked tongue slithering up her cheek once more. But she couldn't allow that to happen.

When the thing reached for her, Ahlvie sliced forward with his blade. It seemed to go straight through the wraith before the thing coalesced into substance once more a few feet away.

"We don't have to play cat and mouse like this," it said with its abused and inhuman voice.

"Leave us alone, and never bother this village again, or we will destroy you," Cyrene said with more confidence than she felt.

But she was crackling with magic and holding on to Avoca like a tether. She had her friends with her and a girl with more inner strength than Cyrene had seen in a long time.

A strange laughed seemed to emanate from the Nokkin. "You cannot hope to defeat me. I will have you. I will."

Then, it disappeared. Cyrene took a breath and waited. Cal shrieked behind her and let loose an arrow.

Cyrene flipped around and saw the Nokkin reaching out for Cal. The arrow hit it in its shoulder, and it screeched and moaned, as if it had not felt any pain in a long time.

Avoca shot a blast of fire toward the creature's face. It choked on the smoke as it dissipated all around the thing. For a second, its eyes had been illuminated in the darkness. All white, all seeing yet unseeing. Disturbing and terrifying.

The Nokkin disappeared again, and this time, Dean and Ahlvie tried to slice through its flesh. But found none there. The Nokkin put its hand on Ahlvie's chest.

"No!" Cyrene and Avoca screamed at the same time.

But the Nokkin hesitated. And then laughed. "You are of my world, I see."

Ahlvie took that opportunity to slice his sword through the Nokkin's neck. It was about as effective as trying to cut through water.

The Nokkin appeared again, reaching for Cyrene. "Let me have my prize, and you can keep your friends."

"Never," Avoca said. "Now!"

Cyrene and Avoca launched an attack at the same time, blasting the Nokkin with a burst of energy that they'd been slowly gathering together. They used the energy to slice through the hurt shoulder Cal had pierced. It shrieked again. And, just when Cyrene thought it was going to blink out and reappear again, something tore out of the trees with a battle cry and sent a fire bolt directly into the Nokkin's chest.

Ceis'f landed in a whirl of long silver-white hair in the exact spot where the Nokkin had just been. It had vanished into thin air, and in its place was the battle-hardened Leif warrior.

"Oh my Creator, did we kill it?" Cal gasped.

Avoca shook her head. "No, I don't think so. We ran it off."

"Can you not even walk home without getting ambushed and needing me to save you?" Ceis'f demanded.

"We were doing fine," Avoca said.

Cyrene was doubled over. Her breath was coming out wild and irregular. She couldn't believe how much energy they'd had to use together. But, with Avoca linked, she hadn't even had to think about it. It had just come. Still, it had been intense.

Ahlvie was crouching on the ground.

Cyrene reached for him. "It touched you?"

"Yeah," he said with a shake of his head. "But…I'm fine."

"Well, I'm not fine!" Cal cried. "I'm awesome! Did you see me hit its shoulder?"

Cyrene burst into laughter. "Our savior."

"No need for the thanks," Ceis'f muttered.

"Thank you," Avoca said softly. "I knew you wouldn't abandon us."

Ceis'f muttered something nasty under his breath before marching into the woods and yelling, "Hurry up!"

Forty

THE CONFESSION

They stumbled back into Fen, exhausted, hungry, and full of questions. But they were greeted with unparalleled fury and despair.

"Caldreva Anamarya!" a woman cried, rushing through their group to grasp her daughter in her arms. She hugged her tight. "You're alive. Oh Creator, you're alive!"

"Mom!" Cal grumbled. "Of course I'm alive."

"You told me you would be gone for fifteen minutes!" she shrieked. "You have been gone for hours! Hours! Do you know what I thought? What your nana thought? What the whole village thought?"

"Yeah," she said, shuffling her feet.

"That you were dead! That a wraith had attacked and killed you. All of you," she said, looking up at their group. "You should be ashamed, taking a fourteen-year-old girl into the woods without letting anyone know where she was or how long you would be gone. At times like this!"

"Mom, I'm fine!" Cal said. She pushed her off of her. "I was gone for half a day! The wolves go out for a whole week! I was with the bravest, smartest, most Creator-blessed group of people I'd ever seen. You should have had faith in me."

"I will hear none of this. Go home right this instant. You're grounded."

Cal opened her mouth to argue, but her mother gave her *the look*, and she dragged her feet back to the house. Her mother followed at her heels.

"I hope our reception is a bit less…exciting," Ahlvie said.

Cyrene watched Cal the entire time, feeling bad that she'd gotten her in trouble. She didn't regret it though. Even though they had been attacked by a wraith. Creator forbid she ever told her mother that!

When Cyrene finally ducked back into Avniella's home, she found their reception not much better than Cal's. Avniella and Lace berated them for leaving without warning and for taking Cal with them.

Ahlvie finally kissed them each on the cheeks and said, "We picked up a stray." He nodded his head at Ceis'f.

"Oh, dear. We'll get you an extra bed for the night," Lace said.

Ceis'f stood tall and proud in the corner, completely uncomfortable with being in human dwellings. Matilde and Vera curiously eyed him when they came out of the bedroom but just grinned.

"Welcome back, Ceis'f," Vera said.

He grunted.

Then, Reeve and Aubron burst into the room.

Reeve grabbed Cyrene around the middle and held her to him. "I thought something had happened to you. I can't lose you, too."

Cyrene patted his shoulder and sighed. "I know. I love you."

Dean collapsed into the corner and promptly passed out, drawing everyone's attention once more.

Vera put her hand on his forehead for a few minutes and then frowned. "I feel as if you all have a lot of explaining to do."

"Start talking," Matilde said, taking a seat of her own.

And so, they did. They told them of tracking the wraith to Aonia and finding Ceis'f, only to discover that the wraith was a Nokkin.

"Impossible," Matilde said.

Vera shrugged. "I believed they were dead."

"Do you know how to kill them?" Avoca asked.

Matilde frowned. "There were very few Nokkin. It was never clear exactly who they worked for, so information on them was scarce. Let us look into it."

"In the meantime," Vera said, "it might be possible to put a barrier around the town to prevent these attacks. I believe Fen is small enough to endure one, if your ancient ones will assist us."

"Let me convene with Mana," Lace said before rising and leaving the room.

"While we were there," Cyrene said, "Dean looked into what Avoca called the Mirror of Truth."

Matilde hissed between her teeth. "What truth was he looking for?"

"What actually happened to his home and his family."

"That is likely only a part of what he saw."

"Is there anything we can do for him?" Cyrene begged.

"Time," Vera said. "When I tried to heal him, there was nothing amiss. Whatever he is enduring, he will have to find his own way back."

Cyrene frowned. She had been afraid of that.

"This is all well and good," Orden said, finally speaking up, "but I believe we have more pressing matters to consider than the threat against this town."

"Yes," Vera said.

"Indeed," Matilde agreed.

"We almost lost Cyrene, but now that we have her back, we need to figure out where to go next. The Nokkin clearly wants Cyrene for her magic," Orden said. "It's the thing no one wants to talk about, but she used blood magic and survived. She needs to train. She needs to figure out what she is capable of."

Cyrene colored slightly but met Orden's hardened eyes head-on. Somehow, coming from Orden, the statement felt right. Anyone else might have said it as a joke or tried to lessen the blow, but the truth was, Cyrene was something different, and she couldn't hide from it.

"You're right," she said, pushing off the wall and walking into the center of their circle. "For the last couple of months, I have been anything but myself. Maelia's death…wrecked me. No, destroyed me. It turned me inside out and made me not want to care about anything. Add Daufina and my parent's deaths to that toll and I've been a shell. I have done some things that I am not proud of, but the only blood magic I ever took was after a Braj slaughtered my parents in front of my brother and sister. I used the power to save the life of the king. It might have been wrong, but I saw no alternative. So, if you want to judge me, then go ahead."

The room was silent at her declaration. No one even averted their gaze from her.

"I might not be the person that everyone wanted to fulfill the damn prophecy, but I'm all you have. I want to bring back magic. I want the entire world to be like Fen! No one here shuns anyone for having powers. Everyone is accepted—maybe not exactly for who they want to be, but they are not murdered because they have magic. It is like the world that used to be before Viktor Dremylon. And…I believe I know the next steps to bring it back."

"Oh?" Vera asked.

Cyrene smiled. "As you know, I have had visions of the Domina Serafina for almost a year. She has shown me glimpses of her past, but when I was unconscious and high on blood magic, she was able to break the barrier between her world and ours. She said that, when I master my spirit magic, I should be able to speak to her myself. That I wouldn't need to black out to reach her."

Matilde leaned forward, and Vera placed her hand on her mouth.

"This way, I was able to personally speak with her rather than just getting stuck in her visions. She told me that I needed to use the coin and not be blinded because there were bigger forces at play. She mentioned a woman but could not speak her name."

"The coin," Avoca whispered.

"Yes, yes," Matilde said. "What else?"

"A woman?" Vera asked softly.

"Yes, sometimes, I would get ripped from my dream with Serafina and find myself trapped in a world of darkness where this woman, I have to assume they are one and the same, told me to come to her. I don't know what it means, but she handed me a coin." Cyrene held her hand out. "It felt so real. So, even though she may be dangerous, it's too much of a coincidence. The first step is that we need to find that coin."

Vera stood and retrieved something from her pocket. "Did it look like this?"

Cyrene gasped. "Where…where did you get that?"

"You were clenching it in your hand," Avoca said.

"But where had it come from?"

Avoca shook her head. "I'd been holding your hand, and you had nothing. Then, when I left to get a drink of water, I came back, and you were holding it."

"It truly came from my dream?" Cyrene's mind reeled. "What is it? How does it work?"

Vera flipped it between her fingers. "It's a talisman. It is used to harness intense energy. Depending on the talisman, it can be used to store power or amplify power or recall memories or any number of other things. They have many functions."

"What does *this* one do?"

Matilde shook her head. "We don't know. To our knowledge, a coin has never been used for a talisman."

"Yet we have two," Vera said, retrieving a second coin.

Cyrene put her hand out, and Vera dropped it into her palm. It was exactly the same as the one she had held in her dream. About half the size of her palm, gold with smooth edges, and a female profile carved into the center with three words traced around the outside in a language Cyrene had never seen. It looked like Doma but…not.

"A second talisman?" Cyrene asked, tracing her finger over the text. She felt as if she should know what it said, but it eluded her. "Where did you get this one?"

"Maelia had it in her rooms," Avoca explained.

"So, let me get this straight," Ahlvie said. "We have two talismans. One from Maelia. One from Cyrene's *dream*. And we don't know how either of them works. But a dead Doma told you to use it? Sounds about right."

"Sounds ludicrous," Ceis'f said. "Your plans are always so shoddy."

"It fits together," Avoca said, chiming in.

"There's more," Orden said. "What did you leave out?"

"How did you—" Cyrene began.

"I have spent a long time learning and observing people, girl. You always have crazy ideas, but they work. Tell us the rest."

Cyrene sighed. "Serafina said she knew the reason that I had magic."

Reeve stood up at that. "That is something I would like to know the answer to. Why you and not me? Not Aralyn or Elea?"

"It doesn't always go straight down bloodlines," Matilde told him. "It has nothing to do with you or your sisters. It has something to do with the right combination of power at the right time."

"What did she say, Cyrene?" Avoca asked gently.

"She said that she had a child."

"Sera had a child?" Vera gasped.

"So…I must be her ancestor."

Everyone stilled at that. To be descended from the Domina Serafina. That was beyond anything she had ever imagined.

"No wonder she has such a strong connection to you," Vera said. "It explains much."

"Though I don't know how she got it past us," Matilde muttered in frustration.

"Oh, and one more thing," Cyrene said, just remembering. "She didn't just say to use the coin. She said to use the coin to find the lost ones. Not that

I know who the lost ones are."

"She said, *the lost ones?*" Vera asked breathily.

"Yes. Do you know what she means?"

Matilde's and Vera's eyes met, and tears gleamed in them.

"Dragons," they said as one.

Forty One

THE SPELL

It took a full minute for everyone to process that word.

Cyrene blinked, and then she blinked again. "Dragons? Like… dragons?"

Matilde and Vera nodded and said together, "Yes."

"There are actual dragons?" Ahlvie asked. "Not just stories?"

"When are you all going to start realizing that all your stories come from somewhere? Everything you've read about exists. Dragons exist," Matilde said.

"We knew that you spoke of your time as dragon riders before the fall," Avoca said, "but we didn't think there were any more dragons left in Emporia."

"There aren't," Matilde said.

"But dragons must still exist," Vera said. "We are bound to dragons, and our lifelines are tied to theirs."

"So, if one of your dragons was killed somewhere else, you could just drop dead for no reason?" Ahlvie asked.

Matilde gave him a deadly look. "You have such a way with words."

Reeve coughed in the corner. "I know that I am new to this group and magic and the lot. It's all a bit much to take in at once. I was with you with magic; I saw that with my own two eyes. I was with you through blood curses and these whole coins that could amplify magic and also mirrors that told you the truth and all of this…but dragons?"

Aubron patted his arm. "You sort of learn to just accept it."

"We don't have time to discuss all of this now," Vera said. "We must meet with the ancient ones to try to get the protection spell up. Tonight, if at all possible."

"Yes," Matilde added. "The Nokkin is still a threat, and I would like to get that in place before we leave."

They both stood and brushed off their dresses, as if that were the end of the discussion.

"Wait…leave?" Cyrene asked.

"They know where to look for the dragons," Avoca guessed.

"We have an idea," Vera said, her eyes twinkling.

Matilde and Vera nodded for Cyrene and Avoca to follow them as they left the rest of the room chattering about the possibility of dragons. Cyrene herself found it impossible.

If dragons still exist in Emporia, then how am I to find them? Wouldn't there have been signs all along? Someone noticing them in the sky? Livestock going missing?

It seemed absurd for Serafina to send her on a wild goose chase. How could she have known through the veil that dragons still existed? But Serafina hadn't been wrong about Matilde and Vera when she sent Cyrene to look for them. Cyrene sure hoped that Sera wasn't wrong about this either.

Ceis'f appeared behind them and reached for Avoca. "I'm not staying in a human village tonight. Come out into the woods with me. When was the last time you had your hands in the earth?"

Avoca pulled her arm back. "I am staying to help the village. I know you might not care what happens to them, but they have been good to us."

"When are you going to get it through your head that humans do not care about you? They want to use you."

"When are you going to get it through your head that not everyone is like that?"

"This village was here when Aonia was sacked, and they did nothing," Ceis'f growled.

"They can hardly defend themselves against one Nokkin. You know that they couldn't have done anything for your people who were trained warriors."

"Are you coming back with me or not?" he asked.

"No. You know my duty is to Cyrene."

"That's funny. I thought it was to that human bastard."

Avoca's eyes narrowed. "Watch what you say about Ahlvie. I am still a better soldier than you."

Cyrene shuffled her feet and felt as if she were intruding. Matilde and Vera hadn't slowed their steps, but she wasn't ready to leave Avoca alone with Ceis'f.

"We should go," Cyrene said. "He's not going to help us."

Avoca lifted her chin and nodded. "You're right. He's not. Absolutely nothing has changed."

Ceis'f's face was a mask of hard planes and deep shadows. His gold eyes flashed in annoyance. "Much has changed. But my distaste for humans hasn't changed one bit. I'll be in the meadow. Find me when you find sense."

Then, he traipsed off, loping through the village and out to the trees, as if he had been born for it. Likely, he had been.

"I'm sorry," Cyrene said, touching Avoca's elbow.

"Don't be. He's…infuriating. How did I ever think that I could marry him?"

"You were meant for each other in Eldora. Maybe you would have made it work there."

Avoca fell into step next to Cyrene as they followed after Matilde and Vera. "We would have always been at each other's throats. It would have been a disaster."

"That's also likely," Cyrene said with a small chuckle.

"And you?" Avoca asked. "What of your men?"

Cyrene flinched at the thought. She had been trying to forget all three of the men who had been chasing her over the last year. Power apparently attracted power.

"I don't know."

"Dean is still in love with you."

"I know," Cyrene said.

"You still care for him."

"How could I not? We were going to get married. I can't help how I feel, but I did horrible things back in Byern, and not all of them were because of Maelia's death. Many of them were because of Dean. I don't know where that puts us. I'm not ready to forgive him, but I know he is trying."

"He might be a fool," Avoca said. "But he's a fool in love. I was hesitant to work with him. I wanted to cut out his throat when I first heard what he had done to you. But we have worked together now for several months, and he is constant and loyal. I don't presume to know your love life, but I would at least talk to him. He deserves that."

"I suppose so," she said.

"And what about Edric and Kael?" Avoca asked. "Those Dremylon boys?"

Cyrene shook her head. "Dead to me."

Avoca's laugh had bite to it. "Hardly."

"When I was there, I realized that I was bound to both of them. A Doma and a Dremylon, just like Serafina and Viktor."

"You suspect that it is the same binding?" Avoca asked intuitively.

"I don't know. I don't even know if that's possible, but when I saved Edric's life, the bond disappeared," Cyrene explained.

"A debt repaid in some way. That is the only way that makes sense to me."

"I don't know," Cyrene said still confused by the whole thing. "It's possible. How else could a bond be nullified."

"Death."

"Well, he died."

"But you brought him back. I suspect it's not that easy and that there is still much that we don't know what happened with Viktor and Serafina."

Cyrene nodded. That was the truth at least. "That means that I'm only bound to Kael now."

"Yes. I can sense him all over you," Avoca said. "I wasn't sure what it was at first, but you must have linked your magic."

"Yes," she whispered, ashamed. "He told me he killed his lover, Jardana, to get powerful blood magic."

"And you think that your blood magic links you?"

Cyrene nodded. "He wanted me to rule the world at his side."

"Ah, then perhaps he does not know you."

"What do you mean?"

Avoca bared her teeth. "You will never need anyone at your side to rule. When you conquer, even the mountains will tremble."

Cyrene grinned at that assessment. Perhaps Avoca was right. Maybe she didn't need a man at her side to rule. But she knew by the matching smile on Avoca's face that she would always have friends.

They finally reached the cabin where Matilde and Vera had ventured into. It was next door to Cal's house and one of the largest in the village. Cyrene could hear voices inside and what appeared to be some grumbling of dissent.

"How powerful is the magic of their ancient ones?" Cyrene asked Avoca. "I only saw a light display by Mana for the lone wolves ceremony."

"Powerful enough. They did help heal you. But it's varying degrees. None of them have been properly trained, but they have a great deal of experience."

"How has Fen survived this long with magic like this if it's in Byern?" Cyrene mused.

"Because we're not a part of Byern," Mana said, appearing in the doorway. She wasn't as hunched or gnarled as she had been that day at the lone wolves ceremony. She stood straighter, and her eyes were lucid and full of fire. This woman clearly ruled the village, no matter what the men might say.

"But Ahlvie and Aubron are High Order."

"Technically, we exist within the borders of Byern. Though the magical barrier you speak of never reached us as our settlement was started after the last war. So, our boys have volunteered to go to the Byern Presenting ceremony. But, if the crown recognizes Fen as a true part of the kingdom, it is news to us."

"Oh."

"That's not why you're here though. You are here because you want our assistance," Mana said. "We have convened and agreed to try to use magic in the way that your ancient ones have instructed. Our magic has never worked in the ways that they have said, and many are wary of trying new things, but if it protects the village, then we will do it."

"We appreciate your help," Avoca said. Then, she touched her fingers to her lips in the sign of deference for her people.

Matilde and Vera herded their group to the center of the village in the same area where the bonfire had been held for the lone wolves. Matilde, Vera, Cyrene, and Avoca added themselves to a shocking twelve other ancient ones, and all but two were women of varying ages. The two men were twins and seemed to have the most reservations about what Matilde and Vera had suggested. But there had apparently been a vote, and they'd lost.

Matilde took a deep breath and then slowly blew it out. "It has been a long time since I have seen so many of my brothers and sisters all in one place."

"A very long time," Vera whispered.

Matilde opened a book, and Cyrene gasped softly. It wasn't just any book. It was the Doma book that she had received on her birthday over a year ago. The book that had led her to her powers and beyond. She had thought that she lost it in Eleysia.

"We've kept it safe for you," Avoca whispered.

Matilde and Vera glanced at the page it was open to and then set it on the ground in front of them.

"We thank you for joining us," Matilde said. "What we are doing is simple. Vera and I can run the mechanics of the endeavor. We need everyone's linked powers to create something this intense."

"So, if you would, please hold hands, close your eyes, and reach for the connection between you and your neighbor," Vera instructed.

Cyrene took Avoca's hand and then Mana's. Cyrene had only ever linked with two people before—Avoca and Kael. It felt deeply personal. At the same time, it seemed that this was only needed in extreme situations and was usually quite rare.

She and Avoca linked up without thinking, and then Cyrene felt it. All around her, the other twelve members of the ancient ones had their eyes closed, their heads tipped up to the sky, and their bodies were blazing with light.

Cyrene gasped. Vera shot her a reassuring look.

No wonder the Doma motto had always been, *Believe in those whose honor doth shine.* Because these Doma actually *did* shine. And it was beautiful.

It felt completely and utterly synchronized, as if each of them were in tune with their magic and with each other's magic. Cyrene couldn't understand their reservations if they were this in sync. Unless they were more afraid of combining with foreigners rather than each other.

But she couldn't think of it any longer. All she could feel was the press of Mana's powers against hers.

Cyrene closed her eyes and let her in. Cyrene gasped.

No wonder Mana was the leader. The light show that she had done at the lone wolves ceremony was nothing. This right here was her true power and the power of their group.

Cyrene floated away into it. It was like seeing smells and hearing colors. As if the essence of who she was and who everyone else was mingled together into this complex new thing. Where mind and matter didn't meet, and fiction became reality. The impossible became possible.

Her powers didn't shake or rattle. She didn't have to try to find that center of fear or anger that had been her focal point for her abilities. Nothing about it was difficult in the slightest. It was as if she were adding to a well. One that didn't leave her hungry and starving when she ran out.

She might not know what the full consequences of her blood magic would be, but right now, they weren't an issue. Right now, she just had a geyser of energy that she could give as needed.

With a breath, she opened her eyes and cracked a smile. An iridescent dome floated over the top of the village, as if they were encased in their own bubble and it might pop at any minute.

Then, Matilde and Vera raised their hands to the heavens. As if following a tidal wave, the entire circle mimicked them. Cyrene tilted her head up to the sky and drank in everything that was happening.

And then something did pop. The magic snapping into place.

Everyone dropped their hands at once, and the magic winked out from each bright bulb of light. But the barrier held. Its brightness diminished when they released their magic, but a faint glow showed over the village. Cyrene was certain that it was only visible to people with magic.

"Thank you," Vera said with a smile. "That should hold, but I have instructed Mana on how to check for weaknesses in case the barrier is probed."

There were a few cheers of excitement, and then the ancient ones dispersed together to discuss what had happened. Mana was the one who stayed behind.

"That was some excellent magical work," Mana said. "I've never seen anything like it in all my years."

Matilde and Vera inclined their heads toward her.

"You give us faith once more that magic can truly return to Emporia," Vera said. "We would love to be able to train all of you in the ways of the Doma when this is all over."

Mana glanced up at the dome once more and then nodded. "I would like that."

Cyrene grinned as Mana disappeared into the night. *We won her over!* That meant, there was hope still for Cal. She hoped tonight had changed everyone's lives.

"You kept my book," Cyrene said with glee.

"It belongs to all Doma," Matilde said.

"But, yes," Vera confirmed as she picked it up and placed it in Cyrene's hand, "I think you are ready for this."

Cyrene cradled it in her hands, as if it were a newborn babe. "That barrier…is it similar to the one constructed to keep magic out of Byern?"

"Similar," Matilde confirmed. "That one was erected after the war and was much stronger, but it didn't prevent anyone from coming into Byern; it just announced their presence to those who might want to hunt them down like the Braj who killed all those people after your Presenting."

"How was it constructed?" Cyrene asked.

Vera shook her head. "We don't know. A barrier that vast would have been impossible to create, even linked, for all those but the most powerful magical users of all time."

Cyrene frowned. "Like Serafina."

"It wouldn't have made sense for her to keep magic out of Byern, but she was capable enough," Vera agreed.

"But she was already dead when it went up," Matilde said bitterly.

Forty Two

THE DEPARTURE

The lone wolves came back at dawn on the seventh day. Cyrene watched from beside Ceffy as a motley mix of bone-thin boys trickled into the village. She couldn't believe that these half-starved feral creatures were the boys who had laughed and danced a week before or that they were now men in their village.

The whole village had turned out at first light to await their return. Ahlvie had said there was always one boy every year who would not return. It was worse in years when a sudden snowfall had hit. The result of so many people being up at this hour meant that Cyrene's departure would also have a large farewell.

After getting the protective barrier up around the village, they had acquired the necessary supplies and decided to head out as soon as possible. Ahlvie was saying heartfelt good-byes to his mother, uncle, and grandmother. Aubron was hanging back, but she could see the fear on his face.

"Are you going to go without saying good-bye to your big brother?" Reeve asked. "Again?"

Cyrene laughed softly. She'd never had an opportunity to leave a place before without running like the wind. Good-byes felt so final. She wasn't ready for good-bye. "How about, until I see you again?"

"I like that better."

Reeve tugged her forward into a hug. "I'm staying here with Aubron for now. Avniella said I was more than welcome to stay."

"Good," Cyrene said, fighting back tears.

"I'm going to try to get information about Elea. Ahlvie said that he could get me in touch with his network contact. Aubron and I might be doing some work for them to keep Fen better prepared for what's to come."

Cyrene stepped back and admired her brother. "You're pretty amazing. You know that, right?"

"Of course!" he said with an arrogant grin. "I'm a Strohm. Just like you."

"That's right. Of course."

"Try to stay out of trouble."

"I'll do my best."

Reeve kissed her forehead and quickly released her. She could see the tears in his eyes as he darted over to where Aubron was standing and pulled him into a kiss.

Cyrene breathed in the cold front that had rolled in the night before. She tugged her cloak tighter around her and pulled on the gloves that Mana had given her. She was going to need them to cross through the mountains.

Another boy was coming down the mountain face. He had blood all over his chest and held a bloody arrow in his hand but no book. Cyrene shivered and didn't want to know what had happened in those woods.

"Cyrene?"

She jumped and turned around to see Dean standing behind her. "Yes?"

"Could we talk privately?"

"Yes. We probably should."

She handed off Ceffy's reins to Orden, who nodded at her. She thanked him and then followed Dean away from the large crowd of people. They tucked away into the patio of the local smithy where some of the warmth from the fire drifted out toward them.

Cyrene looked up into Dean's handsome face and saw a different man than the one she had fallen in love with back in Eleysia all those months before. She wondered how changed she must appear to him. Two dreamers hardened by adversity and death. It was enough to make anyone break.

"I understand why you hate me," Dean said as way of an introduction.

"I don't hate you."

He raised an eyebrow. "I would hate me if I were you."

Cyrene sighed and leaned back against the wooden cabin. "*Hate* is such a strong word. Am I upset that you believed I could have had some role in what happened to your parents? Yes. Am I furious that you drugged me, no matter the reason? Yes. Am I angry that you handed me over to Kael after the last time you saw him when he tried to kill you? Yes. Can I forgive those things? Maybe eventually."

"I'll take maybe," Dean said. He ran a hand back through his sandy hair. "I wish I had a miracle fix for why I did all those things. But the truth is, I don't. I was in shock about my parents. I didn't think that you could have been a part of it, but the way the evidence was portrayed, it was hard not to wonder. But I still loved you, and I wanted you out of the way so that Brigette wouldn't think about putting your head up next. It might have been ill-advised."

Cyrene raised her eyebrows.

"Okay, it was very stupid, how everything was handled."

"It was."

"Yeah. So, I wanted to clear the air with you. I made mistakes. I acted rashly to keep you alive. But I have always loved you." His eyes found hers again before adding, "I will always love you."

"Dean," she whispered, glancing away from him, "I can't…do that right now."

"I know. I don't expect an answer or anything, but I wanted to let you know before I leave today."

"Before you leave? You mean, before we all leave?"

Dean shook his head. "I'm not going with you. What I saw in that Mirror." He shuddered. "No, I have to go back to Eleysia."

Cyrene opened her mouth and then closed it. Of course he had to go back home. Of course he did. That made perfect sense. *Why had I thought otherwise? Why had I hoped otherwise?*

"I'm surprised you stayed for as long as you did."

"I wanted to make amends, and I needed to make sure that you were all right."

"I am," she said. "Or I will be."

"Now, I have to take care of my own family. Look through the wreckage," he said softly. "Try to put the pieces back together."

"I think that's smart," she said, her throat tight.

"I'll regret this moment every day if I don't do this."

"Do what?" she asked, scrunching her brows together.

Then, his hands cupped her face, and his lips pressed against hers. For a second, she thought about pulling away and telling him no. But the truth was…she didn't want to say good-bye.

She opened her mouth to him and let every pent-up emotion crash down all around them. She had loved him so fiercely once, back when they were different people. Now, she didn't know where they stood or where their lives were taking them. Only that, tomorrow, he would be gone, and she might never see him again.

He pulled away too soon and then kissed her nose. "I'll miss you every day."

Her throat constricted, and she nodded.

"I'm still going to make this right," he promised. "I'll be the man you deserve."

Cyrene laughed softly at that. "Don't say good-bye."

"Never," he agreed. "I will always find you."

Then, he kissed her lips once more and left. She watched him walk away, back to his horse, with her head held high. She blinked away the tears that had gathered in her lashes.

His future was uncertain. Hers even more so.

But, at least this time, they'd had a proper farewell.

A proper farewell with everyone.

With Reeve and Aubron staying and Dean leaving, that dropped their numbers back down to her original five. It was probably better to try to move through the pass with fewer people, but it didn't make it any easier.

Cyrene swiped at her lashes and then headed back to collect Ceffy. She could see Avoca huddled up with Ceis'f in the distance. She wondered if they would add him to their party or if it would be another strained farewell.

Cyrene heard weeping in the distance and saw a mother with a boy who was holding out a book to her. She broke down further into sobs when she took it into her arms and clutched it to her chest. She called out his name with a shrill keen.

"Her son didn't make it home," Cal said, appearing at Cyrene's side.

"That's awful."

"Were you going to leave without saying good-bye to me?" Cal asked. Her usually bright eyes were sad, as if she couldn't fathom that all of her new friends were disappearing.

"Of course not. I wanted to save the best for last."

Cal flashed her a quick smile. "Nana says that she's going to train me in magic."

"That's wonderful!"

"But they still don't want me in pants." Cal plucked at the cotton dress she was wearing.

Cyrene thought it looked nice but understood that her pants and shirt fit her more.

"And they won't let me train to fight."

"My brother is staying in town. Reeve is Aubron's boyfriend. He's a very skilled fighter, and he has no reservations about training a girl. I had no interest, but he taught other girls how to fight. It's quite common in the capital."

"You think he'll train me?" she gushed.

"I think that I'll beat him up if he doesn't."

Cal threw her arms around Cyrene. "Thank you. Thank you. Thank you!"

Cyrene laughed. Creator, she was going to miss Cal. "You've earned it. Stay strong. Don't lose any of this fire."

Cal nodded. "Thank you for believing in me."

"You made it easy."

"Come back to Fen, okay? I want to hear about these dragons."

Cyrene's mouth dropped open. "How did you hear about that?"

Cal's cheeks colored. "Did I mention, eavesdropping is my specialty?"

"And sneaking out?"

"Well, yeah," she said with a shrug. "Creator, I would kill to see a dragon!"

"Try to keep that under wraps, okay? We don't want you killing anyone or for anyone to know about the dragons."

Cal laughed. "Got it. No killing. No dragons."

Cyrene smiled and pulled her into a hug one more time. Then, when she released her, Cal frowned before darting back to her mother and nana.

By then, Avoca was striding back toward her with purpose, and it seemed everyone else had wrapped up their good-byes. Avoca hopped onto her horse's back and nudged over to Cyrene.

"Everything go okay?" Cyrene asked.

Avoca sighed. "He is as stubborn as ever."

"So, he's staying here?"

"Yes. Though I don't know what good it will do him."

Cyrene put her foot in the stirrup and hoisted herself into her saddle. "I'm sure it must be hard, being around you and Ahlvie."

Avoca nodded and glanced back at Ceis'f, who was still standing at the tree line. "Yes, I believe it must be. I've asked him to watch the village though. I like it here too much to see something go wrong."

"And he agreed to do it?"

"He didn't want to, but he will for me. Not for them."

"I see."

"He thinks we're foolish to seek out the dragons," Avoca said. Her eyes were shining with questions.

"He thinks we're foolish, no matter what we do."

"Yes, but what if he's right? If dragons have not been in Emporia for two thousand years, don't you think we're tempting fate?"

"Yes. I think that's the point." Cyrene reached out for her hand. "No matter what Ceis'f believes, I believe our mission is Creator-blessed. You should, too."

"You're right. I'm ready to get back to the mission," Avoca said.

Cyrene noticed when she glanced off into Ceis'f's direction one more time.

"He'll be okay."

Avoca shook her head. "I'm not so sure about that."

"Come, you two," Matilde called. "Time to depart."

They waved good-bye to the village that had saved them. Cyrene didn't know what would have happened to her if they hadn't ended up here. But she was glad that they at least had been able to save Fen some strife.

They filed into a line, double abreast. Ahlvie and Orden took the lead with Matilde and Vera following behind them. Cyrene and Avoca took up the rear and tried not to look back at the ease that life could have been.

Forty Three

THE DUNGEON
—RHEA—

R hea hadn't wept.

She refused to let tears fall from her eyes. Though, sometimes, she wanted to. She wanted to break down and pretend that she had stayed the person who enjoyed her work with Master Caro Barca. Who didn't venture beyond the work he had given her. It had been a simple life. An interesting life. One she could be proud of.

Not a murderer.

Not a destroyer.

Not a city killer.

None of those atrocities that were tattooed on her heart. That woke her up, screaming in the night…on the nights she could sleep at all.

She had given the king and prince everything they had asked for in the end. It had barely taken any pressure. She was ashamed that she hadn't been able to withstand even the slightest amount of torture.

At least she hadn't known enough about Cyrene's plan to give her away. Thankfully, Prince Kael had seemed less interested in Cyrene, and since he was the one with the fireballs, she'd appreciated it. He'd already known enough about her work, but he had asked her every last detail about the bombs. And she had given it up. It had been easier than talking about Cyrene.

Then, the news had trickled in.

The capital city of Eleysia was gone. Burned and bombed to the ground.

Her work. Everything she had done to get her bombs working had resulted in *this*.

She should have listened to Master Barca. He had told her that he had no interest in militarizing his Bursts or in figuring out how to harness their blast potential. But she had been determined. Now, people were dead.

Just because you could do something didn't mean that you should do it.

Rhea had taken to making laps in her small cell. Food only came twice a day, and what little news she could acquire from the guards gossiping was more depressing than anything. It wasn't as if they were going to strike up a conversation with her.

Elea had already been gone when Rhea returned from her horrible torture session, and despite the constant gossip, she hadn't heard a peep about her. It was as worrisome as the bombings.

And lonely.

Being alone in a dark dungeon for more than two months was hard. She couldn't deny it. The walls had started to close in. The food was stale. She found that she'd started to talk to herself. She would do anything for a book at this point. But nothing changed, and she was still all alone.

She hated the fact that she looked forward to when her food showed up. At least a real person delivered it. And that time was roughly now.

Rhea straightened and tried to look presentable even though she knew that it didn't matter. A lantern appeared at the end of the hallway, and her heart skipped a beat in excitement. The best part of her day.

But the face that appeared before her was not one of the rotating guards who brought her a tray of food. It was Master Caro Barca!

"Master Barca!" she gasped. "What are you doing down here?"

"I've come to get you out, girl." He slid a key into the slot and turned it.

"How are you doing this?"

"Doesn't matter. What matters is that I won't have them keeping you locked up. It's bad enough that they used my Bursts to hurt Eleysia. I won't let them take this beautiful brain and destroy it down here. Come, come," he said, prying the door open.

Rhea fell into his arms. "Thank you."

Then, they were both hurrying down the hall. She gasped when she saw a guard on duty and stalled her steps. They would be caught.

"Come now," Master Barca said.

The guard turned around, and Rhea gasped.

"Eren?"

The High Order she had fallen head over heels for stared back at her with a rare smile. She had no idea what he was doing here. He had ended their relationship. Or what little relationship they'd had. He followed the rules. He was a thoroughbred High Order who was close friends with the king. None of this made sense.

"Rhea," Eren said, grasping her hand, "it's so good to see you."

"You, too." She blinked back the tears she had been avoiding since being imprisoned.

"The hall is still clear," Eren announced. "We must move quickly."

Instead of turning left, back toward the main part of the castle, Eren veered right and headed deeper into the underground part of the castle. She and Master Barca hurried behind him. She didn't ask questions about where they were going. All she cared about was that she was out of that wretched prison cell.

Byern was not the city that she had known and loved while growing up. Something dark and sinister had taken root in the castle. It was ebbing through the walls and destroying the place she had once adored.

Eren opened up a door and ushered them inside. They hurried down a staircase and then down a long corridor before taking another staircase up a steep incline. Rhea was breathing heavily by the time they reached the top of the stairs. Eren pushed open a door, and Rhea realized that they were in the stables.

It was dark outside already, as the sun had been setting earlier and earlier during the day. Eren had two horses prepared and waiting for them. He threw a traveling cloak over her head to conceal her and then helped her onto the first horse. Master Barca took the second, and then Eren took the seat behind her. It would have been better to have three horses, but it was less conspicuous to have two. She wasn't going to complain when Eren pressed his chest into her back and heeled the horse out of the stables.

The guard at the gate waved them through without ever glancing up into her face. She breathed a sigh of relief as they trotted down the hill that led into the city. Eren took a roundabout way before Master Barca took over and directed them down a side alley. They stabled their horses behind a ramshackle building that Rhea would never have looked at twice.

Rhea had been utterly silent the entire ride. She was too afraid, her heart pitter-pattering in her chest. This felt like a dream.

How many times did I imagine that I would be swept out of the castle and off my feet? How often did I envision myself having the strength that Cyrene had and refusing to be locked up?

"Where…where are we?" she asked. "And how is this possible?"

Eren dismounted and then eased Rhea from her seat. "I couldn't let you rot away in there. When I went to Caro, he already had a plan in place to get you free. Having my help only assured it."

"What they did to you was not right," Master Barca agreed.

Eren pulled her slightly aside. "After seeing what happened in Eleysia, I couldn't stand back and do nothing. It's wrong, what they did to you. It's wrong, what happened in Eleysia. I never thought it would go to such an extreme."

"You've had a change of heart," she said, her own heart swelling.

"Yes. I know that I am proud of my country, but I can't stand by and watch them conduct themselves in such a manner. And I could never leave you behind."

"But I thought…we were…over. I mean, not that we were together, but…" Rhea trailed off as she realized she had been rambling.

Then, Eren moved his hands up into her dark red hair and pressed his lips to hers. She was so caught off guard that she gasped and opened her mouth to meet him. Butterflies flittered in her stomach. Her body seemed to melt at his touch. All the worries and fears she'd had disappeared. It was just Eren and his lips and the enormity of what this all meant.

"I love you," he whispered against her lips.

"You do?" she asked in shock.

"I have for so long. I should have told you instead of pushing you away. Can you forgive me for making you wait so long to know my true intentions?"

She nodded, tears slicking her cheeks. "Yes. Yes, of course. I…I love you, too."

"Music to my ears."

She laughed. "Mine, too."

"I should have said it better…and at a better time."

"No, this is perfect."

He kissed her once more. "I have to get back to the castle. They'll notice that I'm gone, but I'll come back for you. I'll get away as often as I can."

"Okay," she said. "I wish you could stay."

"Me, too. Just know that you have a special place with me, and we'll be together when the time is right."

"Yes," she agreed in earnest.

He finally released her and reluctantly strode back to his horse.

Master Barca appeared then, looking almost a bit sheepish for having intruded on the moment. "I also have to go back with the young High Order. I hate to leave you here, but suspicions will be high when they find you are missing. And everyone believes me too senile to mount any real escape plan."

Rhea laughed and pulled her Receiver into a hug. "I always knew that you were more than you seemed."

"I am everything I seem, and I prefer to be that way." He pulled back and held her at arm's length. "You should learn to accept that for yourself. You are brilliant. The daughter I never had, and I am so proud of you."

"But I created those bombs."

"You do not get to choose how your creations will be used. You did not ignite them on a city. You simply had the genius to create them. Do not ever stop creating. You were born for it."

"I will miss you."

"And I, you." He hugged her one more time. "Go inside. One of my contacts is waiting. He is expecting you. Boss him around a bit. He could use it."

Rhea grinned. "Where have you left me?"

"A house. Find a way to make it a home."

He squeezed her shoulders and then mounted his horse. He and Eren waved farewell one more time and then disappeared around the corner. That meant that she was all alone once more.

She stared up at the derelict building and wondered where Master Barca had brought her. *Who could he trust so much to drop her on a doorstep?*

But she trusted him. So, she would find her own way.

With a gulp, she moved to the door and knocked. A minute later, the door swung inward, and a man stood, blocking the doorway. His figure crowded the space, and his broad shoulders nearly touched either side. He had the appearance of someone who knew an honest day's work but had the mischievous look of someone who also knew how to squander it. His hair was close cropped, but he had a bit of a beard, as if he couldn't decide whether to fit into society or buck standards. His mouth turned downward, but his eyes were alight. He seemed to be a walking contradiction.

"Hello," she said confidently.

"You must be Rhea."

"Yes, that's right."

"Well, what are you standing out here for? Get inside."

She scurried past him and into the building. It looked like a hovel on the outside, but the inside was well maintained.

"Your bedroom is the first on the left. You'll find everything you need in there. Meals are at six, noon, and six. If you're hungry before or after that, sorry."

The man turned away from her, as if that was his entire speech.

"I'm sorry," she said quickly, "but who are you?"

"Oh, right. Introductions." He brushed his hand over the back of his neck. "I'm not that great with those. I'm Fenix."

He held his hand out, and they shook. His hand dwarfed hers, as did everything about him. She quickly retrieved her hand.

"Nice to meet you, Fenix. Um…what exactly do you do here?"

"Caro didn't tell you?"

She shook her head. "We were on a tight schedule."

"Ever heard of the network?"

"No."

"Good. That's how we like to keep it."

Fenix turned and strode away from her then, leaving her puzzled and excited. *What is this new life?*

Forty Four

THE THRONE
—KALIANA—

"How are you so big already?" Kaliana cooed to her little baby girl.

"She's a healthy weight, Your Majesty," Davila, the nursemaid, said.

"They grow up so fast."

"Indeed."

Kaliana sighed when she reluctantly gave Alessia back to Davila. She still hadn't gotten used to leaving her. Though all of the nurses had told her that her attachment was perfectly normal. But she knew that she should never truly attach herself to a girl. They only ever sent them away. Kaliana herself was living proof of that.

"I wish we could move her to my rooms," Kaliana said.

Davila looked scandalized and then quickly masked it. "She's best in the nursery, Your Majesty. You let us look after her. She'll be the perfect little princess."

Kaliana nodded sadly. "She already is."

Then, she turned and fled the nursery before she could take her child and remove her from anyone else's hands. She had this deep gut-wrenching urge to raise Alessia different than how she had been raised. To refuse to listen to tradition and what all these wet nurses said and raise her daughter how she saw fit. Of course, she couldn't. Not as queen. Even the maids could raise their children how they saw fit but not the queen. Creator forbid!

She tried to push all of that out of her mind and focus on what lay ahead.

Edric.

The throne room.

He had taken to sitting in there and celebrating in his victory over Eleysia. A sneak attack in the dead of night that had decimated their capital. Not an honorable battle if they asked her.

But they didn't.

In fact, she was even more invisible now than she'd been before she had Alessia. She had been so determined to be included and feel wanted then. Now, she wanted to get through the parade of activity and get back to her daughter.

Not to mention, she was picking up extra slack since there was no consort for the king. Or at least all the work that his new pet didn't want to do.

Kaliana stepped into the throne room and found Elea resting on a divan between Edric and Kael. *Pet.* That was all she could think of when she saw her. Young, innocent, and utterly stupid.

Cyrene had been a threat because she was intelligent and bold. Her sister was a threat for her eagerness and blind trust.

Kaliana had once hated Cyrene. But she understood Edric's infatuation at least. When she looked at Elea, she felt none of the rage or envy. Only pity.

Kaliana walked up to the front of the room and took her empty seat next to Edric. Kael was doing parlor tricks and making Elea giggle. He'd taken to doing that every time he had an audience now. Somehow, so quickly, he had gone from being shunned to people accepting what he could do. She knew it had to be because Edric was backing him. Also, fear.

The fact that he could do magic…that he had leveled a city was terrifying. If she had been in Edric's place, she would have put Kael down like a lame horse before giving him as much power as he was allowed.

"Hello, Kaliana," Edric said with a bright smile. He'd had a smile for her more and more frequently since Eleysia. "How is our daughter?"

Kael's juggling fireball fumbled, and he nearly caught the divan on fire. Elea shrieked, but he smothered it with air before it even singed the fabric.

"Alessia is healthy and strong, husband," she said with her own smile. Alessia was the true joy in her life. "We should visit her together tomorrow."

Edric nodded. "Yes, I'd like that."

But, as another person entered the throne room, his attention diverted from Kaliana, as if he had never been talking to her. She was used to it. She held her head high and endured the court politics. Perhaps, after an hour or so, she could claim to have some duties for her Affiliates and leave.

"You summoned me?" High Order Eren said once he reached the front of the room. He bowed deeply and then kept his easy smile about him.

Kaliana had always liked him. He was one of Edric's closer friends, especially since he had come back from Trinnenberg as an Ambassador. Eren was steadfast. She felt like he was the right kind of man they needed in their court at the moment, as it was devolving into debauchery.

"Yes," Edric said. "I have a question for you."

Kael patted the top of Elea's head, as if she were a lap dog, and stood to stride around the room. He moved like a predator stalking his prey. Every step important. A current of energy seemed to emanate from him, and Kaliana shivered under the intensity.

"Yes?" Eren asked.

"Where were you last night?"

"I retired to my rooms early after dinner and slept through the night."

"I see," Edric said. He nodded his head at Kael.

A blast of energy smacked Eren in the back and sent him sprawling on the ground. His knees hit hard, and he coughed as he tried and failed to right himself. The room fell silent all around them.

Kaliana held her tongue, but she wanted to scream at them. Tell them no. They couldn't do this! Not to Eren! He was a good man. A good person. This wasn't right.

But she did nothing.

As always.

"Are you aware that Rhea has gone missing?"

"No," Eren said through gritted teeth. "You know that I ended my friendship with her."

"I see," Edric said again. "Then, why did a guard report seeing you leave on horseback with a woman under a riding cloak?"

Eren paled. "I didn't want to concern you. I've been…having a dalliance with one of the local maids."

Kael laughed. "You don't have it in you."

"Truly, Eren, can you not come up with a better lie than that? We all know that you do not sleep around."

"She's special," he said.

Kaliana gave him points for having a backbone. Not many could stand up to Edric, especially not with him working with Kael.

"I'm sure she is," Kael muttered.

"Unfortunately for you, I think you're lying," Edric said smoothly. "Tell me where you took her, and I will spare your life."

"I didn't take her!"

"Make this easy for me, Eren. We have been friends for a long time. Where is Rhea Gramm?"

Eren's eyes darted to the ground and then back up to Edric. Kaliana could see the wheels working in his mind. How she wished that she could reach out and tell him not to give in. But she wasn't strong enough, and she watched in horror with the rest of the crowd.

"In the city," Eren finally said. "I took her to a building off the Laelish."

"What did it look like?"

"Run-down, two stories. I don't know. I'd never been there before. I just dropped her off."

Kaliana narrowed her eyes. There was something in his face that said he was lying. She grinned. Clever. She hoped Edric didn't notice.

"Wonderful. That wasn't so hard," Edric said. "Help him up."

Kael released whatever powers he'd been using to hold Eren down. Then, he walked before Eren and held out his hand. Eren reluctantly looked up at him but put his hand in his. Kael easily lifted him to his feet. Eren dusted off his black pants.

"We'll send someone down to collect her now," Edric said.

He snapped his fingers at Merrick, who had been watching the display with bottomless black eyes. He retreated to a slew of guards and started giving out instructions.

"Thank you for telling the truth," Edric said, drawing Eren closer.

"Of course, Majesty. It was the right thing to do."

Edric tsked. "I have no need for traitors in my midst."

Kael drew the flaming blade that Cyrene had used in their ballroom battle. It had become a bit of a signature for him.

"Edric?" Eren asked with wild eyes.

Then, Kael thrust the blade up into Eren's heart. Kaliana covered her mouth with her hands as her favorite High Order was murdered in front of her. Kael took a deep breath and seemed to be drinking in the madness.

"Someone, clean up this mess," Edric said irritably. "And bring back the music!"

Kaliana watched wildly as everything went back to normal. As if a man hadn't just been killed in front of them. As if a life hadn't been snuffed out. As if they weren't all murderers and accomplices for these outrageous events. But she found no welcoming eyes when she searched for someone who could see how horrible this all was.

Am I the only one who saw the throne room for what it had become?

A trial, court, and execution.

Forty Five

THE MOUNTAINS

"I am freezing my ass off," Ahlvie grumbled.

He blew into his hands and shook on his horse as they passed through the Taken Mountains. Cyrene cringed at the statement. He was cold because of her.

"If Cyrene will just concentrate, we can all be warm," Matilde said snappishly.

She had become more and more irritable, the farther they'd walked through the mountain pass. Snow had started falling on the third day and had been coming down steady ever since. The weather was about as opposite from Eleysia's temperate climate where snow didn't even fall in winter.

"I am trying," Cyrene said.

Matilde humphed.

Vera gave her a sympathetic look.

Everyone else just looked like they were freezing.

And she was trying.

She proved that she was able to conjure all four elements, and now they'd set her to more difficult tasks. Not to mention, they had gone back to the slow and steady approach.

No anger. No fear.

If they sensed even a hint of irritability, they'd cut off all training.

She understood their concerns. No one wanted her to give in to the anger the way she had. To use her magic for evil rather than good. To let that side of herself fuel her powers. Blood magic came with a price, and they weren't sure if she had completely paid it yet.

"Why was this so much easier when I could just imagine Maelia's death?" she muttered under her breath.

"Because you were harnessing your energy at a much faster rate. You burned through your powers," Vera explained for the tenth time. "Using your magic incorrectly comes with side effects—headaches, nausea, depression. When you use your powers properly from your core, you can control it instead of it controlling you. The path of least resistance is not always the correct one."

"I beg to differ," Ahlvie grumbled. "If you ever decide to get angry again, Cyrene, feel free to channel some of that into warming us all up."

Cyrene frowned and glanced down at the open book in her saddle. She'd had all of those side effects. She knew how bad it had been for her. Yet it had been so easy. So, so easy.

"Release from your center," Avoca said again. "When your powers are concentrated and you are in tune with your body, then your powers will energize you, even as they're depleting."

"And they'll run out at a slower rate," Matilde added.

Cyrene nodded. "Got it. The three Cs—concentrate, control, core."

"Now, please, try again," Vera encouraged.

"Okay."

Cyrene closed the book and pushed it back into her saddlebag. It had gone tumbling twice before, and the brutal verbal lashing she'd received from Matilde made her more aware of what she was doing with the two-thousand-year-old book.

She closed her eyes, and then she reached into her center and gathered her magic. Fire was still the most difficult to draw forward, but she knew that was normal. Most people weren't ever completely proficient with fire.

With a sigh, she raised her other hand and conjured a flame in her palm. She opened her eyes and grinned. *Flame, check.*

She closed her eyes again and imagined taking the warmth and energy from the flame and amplifying it beyond her hand. Making it from the small ball of fire that gently heated her hand to a radiating heat for the entire party.

Cyrene pushed out all the extra thoughts and cluttered memories in her mind. She let herself become one with the flame in her hand. She brought her other hand up to meet the glow and stretched them further apart. The fire itself remained the same size, but the energy within it grew to the size of a carriage wheel.

This was the tricky part. She'd gotten here before. Getting the energy past her fingertips was the challenge.

A bead of sweat collected on her forehead as she heated all around her, and her concentration narrowed to a tight focus. She took an easy breath and then released the energy out further and further until it encompassed her entire body and Ceffy below her. The air around her was warm enough now that it was melting the snow as they walked.

She grinned as she looked down at it but knew that Matilde and Vera wouldn't approve, so she reined it back in. She and Ceffy were warm, but the snow was *mostly* intact.

Her concentration wavered as she tried to work outward from there. Warm the whole party. It was like stretching a rubber band. She would pull it far enough until it was taut and then pray that it didn't pop.

Avoca smiled like a fool when Cyrene enveloped her in the warmth. "You've got it!"

"Still cold up here," Ahlvie groaned.

"Just a minute," Cyrene ground out.

"Breathe through it. It's like flexing a muscle. Don't overexert yourself. Let it do the work for you," Vera coached.

Cyrene nodded and tried to listen to her advice. Stretching her magical muscles was more like trying to carry a sack of bricks uphill. But she did it. Her magic covered Matilde and then Vera, and with a burst of energy, she shoved the barrier around Orden and Ahlvie.

Ahlvie cheered, "Thank the Creator!"

"Good. Now, hold it there," Matilde said. "At least until I can feel my fingers again."

Cyrene trotted along, holding on to her magic by sheer force of will. She knew that she could essentially snap the barrier into place and keep them warm for the entirety of the ride. It would be a power suck but more like background noise. The majority of the energy had gone into creating the warmth. She could contain it at a much lower cost. She'd had to do that with Doma Fire, a ball of energy that illuminated about ten feet in every direction. A very useful piece of magic. But they weren't letting her tie the heat off now on purpose.

They had just crested a ridge when they all gasped at the scene below them. The mountains opened up to reveal the Keylani River overlooking Tahne, Carhara's capital city. It was a stunning view with the snow-white landscape brushed with gray stone under the snowcapped spires of the city. Even though Tahne was only a few hours north by boat from Byern, Cyrene had never seen the lauded city with its stunning glass windows that made the entire place gleam and shine.

"Wow," she whispered, shielding her eyes against the sun shining off the glass.

"Cyrene," Matilde snapped.

Cyrene cursed violently under her breath. All of that hard work for nothing. One distraction, and her fire was already down.

"Can you just do it, so Ahlvie stops swearing at me?" Cyrene asked. "Let's focus on the coin instead."

"Uh, guys," Ahlvie said. He snapped to attention. His eyes were bright and searching out the terrain.

"What is it?" Avoca asked, immediately on alert.

Orden retreated a dozen paces down the mountain and then stopped. "It's silent."

"Ambush," Ahlvie said at once.

And then the Indres attacked.

They came out of nowhere. Nearly ten feet long, their fangs as long as arrows, their yellow eyes thirsty for flesh. Their fur was unlike the ones they had encountered in the Hidden Forest; those had been the color of dirt. These Indres blended into the mountainside with white hides that made them practically impossible to see.

Cyrene grasped a ball of fire in her hand and hurled it at the nearest Indres. It squealed at the direct hit, fell to the ground, and turned head-on to face her. The eyes on that beast were as intelligent as any person. It had just registered her as the threat and was growling something to the other Indres.

Not good.

Cyrene's heart pounded as she watched the Indres regroup and focus in on her. Matilde and Vera joined hands and were muttering something under their breath. Avoca reached out and linked with Cyrene. She tugged on their bond, communicating their next objective without words. Orden had a blade in his hand and was facing off with two of the beasts. Ahlvie was lost behind her. She knew he could hold his own.

When she tried to tally up how many there were, they all began to blur together, and she lost count. It was a lot. More than the last time she had seen them. Not an encouraging sight.

The beasts moved as one as they bounded toward her. She shot a fireball at one, but by the time she had another one up, they were upon her. Ceffy reeled in fear, and she skidded backward in the snowy terrain. Avoca rushed in, using her blades to slash throats and magic to push the creatures back.

Matilde and Vera finally finished and then pushed their magic outward. It rattled the Indres, blasting them back into the mountain and blowing the snow and debris away from them in a perfect circle.

"Retreat!" Orden yelled.

No one argued with that assessment. They were outnumbered.

Cyrene wheeled Ceffy around and took off at a gallop down the mountain. Her hair whipped in the wind. Her cheeks hurt, and her lips were chapped, but she didn't look back, and she didn't stop.

By the time they reached the bottom of the mountainside, Ceffy was panting and slowing down. She couldn't blame her. Her own adrenaline was ripping through her system. She had no trouble with keeping warm now.

"How did they know where we would be?" Cyrene asked.

"The Nokkin," Matilde guessed.

Orden nodded. "Generals whispering to their beast armies."

"Yes."

"Abhorrent," Avoca muttered.

"Indeed," Vera agreed.

Cyrene looked back at her friends. Then, she turned her head to look back up the mountain. "Where is Ahlvie?"

Avoca swore. "He was right beside me."

Cyrene cursed, and then she wheeled Ceffy around and set off at a gallop. She could hear Avoca thundering behind her. Their horses were panting when they finally made it back up the mountain to where the dead Indres lay. There were tracks everywhere, in every direction.

"You go that way," Cyrene said, pointing toward the second largest group of tracks. "And I'll follow these. Tug on the bond if you find anything."

Avoca nodded, and then they swiftly departed. Cyrene searched and searched, but there was no sign of any of the Indres who had just attacked them. It was as if they had vanished. And, by the time she made it back to the place where they had been attacked, it was nearly nightfall.

Orden was waiting for them along with Matilde and Vera.

"Did you find him?" Cyrene asked.

"No," Orden said. "I found nothing."

Matilde and Vera shook their heads. They hadn't seen anything either.

Avoca returned, looking defeated. "The tracks went every direction. Even with my good eyesight, I would not be able to follow them at night."

"So, what? We just hope it doesn't snow tonight? That we don't lose the tracks?"

Orden sighed. "I think that is all we can do."

"He'll be back," Matilde said.

"He knows what he's doing," Vera confirmed.

"He was just attacked! He could be bleeding out," Cyrene said.

"You saw no blood," Vera said. "I suspect he will find us by morning."

"But *how* will he find us?" Cyrene asked.

"He will know that we went into the city, and he will find Avoca."

"I'm so confused."

Matilde sighed and glanced over at Vera. "I'm sure he would prefer if he told you."

"Told us what?" Avoca asked. Her eyes were wide with worry.

Orden trotted between them. "The boy has secrets a plenty. But we should be on our way if we want to reach Tahne by sunset."

Avoca's and Cyrene's eyes drifted up to the mountainside. No Indres were visible. Nothing was visible. Cyrene couldn't believe that they were going to leave Ahlvie behind. But they had done all that they could. If they weren't in the city by sundown, they'd have nowhere to rest.

She reluctantly turned her horse back toward the city and followed them to the enormous Carharan wall that Tahne was famous for. From inside, the city was lit up like a Burst. From the outside, the city could hold a siege for years. The walls were twenty feet tall and two feet thick and encompassed the entire city. There were only two entrances, and both would be closed by sundown.

A dozen guards were stationed at the entrance, and just as many other were on the top of the wall with bows and arrows aimed in all directions. Carhara had always been known for their military. Cyrene knew that they were constantly attempting to gain more territory for themselves but never made much headway. Tiek was always pressing back at their borders, and the mountains kept them out of Byern.

"Business?" the man asked.

"We're looking for an inn for the night. We'll be on our way at first light," Orden promised. He smoothly passed a bag of gold into the man's hand.

Cyrene almost laughed. You could take the lord out of Aurum, but you couldn't take Aurum out of the lord.

"Excellent. I recommend the inn down the main street, The Crow and the Ax. Can't miss it."

"Much obliged," Orden said regally.

Then, they were hastened into the city.

Cyrene was captivated by the interior and how much the city bloomed, despite being confined to this one space. They couldn't sprawl out, so glass buildings had been built up, up, up to dizzying heights that were usually reserved for castles. Friendly faces mingled with hardened military men, and fragrant spices wafted toward them with the sound of laughter from children running. It was much the same as all the other cities that Cyrene had seen, except buildings were stacked on top of each other. It was enough to make anyone feel claustrophobic.

"I'm glad we're only here for a night," she whispered to Avoca.

"You and me both. The air always feels wrong in a city. And the earth is so trampled, it can hardly breathe."

Cyrene nodded. This time, she knew exactly what Avoca meant.

They found The Crow and the Ax with ease, as the soldier had said. Orden dismounted and walked up the few steps before he was greeted by a curvy woman of middle years with a heart-shaped face and a broad smile.

"Gerild send you?" she asked, eagerly looking Orden up and down.

"He did," Orden confirmed.

Though Cyrene knew he hadn't heard the man's name before.

"He has good taste. I'm Margrite. You'll need a night for you and your"—Margrite looked up at the rest of them—"wife and family?"

Orden's eyes smiled for him. Cyrene could see he was trying not to laugh at the woman. Other than Matilde and Vera, none of them looked related in the slightest. Margrite was fishing for information.

"Just my sisters and their apprentices. We'd appreciate three rooms for the night."

Margrite smiled. "Sisters, sisters. All right. I can do three. I'll get some lads to stable the horses in the back and bring your things in. Come inside and get yourself warm. Can't imagine being out in this weather."

Margrite made three more blatant attempts to gain Orden's attention before dumping us all in our rooms and storming off.

"Well, she's pleasant," Orden said.

"We'd probably get free rooms if you were interested in a fancy," Matilde said with a snicker.

Orden held up another bag of money. "I'd rather pay her coin than warm her bed. She must have that Gerild at the front poaching for her."

Cyrene cleared her throat. "That is all well and fine, but what about Ahlvie? We *left* him on that mountain."

Matilde and Vera glanced at each other and sighed.

"If we had thought he was in trouble, we would never have left him. Trust us. If he does not return tonight, then we will march right out there and kill every last feral beast to get to him," Matilde promised.

Avoca twirled her blade. "I will kill them with my bare hands if they hurt a hair on his head."

"In the meantime," Vera interrupted, "we should all try to get a good night's sleep. We have a long journey ahead of us before we even reach the Aude River through Mastira. We should all pray to the Creator that it has not frozen over yet."

"At least Cyrene will have mastered her talent of heating by then," Matilde offered with a sly grin.

"I will master it," she said confidently.

"I believe you, child."

Cyrene and Avoca retreated to their rooms, and both collapsed back into the bed. It wasn't the nicest thing either of them had ever lain on by far, but it felt like it after so many days on the ground.

"Why do you believe they are so calm about Ahlvie's disappearance?" Avoca questioned.

Cyrene shook her head, pulling out the Doma book and skimming the pages, as she had taken to doing every night before bed. "Only Ahlvie will be able to tell that tale. You know how they get when they've decided on a course of action."

"Don't think for a second they're more stubborn than you are."

"I'd never dream of it, but I know which battles to pick."

"Perhaps."

Avoca's eyes slid closed. Almost instantly, her breath evened out, and she was asleep. It was a skill Cyrene wished she had.

When she finally fell asleep, she was tossing and turning. Nightmares plagued her as she was torn between a vision of Serafina begging her not to use the coin and that disembodied darkness urging her to come to it.

She woke with a scream before first light, and Avoca shot up in her bed, a blade in her hand, ready to kill a threat that wasn't there.

But then they both realized that the window was open.

"Did you open that?" Cyrene asked.

Avoca shook her head. Their eyes gazed around the room, and they startled, pressing their bodies back against the wall, as a full-bodied Indres lay, sprawled out, on the floor of their room.

Forty Six

THE INDRES

Cyrene's scream was full-bodied and terrified. Her magic burst to life in her core, and she pulled energy tight to her as she prepared to attack. Avoca held her blades in her hands and crouched in a defensive position, like a predator.

But her scream had startled the beast. It rose on its haunches and looked at them with the same intensity that the last Indres had in the mountains. Much too intelligent for a normal beast.

Avoca let loose a blade, and it struck the creature in the shoulder. It roared in pain. But, instead of charging her and taking her out, like Cyrene had always seen them do before, it backed further into the corner. Further away from them.

As if to say, *No, please, not me. I'm sorry.*

"Wait," Cyrene said when Avoca went to land the killing blow. "Its eyes."

"Gold," Avoca whispered.

"Human," Cyrene added.

And then, before their eyes, the creature shifted form. At one point, it was a ten-foot-long beast, ready to rip their throats out, and the next…it was a naked man, trembling in the dark room.

Not just any man.

"Ahlvie?" Avoca gasped.

The door burst open then.

Orden had his blade at the ready. "I heard a scream."

His eyes darted to Ahlvie lying naked on the floor. He immediately removed his cloak and covered him up. Both girls were too shell-shocked to understand what they had just seen.

"I'll get him cleaned up," Orden said, taking charge. "Meet in the twins' room." When he saw that neither of them was moving, he barked louder, "Now!"

Avoca and Cyrene jumped, as if they had just been shaken awake. Cyrene nodded her head at Orden, and he hastened Ahlvie out of their room. They each changed into something more presentable and then walked, uncomprehending, into the next room.

Matilde and Vera were seated in a corner, serving tea, as if nothing at all had happened in the hours since they last saw them.

"How is he?" Vera asked.

"An Indres," Cyrene said, wincing at the words.

"I don't…I don't understand," Avoca said. Her face was grim. She looked more like Ahlvie had died.

"Orden will bring him in when he's prepared to talk. I know this is a long time coming for him," Vera explained.

"How long?" Avoca demanded.

"Patience," Matilde snapped. "Drink this. It will help with the nerves."

"What's in it? A spell?" Avoca asked, taking the drink.

"Very similar. It helps loosen the muscles and releases tension and inhibitions. We call it whiskey."

Avoca shot her a humorless look before taking a drink. She coughed heartily and then downed the whole thing. She passed the cup back. "I'll take another."

"Cyrene?" Vera asked.

"No."

"Suit yourself," Matilde said.

When Ahlvie finally entered the room, he looked like a hollowed out shadow figure of the man he had been. Orden took a seat next to Vera, and then they all waited. Ahlvie stared at the ground, at his hands, at his shoes, at anything but them.

"So, I guess you know now," Ahlvie said with a short laugh, as if the whole thing were one big joke.

"How long?" Avoca demanded. Her voice was tight and clipped.

Ahlvie winced at the venom in it. "Maybe I should start from the beginning."

Cyrene could almost see him putting on his tattered mendicant costume before a performance in the pub back in Eleysia. He seemed able to tell a story if he became someone else. Not the man who had been an Indres, but the charade he concocted around himself. The one Cyrene always saw as the pomp, bombast, and bluster that made Ahlvie, Ahlvie.

He finally lifted his gaze and searched them out, one by one. He flinched at the intensity in Avoca's eyes, but he seemed relieved that Cyrene was facing him head-on. She could only imagine what was running through his head.

"The year I was born, a devastating attack hit Fen. Wolves came out of nowhere and slaughtered dozens of people. Huge wolves. Enormous wolves. Wolves that no one had ever seen or would ever see again. We had a name for them, passed down through legend, but no one dared speak it at the time. Not with so many dead. My father included," Ahlvie said. "That was about twenty years ago."

Avoca startled. "Was that the night Aonia was sacked?"

"As far as I can tell, it is in the right time frame from what you've told me." Ahlvie chuckled once. "I guess Ceis'f and I have more in common than he thinks."

"But you survived the attack," Cyrene said.

"Yes, and no. Growing up, I had this wicked scar on my stomach. The kind that ran from chest to navel. As if someone had opened me up and then incorrectly closed me. It wasn't until my lone wolf ceremony when I really realized that I wasn't like anyone else my age. I always had keen eyesight. I could hear conversations I knew I wasn't supposed to hear. My brain cataloged information that I never forgot. But I thought nothing of it until I was the first person back that day, and my mother finally told me about the attack."

"You were bitten?" Matilde guessed.

"Yes."

"But bites don't make you do…that!" Avoca cried out.

"No. Many others were bitten that night. Some died. Some didn't. No one else was affected. But I was a baby. I should have died by that bite. But a man was traveling through our village, who stayed there that night. Without him, the Indres certainly would have slaughtered our entire village. He imbued my body with magic, which held the Indres venom in my bloodstream. That man saved me and damned me."

Avoca gasped softly. Her eyes were wide. "You don't mean…"

Ahlvie nodded. "Ceis'f."

"He saved your village and your life, only to return to Aonia to see it gone," Avoca whispered.

"Another reason he must hate humans," Cyrene whispered. "To think, if he had not helped you and just gotten to Aonia a night sooner, he might have helped them."

"Or died," Vera added. "He very likely would be dead."

"He'd be smart to see it as a blessing that he had stayed back an extra night," Matilde said.

"That doesn't sound like him at all," Avoca said. "Are you sure it was Ceis'f? It might mean that there is another Aonia Leif alive."

Ahlvie shook his head. "My mother recognized him from twenty years ago. She says he looks the same. She tried to thank him, but he said he didn't remember her. Or he chose not to acknowledge her."

"Does…does he know that you're the baby he saved?" Cyrene asked.

Ahlvie nodded gravely. "He does now."

Cyrene winced. Ceis'f had saved Ahlvie's life only for Ahlvie to end up with the woman that Ceis'f loved. He must hate himself for that. Among many things.

"So…Ceis'f kept the Indres venom in your system, and now, you're an Indres?" Avoca asked in disbelief.

"Not…exactly. I would say up until then, the venom had been dormant. I got some of the benefits. They really helped me in Byern when I needed them. Sneaking out was especially easy."

"Of course you would be given powers and use them to sneak around and cheat," Cyrene muttered.

"What's the use of having superpowers if I can't have a little fun?" Ahlvie shrugged. "Anyway, when we were in Aurum and you were attacked by the Braj at the castle, I disappeared into the gardens and was met with the Alpha."

Matilde and Vera perked up at this knowledge. "The real Alpha?" Matilde asked.

"The big, bad himself. There are pack Alphas, and then there's the top Alpha," Ahlvie explained. "They could sense that I was one of them. That I was inherently prepped to join them. And they sent their best to force me to join or to take me down."

"And you won?" Vera asked, practically giddy.

"Killed the bastard," Ahlvie confirmed. "Then, the pack invaded my mind and made *me* Alpha, all because I'd killed him. The symptoms have been getting worse ever since. I've been trying to fight them off to ignore their calls. But, up on that mountain, with so many of them with us and nothing but the call of the wild, I lost it and shifted."

"And that likely saved our lives," Matilde said, inclining her head.

Vera smiled and did the same. "Thank you for getting your pack in line. Perhaps that will keep them off our tail for some time."

"So, just like that?" Ahlvie asked. "You're okay with this?"

"We've had some time to consider. We've known all along," Vera told him. "You're not the first half-breed we've come across in our years."

"Really?" Ahlvie gasped. "There are others like me?"

Avoca jumped to her feet. "Are none of you going to acknowledge the danger of what we witnessed? Indres are evil. In Eldora, we hunt them for sport. They killed six of my men in the Hidden Forest. They would have killed us all if Cyrene had not saved us. And, now, you are one of them?" She looked disgusted and horrified.

"I didn't choose this," Ahlvie said with his arms wide.

She shook her head and stormed from the room. Ahlvie reached for her, but she sidestepped him, being careful not to touch him before she left.

"Let me," Orden said, swinging on his cloak and following after Avoca.

Ahlvie looked downtrodden. "I was afraid of that," he said, plopping down into his seat.

"She'll come around," Cyrene said. "She loves you."

"This is something worse though. I'm her enemy. I knew it; I did. That's why I didn't tell her."

"Maybe, if you had told her, then you wouldn't be in this mess."

Ahlvie shrugged. "Maybe. But you? How do you feel? Am I still part of the party?"

"You once told me you were a cheat but loyal. I trust you." She reached out and put her hand on his. "I always have. I don't think being Indres inherently makes you bad. You still have a human heart. Use that, and you'll be fine."

THE TALISMAN

A voca was still gone an hour later.

Orden returned empty-handed and shrugged. "You try to keep up with a Leif who doesn't want to be followed."

Ahlvie stood up and made for the door. "I'll go after her. I'll explain. I'll, you know, charm my way out of this."

Cyrene stopped Ahlvie. "I don't think so. Even if you could find her…"

"I found her in your room last night from a league away after leaping over a twenty-foot wall into the city. I think I can find her now."

"I'm sure we'd all like to know exactly how you did that," Cyrene said with a raised eyebrow. "But, last night, you were in your Indres form. Even if you could find her as you are now, she doesn't want to be found. Take it from me. Sometimes, it's best to back off and let her come to you."

Ahlvie grumbled and cursed. "Fine. I'm going to go downstairs with Orden and get us some breakfast then."

"Don't do anything stupid."

"Me?" he asked with that confident look in his eyes. "I'd never."

Cyrene laughed at him as he and Orden disappeared back downstairs. "How long do you think Avoca will be gone?"

"Not as long as her anger will last," Matilde said.

"If she's gone too long, you can call her back," Vera said.

"How long did you two know what Ahlvie was?" Cyrene asked, taking a seat before them once more.

"From the first," Vera said.

"Yes. He has the look about him," Matilde confirmed. "Half-breed."

"You know," Vera continued, "I had a thought about the coin."

She held up the little thing in her hand, and Cyrene gazed at it with earnest. She didn't know why she felt so drawn to it. Probably because the infuriating thing showed up in her dreams every night.

"Yes?" Matilde asked.

Vera flipped it in her hand as elegantly as Ahlvie did with dice at an inn. "Why would Maelia have this talisman in her possession?"

Cyrene shrugged. "Chance?"

"No," Matilde said. She raised her finger and touched her cheek three times. "Very few talismans can be used by non-magical people, and that girl didn't have a lick of magic about her."

"There are talismans that can be used by people without magic?"

Cyrene asked.

"Well, of course. You've seen one yourself," Matilde said.

Cyrene blankly stared back at her.

"The Mirror of Truth," Vera filled in for her. "Dean doesn't have magic, and he looked into its depths. The Doma book in your possession is a talisman as well."

"The book is a talisman?" she gasped.

"With dire consequences for those who use it who are not worthy."

"They lose time," Cyrene said intuitively.

"But most talismans, including your book, were thought to have been lost before or during the war. Eldora, of course, still has a stockpile, but so many of the others have been lost over time."

"So, the Mirror can be used without magic. Are there others like that? Could this coin be one of them?"

"We're not sure," Vera said with a disgruntled sigh.

"The most notable one is the bridge," Matilde said.

Vera shot her a look of disgust. "Oh, do not even talk about it."

"What's the bridge?" Cyrene asked. She felt like she could sit here and soak up information from them all day and night and never know enough.

"Our own sort of fairy tale," Vera told her.

"Didn't you say all fairy tales were true?"

Matilde shot Vera a look of triumph. "You did, didn't you?"

"Fine," Vera muttered. "The bridge is rumored to be one of the most powerful talismans in the known world. It can take a person between dimensions."

Cyrene stared at her in confusion. "Dimensions?"

"Imagine that there's an infinite number of worlds beyond our own,"

Matilde said. "Other places than where we are right now that exist at the same time as our world."

"Okay," she said reluctantly.

"The bridge is said to transport you to the other side. Essentially, to take you to hell and back," Vera said.

"Why would anyone want that?"

"For one," Matilde told her, "it's rumored that other dimensions have different kinds of magic. That dragons came from another dimension. That you can go through the bridge, and if you prove yourself, you can come back with more power."

"So, as you see," Vera said, "it's a myth. If such a bridge existed, only a fool would enter. Sacrificing your life for the potential payout."

"Or they might have nothing to lose," Cyrene offered.

"Perhaps. Though that is not the here or now. The bridge has never been seen. Even when we were girls, the bridge was just a story. No one had ever actually seen it or knew anyone alive who had gone across it."

"Okay. So, talismans can work for people without magic. Can't we just test it out?" Cyrene asked.

"The problem is," Matilde said, starting the lecture Cyrene knew was coming, "we don't know if these pair of coins could have the same horrid side effects like the Mirror of Truth. I personally knew someone who used a gemstone, expecting it to be an amplifier, and was blinded."

"Oh, poor Marten," Vera whispered. "He was never the brightest."

"What did it do before it blinded him?" Cyrene gasped.

"Eventually, someone realized that it was mirroring visions. You could see what happened through someone else's eyes. Messy business."

"Well, we can't just do nothing," Cyrene told them, standing in frustration. "Serafina told me to use the coin to find the dragons. She couldn't have said that for no reason."

"That's true," Vera agreed.

"Do you recognize the figure or the language on the coin?" Cyrene asked, admiring the female figure and the three mysterious words. "The words feel almost familiar."

"Ah, that," Matilde said with a shake of her head. "It seems as if it's a derivative of Doma."

"Or," Vera added, "Doma is a derivative of it."

"There was something pre-Doma?" Cyrene asked.

"Well, it is possible. Legend says that there is a language of the gods."

"And *this* is a language of the gods? Like, when the Creator herself walked the earth, this is the language she used?"

Vera nodded. "It's possible. We know all known languages, and we don't know this one. Thus, we have to assume it predates even our knowledge."

Cyrene blinked rapidly. *Could I be holding a coin that belonged to the gods? And if I was…was the person in my dream who had given me the coin a god?*

It was too outrageous to even consider.

Gods on earth! Creator!

Vera took a sip of her tea and set it back down. "Cyrene, will you retrieve the book for us? Perhaps there's something we've overlooked in there."

Cyrene nodded and then hurried back to her room. The book was waiting right where she had left it. She snatched it up just as Avoca climbed up through the open window.

"Creator! Can't anyone use the door?" Cyrene gasped.

"Apologies," she whispered.

"Where did you go?"

"Nowhere. I wandered. The city is very dirty."

Cyrene smiled. "You'd think they'd clean that up with all the glass buildings."

"The glass confuses me as well. Why have glass when it's so often covered in snow?"

"I have no idea."

"What are you doing?"

"Ahlvie and Orden went downstairs for food. Matilde, Vera, and I were working on the coin until you got back."

"Well, don't let me keep you."

Cyrene grasped the bond between them and tugged.

Avoca slipped her a smile. "I'm not ready to talk about it."

"Come with me then."

Avoca nodded and followed without complaint. Matilde and Vera didn't seem surprised when she took a seat in the corner and started sharpening her knives. Cyrene passed Vera the book.

"Thank you. You hold on to this and see if you sense anything from it," Vera said.

Cyrene took the coin, and her magic practically sighed with relief. She didn't know what that meant exactly, but she felt connected to this somehow.

"It feels right," Cyrene said. "I wonder if it's because I was given its pair in my dream."

"I wonder if they work together," Matilde hypothesized.

Vera shrugged and flipped the page. "This wasn't exactly our area of expertise. Two thousand years is a long life span, but without tomes such as this one, we were only able to glean new information from the remaining sources in Emporia."

"You could be doing that forever," Avoca muttered.

Cyrene sighed. "We don't have forever."

"We should probably just get the boys and get to the gate before first light. That way, we can be the first ones out of this city and on our way," Avoca said.

"You can do that," Cyrene said with a raised eyebrow.

Avoca shut her mouth and glanced back down at her blade. "Fine."

"*If you channel raw energy from all four elements into the talisman,*" Vera read under her breath, "*the talisman will begin to glow, revealing its true meaning.*"

Cyrene frowned and stared down at the coin. *Is that it? Just channel my energy into the talisman? Well, that's easy.*

She pulled all four elements to her and then pushed it toward the coin.

"No!" Matilde and Vera shrieked at the same time, jumping to their feet.

Avoca was beside them with a blade, ready for whatever was to come.

"What have you done?" Matilde cried.

Cyrene glanced up at them and then down at the coin as it started to rattle and glow fire red. "I…I thought I was following Vera's instructions!"

"I wasn't finished reading!" Vera cried.

"Drop the coin!" Matilde said. "Throw it down! Everyone, take cover."

Cyrene's mouth flew open as she tossed the coin into the center of the room and took a diving roll to avoid whatever she had unleashed. She was huddled behind the chair, shaking from head to toe. She couldn't believe that she had been that stupid. She had thought that the instructions were so clear. But, of course, she should have listened to them and heard the consequences. *I could go blind or insane or be thrust into another dimension! Anything is possible!*

Why did I have to be so reckless? Why couldn't I control the insane urges that took over me?

All she'd had to do was listen, and instead, she'd set the talisman loose with no knowledge of what it could possibly do.

Cyrene's eyes darted down to the innocuous coin in the center of the room. It was as red as hot coals and turned in circles round and round, like a top, before finally falling flat with the figure face up.

Then, before she could cover herself again, she watched the world cleave in two.

Forty Eight

THE COIN

Cyrene screamed and fell backward to get away from whatever was happening. One second, she had been staring at the other side of the room where Matilde, Vera, and Avoca were standing. Now, she was looking down a long hallway. It was made of dark stone, and at the end, she could see a closed door.

She had split the fabric of space.

The coin had taken her…somewhere else.

Of course, she didn't know if the hallway was of this world or if she was staring at the mystical bridge that Matilde and Vera had mentioned.

"Cyrene!" Avoca yelled. The noise sounded muffled, as if coming from a long way off.

"I'm here!" she shouted back.

She tugged on her bond and felt an immediate response. Avoca was fine. They were all fine.

"Do you see this?" Cyrene asked.

"Yes! We're working to fix it!" Avoca called back.

Cyrene finally rose to her feet. Nothing was coming out of the hallway. In fact, there wasn't even anything in the strange hallway, except for some bracketed lanterns. She kept expecting for something to crawl out of the space at any minute. For the darkness she'd had in her dreams to seep into her world and take over. For that hand to reach out and snatch her.

But, besides the crackling of the edges of the space, it was empty. Whatever the coin did, it didn't seem to be inherently dangerous. Perhaps it would have been had she been holding it when the hallway opened. Maybe it would have sliced her body in half as easily as it had popped open in the room.

She had no idea.

But she wondered why Serafina had told her to use the coin to get to this strange hallway. *Were the dragons on the other side of that door? Could it possibly be that easy?*

Her life was never that easy.

She trembled as she neared the strange doorway. When she had first glimpsed it, she had been too afraid to really see what she was looking at. She frowned as she got closer, careful not to touch anything in case it made the vision do something else…like suck her in or kill her. Then, she watched the image ripple before her.

Something about the rock that had built the hallway felt familiar. In fact, the brackets even felt familiar. She narrowed her eyes to look at the door at the end of the hall.

Have I seen that door before?

Then, the handle turned, and she jumped backward.

"Hurry! There's someone at the door!" Cyrene shrieked.

Then, as the door opened and a figure dressed in all black with midnight hair appeared, the vision shook and then vanished. Cyrene gasped, falling backward at the sudden loss of the barrier between her and the other side of the room. She had just been about to see the person in the door, to identify who was there, but it was gone.

"What in the Creator's name was that?" Cyrene gasped. Her eyes were wide with wonder and terror. She felt both excited and sick to her stomach. Whatever she had witnessed was beyond anything she could have ever thought possible.

Matilde grasped the coin between her fingers and shook her head in disbelief. "A portal."

"A...a portal? What does that do?" Her hands were shaking, and she tucked them into the folds of her dress.

"The talisman opens up a passage to a portal."

"It can take you anywhere?"

"No," Vera said. "Talismans are limited. Each portal has its own talisman that allows people to move from one portal to the next. From Eleysia to Eldora, for instance. But this one is an independent talisman, though they were few and far between, even in the magical heyday. It can transport you from a portal to anywhere in the world and then back to any portal you choose."

Cyrene was gaping at them. "You mean, wherever that hallway is...it's a real place?"

"Very," Matilde said.

Avoca looked shaken. "I've seen the portal at Eldora. Mother said all the portal doors were closed after the fall of magic."

Vera nodded. "Yes, that was my understanding. It seems…someone has opened them again."

"Who?" Cyrene gasped. "Who could do that?"

"Did you not recognize the hallway?" Vera asked.

Cyrene racked her brain. It had looked familiar, but she didn't know where it was. But, now that she realized she had been looking at a real place, she knew why it had looked familiar.

"Byern,"

"Yes," Matilde said. "That was the portal door in the Nit Decus castle."

"So…someone opened the portal in Byern," Avoca said.

"Kael," Cyrene said at once. "Kael opened the portal. That was who was in the doorway. But why?"

Matilde and Vera were silent. Their eyes were sad, as if they had already put the pieces together and she was too far behind.

Cyrene glanced from one to the other and then Avoca. *What am I missing?*

"Maelia had the coin, Cyrene," Avoca whispered.

Cyrene stumbled back and took a seat. Her chest ached. "No, you don't think…" She trailed off, unable to say the words clouding her mind. It couldn't be true. It just…couldn't.

"Kael gave the coin to Maelia. He used it to reach her," Cyrene said.

Matilde nodded.

"Do you think he…controlled her? Do you think he's the reason she killed the Eleysian monarchs?"

Vera stood and placed a gentle hand on Cyrene's shoulder. "If it fits together that easily, it is likely the truth."

Cyrene thought of all the times that she had seen Maelia and Kael together. In the gardens back in Byern when she had come across them, unexpected. Maelia had said that she could handle herself. That wasn't true. Then, Maelia had spent all that time with him in Aurum. He'd collected her at Strat, and she'd been in the Aurum capital with him for so long before Cyrene rescued her.

Creator, had any of it been real? Had Kael planted Maelia there that next morning in the Vines to direct me to see Kaliana? Had she been there, waiting for me to get there, knowing I would need directions? She didn't want to believe their friendship was false, but it could have started on false terms. And ended because of him, too.

"He's the reason for her death," Cyrene gasped. "He forced her hand. Made her kill them. Who knows his reasoning for it all? How could he do something so horrible and then take me back to Byern and pretend to be my ally? My friend? To love me?"

Avoca reached for her in the bond, and Cyrene felt so connected to all of them at once that it was almost too much. She shoved to her feet and pushed away from everyone. Her anger grew and grew and grew. All the pain that she had felt all those months. All the anguish.

And she had been content to be around the one person who had caused it all. The person who had shattered her happy life. Who had demanded her return and then made her feel as if *she* was somehow responsible for what had occurred.

Her fingers and hands twitched as magic burned and ignited through them. All she felt was the rage and betrayal. She had actually felt bad for leaving Kael behind in Byern. She had thought that, deep down, he always really wanted her for *her*. He was the only one who never really feared her magic. Who had embraced her as she was.

But she was wrong.

So wrong.

Utterly and unequivocally wrong.

She had sung to his tune. Fallen right into his trap. And been perfectly fine to stay in that state. To even learn magic from him.

"Cyrene!" Avoca called out to her.

She glanced up and realized that they were all trying to reach her, but she had erected some kind of involuntary barrier between her and them. She had shrouded herself in silence and anger.

It hurt that much worse from Kael because he had tricked her. Tricked her into feeling for him. Tricked her into believing in him.

How could she have thought for one minute that she was a child of darkness? There might be darkness in her soul that rattled around like a caged bird. But she was a child of the light.

So, perhaps Kael was right.

They were a matched set.

The Heir of the Light and the Heir of the Darkness, drawn to each other like magnets. Destined to battle at the end.

And she was going to make damn sure that she won.

Cyrene dropped her barrier. She felt a considerable drain on her powers. She had been using anger, the remnants of her blood magic.

"Are you quite through?" Matilde asked.

"You're only going to hurt yourself if you continue to use your energy in that way," Vera said softly.

"I'm fine. I realized why the prophecy is a prophecy," she muttered. "Destiny has a way of catching up with you."

Just then, the door flew open, and Ahlvie and Orden traipsed into the room. They both stopped when they saw all of them standing in a circle around Cyrene with the room a disaster area.

"Uh…did I miss the party?" Ahlvie asked.

"Something like that," Cyrene said.

"We've found a way out of Tahne," Matilde said, straightening her skirts.

"The front door?" Orden asked.

Vera sent him a disapproving look. "We'll need to leave as soon as possible."

And that ended the conversation.

Their bags were swiftly packed, and their horses were removed from the stables.

Cyrene was still in a mood when they rode out of the gate and left the city of Tahne behind. She had barely seen anything in the city itself, and for once, she was grateful. Staying any longer than necessary in a city usually meant trouble. She'd had enough of that for one day. Between being awoken from bed by an Indres and finding out that Kael had sent Maelia to her death, she was glad to not run into any more trouble.

It was leagues of silent seething before Matilde and Vera gestured for them to move off the road. Cyrene had been so lost in her own head that, if Ceffy hadn't been doing all the work for her, she never would have followed in line with everyone else.

"Can someone explain what is going on?" Ahlvie asked finally.

"Oh, you want answers?" Avoca snapped. "Perhaps you would get them if you gave them."

"Avoca," he murmured, "please."

"No!" She held her hand up.

"We're going to use the coin," Vera said to end the argument.

"You figured out its use?" Orden asked in surprise.

"Quite by mistake."

Matilde held the coin in her palm. "I think I've corrected it."

"Corrected it?" Avoca asked.

"Rerouted the end destination," Matilde said.

"Everyone stand back," Vera directed.

They all moved into a single file line, facing an open field.

Matilde took a deep breath and then channeled her energy into the coin. Cyrene could see it flare to life before her eyes, burning red hot. Then, Matilde directed its energy at the open field. Out of nowhere, the field disappeared, and in its place was an empty nothingness.

"What the..." Ahlvie demanded.

"What kind of magic is this?" Orden asked. He didn't sound frightened, just interested.

"Portaling. The talisman allows us to move to any portal in Emporia," Vera explained.

"And from any portal to anywhere we choose as long as we know our destination," Matilde added.

"That looks like we're walking into darkness," Ahlvie said.

"Thank you for pointing out the obvious," Avoca muttered.

"It's dark because the place we are traveling to was destroyed long before we were born," Matilde said. "Now, move through before I break the connection."

Vera used her magic to light a Doma Fire and then moved her horse through the open portal. As soon as she was through, the portal revealed a large moss-covered room.

"It appears deserted," she called to them.

One by one, they moved through the portal. Cyrene lit her own Doma Fire and then went in second to last. As she stepped through, she expected some resistance, like a barrier, but there was nothing. It felt exactly the same as if she had just stepped into the field beyond.

Finally, Matilde entered through the portal, whispered a few words, and then closed her fist over the coin. The open field with Tahne off in the distance disappeared from view, as if they hadn't even been there.

Cyrene glanced around the room. It was even worse than what she had witnessed in Aonia. The place was caved in and had been in such a manner for so long that nature took back over the ruins. The room smelled moldy and stagnant, and she could hear water drip, drip, dripping in the corner.

"This way," Vera whispered, guiding their horses to a closed doorway.

She didn't bother trying to wrench it open. She pried it open with her magic and guided her horse out into the sunlight. They moved out into the open and found themselves at the crest of a hill, surrounded on all sides by an unruly forest. Even in daylight, the trees and forest creatures seemed to lean in to see who their unwelcome visitors were.

"Where are we?" Cyrene whispered.

But it was Avoca who responded with awe in her voice, "The lost Leif city of Isola."

Forty Nine

THE HEIR
—DEAN—

Eleysia was a wasteland.

Dean's heart plummeted at the sight of his once prosperous and flourishing home. It was hard to reconcile the ruins he had seen in Aonia with his home here.

After trekking by horse down to the Keylani, he'd hopped on a Tiekan fishing boat traveling to Albion. From there, he'd found a merchant who agreed to take him as far as Aurum. There, he'd paid to sail a boat into Eleysia. No one would charter into the city. And Dean could see why.

He'd seen it in his vision in the Mirror, of course, but it was entirely different in person. It was desolation and destruction and despair. The buildings were rubble, and the waterways were nearly impossible to wade through. At least one of the districts was still burning.

He finally made it to the heart of Eleysia and to the Lombardy Palace.

His home.

His sanctuary.

Destroyed.

It had taken a direct hit to its structure, destroying the palace and bringing the whole thing to the ground. Anyone who had been inside, including all eleven of his sisters, would have been trapped and killed.

He got out of the boat and searched through the wreckage for a sign of life. But there was nothing. Either everyone was truly dead or no one lived on the Eleysian capital island any longer.

Being here was somehow worse than the vision. That horrible vision.

What had compelled me to look in the Mirror? It was foolish, but he'd had to know. And he'd learned more than he'd ever wanted to. Learned beyond the imagination.

But that wasn't for the here and now.

As the last living heir, he needed to claim the birthright he never thought he would come close to. Though Eleysia was a queendom, without the presence of a female monarch, a male could take the throne as regent until such a time when a queen was crowned.

With a wistful glance at the home he was leaving behind forever, he set his sailboat back onto open waters. Sasra was the closest major Eleysian city to the capital, and he assumed the majority of the survivors had gone there. It was closer than Rasine, though less defensible. Something they'd rarely had to think about until now. Sasra had never been a target before. An army would have had to go through Eleysia, and up until recently…they hadn't believed that to be possible.

It was a short trip into Sasra, but he didn't arrive until late.

Dean could tell immediately that the city was in upheaval. Signs all over the city claimed to have no vacancy. All the inns were full. Food hadn't yet come in to feed the larger population, and prices were astronomical. All for people who had nothing.

He tugged his cloak tighter around him, not wanting to draw any attention to his fine clothes. A hungry crowd could turn into a mob quickly if they were desperate enough.

He turned into the first inn he could find that offered food for good coin. Taking a seat in the dining room with his back to the wall, he observed what had become of his country. The main area of the inn seemed like any other tavern he'd ever been to. Men flirted with the barmaids, loud boasts came from a corner of the room, a handful of men were playing a card game he'd learned in his youth, and a doxy or two roamed the room, hoping someone would have enough coin to pay.

One approached him, dropping her foot on the stool next to him and adjusting her slipper so that he could glimpse up her nearly sheer Eleysian gown. He was more concerned with how thin she was. He could see her ribs, and her arms were beyond frail.

"Need a companion for the night, sailor?" she asked.

Dean flipped her a few coins. "Get some real food and a night's rest."

She trailed her hand down his front. "And what do *you* want in return?"

"I want to know everything that has happened since the capital was bombed."

She batted her eyelashes. "We can have more fun than that."

"Answers. Now."

She narrowed her eyes and glanced around. "That's it? Really?"

"Yes. And be quick about it."

"Well," she said, taking a seat next to him, "after the warships blew up the city, ships were sent in to defend the capital, but there was nuthin' left." Her thick Eleysian accent spilled out of her words when she wasn't trying to seduce him. "There was nuthin' to do but round ever'one up and take 'em here. I know some got through to Rasine, too. But, mostly, we don' have enough food or money or liquor for all the new people. Lot of people are tradin' services for goods."

"I see that," he said. "What about the royals?"

"There ain't no more royals," she said with a grating laugh. "Ellison family was wiped out, and they moved court to Rasine."

Dean grunted irritably. Rasine was another day's trek.

"Who is ruling then?"

The girl shrugged. "Don' know. Some say Anders, and some say Mayhews."

Dean nodded and tried to reel in his anger. Anders and Mayhews. As if either had a right to the throne.

He tossed the girl another coin. "Thanks for all your help."

He disappeared into the night and found his boat exactly where he'd left it. It would have been nice to have another pair of hands, but he'd have to make do. He'd been taught to sail alone if need be, and he was grateful for all his training at this point.

Dean pushed off and traveled farther north. He knew that he probably should have slept through the night in Sasra while he could, but he was too anxious to reclaim his birthright. Eleysia was in desperate need of help.

He docked his boat later the next afternoon, bone-weary and falling over. Making the voyage had been a bad idea. He'd get nothing accomplished in his state. Luckily, he knew Rasine better than Sasra and remembered an inn he'd been to before. Half-delirious, he located the inn, paid the exorbitant price for a room to himself, and promptly passed out.

Dean woke to the sound of the gulls calling and the smell of the salt and sea lingering in his nostrils. The night before came back to him with a sigh. He was not looking forward to what he had to do next.

He stretched and rolled over onto his back. Then, he opened his eyes to face Rasine, ready to take on the city. But he wasn't alone.

Dean swore as filthy as any sailor and sat up. "Darmian!"

"Morning," Darmian said with a grim smile.

Dean's jaw was hanging open. He couldn't believe what he was seeing. Darmian was his guard, his best friend, the man he would do anything for. He'd had to leave Darmian behind when Avoca threatened Darmian within an inch of his life, but Dean had always worried about his safety. In fact, Dean had worried that Darmian was dead.

"I have never been so glad to see you."

"And I, you, sir."

Dean grabbed his shirt off the floor and threw it back on over his head. He reached out and grasped forearms with Darmian, and then he drew him into a hug.

"How did you survive the attack?"

"Good fortune."

"I just passed through to see it. I can't imagine how you could have made it out of the castle. It was demolished." He ran a hand back through his messy hair.

"With luck, we had left the castle and were on our way to a neighboring island for a name day ceremony. We heard the first attack and made it out of the city before it reached us."

"We?" Dean asked. Hope bloomed in his chest, but he didn't want to acknowledge it.

"That's why I came to collect you."

"How did you know where I was?"

Darmian grinned and nodded toward the door. "I've known you your entire life, Captain. When I heard of a sailor dressed finely, wandering around the market district, I hazarded a guess. A hopeful one."

Dean shook his head. "Only you would figure all of that out from such little information."

"I swore an oath to protect you. That hasn't changed. With you gone, it nearly killed me the last couple of months, but I did the best I could."

"You're alive," Dean said. "That's good enough for me."

They exited Dean's room, and Darmian directed them out of the inn. They walked down the crowded market streets. Even this late at night, Rasine hadn't gone to sleep. It was a busy fishing town with the wealthiest district besides the former capital. With the capital gone, the wealthy had just become even wealthier.

"They can still drink and party, despite all that has happened," Dean muttered.

"I think…*because* of what happened, Captain."

"Darmian, how many times have I asked you to call me Dean?"

"Titles are important, sir."

Dean supposed he was right. They moved out of the market district and into one of the more ramshackle parts of town. After a few blocks, Darmian drew Dean down a back alley and through a defaced door.

"Where have you taken me?" Dean asked as he followed him through.

But he stopped dead in his tracks when he saw who was waiting for him.

"Hello, dear brother," Brigette said with a strained smile.

"Your Majesty," he said with a bow.

"Oh, come here!" She pulled him into a hug and seemed to collapse into his weight. "We are the only two left."

"I thought you were gone, too," he whispered in horror. "Why are you in this hovel and not sitting on the throne?"

She glanced at Darmian. "No one knows I'm alive. I was worried…well, Darmian was worried that there would still be a target."

"You let the Anders and Mayhews threaten our queendom?" Dean asked.

"We were waiting for the right time," Darmian interjected. "We have been rallying support behind the Ellison banner. If we had the pair of you together, it would be an even better claim."

"What claim?" Dean demanded. "You are the rightful ruler of Eleysia. No one could challenge your claim."

"It is always better to go into a fight with a trained warrior at your side," Brigette said. "You will be at my side, right? Your ex-fiancée sent her dogs after us, and now, we're ruined. I need you."

"Cyrene didn't do this," Dean said. "The king and prince of Byern did this after I saved her from court."

"It appears that you have a habit of doing that."

"She wasn't a part of Mother's and Father's deaths."

"Death follows that girl everywhere!" Brigette snapped.

"She wasn't in on the plot, and she didn't know that Edric would retaliate. You can lay the blame at my feet if you prefer. Cyrene is innocent."

"You defend her? After all of this? After our parents and then ten of our siblings were slaughtered along with all of our nieces and nephews and thousands of Eleysian citizens?"

"I put the blame where it's due—on the Byern throne. And I think it's time to take the fight to them," Dean said.

"I agree wholeheartedly," Brigette said with a wicked smile. "I cannot believe I ever considered diplomacy. I'm ready to take back my throne and topple those bastards and whoever else thought they could tear us down."

Fifty

THE LOST CITY

"Is it just me, or does this place feel…alive?" Ahlvie whispered, hunching over his horse and peering into the trees.

"No, it's not just you," Cyrene said. "I sense it, too."

"The city has been abandoned for millennia. Civil war tore it asunder. Thousands of Leifs were killed in the great battle, and Isola was ripped inside out. What you are feeling is all the death and slaughter," Avoca said before heeling her horse forward.

"Well, on that pleasant note," Ahlvie said.

He followed behind Avoca regardless. Orden trotted after them, probably to make sure they wouldn't rip out each other's throats.

Cyrene turned to Matilde and Vera, who were conferring with one another. "How did you know to bring us here?"

"We were able to reconfigure the coin to portal us to a different door. I've done it in the past," Matilde said. "Though it was always when I was standing at the gate myself. I've never had an independent portaling talisman. So, I wasn't sure if it would work."

"But we knew that Isola had a gate, and it would be the least likely to have people around it. Also, it was the closest to the human settlement in Alba," Vera said.

"The capital city of Kell?" Cyrene gasped. "We just traveled all the way across the world in one step?"

"The joys of portaling," Matilde said with a keen smile.

Cyrene shook her head in disbelief. It was unbelievably efficient. She couldn't imagine walking all the way anywhere ever again. Not if she could just open a door and walk straight through it to wherever she wanted to go. Or at least anywhere where there was a portal.

"Cyrene," Vera said, "will you take a look at this?"

She turned to face the twins again and peered over Vera's shoulder. She was holding the two coins in her hands.

"Did you figure out what the words mean?" Cyrene asked.

"No," Matilde said irritably. "Vera is the scholar though."

"You always were the politician, which baffles me." Vera grinned at her sister. "What we wanted you to look at is whether or not you see any differences. We were able to change the location of our portal with Maelia's coin, but this one, the one you received in your dream, it doesn't seem to work. Or if it does work, it will not let either of us open it up."

Cyrene frowned. "Do you think I should try it?"

Matilde shook her head. "If it were a regular portal, it would open up for us as well. It should open up for anyone with enough energy to power it."

"We worry about this woman you described. If Serafina was trying to keep you away from her, I'm not sure we should use the coin she handed to you," Vera said. "It might be best to wait until we have more information."

Cyrene nodded. "I won't use it."

She understood where they were coming from, but she didn't know how long it would take for her to access her spirit magic. But using the coin and possibly meeting the woman that Serafina was warning her against didn't sound like her idea of a good time.

Vera handed the coin over to Cyrene, and she observed the front. It didn't feel any different. Holding the coins in each hand, she couldn't see anything at all that marked them differently. The only difference was that one had been given to Maelia by Kael and one was given to Cyrene by a strange woman. If it couldn't open or work for the twins it had to be because of that.

"Nothing. I'm sorry," she said, passing them back.

"We wondered," Matilde said with a pensive look, "if we might be able to put you under in a sort of trance. It seems that your visions hit you when you are at your most vulnerable, like after passing out or during your blood magic detox. We could see if we could put you into a state where you could communicate with Serafina before you mastered spirit."

"You could ask her more questions, and you might be more prepared if you can control when you enter the vision," Vera added.

Cyrene's face split in two. "Absolutely! I would love to be able to get more answers. She was always worried about having enough time. We were always getting torn apart. I think it would be—"

But she didn't get to say what she thought because a savage war cry went up all around them.

Cyrene instantly reached for her magic, calling it to her with ease after hours and hours of practice. It still wasn't perfect. She still had her moments of weakness. Sometimes, she could even feel the craving of the blood magic seeping through her, but right now, she was in her element.

They rushed as a unit to where they had had heard the cry. Ceffy broke through the tree line, and Cyrene gaped at what she saw before her. The view was stunning. Isola stood on the top of a long, sloping hill. From so high up, they could see all the way down the grassy slopes to Lake Mische, which was so large that it was impossible to see the other side from any point around its mystical depths.

But even more shocking were the thirty or so warriors clad in all black, surrounding Avoca, Ahlvie, and Orden. Avoca's wrists were bound before her. Cyrene could feel her holding on to her magic tight, but there was something…odd about it. It didn't feel quite right. Ahlvie and Orden, it seemed, had been completely disarmed, which was truly *incredible*. Both were excellent swordsmen. Ahlvie was practically rippling as he tried to control himself from turning into an Indres.

Cyrene was about to move forward to attack, not even caring that they were all clearly outnumbered, but Matilde reached for her.

"No," she whispered.

Vera was stark white in shock, but her voice was strong. "We mean you no harm. We believed the area to be deserted. If you will release our friends, we will leave here and never speak of this meeting."

A man as broad-shouldered and muscular as Cyrene had ever seen moved forward to take point. "Unfortunately, we cannot allow that to happen. Your people must suffer the consequences for attacking a Guild member and trespassing."

"What are the consequences?" Matilde asked, docilely holding her hands before her.

"That is up to the leaders to decide." He nodded his head at a few of the people to his left. "Tie them up. We'll see what the Honorary has to say about this."

"What should we do?" Cyrene hissed.

"Nothing," Vera said.

"What the hell do you mean, nothing?"

"If we act, they will kill the others."

"How do you know that?"

"Because we've encountered them before," Matilde said. "Many years ago. Many, many years ago."

Vera sighed. "We left them unchecked, and the problem has only gotten worse. I knew that we should have come to Kell sooner. Two hundred years is too long between visits."

"Don't try to blame this on me," Matilde said.

"You do hate the snow."

"Everyone hates the snow."

"Can you two stop it for one minute?" Cyrene snarled. "Who are these people?"

A man approached her to tie her up, and she retreated away from him. She was not going to go down easy for nothing.

"Do not touch me," she warned.

The man gave her a piercing look. "You are only making this harder on yourself."

"Thanks for the tip," she said before shooting past him and blasting her way through the first row of people in her attempt to reach her friends.

She made it as far as the incredibly built man before she was thoroughly knocked off her horse with a blast of something so sharp that it felt as if her entire body had been sliced open. She cried out as she hit the ground and rolled out of the blow. She stared down at the dress she'd worn out of Tahne, expecting to see a slash down the fabric…but there was nothing.

Her mouth opened wide in shock as she stared at the man. He'd dismounted in the time that it took her to get her bearings again.

"What did you just *do*?" she gasped.

The man flicked back his hood, and she stared up into his churning gray eyes. His dark hair was pulled back into a topknot. From top to bottom, he was sculpted and etched and chiseled into a weapon.

"Someone should teach you some manners." He snatched up her wrists and bound them in a tight black rope.

She struggled against him, but after the knot was tied…she couldn't seem to manage it. She reached for her powers, but nothing was there. She could sense her magic. It hadn't been stripped from her, but it was out of her reach.

"What is this?" she demanded.

"A necessary precaution, spitfire," he said with a cocky grin. "Now, get on your horse, and try to keep your tongue under control, or you might have another tumble, and I might not be so gentle next time."

Cyrene glared at him, and called him a pretty spectacular list of vulgar names, but he grabbed her by the waist and threw her back up onto Ceffy. Ceffy bucked against him, and he just laughed. He stroked her nose twice and then gave her a treat from his own bag. Ceffy sidled right up to him after that.

Traitor.

The Guild, as they called themselves, pushed them into a single file line. Matilde and Vera willingly offered up their hands to be tied, but Cyrene had no idea why. How could they want to be taken away from their magic?

But she never got a chance to ask. The big, muscular brute had decided she was the troublemaker, which wasn't entirely wrong, rode next to her.

"Where are you taking us?" Cyrene demanded.

He grinned at her. All feral predator and barely contained aggression. "To the Guild leader."

"You're not the leader? I'm shocked."

"I lead these people but not everyone."

"How many more of you are there?"

He pulled his hood back up. "Trying to assess our numbers won't help you."

Cyrene humphed. "Are you at least going to tell me your name?"

"Names are very expensive," he said with a look that said he wasn't joking. "What will you give me for it?"

"What do you *want* for it?" she asked, befuddled.

This man was even more confusing than Ahlvie, and that was a feat.

"Don't ask questions you won't like the answer to, spitfire."

Cyrene snapped her mouth closed. Perhaps antagonizing their leader wasn't a good place to start. But she couldn't believe that they had been outmaneuvered so efficiently. *Who are these Guild people? What are they doing in Isola? And what did they want with us?*

She got no answers the hours that they trekked through the forest around Isola and out onto the open plains that led toward Alba. They came upon the sprawling city at twilight, and Cyrene barely got to see anything. As soon as they were inside the grounds, a hood was thrown over each of their heads. Cyrene swore at their leader when he did it, but he chuckled and hurled insults back at her.

Cyrene tried to memorize all the twists and turns they were taking, but it seemed they were purposely taking her on an indirect route. Soon, she lost track and sat back hard into Ceffy with frustration. She was lost, imprisoned, and without access to her magic.

Finally, they entered a room, and their hoods were ripped off. Cyrene's eyes adjusted to the dim lighting. They were in a cavernous room about the size of three ballrooms back home. At least a hundred people were inside. Almost all of them were fighting or going through some kind of exercise. A few trainers walked around the room and made corrections.

But, from what Cyrene could gather…*all* of them had magic.

Every. Single. One.

"How is this possible?" she whispered.

Her new *friend* shook his head and dragged her past the trainees. They moved to the front of the room where a panel of men and women were watching what was going on with keen eyes.

"Good to have you back, Commander," a man said. "Though it is unexpected. Did your men complete the exercise so quickly?"

"Unfortunately, our operation was cut short due to these six trespassers on Guild land."

A woman raised a highly arched eyebrow. "You allowed six people into your camp? How?"

"They appeared out of nowhere. We had wards up, and they didn't trigger them until they were already in the heart of Guild territory."

"Hmm," the woman said, tapping her finger to her mouth. "Interesting."

"Who speaks for these people?" a man with a thick, bushy mustache asked.

"I do," Cyrene spoke up.

She heard a groan from behind her. Yes, she was sometimes rash, but these *were* her people. She had brought them here, and she would put herself in the line of fire for them.

"Very well. What are you doing in Guild territory, and why were you trespassing on our ancient grounds?"

"We were unaware that this was Guild territory. By the time we realized it, we were ambushed and dragged here against our will," Cyrene told them.

"This girl," he said, pointing to Avoca, "injured one of my men as well."

The woman's mouth popped open in surprise. "A mere human managed to touch one of you?"

"She has Guild energy," he added reluctantly. "Along with these three. We have them tied off, so they can't do anything rash."

"Four foreigners with the energy," the man said, "and they just *happened* onto Guild property while you were there. That seems rather suspect. Are the lords conspiring again? I would love to cut off Dahl's head and deal with his arrogant but obedient son."

"Truly, I have no idea what you're talking about," Cyrene said. "We were simply passing through."

"What she says is true," Matilde cut in. "We submitted to your men without a fight."

The commander scoffed.

"It was a mistake, and it will not happen again. We thought that the area had been abandoned for some time," Vera added.

The woman held up her hand. "Foreign trespassers are subject to Guild law, as is everyone in the Triangle."

Cyrene glanced from person to person. The Triangle was the three war-torn countries of Kell, Mastira, and Harthrow, but she had never heard anything about this Guild.

"We apologize for anything that we did wrong. We were unaware of this Guild or Guild law," Cyrene added.

The woman turned to the man, and he nodded.

"The girl," she said, pointing at Avoca, "will be broken like a prized horse. If she survives, then you can go free."

Avoca seethed. "I will not be broken."

The man leaned forward and grinned. "We'll see."

"The rest of you can try to earn your own freedom once she fails," the woman added. "Except you." Her eyes were fixed on Cyrene. "I believe my commander wouldn't mind keeping you."

Cyrene balked at the suggestion. "She will win. We will all win. And, when we are done, I will teach you what it means to be broken."

Fifty One

THE RING
—AVOCA—

The commander cut the ties on Avoca's wrists. She flexed her magic like a living, breathing extension of her body. She never again wanted to be parted from it.

She rolled her shoulders and glared at the commander. "You have made a terrible mistake."

"We'll see." He grinned. "You're to fight a trained Guild member to the death. You can use anything at your command. There are no rules."

Avoca snarled at him, "I would like my blades back then."

His head snapped to the administrators of their fate. The woman nodded. Someone went to retrieve her blades from a pack. Suddenly, they were flying across the room, aimed straight at her head. She grinned at the challenge and then unleashed her Leif abilities, launching her body into a twisting roll and catching them midair.

The commander had the good sense to look impressed. It was damn good that he did. She had had more than a hundred years to sharpen her fighting skills. And she had done it for much of that time without magic as a crutch. She doubted some newborn assassin had a chance against her.

"Who will take on the woman?" the commander called into the crowd.

Avoca turned to face that crowd with the poise of her people. She was ready for slaughter. Then, a woman stepped up to face her. She was at least six feet tall and built like a mountain.

"I will take on the bitch," she said.

A war cry went up around the room, and all Avoca could hear over the stomping of feet was one word repeated like an anthem.

Lynx.

Avoca didn't know who this Lynx was, nor did she care. She was dressed in all black, like the rest of them, and had a huge staff in her hand that had an arrowhead on one end.

The room cleared as a ring opened up for their match. Avoca brushed past Cyrene, who was staring at the commander with murder in her eyes.

The commander turned his eyes on Cyrene. "You. Here."

"I'm not a dog," she bit out.

"Shall I make you into one? You'd look nice on all fours."

Avoca shook her head. Cyrene and the commander were a complication. She could already tell that he was attracted to her. If she didn't get them out of this, then she was sure he would take Cyrene for himself. That was absolutely not something she could live with. She would win this challenge, and that would be the end of it.

Avoca stalked Lynx in a tight circle as she assessed her opponent's skill and weaknesses. Lynx was heavier, which meant that she was slower. Avoca knew that it was to her advantage that she was slight and appeared young and innocent. No one suspected that she was over a hundred years old, and clearly, they believed her to be human. Lynx had strength and muscle going for her, which meant she had bulk and reach. Avoca needed to be light on her feet. Get in and out and never within arm's reach.

Avoca waited. She could see the girl tense before her. Not the best of their lot if she was showcasing where she was going to strike. Avoca held on to the fierce, quiet calm that settled in her bones before a fight. She was ready.

Lynx jumped forward, exactly how Avoca had anticipated. She was ready for her opponent. Though not as ready for the amount of speed and agility that she demonstrated for a girl of her size. Avoca let her surprise show blatant on her face. She always kept her emotions under tight guard, but she knew that she could use them to her advantage.

The girl saw Avoca's face and took the bait, rushing right into Avoca's defenses. Avoca's smile was feral when she aimed a quick jab for the girl's throat. Lynx barely blocked it before dodging the next hit Avoca threw as well. But she had thrown Lynx off.

Right from the start, it was clear that Avoca would win this. However, with the way she and her friends had been treated, Avoca had no intention of letting her go easy.

Lynx dashed for her again, throwing her spear up at the last second. Avoca met her with her blades. She backed up as the assault continued.

Then, with fluid agility, she whirled in place, batted aside the staff, and sliced across Lynx's cheek.

Lynx bared her teeth. "That's the last time you'll get close enough for that."

"We'll see."

Lynx took more caution in her second pass. Avoca had an advantage that Lynx hadn't been expecting, and Lynx couldn't just barrel in. With more finesse, she came forward with her staff. Avoca took a small breath before digging into the battle. She parried the blows with her blades. The girl was trained; Avoca would give her credit for that. Whatever was happening with these Guild members, they knew how to fight at least. Not like a Leif but well enough.

Avoca was lost in her head for half a second too long when Lynx took a practiced swing and knocked one of Avoca's blades from her hand. Avoca ground her teeth together. *Clumsy.*

Lynx jabbed forward, and Avoca was still reeling from the blow that she couldn't get out of the way quick enough. The blunt end of the staff rammed into her stomach.

Avoca took the hit, and with a whoosh, all the air left her lungs. Not good. She needed to keep her head in this. Lynx came at her while she tried to catch her breath, and Avoca pivoted. She dropped to the ground and swept her leg out at Lynx. Her legs buckled, and all six feet of her toppled over. It was like watching a tree fall.

Avoca jumped to attack with her blade, but Lynx rolled away from her and came to her feet in a crouch.

There were no more chants. No more jeers. This was life or death. They had thought she was an easy target, and with one of their fighters, it should have been easy. But she was anything but an easy fight. This was what she had been trained for her entire life.

Lynx leaped to her feet and raised her staff. Now, she fought with anger. Avoca could see it gleaming in her eyes. She rushed forward, slamming into Avoca. She pushed her back and back and back. Avoca let her. She let the girl think that she was making headway, but instead, all Avoca was doing was tiring Lynx out. Making her use up all her stored energy, burn it out on the anger. Then, when she least expected it, Avoca shifted and pressed her out of the circle. As she shoved Lynx, she brought her blade down on her arm, slicing it open from shoulder to elbow.

The girl snarled like an animal and jabbed the tip of the staff toward Avoca's arm. It grazed across her milky-white skin, and Avoca gasped. The jagged edge cut deeper than even her blades. She sidestepped the next pass and took the defensive as she eased pressure off that arm. Back in Eldora, it would have been an embarrassment to suffer such a cut. She would not allow it a second time.

Just as Lynx shot out for Avoca again, a roar erupted from nearby. Goose bumps exploded on her skin, and her eyes cut away from the fight.

Her eyes locked on Ahlvie as he shifted fully into his monstrous Indres form. Everyone was paralyzed with fear and confusion. It was practically palpable as they beheld the beast who had just stood as a human moments before.

Ahlvie took off toward her, as if the scent of her blood had triggered some innate reaction within him. She knew that she could do nothing to stop him as he pounced on top of Lynx. The girl's screams were drowned out by the sound of him ripping out her throat.

The room erupted into chaos. Avoca went into fighting mode. Though her thoughts about Ahlvie were jumbled at the moment, she could not deny that he had acted to save her life. No matter that she'd had the fight exactly where she wanted it, he'd rushed for her, and now, she would fight at his side.

Time had no meaning as she fought against the Guild members all around her. Ahlvie was taking on many more than would have been physically possible in his human form. She felt a tug from Cyrene and knew what she was trying to say, even from a distance, even without looking for her.

They were outnumbered, and they had the advantage of surprise.

"Let's get out of here!" she shouted at Ahlvie.

He roared and then scattered the crowd before her. He was cutting them a path for the exit, and she followed in his wake, scooping up her discarded blade as she ran.

They were out of the warehouse with only a few remaining Guild following them. She made quick work of them now that she was not on display and then hurried down the unfamiliar corridors. It was clear that Ahlvie was locating the exit by scent alone. She didn't know if they would have found it so quickly otherwise.

They exited onto an empty street and moved into the shadows. They dashed into the nearest stable. The horses nickered at Ahlvie's appearance. Then, Ahlvie rippled and changed before her eyes. She still wasn't used to this new version of him. The change that had taken over him. The enemy under his skin.

He lay on the ground, his body covered in blood, naked as the day he had been born.

Avoca tossed her cloak over him. He groaned and tugged it tight around him before slowly rising to his feet.

"I…I don't know what came over me," Ahlvie said.

"I do not either," she said.

He frowned and glanced off. "I couldn't stand to see you hurt. I had to protect you."

"I was doing fine. I can protect myself. You know I would have won."

He nodded. "I do. It wasn't because I believed you were not formidable."

"Then, why?" Her voice was tight.

She didn't know if she could endure this. This was *Ahlvie*. The man full of sunlight and lies, trickery and savagery. The man who made her skin tingle and a smile touch her features. The man who knew her, understood her.

Yet Indres were her enemy. And keeping that from her was a different sort of lie. One she could not possibly understand…and had no idea how she could forgive. Did not believe she would ever forget.

"When I smelled your blood and knew you were in danger, it was like my brain exploded. I went completely insane. Something snapped, and I had to protect you. I didn't care what I had to do or who I had to kill to get to you. You were the only thought in my head."

"So, it was your Indres instincts," she said, shuddering at the idea.

"Not entirely, but I can no longer deny that it is part of who I am. No more than I can deny that I love you."

Avoca nodded once. She didn't have words for that. She didn't know how to respond to it.

Love was…

It was enough.

For now.

She nodded her head at him and then glanced away.

"Avoca, please," he said, reaching for her.

"No." She shook her head. "I need more time."

"I am still the same man that you fell for."

"Are you?" she asked.

"Aren't you tired of the prejudice against Leifs, against you? Can't you imagine that I have been sick of the way people have treated me my entire life, and *this* only makes it worse?"

"I cannot help how I feel."

"But you can help how you react to it. I didn't choose this," he said vehemently. "It chose me."

"And I chose you," she reminded him. "But I don't have to."

He stumbled back a step. "Avoca…"

"I…cannot come to terms with being with a monster."

"That's what I am to you?" he asked in disbelief.

"You are a six-sided die." Their eyes met as she spoke his language, "Every time we are together, you roll the dice, and I only have one chance of winning."

"I'm not wagering on our love."

"Why not? You wager on everything else," she whispered as she moved back to the entrance to wait for Cyrene.

She could sense him behind her, desperate to reach out, desperate for more. But she was glad that he didn't approach her. Didn't see the silent tears running down her face.

THE GUILD

Chaos broke out around the room, as if the place were up in flames. Cyrene's mouth dropped open, but instinct took over. She shouted through the bond for Avoca to get herself out as soon as she could. Orden had somehow wrestled a sword from an unsuspecting victim and was slicing through the bindings on Matilde's and Vera's wrists. She rushed to their side but was hastily scooped up by the commander.

"What in the bloody hell did you bring here?" he demanded.

She elbowed him in the side. "Let me go."

"I'd do as she said," Matilde ruthlessly said with a fireball in her hand. Her dark hair had fallen out of its bun, and she looked like a fire-wielding goddess.

"I could kill her before you ever hope to reach me."

"But you won't. That is not in line with your code," Vera said. Ice had started crawling its way up her arms, and the path around her was frozen solid.

"Release her. Now," Matilde said.

Orden was holding the rest of the group at bay while Avoca and Ahlvie fought their way out of the room.

"You will regret this," the commander said, pushing Cyrene toward them. "The Guild does not forgive slights. We will come after you tenfold. There is not a place in all of Emporia that we do not touch."

"I find that hard to believe," Vera said before freezing his feet to the ground.

His eyes widened at the ease with which she had done it. He opened his mouth, as if to ask a question, but Matilde released her fireball, and suddenly, the place was *actually* on fire.

Orden grabbed Cyrene's wrists and snapped through the rope. Her magic released, and she sighed with relief. She used her pent-up energy to blast the wave of fighters away from them. Then, as they were disoriented and the ceiling started to cave in from the fire, they made a dash for the exit.

Cyrene could feel a tug from Avoca, guiding them out of the Guild headquarters and through the maze. They exited onto an empty street in an abandoned part of town. They barreled down the road, keeping to side streets as much as they could, before they came upon the stable where Avoca was standing watch. They all ducked inside and out of the cold.

"You're safe," Cyrene said, embracing Avoca.

"Yes. We made it fine."

"Where is Ahlvie?"

"Here," he said, returning in ill-fitted breeches and an unbuttoned shirt.

"Had to sneak into the house and find something to wear. Imagine if one of the ladies had walked in on me, naked and rummaging through their drawers."

"In Kell, it would be tantamount to losing your head," Vera said. "Kell is extremely prudish and undeniably religious. They take their prayers to the Creator very seriously."

"What in the Creator's name was that place?" Avoca demanded, turning her back on Ahlvie. "Fighting for my life after *they* ambushed us?"

"The Guild," Orden said with a sigh.

"You know of it?" Matilde asked in surprise.

"I don't just know it. My master was trained in it."

Everyone stared at him, agog.

"They're practically a sacred organization within the Triangle."

"But what are they?" Cyrene asked.

"Assassins," Orden said simply.

"You were trained as an assassin?" Ahlvie asked. "Come on! You've been holding out on me."

"I was not trained as an assassin. I am a man of honor. After my sister, Lissa, died, I left the court at Aurum, and I disappeared into the Sand Plains, determined to end it all. I came across a man who saw my potential and offered to train me. I was foolish and believed myself already a skilled swordsman. I spent five precious years learning I was wrong and heard more stories than you could possibly fathom about my master's life here in the Guild."

Cyrene's heart broke. Orden offered very little about his history. She had always respected his privacy but found his backstory to be so fascinating.

"I think the important thing that has changed about the Guild since we were last here," Matilde said, "is that they train with magic. Though they have little knowledge of what they're actually doing. It is clear that they believe their energy, as they call it, is bound to their fighting skills. The ropes, once sliced, couldn't tie off our powers any longer."

"A huge misstep in their magical education," Vera said.

"That's why you weren't worried?" Cyrene asked.

Vera nodded once. "For all their skill, they are untrained in the ways of the Doma."

"But are formidable as assassins here," Orden said. "They freely walk around without retribution. People allow them into their homes without complaint. Assassins are the way of the world here, and *no one* turns against them."

"Well," Ahlvie said with an indulgent shrug, "there's a first time for everything."

Cyrene shook her head at Ahlvie. Of course, that would be his takeaway. "We need to find a safe place for the night and then get out of Alba as soon as we can."

"An inn would not be a good idea," Matilde said. "Not if what Orden says is true of the Guild."

"We no longer have contacts in the city," Vera said. "I knew we should have come here sooner."

"I truly do hate the snow," Matilde said.

They continued quarreling when a light bulb struck Cyrene.

"Creator! Why didn't I think of it before?"

"What?" Ahlvie asked.

"We're in Alba."

"Yes. Thank you for that assessment."

"My sister Aralyn lives here. She is the Ambassador to Kell."

"Do you know where she has been staying?" Orden asked.

"Would she house us?" Vera asked.

"Can she be trusted?" Matilde added.

"Yes, I believe so. The Ambassadorship comes with accommodations, usually in the castle, but I know Kell is different because they are an aristocracy and run by a group of lords. The last I heard, she was staying with Lord Berg."

Orden startled. "Berg? As in, Larsen Berg?"

Matilde pursed her lips. "Even we've heard of him."

"Yes, he's merciless," Vera confirmed.

"Do we have another option?" Cyrene asked.

Everyone looked around at each other and then shook their heads. No, this was the only option they had. No one else was familiar with anyone who was still living in Kell. Even Matilde and Vera hadn't been in the city in two hundred years.

"I know where the Bergs live," Orden said. "I can take us to their residence."

"How much time have you spent in the city?" Cyrene asked.

He shot her a cunning grin. "More than I care to admit."

"Then, let's go before the Guild puts out the fire we started."

Everyone filed out of the barn. They took off at an easy jog through the streets of Alba. Cyrene was terrified about their tracks being visible in the snow, but Matilde waved her hand at the road, and they vanished.

"How did you do that?"

"Wind. You do it," Matilde said. "You have enough strength."

Cyrene sighed and wished she hadn't asked. But, by the time they reached the mysterious Lord Berg's house, Cyrene was an expert at covering their tracks. And she felt light as a feather. As if she could have done that all day. Magic might be the most addictive substance on earth.

They looked at Lord Berg's impressive mansion from a side street. Orden wanted to sweep the perimeter before approaching the house. He, Avoca, and Ahlvie disappeared, promising to make sure they hadn't been followed as well. Cyrene huddled in her cloak and wished she had poor Ceffy and the winter gloves that she'd received from Mana back in Fen.

"There's one thing I don't understand. How do they all have magic?" Cyrene asked. "I thought magic was gone."

Matilde frowned. "Magic has never really disappeared, but we were as baffled as you were by the amount of natural-born Doma users."

"It seems magic has gone underground. You can still find it, but no one is using it in plain sight any longer," Vera added. "The Guild is a trained assassin group. They are respected, but no one, not even them, realize what they're doing is magic."

"Then, they're fools," Cyrene said.

"The most dangerous ones always are," Matilde said.

Orden appeared at her elbow then. "I think it might be best if I approach the lord first. He will respect a title that he understands. Then, I can find out if your sister is in fact in residence still."

Cyrene nodded. "Be careful."

She watched as Orden crossed the empty street and knocked on the door. A butler answered, and they had a quick conversation. From the looks of it, the man didn't want to speak with Orden at such an hour. Cyrene was ready to break into the house herself when the man finally gave a disgruntled nod and allowed Orden to move inside.

Ahlvie and Avoca appeared a few minutes later. It was a freezing half hour in which they were all blanketed in snow before Orden appeared at the door once more. He looked worried. Even for him.

"Thank you, Lord Berg. I greatly appreciate your assistance."

Orden bowed crisply and then walked across the street.

"What happened?" Cyrene demanded when Orden appeared.

"Lord Berg refuses to house us. Also, he claims to have never heard of an Ambassador Aralyn from Byern."

"What?" Cyrene asked. "How is that possible?"

"However," Orden continued, unfazed, "Lady Berg briefly spoke to me while Lord Berg went to fetch us some fine Kelltic vodka and told me not to listen to her husband. That she would be happy to house me and my friends for the night."

"That's nice of her," Matilde said with suspicion in her voice.

"She told me to come around to the back after Lord Berg went to sleep, and she would bring us inside and deal with Lord Berg herself."

"I'm shocked that a lady would sidestep her husband in such a way," Vera said.

"She is a formidable woman."

"Well," Cyrene said, "my gut says to go with it. What do you all think?"

"We have no other choice," Orden said.

Everyone nodded, and then they set out to wait for Lord Berg to retire. Orden claimed that he took a cigar out on his balcony every night and then promptly went to bed afterward. Cyrene practiced warming them all up while they waited. She was getting better and better at it. Even Ahlvie didn't complain as she worked on it.

"This is getting good," Vera said with a warm smile. Probably because they weren't all freezing now.

"Why do you think that is? When we first started, I could barely do anything that wasn't catastrophic."

"Magic has a way of things. You had a block against your powers. You didn't believe in magic, and you didn't believe in yourself. You might have learned your powers wrong in Byern, but once you started over, you retained that confidence about your abilities. You complain, but you don't second-guess yourself. You are strong," Matilde said. "You learned that yourself, and now, your abilities and the way you master them *should* happen more naturally."

"Plus, you have me," Avoca added. She reached through the bond and turned up the heat on Cyrene's magic.

"Yes, the bond definitely helps. You learn faster together," Vera agreed.

"I think it's time," Orden said, watching Lord Berg snuff out his cigar and then disappear back inside.

They waited another ten minutes before hurrying to the back of the house and waiting for Lady Berg to let them inside. Cyrene prayed to the Creator that this wasn't a trap. Her little band of followers needed one easy break right about now.

Miraculously, the door swung open, and Lady Berg's face appeared at the door. She was dressed in a fine dark green dress, and her hair was pulled back into a twist. Her eyes were wide and blue and startlingly familiar.

"Aralyn?" Cyrene gasped.

Fifty Three

THE AMBASSADOR

"Cyrene?" Aralyn said, her mouth falling open.

"*You* are Lady Berg?"

"Yes!" Aralyn said. "I…I wanted to tell you. I did!"

"Oh my Creator!" She tugged her sister into her arms.

It had been a year since she had seen Aralyn. The last time had been at her own Presenting back in Byern. Aralyn hadn't even been able to make it for Elea's Presenting…nor for their parents' funeral. Now, she was…married?

"You came all this way?" Aralyn asked in shock. "I know I should have made it back for Mother and Father. How awful!"

"It was," Cyrene said solemnly.

Thinking about her parents opened up that gaping wound that she always associated with her blood magic. She never really had time to grieve what had happened, and instead, she'd just been soldiering forward at a relentless pace.

"How was the service?"

"It was…" Cyrene shook her head. "It was."

"I know."

"You missed Elea, too," she said quickly.

"Yes. But she made Affiliate, of course."

"She did."

Cyrene almost came out and said that she was consort now, but then she realized that wouldn't help anything. Not why she was here or what she was doing. She was still in shock, just seeing her sister. All she wanted to do was divulge all her secrets and be kept close for once. But that wasn't her destiny.

An abrupt cough sounded behind them.

"Oh, where are my manners?" Aralyn said. "Please come in, out of the cold."

Aralyn stepped back, sweeping her long skirts out of the doorway, and ushered Cyrene and all of her traveling companions inside. They entered a great room with a crackling fireplace on either end. The marble beneath their feet was white and gleaming, and the incredible stonework had to have come from the Barren Mountains. Kell was renowned for its stone masonry.

Aralyn closed the door behind them and escorted them across the room. They entered a lavish sitting room where tea and biscuits were set out for guests. The party appropriately arranged themselves around the room, but Cyrene turned back to Aralyn.

"So…you're married," Cyrene got out.

Color rose in Aralyn's cheeks, and her hand went to her stomach. "Yes. We were married in a Kelltic ceremony two years ago."

"Two…years ago!" Cyrene gasped. "You came home for my Presenting last year and told no one?"

"You seem to be keeping quite a few secrets yourself," Aralyn said. Her eyes flickered over to Ahlvie's face in the corner. He had been trying to hide himself from her. "Like consorting with criminals."

"Ahlvie is not…" Cyrene began and then stopped. "Ahlvie did not kill Leslin. That was a misunderstanding."

Ahlvie grinned and gave her a low bow. "Lady."

"I believe all of this is beside the point," Vera said smoothly. "We are quite grateful for your hospitality."

"It is a rare gift in this world to have such a way with people," Matilde added.

"We are much appreciative," Avoca added.

"Well, I believed that I was helping an Aurumian lord and his close friends who had gotten in late. My husband is very strict with his rules. Calling on him after hours went against his sensibilities, but I couldn't let you all stay out in the cold. I hardly expected my sister, who is supposed to be studying in Byern, to be here."

She looked from one person to the next, as if expecting an explanation. She finally settled on Matilde and Vera, gathering that they were the leaders of this bunch. But their eyes shifted to Cyrene to ask what was appropriate to say to her sister.

Her other two siblings knew about her magic now, but could she tell Aralyn? Burden her with the information? Aralyn was the most logical and sensible of the four of them. Cyrene knew how she would react. Poorly. It wasn't worth the risk.

"Well?" Aralyn asked, shifting to Cyrene.

"It is part of my Affiliate training," she lied.

"Part of your training? No, the queen would never have let you leave before your two years in residency were up."

"Kaliana recently had a baby girl. She is a bit more lenient than she was when you were last there."

Again, Aralyn's hand drifted to her stomach. "A royal princess?" Her eyes lit up. "How wonderful! I am sure that she and King Edric are so pleased."

It took a great deal of effort for Cyrene to keep her face passive. Aralyn truly knew nothing of court.

"I can't really speak about what I'm doing here, Aralyn. I'm sorry."

Aralyn sighed and waved her off. "If it's important, then you'll share it with me. I am not going to leave you on the streets because you refuse to be frank with me. But you will have to give a better explanation to my husband in the morning. Lord Berg is *excellent* at detecting a lie. He is renowned for it. So, pick a truth, and stick with it."

"Thank you, Aralyn," Cyrene said, pulling her sister in for another hug.

Aralyn opened her mouth to respond when a pitter-patter of feet was heard down the hall. Then, a little boy burst into the room. He only came up to Aralyn's knee and kept tripping over his white dressing gown while tugging on his cap.

"Mamá! Mamá!" the boy cried. "The demons are trying to get me again."

"Laine, darling," Aralyn said, hoisting the boy up onto her hip, "what have I told you about demons?"

"But Papá says they do exist!"

She brushed his blond mop of hair back off of his face. "Demons are not real. But I will come up to check under your bed if you like."

The boy nodded vigorously and then seemed to notice he had an audience. Cyrene was staring at him, slack-jawed. Everyone else had seemed to grow still.

"Mamá, who's this?" Laine asked with wide-eyed wonder.

"Oh, you will never go to sleep now," she said with a sigh. "Might as well explain. Laine, darling, this is my sister Cyrene."

"You have a sister?"

"Yes. Two. Remember I told you they lived very far away."

"Why's she here?" he asked with the inquisitiveness only small children mastered.

"She's here to visit. She was desperate to meet you," Aralyn said, nuzzling his neck. "Well, Cyrene," Aralyn said, seeming as if she was bracing herself, "this is your nephew, Laine de Boer Berg."

"Hello there," Cyrene said.

"You're pretty," Laine said with a smile.

"Why, thank you. How old are you?"

"Almost two!" he said, holding up three fingers.

"Two!" she said with round eyes at Aralyn. "That's amazing."

"Okay, enough excitement for one night. Time for bed."

"But, Mamá," he whined.

"Now." She weakly smiled at them. "I'm going to get him in bed, and then I can get you to your rooms for the night. We have plenty of space."

Cyrene took a step forward. "Do you need help?"

Aralyn smiled faintly. "That would be nice."

Cyrene nodded at her friends, who finally dug into the biscuits.

Aralyn and Cyrene were silent as they walked through the foyer and up the grand staircase that led to the second story. Laine's room was the first on the right, and after Aralyn checked under his bed, she kissed him once on each cheek and then his forehead before closing the door again.

"Well, I was going to tell you in the morning," Aralyn whispered as they walked away from Laine's door.

"You have a child."

Aralyn nodded. "And I'm pregnant with my second. That was why I couldn't come home."

Cyrene put her hand out on her sister's stomach. She could feel the small bump there. "I'm so happy for you. You're in love? Lord Berg treats you right?"

"Yes, he is the best husband I could have ever hoped for. It started out… unexpectedly. I didn't think that the lordship would allow him to marry a foreigner, but when I became pregnant, there was no other choice."

Cyrene's jaw dropped. Aralyn—her prudish, reserved, withdrawn, bookworm sister—had gotten pregnant out of wedlock.

Aralyn laughed. "Oh, don't look at me like that."

"I am not judging. I simply wish that you had told me." Cyrene took Aralyn's hands in her own. "I am happy for you."

"I know." She turned her face away from her sister. "I think I was ashamed."

"Of this wonderful life?"

"Not exactly. More that I had gone away and done precisely what I was told not to. I am no longer objective about the subjects. I am a member of the family now. I might be a dual citizen, but I am Kelltic now. My heart belongs here. I worried every moment I was home that you or Leslin or Mother would notice. And then, after Leslin died, I wanted to get away, to get to my family, to be consoled by my husband. So, I fled."

"That's why you left so quickly."

Aralyn nodded. "Do you forgive me?"

"Of course. You have done nothing wrong."

"Are you going to tell me why you are really here, Cyrene?"

"There is more going on in Byern than you could possibly understand."

"Like what?" she asked, narrowing her eyes.

"Daufina is dead."

Aralyn gasped. "The consort? Who is replacing her?"

Cyrene sighed and glanced down. "I did."

"You? But why?"

"Because…both Edric and Kael were…are infatuated with me."

Aralyn crinkled her nose. "Are you telling tales, Cyrene?"

"I wish that I were." Cyrene shook her head with a sigh. "I was not in Byern much of this year. Surely, you heard that?"

"Yes. You were kidnapped, but Reeve wrote to me to say that you were home and well."

"I wasn't kidnapped. I left and fell in love with the Eleysian prince. When Edric found out, he threatened to wage war if I didn't return. So, he sent warships to collect me. When I got back to Byern, I tried to flee, and he killed Daufina because she tried to help me. Reeve is on the run, and Elea is trapped with Kael, who she is infatuated with. Something evil has taken root in Byern, Aralyn. It would be better for you not to return."

Aralyn put a hand to her mouth. "This is all…so much."

"I know. It's unbelievable."

"No, you always had a way with men. Now, you are on the run from your own country?"

Cyrene nodded. Almost the truth.

"Well, you may stay with me for as long as you choose. I will have to speak with my husband in the morning but know that you are always welcome with me. I will not send you back to Byern if that is not what you wish."

"Thank you, Aralyn."

"Now, we've kept your friends waiting for far too long. Let me get them settled. You and I will speak more about all of this tomorrow."

They returned to find the tea and biscuits gone. Ahlvie was dozing in an armchair. Matilde and Vera were bent close together, whispering. Avoca was straight back and attentive. Orden stood like a sentinel in the corner.

Aralyn bustled them all upstairs, stuffing Ahlvie and Orden in one room with two beds. Then, incredibly, all four of the women were given their own rooms. Cyrene didn't even want to know how many rooms this house had if it could comfortably sleep nine with space to spare.

"I'll have baths drawn for the lot of you tomorrow. I will wake you all to break your fast at eight. If there is anything else that you need, please do let me know," Aralyn said. She leaned forward and kissed Cyrene on each cheek and then on the forehead in the Kelltic manner, and then she disappeared for bed.

As soon as Cyrene's head hit the pillow, she thought she would be able to sleep forever. It felt like weeks instead of a mere day since she had last been woken up in Tahne with Ahlvie as an Indres. Just as she was beginning to relax, Matilde and Vera barged into her room. They closed it, and she sat up straight.

"What is it?" Cyrene asked. "Has something happened?"

"We sent Ahlvie, Orden, and Avoca out to scour the streets to see if they could locate our horses and saddles," Matilde said.

"They knew to wait until you returned with your sister," Vera said.

"Good thinking, leading her away so that we could plan."

That hadn't exactly been what she was doing, but at least it'd worked out.

"If they're able to locate our things, we should leave at first light," Matilde went on to say.

"First light? But we just got here."

"Cyrene," Vera said gently, "I know you wish to learn more about your sister's new life as a lady, but we never intended to come into Alba."

"In fact, Alba is one of the most dangerous cities in the world."

"Unless you count Bienco."

"Or perhaps Yuve."

Vera shook her head. "Besides the point."

"Undoubtedly."

"What is the point?" Cyrene asked.

"An Alba run by the Guild is worse than when we were here two hundred years ago, and it was horrible then. The lords rule this land with an iron fist, but even they are subject to the Guild. No one takes kindly to visitors. No one takes kindly to women. And an outlaw to the Guild is as good as dead to the lords," Matilde told her.

"So, if they find out who we are, we will be right back where we started," Vera said.

"Okay. What happens if they don't find our things?"

"We'll have to find an alternative means of transportation," Vera said.

"I'd hate for the book to end up in their greedy hands," Matilde grumbled.

"But it will not work for them. Their magic is—"

"Ridiculous," Vera finished.

"I don't understand it," Cyrene admitted.

"Their magic seems to be tied to their fighting skills. Instead of training to become Doma, they have used their powers to become fighting machines. So, they cannot control the elements because they do not believe that is what their energy is for. Magic is a weapon to them. They used the ropes to keep us from accessing our energy, but they don't actually know how to tie off magic."

"So, you can tie off magic like they did?"

They nodded.

"It is possible but a heinous offense. We will show you at a later time. The more important thing is that using the ropes or their swords or staff as a crutch limits them and makes them vulnerable to an attack from us. If they truly knew what they were doing, they wouldn't need the ropes. Do you understand?"

"Yes. That explains why the commander was so shocked by your displays of fire and ice."

"Indeed," Vera said.

"More importantly, this means, we have one clear night before we leave," Matilde said. "You said that you would be up to trying to enter a trance to speak with Serafina. Would you be willing to try now?"

Cyrene's stomach dropped. She was nervous about this trance, but she trusted the twins. "What do I have to do?"

"Just lie back and think about the last place you saw her. You will appear there in the trance and then call Serafina to you," Vera explained.

"You will need to remember yourself once in there and be sure to ask specific questions about where the lost ones are and why we need to see them.

Also see if you can get any more information about the second coin and the woman Serafina mentioned. Breaking through the barrier between life and death is not going to be easy for you," Matilde said with a nod of reassurance. "Just try to be patient and specific."

"Are you ready?" Vera asked gently.

Cyrene nodded. Though fear crept through her without warning. She had never reached for Serafina herself. She had always been bombarded by her presence. On one hand, it felt good to have the upper hand and to know what she was getting herself into. On the other...the idea of breaking the barrier between life and death frightened her.

"You will be fine. If anything happens, we will pull you out," Matilde told her.

"Okay"—Cyrene lay back, facing the ceiling—"I'm ready."

Fifty Four

THE TRANCE

Cyrene didn't remember falling asleep.

But, suddenly, she was standing on a bridge in Eleysia. A bridge that no longer existed. In a country that had now been burned.

"Serafina," she called out.

Matilde and Vera had told her to have patience and to be specific. Maybe Serafina wouldn't even hear her, and this would all be for nothing.

She called out her name twice more, but Serafina never appeared. Perhaps she couldn't bridge the distance between their worlds when Cyrene was in control. Normally, she was completely out of it when Serafina was able to reach her.

She didn't have a plan for failure.

She couldn't call for Matilde and Vera and tell them it didn't work. She was stuck.

With a sigh, she tried one last time. "Serafina, can you hear me? I need to speak with you!"

"You don't have to yell so loud," Serafina said, appearing behind her with a small pop.

Cyrene whirled around with her hand on her chest. "Creator!"

"How did you manage it?" Serafina reached for her wrist and held it. "No, you haven't gotten to spirit so soon. That would be…incredible."

"Matilde and Vera have me in a trance."

"I see," Serafina said with a sigh. "That is tricky. They should know that."

"Why is it tricky?"

"This link between us means that, *normally*, I should answer you first, Cyrene. But someone else could have. Someone with much more sinister intentions."

"Like the woman you mentioned."

Serafina tensed. "Yes. Like the woman. We should not speak of her here. You need to learn to reach into your spirit magic. Only then will you ever be truly safe."

Cyrene nodded. "I'll put it on the list."

Serafina barked a laugh. "Yes, I suppose you will. You sound just like me."

"Well…I am your ancestor, aren't I?"

Serafina smiled. "Indeed. Magic never dies. My magic was passed to you. It passed many times before reaching you, but no one harnessed it. You are the only one who wanted more."

The world shimmered all around them, and Cyrene gripped the railing.

"What is going on?"

"I am going to show you something."

The world around them disappeared, and they were on a beach, staring up at a small thatched cottage. The waves beat against their feet, and the weather was balmy but comfortable. It was a dream location.

"Where are we?" Cyrene asked.

"This is where I had my child," Serafina said wistfully. "Her name was Anne. She was the most beautiful thing I'd ever seen. And this cottage was my safe haven during those months."

"You had the baby in secret?"

"I had to. If Viktor ever…" She broke off and swallowed, the clouds turning stormy and the waves churning at their feet. "Well, he eventually did find out."

"It wasn't his."

Serafina shook her head.

"Was it…Jon's?" Cyrene asked, racking her brain for the name of the man she had seen in her last vision in Eleysia. "The man you met in Eleysia."

"Yes." Serafina wistfully glanced off to the ocean. "He was a man that I met while I was training with Matilde and Vera in Eleysia. I was there for several years."

"But you were already bound to Viktor?"

"I was. I think it was how he knew."

"What did he do when he found out?" Cyrene asked, caught so profoundly in this memory.

Serafina took a deep breath and closed her eyes. "He killed Jon and would have killed Anne too."

"But…what happened?"

"That is for another day," Serafina said with a sigh. "Come."

They walked out of the surf, across the sandy beach, and into the cottage. It was a simple place with one big room and a kitchen. A woman sat, nursing, oblivious to their presence.

"That's Maribel. She was my closest friend and confidant in the years that I was training. She took care of my babe and raised her as her own for Anne's protection." Serafina touched Cyrene's arm, and they took a seat. "We should be safe here. I am deeply connected to this cottage."

Cyrene had gotten completely caught up in her vision here with Serafina. She was supposed to be specific and ask about the dragons. Yet she felt Serafina leading the dream about like a horse by the reins.

"You are troubled," Serafina said intuitively.

"Yes. You told me to use the coin to find the lost ones. I am on the path. I used the coin, but there is a second. The woman in the darkness gave it to me."

"It must be Viktor's," Serafina said with a sigh. "We had a matched set."

Cyrene flinched at the words. That was what Kael had called them. Were she and Kael as much a matched set as Viktor and Serafina?

"Do you still love him?" she asked.

Serafina nodded without an ounce of reluctance. "He was and always will be my love. If his jealousy of my magic had not changed him, we would have found a way to truly be together, despite the prejudice against non-magical people."

"The lost ones," Cyrene forced herself to say. She needed to stay on track. Considering what once had been wouldn't help her current situation. "Why do I need to find them? How do I find them?"

"You are something new. They are something old. The oldest creatures still known to man," Serafina said. "If you hope to contain the darkness inside you, no one else will do."

Cyrene clutched at her skirts. "The darkness…but I thought…I thought I was the light."

"It's a funny thing about prophecies," Serafina said. "They're open to interpretation."

"And *you* interpret me as darkness?"

"I see you as a person—a Doma, a sister, a friend, and an ambitious, beautiful young woman—Cyrene," Serafina told her, pressing her fingers against her shoulder. "You choose your destiny. You walk your path. Seers have been wrong in the past. It does not do well to focus on what might happen and forget to live."

"I like the idea of choosing my own destiny."

Serafina smiled. "I felt the same way. But take care. You do not know all that is happening in your world. Forces simmer in the background, and I would hate to see your life torn asunder, as mine once was."

"Where…where do I find the lost ones?" Cyrene asked.

"Some things were lost for a reason," Serafina said. She folded her hands and stared back at her lost daughter, Anne. "They do not want to be found."

"That's not an answer."

"Perhaps. Shall I tell you another story?" Serafina asked with a glint in her eyes.

"No, I want an answer. I don't need to know more about the past. I need help with the future."

"I'm afraid that the past is much more informative than the future."

"Hardly. The past, your past, is a love story."

"A love story that broke the world," she said sadly. "Love is the most powerful force on earth."

Cyrene sighed and nodded. "I've seen that to be true."

"Your guides know of the lost ones. I believe that they have been waiting for the right person to find them, Cyrene."

"But where can I find them? Please, Serafina!"

Serafina opened her mouth, but then the cottage began to shake.

"What's going on?" Cyrene gasped, jumping to her feet.

"Our time is up."

"I'm not ready to go."

Serafina pulled her into a hug. "I will never be ready."

"I feel like you haven't told me enough."

She nodded. "You're right. There is so much more for you to learn. Come back to me when your spirit magic makes you safer. I promise to reveal as much as I can. And, Cyrene?"

"Yes?"

"Don't use the second coin."

"What? Why not?"

"I made that mistake once. Do not repeat mine."

"But that's not an explanation," Cyrene cried as the cottage disappeared.

Then, Serafina winked out of existence, leaving Cyrene alone in the cottage, wondering what in the Creator's name that coin did.

Cyrene awoke with a gasp. Light was streaming in through the shuttered windows. Hours had passed, and it had barely felt like a full hour with Serafina. Clearly, time worked differently there.

"Did it work?" Vera asked.

Cyrene nodded. "Yes."

"What did she say?" Matilde asked eagerly.

They both looked deathly tired but excited about a new magical discovery.

"She…she told me the lost ones don't want to be found. That my guides, you, know of the lost ones. That they have been waiting for the right person to be found. It was riddles again. I'm sorry. She is only truly informative about her past."

Vera sat back on her heels and sighed. "Gods!"

"Gods!" Matilde spit out. "She wants us to go to the caves."

"The caves?" Cyrene asked. "How did you get that from what I said?"

"She said we were guides, and we know the way. We do," Vera told her.

"You do?"

Matilde nodded and chewed on her bottom lip. "There are two places in all of Emporia that she could mean."

"We've checked there hundreds of times," Vera complained.

"But, if it is true, then perhaps only Cyrene can find the caves once more."

"What caves?"

"The caves of the lost ones," Matilde told her. "An ancient settlement for the dragons before their race was hunted down and nearly destroyed. Before the dragons fled. Well, at least we have a destination."

"We do?" Cyrene asked.

"The Drop Pass through the Barren Mountains."

Cyrene shivered at the idea. "Isn't it haunted?"

"It received its reputation from the dragons. Now, most take care when going through the mountains," Vera said.

"The dragons were alpha predators. The creatures of the Pass thrived in their absence, and now, it is a place of horrors."

"And we're to go in there?" Cyrene asked with a gulp.

Matilde and Vera nodded. "At once."

Fifty Five

THE FUGITIVES

Avoca dropped into the room through the window with a sigh. She looked run-down but straightened and dusted off her dress. "Nothing. There's no sign of our horses or belongings"

Cyrene's face fell. "I'll have to ask Aralyn then."

"She won't like it," Avoca said.

"I know."

"It'll delay us. Possibly a day. Maybe more."

Cyrene chewed on her lip and stared out at the city of Alba. She'd hardly seen any of the city last night when she was dragged in by the Guild.

It was…drab.

There was no other way to put it. The buildings were dark and foreboding, glistening with fresh snow. Spires topped the spiraling towers that jutted from the forbidding churches that dotted the city. She had seen a half-dozen men dragging black robes enter the church down the street before the sun was fully up. The day was bitterly cold, bleak, and dreary. Whatever trickle of sun that had edged over the horizon was already obscured from view from the snow-heavy clouds blotting out the sky.

A knock at the door broke them apart. Avoca quickly hid her dagger, and Cyrene reached for the serenity that constantly evaded her.

Aralyn poked her head in. "We break fast in the formal dining room. Baths will be drawn for everyone henceforth. My husband has agreed to allow you to remain here on one condition—that he speak with you all first."

Cyrene caught Avoca's gaze, and she felt a warning tug through the bond. "That would be wonderful. Thank you for everything, Aralyn."

"Of course. You're my sister."

Then, she was gone, and they had nothing to do but follow her downstairs. Orden and Ahlvie were already at the dining room table, and Orden seemed to be working over Lord Berg, as was his specialty. Cyrene remembered more and more why he was so valuable to their party. He could charm a snake.

Ahlvie seemed to be on his best behavior, which was never too far from his worst behavior. He sighed in relief when she and Avoca entered the room though, as if he knew he wouldn't be able to control his mouth or inevitable facial expressions without them.

Avoca carefully moved around him and took the seat next to Orden instead. Cyrene grimaced. She had thought that Avoca and Ahlvie had fixed their issues, but it didn't seem so. Cyrene quickly cleared the room and filled the gap next to Ahlvie. He shot her a grateful look, but she knew it was tinged with sadness. This was clearly eating at him.

"Lord Berg," Cyrene said, nodding her head at him, "thank you so much for allowing us to remain in your home."

He gave her a stern, reproachful look. "That remains to be seen. You're Lady Berg's sister then?"

Cyrene stifled a glare. "Yes."

"Yes, sir," he ground out.

Cyrene startled. "Yes…sir."

"My wife is a kind soul. She doesn't think about the consequences of her actions or how having foreigners on our doorstep might appear to the other lords and the citizens we represent. So, you'll have to forgive me if I'm none too pleased that she went behind my back and allowed you all to stay here last night. Or that I'll have to make explanations for your visit."

"We understand that circumstances are not entirely satisfactory, but we hope we can help in any way that you need," Orden said before she could open her mouth. He darted a quick glance at her that told her to keep her mouth shut and let him do the talking. "We're here to assuage any concerns that you might have."

"Don't beat them down before I even arrive for the meal," Aralyn said, appearing in a gorgeous black silk gown with full lace sleeves.

"My darling," Lord Berg said with an affectionate smile.

She moved to his side and chastely placed a kiss on his cheek before taking the seat at his right. "Now, what is this business?"

"We're waiting for two more," Lord Berg told her.

And then the twins appeared, serene and pious, dressed head to toe in

Kelltic fashion. Cyrene's mouth nearly fell open. She had no idea where they had gotten such dresses in such a short period of time. It would have been nice for her to be outfitted to please Lord Berg as well. Because she could see on sight that he was much happier with their attire than Cyrene's close-fit dress. At least Avoca had chosen not to wear pants.

"Good morning, Lord Berg," Matilde said sweetly.

Cyrene gaped. Sweet was not in Mati's repertoire.

"We're pleased to be breaking fast with you this morning," Vera said.

"Yes, well," he said with a smile, "please take a seat. We have business to discuss."

Aralyn sighed. "Business this early?"

"I know how you feel about this, darling. Please, keep out of the lord's business."

Aralyn shot him a derisive smile. She had never been known to keep out of anyone's business as far as Cyrene knew.

"Now that you're all here, I need to clear up one thing before we can allow you to remain in my residence," Lord Berg said. He steepled his fingers in front of his face and leaned his elbows on the table. His sharp dark eyes peered down at each of them from the length of the mahogany table. "Are you or are you not fugitives of the Guild?"

Aralyn gasped. "What?"

No one else said a word. They all stared straight ahead at Lord Berg, wondering who was going to field that question.

"Cyrene, is that true?" Aralyn demanded.

Cyrene slowly turned to face her sister. Clearly, the notion was tantamount to treason in this strange land. Admitting that, yes, somehow, they had become embroiled with the enemy could mean they would be handed over. Lying and saying they hadn't could hardly be a better alternative.

"Silence?" Lord Berg asked. "Well, that's confirmation enough."

"How?" Aralyn sputtered. "How could you have gotten tangled up with…them?"

There was real fear in her voice. Cyrene wondered what Aralyn would think if she knew what Cyrene could do.

"A mistake," Cyrene said. "We traveled onto land that we were unaware belonged to them, and they enslaved us for it without explanation."

"A grave offense," Lord Berg said.

"Cyrene, how could you?"

"This is not her fault," Matilde smoothly cut in. "It was a tactical error on our part. By the time we realized where we were, it was too late."

"My Lord, if I may," Orden said with a flourish, "we need not bring you into this matter at all. The Guild doesn't know where we reside at the present. We'd be happy to keep it that way."

"And how do you suppose you will be able to do that?" Lord Berg asked with a pointed stare.

"We plan to leave to ensure your safety in the matter," Cyrene said.

She knew it was the only way to keep them out of it. She didn't want her sister tangled up with the Guild. She had a happy life here. Someone should at the very least.

"You're leaving already?" Aralyn asked. Her voice was tight.

Cyrene could already see her withdrawing back in on herself.

Lord Berg put his hand on hers. "It's for the best. Think of Laine."

"If you could spare horses and supplies, it would be greatly appreciated,"

Vera said.

"Yes," Aralyn said, strong but distant. "I'll arrange it all myself."

She pushed her chair back, as if to leave at once to attend to it, but Lord Berg stopped her.

"You have put my family in grave danger. We can harbor you for one more night, but if you remain, we will be forced to turn you in."

Aralyn was shaking by his side, but she didn't defy him. Not in this.

"We understand," Cyrene said.

Her eyes followed her sister as she wrenched her hand free of her husband's and walked briskly out of the room.

Cyrene shoved her chair back to follow, but a tug on the bond from Avoca told her to stay where she was. She remained seated. Her heart was pounding, and she ached to go after her sister, but all she would bring her… all she'd brought anyone was disaster.

That black pit opened wide in her core, and she felt herself spiraling. Sitting in a roomful of people, demands being met, plans being made, and she was lost. Her blood magic called to her like an itch she couldn't scratch. It whispered and taunted and teased. If she could just fill that void, then she wouldn't have to sit idly by and take orders from some trussed up lord. She could comfort her sister. She could rule.

Dark, deep thoughts.

Buried.

Forgotten.

Once, she had been encased by them because of Maelia's death. The feeling of emptiness, of fault. Here again, this was her fault.

But…

But Maelia wasn't her fault.

She slowly retreated out of that darkness.

This was an accident. She hadn't even known she would see her sister. Had never considered that fact. She loved Aralyn and would do what she could so that her own problems didn't fall on her sister's shoulders.

"Then, it's settled," Orden said.

And it was over.

Aralyn returned when food was served. She ate scarcely for a woman in her condition and said not a word.

"I should say something to her," Cyrene said, edging for the door again.

"If you think you must," Avoca said.

Hours had passed. Aralyn had busied herself with their preparations. They were going to leave before dawn and try to sneak out of the city before anyone got wind of them. That meant a whole lot of sitting around and doing nothing.

Patience had never been one of her virtues.

"She must be so upset with me."

"She's not upset with you. She's sad that she won't get more time with you."

"That makes it doubly horrible. My sister has never wanted to spend time with me."

Avoca grinned. "There is not a person alive who wouldn't want to spend more time with you."

"Ceis'f?"

"He's a Leif. He doesn't count."

Cyrene laughed. "Fine."

"I know you love her, but it is best that we depart now. Make amends with her in the morning when she has cooled down." Avoca gripped her shoulder. "Our mission is important for the safety of all of Emporia. You are on a Creator-blessed journey. We will find a way to make this all right for the rest of the world so that you will never again have to be separated from your sister like this."

Cyrene gave her a sad smile. She wished she were so sure about what Avoca had said. Was she on a Creator-blessed mission? Was she this preordained Heir of the Light? Even though she knew that Kael was a Dremylon, following in Viktor's footsteps, she sometimes wondered if she was the dark side of the coin.

If the darkness that swept through her would blot out the light for good.

If she were destined to love him…and break him.

Just as Viktor had done to Serafina.

Her nasty thoughts chased her into a whirlwind nightmare.

A hand reaching out through the darkness.

A beachside cabin in ruins.

The tears of a grief-stricken mother aching for her baby.

Her mind going blank.

A coin flipping in her hand. Heads or tails? Heads or tails?

She waited for it to land. She craned forward, desperate to find the answer. But it was snatched midair. And then she was screaming. In pain or madness?

She was wrenched out of bed. A hand slapped her face.

"Wake up," a gruff voice barked.

Her body was coated in a film of sweat. Her hair matted to her face. Her eyes wild with alarm and the lingering disorientation of the nightmare.

But then she realized who had woken her…and she wanted to scream all over again.

"You," she managed to get out. Her voice was rough, as if she'd actually been screaming.

"Me," the commander said.

His grin was feral. His cheekbones sharp and dangerous in the shadows. He was in all black with a hood covering the dark hair underneath. His muscular body weighed her down, and she suddenly realized that they were alone, in her bedroom, and he was on top of her.

"Get off of me," she said, struggling to free herself.

He laughed harshly. "You think I'm going to let you go, spitfire? After what you did to the Guild?"

"You got what you deserved," she snapped.

"Burning down our building and murdering our people is what we deserved?"

"You would have done the same to us."

"Perhaps. But it is not what I deserved."

His eyes traveled down the length of her body. She hadn't realized how exposed she was. In her nightmare, she had kicked off her covers, and she was now lying in nothing but her thin shift.

"Then, why haven't you killed me already?"

"There are many things I would like to do to you, but killing you right here, like this…low on my list."

Cyrene flushed uncomfortably as his gray eyes probed her.

"Killing you slowly is much higher on my list."

"How did you even find me?"

"I followed your pretty blonde friend last night."

"You've known all day, and you're just *now* here?"

Warning bells rang in her head. Something felt wrong about that.

"They don't know that you're here," she said slowly as it dawned on her. "You're here on your own."

The commander tensed like a coiled viper waiting to strike. "Don't speak of what you don't know."

Cyrene eased out from under his taut body and sat up. Their eyes locked. "You're here for something else."

"Are you offering?" His hand landed on her thigh, and he arched an eyebrow.

She doubted many women had said no to that face. And, with the sexual tension between them palpable, she wasn't sure if she would have said no if they had met in another way.

She placed her hand on top of his. "What would you do if I was?"

He edged forward until his lips were a breath away. She stayed stark still, knowing she was prey to a predator.

"You couldn't handle it."

She laughed to ease the tension between them. "You're here about the magic, not me."

"Maybe both."

"If you were going to turn us in, you would have done so already."

The commander closely assessed her for a long-drawn-out minute. "How did you do it? How did you manipulate your energy in such a way?"

"Answers are currency, Commander. What are you going to give me for them?"

"Your life," he spat.

"How about our horses, belongings, and a way out of here?"

Cyrene wasn't sure if the commander was going to either stab her or kiss her, but he stalled and then stuck out his hand.

They shook.

Deal.

Fifty Six

THE COMMANDER

"Are you out of your mind?" the commander asked when Cyrene allowed him to turn around.

"They're just pants, Commander." She rolled her eyes. "Don't all of your female Guild members wear them?"

"Yes, but—"

"Then, it shouldn't be a problem."

"But I can see your legs."

"You saw them a minute ago, and it wasn't a problem."

The commander cursed violently and then tossed his black hood at her. "You'll blend in better with this. Don't open your ruddy mouth."

She grinned fiercely as she followed him to the open window. "I've never had much luck with that."

"Trust me, I've noticed."

The commander went out the window first and landed silently on the snow-coated ground. Cyrene sighed and trembled slightly as she stared down at the landing. She could take on Kael Dremylon and conquer blood magic, but climbing out of a second-story building was a feat.

With a deep breath, she wrapped her hands into the trellis and swung gingerly out of the window. She forced herself not to look down as she climbed. When she was about six feet from the bottom, she realized there was nowhere else to go. She was hanging, suspended from the trellis.

"Just drop. I'll catch you," he hissed up at her.

She held on tight, feeling utterly ridiculous. She should be able to use some air magic to gracefully drop herself to the ground. Usually, her anger boiled up, and she acted recklessly to get herself out of a stupid situation. But she wasn't angry.

"We don't have all night."

"Fine," she spat.

Then, with a deep breath, she dropped the remaining feet. The commander caught her, as if she were a pillow, and cradled her against his chest.

"Told you I'd catch you."

She nodded and then landed on her feet. Hastily obscuring their footprints, she dashed after him, down the narrow street next to Aralyn's home. They were almost around the first bend when a figure dropped out in front of them.

"Hello, Commander," Avoca said, straightening from her crouch. "Where do you think you're going?"

"It's not what you think," Cyrene said. "He's going to help us."

Avoca narrowed her eyes. "Really? Why would he do that?"

"In exchange for information on our magic."

"No," Avoca said, sliding one of her blades out. "I don't trust him. He's playing you. He's going to turn you in."

"He's not going to do that."

"Are you blind?" Avoca brightened with the magic that she held on to.

Cyrene could feel it through the bond. Instead of being a punch to the gut that it once was, it was like a caress. A window into her intentions. And she was furious.

"What kind of assurances could this man—the one who had our magic tied off, dragged us all into this mess in the first place, and then had me fight for my life—possibly give you?"

"My word," the commander growled.

"We don't even know your name," Avoca spat. "Your word means nothing."

"We really don't have time for this," Cyrene said. "Do you want all of our things and a way out or not?"

"What I want is for you to be sensible for once! To not run off into trouble, *alone*," Avoca snarled. "Why are we even..." She trailed off, not wanting to use the word *bound*. She snarled something under her breath and then looked back up at them. "Why are we all even together if you will not let us help you?"

Cyrene opened her mouth and then closed it. *How could I explain? How could I possibly explain how I feel?* That she loved them...all of them. But she constantly felt as if she could never make up for all they had done for her. The escape in Byern, the magic given to her in Fen, the life they'd saved.

She wanted to give back. She wanted to get them out of the situations that she'd kept throwing them into time and time again. If she was prophesied, then it was *she* who was drawing them into danger. It was *she* who was responsible. And, if she did it alone, then she wouldn't have to keep hurting anyone.

Avoca must have felt some of that through the bond because her anger softened. She sighed, and a tinge of sadness crept between them.

"If we're going to do this, we're going to do this together. You're not going to have some assassin play you double," Avoca said. Her eyes were sharp on the commander.

"Your wolf going to come out of the shadows then?" the commander asked.

Ahlvie appeared then, bristling from head to toe. "This should be fun."

"It would have been easier for just the two of us to go, but if you must join us, then fall into line."

Cyrene's eyes shot to Ahlvie's, and she could see that he was equally hurt that she would sacrifice herself.

"Don't you think you've done enough?" he muttered as she passed him.

No, I didn't.

The run through the city was as awful as Cyrene remembered it. The commander kept them in the shadows and out of the main thoroughfares as much as possible. He obviously knew Kell better than Orden did, but it didn't make it any better. She swore that, if they all made it out of here alive, then she was going to start exercising. She had to run for her life far too much to continue to be this winded.

"Stay here," the commander ordered. "We don't want to raise an alarm."

Then, he darted out from around the corner and strode up to a large stable guarded by two young men.

Avoca smacked her arm. "Are you out of your mind? Running off with this strange man?"

"It seems to be a specialty of mine," Cyrene said, not taking her eyes off the stables.

"You trust way too easily."

"I trusted Ahlvie this easily."

"Hey!" Ahlvie protested. "I'm offended by that."

Cyrene shook her head. "I'm just saying…I trust my gut. Something tells me that he is not going to hurt us."

"Your gut isn't always right, Cyrene!" Avoca groaned. "You were going to stay behind in Byern with Kael Dremylon."

Cyrene shot around and glared at Avoca. "Yes, I know perfectly well what I was going to do. But this is not that same situation. He wants to know about his magic. I want to get us out of here. That's all." Avoca opened her mouth to argue, but Cyrene cut her off, "Now, quiet, so I can watch what's going on."

She swung back around and came face-to-face with the two stable hands.

"Creator," she muttered before reaching for her magic.

Avoca leaped forward and slammed her fist into the face of the first, sending him tumbling to the ground. Then, while Cyrene held his tongue to keep any noise from coming out, Ahlvie crashed the other one into the side of the wall. His head hit with a sick crunch, and he collapsed, blood trickling out of his nose.

Cyrene felt a compulsory pull from her blood magic, and she had to physically retreat a few steps away.

"They're out," he said. "But the commander?"

Avoca shook her head and hoisted one of the boys over her shoulder. Ahlvie grabbed the other, and Cyrene hastened after them.

"Come on," Avoca said. "Let's go find your double-crossing son of a…"

When they entered the stables, Cyrene's hands were shaking, and she fisted them at her sides. She had this under control. She could do this. She wouldn't give in.

Ahlvie and Avoca deposited the boys in a corner, and Cyrene darted away from them.

"Are you okay?" Ahlvie asked, approaching her in the dimly lit room.

"Fine," she lied.

"About as fine as I was the first time I shifted."

"About," she agreed.

Avoca had her knife an inch from the commander's neck. "You sent them after us."

The commander cursed. "Did they raise an alarm?"

"Did you?"

"I know you don't trust me," he said, harmlessly batting her blade aside, "but if we have the whole of the Guild against us, then you're never getting out of the city."

"I didn't hear an alarm," Cyrene said.

"Good. Now, help me tie the horses to their leads."

They worked diligently for a few minutes to make sure everything was accounted for. It appeared someone had been through their belongings, but the book was still there. So, either they were only looking for money or they didn't realize its value.

"Let's get these back to Berg's house," Avoca said.

"We're going to meet up with his contact," Cyrene told her.

Avoca's eyes were venom. "How can you trust his contact?"

"Don't trust him, but he's your only way out. He knows this land like the back of his hand, and he's not Guild, so don't look at me like that," the commander said.

Avoca's blade was at his neck again. "Why are you really helping us?"

He looked directly into her wide blue eyes. His body seemed to be rippling with tension, ready to slice her open at a moment's notice. "When people show you who they really are, believe them."

"That's not—"

"He means the Guild," Cyrene said intuitively.

"If you've been lied to your whole life, you start to get good at picking out the truth," the commander said, glancing sideways at Cyrene.

"And *we're* the truth?" Avoca asked with a snort. "How foolish do you think we are?"

"Avoca," Ahlvie said, "just because you're upset, it doesn't mean you can't trust anyone."

"Don't try to make this about you," she spat.

He held his hands up. "A man would truly be a fool if he tried to make everything about himself. All I'm saying is, we've always trusted Cyrene before. If she trusts him, then I trust him. Because she was the only one who trusted me when she had no reason to."

"You'd better be deserving," Avoca said to the commander.

The commander didn't say anything to that. "We'll never get the horses through the city unnoticed. Someone will have to go to the contact with the horses. We'll meet there as soon as we have the others."

"I'll go," Ahlvie volunteered. "Avoca, perhaps you should go with me."

She looked as if she was going to disagree but then seemed to think better of it. "Fine. You know what to do if you're in trouble," she told Cyrene.

Cyrene nodded. The commander sketched them a hasty map with directions to his contact who would get them out of the city. Cyrene felt reckless, trusting him like this. They could have easily gotten out of there with Aralyn's horses, but it felt like more than that. With the commander, even though there wasn't exactly trust, she knew that she had an ally. And allies were in short supply these days. She felt a tug, like she would need as many friends as she could get.

"You're sure they'll be safe?" she hastily asked the commander after Ahlvie and Avoca departed.

"As long as they follow the directions," the commander said. When he seemed to realize that wasn't sufficient enough for her, he added, "That route avoids Guild patrols. Now, we need to move."

She reached out for his arm, and without notice, he grabbed her wrist, twisted, and had her arm nearly out of the socket.

She cursed. "Let me go! You're hurting me!"

"What were you going to do to me?" he demanded.

"Touch…touch you," she said. "Please, let me go."

He loosened his grip and then released her entirely. She rubbed her sore shoulder and wrist with a wince. She was glad that she healed quickly.

"That's going to bruise."

"You shouldn't sneak up on a man like that."

"You're a rather touchy bunch."

The commander glared at her.

"I was going to thank you," she said. "For helping me. I know it is a deal, but I like to think you would have anyway."

"I wouldn't have." His gray eyes smoldered in the darkness.

"I don't believe you. But I think we could be…friends," she said, offering him her hand.

He winced. "Friends?"

"Yes."

"Never make friends with your enemies, spitfire," he said with a feral smile. "It hurts twice as much when they cross you."

Cyrene let her magic infuse her. The wind picked up around her hair, wildly blowing it. The earth trembled under her feet. Her fingers were wreathed in fire. She could have reached for water, too, if need be. She could sense it sitting in the trough for the horses. It was pure heaven, her body responding to his barely veiled threat.

"If you cross me, you'll regret it for the rest of your sad, miserable existence. And, worse, you'll never get the answers you need." She brought her hand up to his face and watched as the light danced on his sculpted cheekbones. "I wouldn't underestimate me."

He had the good sense to conceal the fear that sparked in his eyes. "You'll have to show me how to do that one day."

"One day," she said, letting her magic extinguish as easily as it had come.

She didn't know what she saw in his eyes now. Perhaps he was afraid of her. Perhaps he liked being a little bit afraid of her.

"Now…we should go," Cyrene said.

Fifty Seven

THE FLIGHT

The commander nodded once, and then they were back out in the snow. Cyrene hastened to cover their tracks as they left. They moved down the windy snow-covered roads, past the tall black buildings, and around tight bends. The sun was about to set over the horizon, and she picked up her pace, attempting to match the commander's speed. He was a beast, carved out of muscle, unyielding.

"Wait," he said, pushing her backward.

She bent and heaved a sharp breath. There was a stitch in her side. "What is it?"

"Guild."

She cursed and then peeked around. Guild were stationed on all the corners in this block, and three were at the front door of Aralyn's home. Cyrene could sense the magic brimming all over the square.

"How did they find us?" she whispered.

He shook his head. "We were patrolling. I found you first. Anyone else could have followed you back to this residence."

"We need to find out what's going on."

"What we need to do is get you as far away from here as possible."

"My friends are still inside. I won't leave them behind."

Just then, the door opened, and Aralyn stepped out into the dark night. Her chin was held high, and to her credit, she didn't look as afraid as Cyrene was sure she felt.

"Can I help you?" she asked loud and clear.

"Apologies for the inconvenience, Lady Berg," the man at the door said just as loud, "but we have news that you're harboring fugitives."

"Fugitives? That's absurd!"

"So, you never took in a group of foreigners?"

"Well, of course I did, as any good Kelltic woman would."

The man bristled at her tone. "Then, you wouldn't mind if we escorted them to the gallows?"

"I wouldn't mind at all," Aralyn spat, "if they were still here. I turned them out before I ever even knew there were fugitives in the city."

"Indeed," the man said with venom in his voice. "Search the place."

Without warning, the other two people with the man barreled past Aralyn and into the house. Cyrene watched with fear. She wanted to go to Aralyn, to apologize for the position that she'd put her in. The lies she had to tell. But there was nothing she could do for her sister at this point. Interfering would only harm both of them.

"They're going to tear their home apart. You could have chosen more wisely. The Bergs won't stand for this in assembly. They're extremely powerful."

"Perhaps I should have chosen more wisely," she agreed with a sigh. "If you were sending three people on horseback out of the city in a hurry, which direction would you go from here?"

He shook his head and then considered. "This way."

She took one last deep breath. "Wait."

She grabbed on to his arm, and he only flinched this time.

"What is it?"

"I need you to promise to look after Lady Berg and her family when I leave this place."

"Didn't you just hear me? They're extremely powerful."

"Please. Promise that you'll make sure they come to no harm."

The commander narrowed his eyes. "You didn't come to the Berg's house by chance, did you?"

She shook her head, letting him in on another secret. "She is my sister."

"That sort of information is very valuable. You must trust me if you trust me with your sister."

"I put her in this position. If you can, will you help her out of it?"

"If I can. I swear it on my name."

"And that is?" she asked coyly.

"Not something you've earned yet."

Cyrene choked on a laugh. Of course not.

He directed her away from Aralyn's house, and as they turned the corner, they came face-to-face with a Guild member. She was no older than Cyrene and dressed in black from head to toe, but her hair was silver, nearly to her waist, unbound and breathtaking.

"Commander," she said, her voice low and threatening.

"Haeven," he acknowledged.

Cyrene was surprised he had used her name if names were that important to them. Maybe it wasn't her real name, like Commander wasn't his real name.

"What I see is treason," she said, pointing a wicked blade at his feet.

"Maybe you don't see anything at all."

"You might have picked me up out of the death camp in the mountains, Commander, but I swore fealty to the Guild. Not you."

"If anyone understands what we need here, Haeven, it's you. They tortured you nearly to death to release your energy. What if there was another way?"

She gritted her teeth, and Cyrene could see the feral animal hiding underneath her skin. "If there was another way, wouldn't we have found it already?"

"Show her," the commander barked at Cyrene.

Cyrene reached for her magic. She shot a perfectly executed blast of wind at her wrist, forcing Haeven to drop her sword. Then, she spiraled the snow at Haeven's feet and up into the air to mirror snow falling all around the girl. She snapped her fingers, and the snow turned into a downpour, soaking her through. She concentrated, knowing this was the tricky part. Then, she created a ball of fire and slowly dragged it out until all three of them were bathed in its warmth. It lasted only a split second before disintegrating. She was still rusty, but it was enough. It would have to be.

"What camp did you come from?" Haeven asked. Her eyes were flat and emotionless. She didn't seem to be the kind of girl who ever showed her feelings. Wherever she had come from took that from her.

"No camp," Cyrene told her. "I have two tutors. They taught me the ways of my powers."

"I don't believe it."

"Yet you see it before you," the commander said, his voice lowering. "We are destined for more than this."

Haeven considered that for a moment. "This will mean civil war in the Guild. Are you prepared for that?"

"Some things have always been inevitable."

Haeven nodded, as if they had had this conversation. "Should I go collect the others then?"

"The others?" he asked with a note of surprise.

"The others who have been waiting for you, for this moment."

"Start with their sentinels."

"Blood will spill in Kell tonight," she said with a grin.

"May the river run red," he responded like a benediction.

She darted off past them, not looking back once, as she appeared nearly invisible in the shadows.

"Who is she?" Cyrene asked, slightly terrified and in awe of such a soldier.

"I suppose, now, she's my second."

"And before?" she asked as he maneuvered them through the streets.

"She was a mouthy know-it-all, like you."

"Ah…so you like her?"

The commander cut her a sharp look. "Haeven is…complicated."

"Why do you use her name?"

"Haeven isn't her name," he said, his voice going to that soft, distant place. "It's where she was found—in the Haeven Mountains—after she slaughtered her way through a Biencan warrior camp."

Cyrene gasped. "A…warrior camp?"

"Trust me. You don't want to know."

She trusted that she didn't. If that was the kind of creature that had come out of it, then she didn't want to know what Haeven had had to go through to become that way. Cyrene could only imagine the atrocities.

By the time they weaved around the Guild patrols and through the streets to the three different places that the commander had suggested her friends might have gone, Cyrene was giving up. "Maybe they're still in the house."

"I doubt it," he said.

And that ended the discussion.

Cyrene shook her head and followed him on another route. They ran into a pair of Guild but hastily blended into the shadows as they passed. Cyrene held her breath as the commander's body enveloped her to keep her hidden.

When they were finally out of sight, the commander shook his head. "Pathetic. They should have seen us if they had been paying attention."

"Well, let's hope they're all like that."

"They're not," he insisted.

A commotion a street over alerted them to trouble, and they dashed toward it. By the time they reached the street, three Guild members lay in a heap in the snow, and the twins smiled down at them in glee. Orden hadn't even had a chance to remove his sword.

"There you are," Matilde said.

"About time," Vera agreed.

"What the bloody hell are you doing with him?" Orden asked.

"Change of plans," Cyrene said hastily.

"I shouldn't even be surprised," Matilde muttered.

Vera shushed Matilde.

Orden actually rolled his eyes. "What crazy idea have you come up with this time, girl?"

"The commander is getting us out of the city. He has a contact where we can meet with Avoca and Ahlvie, but we have to be quick. We'll be much easier to spot when the sun rises."

"I must impress on you that being caught by the Guild in this city is a death sentence. You were lucky the first time when you escaped. Pandemonium saved you. Leaving is not just your best option. It's your only option."

"Well, let's get on then," Matilde said with a sigh.

Cyrene and the commander grabbed horses, and then he took point, making a mad dash through the city. They kept pace with him. Already, people were filing out of their homes and going about their day. The sun was cresting the horizon, and if they weren't careful, they wouldn't ever make it out of this blasted city.

The commander pulled up his horse at a ramshackle house on the outskirts of the city. It was dilapidated and barely held up. A wagon with a purple tent hung over it, obscuring the insides. A dozen horses moved around in a gated pen for grazing.

"Have we outpaced them?" Cyrene asked.

"For now," the commander said, jumping down from his mount. "Their territory reaches this far, but Haeven will occupy them for the time being."

They tied up the horses and hurried up the shaky stairs as Ahlvie and

Avoca burst out of the front door.

"Cyrene!" Avoca said with a gasp, pulling her in for a hug.

"We're okay," she assured her.

"And Aralyn?"

Cyrene shook her head. "I couldn't see her."

Avoca's face fell. "I'm so sorry."

"But, more importantly," Ahlvie cut in, "wait until you meet your commander's contact."

"What does that mean?" Cyrene asked suspiciously.

"Oh, he's a real treat."

"I'll take that as a compliment, good sir," the man said, standing in the doorway to the dilapidated house, looking every inch the enigma he always appeared to her.

"Basille Selby," she gasped.

"In the flesh."

Fifty Eight

THE DEAL

"What in the Creator's name are you doing in Kell?" Cyrene asked.

When she had first met Basille Selby, he'd been an Eleysian peddler hawking knickknacks at the Laelish Market in Byern. He'd sold Elea Cyrene's birthday present, the very book that had belonged to the Doma all those years ago. He had been the one to tell Cyrene to find Matilde and Vera to begin with. Then, of all things, she had found him again in Eleysia, only to discover he was a disgraced noble after having an affair with Princess Brigette. Now…Queen Brigette. Now…dead.

Even though Cyrene hated her for killing Maelia, she did feel sorry for

Basille that his lost love had perished. And…he probably wasn't even aware of it.

"Hard times, my dear," he said. He waved his hand in a flourish, as if he'd never truly seen hard times.

"Is that why you ran in Eleysia?"

"Ran? Me? No, I found a better opportunity."

"But Brigette…"

"Don't speak her name," he said tightly.

"You've heard?"

"Heard?" he asked coyly. "That the Eleysian throne has been wiped out, the countryside is in turmoil, and all the warring parties are clamoring for the crown? Believe me…I've heard."

Cyrene wilted. "My apologies."

"Anyone going to tell me what is going on here?" the commander asked, his eyebrows knit together in confusion.

"Ah, I see you're the culprit who dropped this group at my door," Basille said to the commander.

"You already know them?"

"Indeed. This is not our first run-in."

"I don't understand how we keep ending up in the same place," Cyrene said with a shake of her head. "Once was chance, twice was coincidence, but three times…"

"I think the word you're looking for, my dear Affiliate, is *fate*."

"Affiliate?" the commander said with a raised eyebrow.

"I don't claim that anymore," she said to Basille.

"Ah, yes, I did hear rumble of something else," he said, gesturing for them to all get out of the street. "Consort?"

Cyrene's eyes snapped to him. "How exactly are you so well informed?"

"I am a simple peddler. Information is my favorite currency."

Matilde bustled past Basille and tipped her head at him. "Are you working with these assassins, too, now, Selby?"

"I don't discriminate on clientele," Basille said.

Orden snorted in the corner.

"We're pleased to hear that," Vera said, "because we need you to take us through the Drop Pass."

Ahlvie coughed himself hoarse. "You want to take us *where*? You know the Pass is haunted, correct?"

Avoca knocked her shoulder into his as she passed into the room and took a seat. "Scared?"

"I've heard the stories. And, no offense, but when we travel with Cyrene, things tend to be worse than expected rather than better."

"Thank you for that," Cyrene grumbled.

"I was going to suggest the Pass as well," the commander said. "It's the fastest way out of Kell, and the Guild won't follow you through. You'll be off to Yarrow and beyond in no time with the right guide."

"And you all think I am the right guide?" Basille asked in his drawling Eleysian accent. For once, he wasn't dressed head to toe in the Eleysian garb—loose fit pants and a shirt, fitted around the ankles and wrists. Much too cold in Kell for that attire, but he still managed to make the tailored Kelltic clothing suit his tan skin and dark features.

"Is there another one around?" Avoca asked with that heightened intensity that only she could master.

With her own anger simmering just under the surface, Cyrene worried that she might erupt.

"Certainly no one as well traveled as I," Basille said.

Cyrene had a feeling she knew where this was going. "What's your price? There's always a price."

"Gold?" Orden asked. "We have plenty."

Basille barked out a short laugh. Cyrene shook her head. No, that was never what he was after. He always wanted something more.

"What is it?" Cyrene asked. "There's something else. Last time, it was an invitation. And this time?"

"I find myself in a room with some very important people. I should think they have something valuable to me."

The commander moved with the fluidity of a wraith. He grabbed the merchant by the throat and raised him onto his tiptoes. "I bring these people here on good faith, and you are swindling them, crook?"

"Put him down," Cyrene cried at the same time Vera said, "Control yourself."

Basille's eyes were bugging as the commander slowly eased him back onto his feet. He released the peddler, who coughed and choked.

"That was unnecessary," Avoca muttered.

"I quite liked it," Ahlvie said with a lopsided grin. "I could get used to this guy."

"Before the brute attacked me, I was going to name my price," Basille said, straightening and rubbing his throat.

"Well, spit it out then," Cyrene said. "He is the least of your concern in this room."

"Ah, so you went beyond your manifest then? I knew you'd find the right tutors."

"Enough," Vera said. She waved her hand in the air. "We are at the end of our wits. You always did like to hear yourself speak. Say your price."

"Guess," he said with a twisted smile.

"Can I cut him?" Avoca asked. Her blade was in her hand, and she looked poised to throw it into Basille's chest.

"Wait," Cyrene said, holding her hand up. There were too many voices. When she had been in Eleysia and struck a deal with Basille, it had been for something innocuous but with dire consequences. She needed to think on his level. If he was their only way through the Pass, then she would figure it out. "Something about home."

"Yes?" he asked.

"You want to go home?"

He scoffed. "I can go to Eleysia anytime I please."

"Then, something more than that?"

"I want you to write a letter," he said simply.

Cyrene furrowed her brows. "To whom exactly?"

"I want my name cleared and to be reinstated as a noble on the Privy Council."

"How exactly am I supposed to do that?"

"You know a certain prince," he said with a smirk.

Cyrene sighed. "Dean."

She didn't even have to ask how he knew that Dean was still alive.

"See it done, and I'll take you through the Pass."

"I can't guarantee that he'll do it."

Basille grinned. "Oh, he'll do it."

Cyrene shook her head in disgust. Deals made her feel slimy. "Fine. But we must hurry."

Basille disappeared to retrieve pen and paper.

Avoca strode across the room to stand in front of Cyrene. "You do not have to do this."

"It's just a letter," the commander said. "I've seen him deal with much worse."

Cyrene paled. If only it were just a letter. She and Dean might have parted on good terms in Fen, but that didn't mean that she was anxious to open that connection between them. She didn't even know if she would ever *see* him again. Or why it made her so anxious to consider that she wouldn't.

"Maybe you should mind your own business," Avoca snapped at him.

Matilde and Vera materialized before the commander. "We believe that you were promised information in exchange for your own help. While Cyrene prepares, we would be happy to explain what your Guild training has been sufficiently lacking."

The commander looked as if he were about to snarl at them but eventually disappeared. Cyrene was grateful that she wasn't the one who would have to explain everything to him. Matilde and Vera had years of experience. She would be better off writing one measly letter.

Cyrene folded the letter and addressed it to his Royal Highness Prince Dean Ellison of Eleysia. She had no mark of her own, so Basille used his own seal to close it.

"You'll need one of these," he told her. "I could give you a fair price."

Cyrene rolled her eyes. "How will we send it?"

"The commander will do it," Basille said, as if it were obvious. "Now, let's go, Consort. Much to do and little time to do it."

Cyrene backed out of the drawing room and carried the letter outside. Her friends had saddled their horses, packed the saddlebags, and consolidated their belongings. The commander was hastily scribbling into a worn book, looking suddenly out of place in the light of day.

She cautiously approached him. "Commander."

His head darted up. "Are you finished?"

"Basille requested for you to get this into the right hands." She passed him the letter.

He took it and stuffed it into the notebook. "It will be done. Your tutors are remarkable."

It was the first real compliment he'd given anyone.

"Yes, they are. Did you learn much?"

"Enough. If I need more, I'll send a hawk."

"A hawk?"

"They're incredibly smart. My hawk could find anyone in Emporia. He will find you, and he will find the person to deliver this letter to."

"Thank you for not double-crossing me," she blurted out.

"Not yet at least."

"So, do I get your name yet?"

The commander tucked away his notebook and pulled her into his arms. She wrapped hers around him, surprised at how close she felt to this total stranger.

"When next we meet," he promised.

Cyrene laughed. "Be safe."

"An assassin's life is never safe." He released her with hooded gray eyes and a warm smile. "May the river run red."

"I'll take that as a benediction."

"Keep your wits about you in those mountains, spitfire. You'll need them."

With those chilling words, the commander stepped back and disappeared into the distance. She shuddered at the thought of him becoming Doma. With his power and unbridled ferocity, he could do anything. She was glad to leave him as an ally and not an enemy.

"Ready?" Orden asked as she marched over to retrieve Ceffy.

"Ready to get this over with."

"Mountain ponies would have been better," Basille said, "but we work with what we have."

And then they moved out and away from the nightmare of Alba, toward the dark and foreboding hell awaiting them.

Fifty Nine

THE PASS

"Did you hear that?" Ahlvie asked, his eyes scanning the mountains closing in all around them.

"You are making everyone jumpy," Avoca ground out. "There is nothing in these mountains."

"Actually—" Basille said from the front of the line.

"Shut it," Cyrene snapped at him.

Ever since they had set foot in the Drop Pass, Basille had been hinting at ghost stories and monsters and all manner of creatures that would swoop in and destroy them. It was making everyone jittery. Even Matilde and Vera, who were never ruffled.

Cyrene heeled her horse forward to come to the outside of Vera. "Do you know what we're looking for?"

"We'll direct Master Selby in the right direction, but we were here many years ago, and the passage into the caves was completely obliterated," Vera told her.

"Obliterated?" Cyrene asked uneasily.

"Blasted off the face of the earth."

"How?"

"I believe you mean…by what?" Vera said grimly.

Cyrene leaned in closer. "Are you saying there actually *are* creatures that haunt this pass?"

"I'm saying that the stories aren't for nothing."

"Keep your eyes open and your senses sharp," Matilde said.

"And your magic close," Vera added.

"Wonderful," Cyrene muttered under her breath.

She held her magic on a short leash as she moved back to Avoca's side. Though the Pass wasn't narrow by any means, the snowdrifts kept them two abreast as they tramped through the snow. And, even though it was daylight, time seemed to move differently here. Dark clouds hovered overhead. A storm was brewing. Cyrene could practically reach out and touch the intensity of the current. She had learned the hard way not to meddle in weather if she didn't have to, but something about this called out to her.

"I seriously heard something this time," Ahlvie said.

Cyrene groaned.

"His ears are sharper than ours," Orden reminded them.

She hadn't heard a thing, but Orden was right. Maybe Ahlvie could hear something they couldn't. All she saw all around her were white snowdrifts, tall evergreen trees, and endless black granite that the Barren Mountains were known for. Its highest peak was called the Black Mountain of Death. Real cheery.

A twig snapped in the distance, and Cyrene's eyes darted to where the sound had come from. "Okay, I heard that," she whispered.

She held her magic taut, like a bow ready to fire, and waited. Avoca also grasped her magic, and a blade slid into her hand. Heeling Ceffy toward the source of the noise, Cyrene held her breath as she approached. Whatever was hiding in these mountains was making them all insane. She could feel the tension in her group. They needed to find these caves and get out of here. Nothing good could come from somewhere like this. And certainly not if they had to stop at every stray sound.

Another crack sounded a half-step from where she was standing on the tree line. With a quick jolt, she snapped her magic out at the unsuspecting victim. A yelp came from the trees, and then an average-sized white rabbit darted out of the clearing before hurrying out of view.

She released her breath in a gasp. A few chuckles were heard behind her.

"See? It's nothing," she assured them.

Ahlvie looked sheepish. "It felt like more than a rabbit."

"Maybe your senses are wrong here," she suggested, urging them forward again.

They had a lot of ground to cover.

"Everything feels wrong here," Basille said from the front. "It always does."

"But you've been through before. So, we'll make it this time," Cyrene said with feigned confidence.

The higher they got up in the mountains, the harder it was to breathe.

The Pass was overrun with snow already this early in the season. Basille threw back a long rope once it became clear that, if they stepped off his trail, they could be lost in the snow. They each tied together their horses and moved single file through the cold. The weather was so damp and uncomfortable that even Matilde and Vera were helping to heat the whole party and their horses. A task they normally considered built character.

"Once we cross the high point, we'll head toward Black Mountain," Matilde called to Basille.

He turned back toward them and sneered. "There is no path to Black Mountain. I've already told you."

"We'll have to make one then."

"There's a reason it's called the Black Mountain of Death."

"Death was added as a scare tactic," she said. "I assure you."

"It worked," he grumbled.

Cyrene couldn't shake the feeling of dread settling over her. She didn't know if it was the tall tales of the Drop Pass that she'd heard as a child. Horrible tales of creatures coming out, endless darkness turning people into ash, and ghosts. Always ghosts.

She shuddered at that thought. Even though she herself had been speaking to a two-thousand-year-old dead ancestor for the last year, the idea of ghosts made gooseflesh dance on her skin and the hair on the back of her neck stand on end.

"I still hear something," Ahlvie muttered.

"It's probably another rabbit," Avoca said.

But, when Cyrene glanced back at her, she could see that wasn't what Avoca believed at all.

By the time they were heading to the top of the Pass that afternoon, the cloud had darkened entirely. Each of the girls held a ball of Doma Fire in her hand to lead the way. But the darkness only escalated, as if it had a physical presence pushing in on their magic. The shadows began to shift. The night crept in. And, soon, the bunny was the least of their concerns.

"It's not ghosts. It's not ghosts. It's not ghosts," Cyrene whispered under her breath.

Lightning cracked overhead, illuminating the mountain for a brief moment. Everything looked normal. Just as it had appeared this morning. But, once the thunder boomed in warning, the answering call was clear.

There was something else out there.

And they were blind.

Then, she heard it.

Swoosh.

"Arrows!" she yelled. "Attack!"

But it was too late.

A distinct *thunk* said that the arrow had landed into its target. Avoca screamed behind Cyrene.

"Avoca!" Cyrene cried.

She reached for Avoca through the bond and probed for the wound. Through her shoulder. A direct hit, and she was already losing blood. Cyrene could sense the blood as well as her own magic.

Orden took charge in the madness, ordering them out of the open pass and up to the top of the mountain where they would have a better position. They hadn't gotten to choose where this battle was fought, and it was leaving them at a distinct disadvantage.

Arrows whizzed past them as their horses heaved upward through the snow. Cyrene called wind to herself and blasted the arrows out of the way before they could fall on them again. Matilde and Vera were already working on setting up a barrier, but their group wasn't stationary, and since they were drawn out across such a wide swath of space, it was difficult to keep in place.

Cyrene put up her own shield in front of Avoca, who couldn't defend herself. She was doubled over on her horse, breathing heavily into her wound.

She held her Doma Fire at the same time, lighting the path before them, but it gave her no better view of who…or what was behind them. They needed to be able to see. They needed this storm to pass. She was already having difficulty managing too many spells at once. She would have to drop the shield around everyone to open up the sky for them. It wasn't a risk she could take while Avoca was in danger.

Just before they reached the top of the Pass, an explosion rocked the ground before them. Basille wheeled around to escape the onslaught. His horse bucked and tried to free itself to escape. All of them pulled up tight together, their way barred.

Then, out of the smoke, came dark shadows that moved as smoothly as ghosts and struck fear into Cyrene's heart.

She swallowed hard and herded Avoca behind her. Their group cut their lead line and then made a circle, facing off with the deadly shadow figures. With their shields up, they were prepared to unleash whatever power they had to stop these ghosts from killing them all.

"How do you kill a ghost?" Ahlvie muttered.

She could feel him bristling, ready to transform at a moment's notice.

"Those aren't ghosts," Matilde said.

"An ambush," Basille said, shaking his head. He had a thin blade in his hand that he held as if he had been born with it.

Cyrene would never have guessed that he would put himself in a position where he had to actually fight.

"Who are you?" Cyrene shouted into the dark. "Show yourself!"

Then, figures moved from the shadows and toward the light. Armed to the teeth, a woman entered the clearing. A woman Cyrene recognized.

"Guild," she muttered like a curse.

"Did you think we would let you walk out of our city without paying for your transgressions?" the woman asked.

"Honorary!" the crowd cheered as one.

"So, *you're* the Honorary," Cyrene said, sizing her up.

She'd thought that the group of leaders at the Guild shared power or that they were the face for the true leader. No one had named her as such.

"Yes, of course I am the Honorary, leader of the Guild. And *you* are here to die."

"I wouldn't count on it," Ahlvie said with a laugh.

"You're a long way from your pack, dog," she bit out.

Matilde moved, as if she were about to strike the Honorary down, but the Honorary held up a finger and wagged it back and forth.

"Uh-uh, I wouldn't do that. Your magic might be fast, but our arrows are faster."

"I doubt it," Vera said boldly.

The Honorary waved her hand, and suddenly, all of their shields were gone. Cyrene startled and reached to replace hers. Once again, it disappeared.

"We can play this game all day," the Honorary said. "You're outmatched.

Drop your weapons and come quietly. This will all be over soon."

Her friends scoffed. As if they were going to turn themselves in to these monsters.

"How did you even know where we were going?" Cyrene asked.

"The commander told us, of course."

Cyrene froze. No. He wouldn't have done that. He couldn't have.

The Honorary laughed. "Did you believe he cared for you? That he was on your side?"

Yes. No. Maybe she'd thought that. Despite all of his warnings that he would betray her, she still hadn't believed that he would do it.

It hurt worse than she wanted to admit. He was right. It was much worse to be double-crossed after making your enemy a friend. She hoped that he had done it for a good reason, but right now, she couldn't think of a single one. She just felt sad that, once again, her judgment was off.

She should have listened to Avoca. The commander had used her and set her up to be betrayed. He'd wanted knowledge about their magic, and after he had gotten it, he didn't care.

Her heart constricted. Could it be that simple? Or was he protecting his people, his friends? Did he think she'd already be gone? Was she too hopeful that he wasn't the villain he'd painted himself as?

"Don't look so surprised. The commander is an excellent actor. Gaining your trust and then plotting against you once he got what he wanted from you. Truly inspired."

"I don't believe you," Cyrene said.

Avoca groaned behind her. "Just kill the bastards."

"Your choice," the Honorary said with cold, dead eyes.

Cyrene didn't think twice. She launched her energy toward the Honorary, but Matilde beat her to it. She blasted through the defenses the Honorary was holding up. Whatever magic the Honorary was capable of clearly outmatched what the commander had been trained in. Matilde effortlessly weaved the elements together, taking on the Honorary with skill and precision honed over thousands of years.

But Cyrene didn't have time to watch her skill. They were soon engaged on all sides. More than a dozen Guild members threw themselves at them. These were the dazed and confused lot that had been training the day they met the Honorary. These were their top-notch assassins. The ones that gave the Guild their treasured name.

Ahlvie vaulted off his horse and exploded into fur and claws and fangs. He shredded through the first assassin with ease but was quickly crowded with fighters as he worked to keep people away from Avoca. Cyrene was doing the same thing. Avoca was wielding small amounts of magic, but Cyrene could practically feel the intense pain that she was in. They needed to get that arrow out of her shoulder and quick.

A Guild member threw himself at Cyrene. She reached for the fire sword that she had used all those months ago on Kael. She might not be a master swordsman by any means, but a flaming sword was its own trick. She had killed a Braj out of sheer force of will. She could hope to best this assassin.

She parried with her sword, but the assassin came at her with a whole other tactic. It was clear that she was out of her depth. But she drew on her wealth of magic and pushed back with air, blocked with water, slammed into him with earth, and lit him on fire as often as she could.

She was holding her own but lagging. And more kept coming. When she slew one, another one took its place. The battle became a song, a rhythm, a heartbeat. The tempo rose and fell, hit a crescendo, moved to a feverish pitch, and then settled into a dance.

Her mind and heart and soul all fell into perfect synchronization, and suddenly, she was free. Set sails and open skies and summer days and true love's kiss. She was soaring in motion. Alight with energy and pulsing with the feel of it all.

It was terrifying and horrible. Blood and blood and blood. Destruction and torment and finite.

Yet she felt more alive than she ever had in her life. More alive than the first time she'd ever found her magic. This spoke to her in a way she'd never experienced. As if she were one with herself. Drinking in the energy all around her—Doma, elemental, blood—all of it crashing into her, using her as a vessel.

As she reveled in her own perfect equilibrium, she knew she was powerful enough to control it all. Strong enough to carve her own path. New path.

She had long wondered if she was the light or dark.

The good or the bad.

Perhaps to win this battle, to end this war, she needed to be both. To be more than separate halves and instead be whole.

Sixty

THE GOOD

Blood coated Cyrene's hands and was splattered all over her clothing. She had lost track of time and her friends and everything in the heat of the battle. But they were winning. She could feel the tides turning, the edge slipping away.

Her flaming blade slid through the chest of her last opponent, and she yanked back, letting the figure fall down dead. Death was everywhere. She turned to face her friends, ready to help where she was needed, but then she felt the energy crackle in the air around them.

Her eyes rounded with horror as the air sizzled, and then everything shrank to that one moment. She reached out with her magic to test the energy and gasped.

"No!" she screamed.

She launched herself toward Avoca, knocking both of them off their horses and landing with a crunch onto the blood-soaked earth. Avoca cried out from the impact to her shoulder. But they had barely touched the earth when a lightning bolt smashed into the ground exactly where Avoca had been only a split second earlier.

The blast rocked the ground all around them, shaking and rattling it from the heavens. Cyrene covered her eyes as the light seared them. She was seeing stars when she tried to orient herself.

Lightning.

Someone had controlled the lightning.

Not possible.

Her mind felt fuzzy. Cyrene knew that she was one of the few capable of it. But she had felt the energy in the air. Tasted the tinge of magic directing the blaze to that exact spot. It was pinpoint accuracy. Beyond anything Cyrene had ever mastered. Whoever had controlled it was well beyond her, which was even more terrifying.

"Cyrene," Vera called, rushing to her side.

"What…what was that?"

Vera shook her head. "We need to get out of here. Get Avoca back on her horse, and we'll retreat."

Cyrene wanted to argue, but the look on Vera's face stilled her. Cyrene hauled Avoca up. She was panting and delirious. The arrow through her shoulder had shifted when Cyrene landed on her and was bleeding again. Cyrene put a protective shield around her and then went for Avoca's horse.

The mayhem around her was suddenly shockingly clear. Bodies littered the ground. Ahlvie and Orden had a group of Guild members engaged.

Matilde was still fighting with the Honorary. Vera was interjecting where she was needed and holding people off so that they could get away.

Cyrene darted for the horse and dragged it back toward Avoca. Her eyes were glazed.

"I'm going to need your help," Cyrene told her, shifting Avoca's weight onto her.

"I…can't," Avoca muttered. "Leave me."

"You know I won't do that."

Cyrene had her halfway into the saddle before Avoca slid back down and landed in the snow. Cyrene snarled in frustration.

Just as she was attempting to find an easier way of doing it, she felt the energy sizzle again. Cyrene cursed and then threw herself on top of Avoca. Her energy shield activated, and she prayed to the Creator that it would be enough.

When the lightning hit her shield, it was like being cleaved in two. She gritted her teeth, glad that she was full to the brim with magic, and held on for dear life. The hit only lasted a few seconds, but it felt like an eternity.

Cyrene was left trembling and shaky. She released her battered shield and collapsed forward over Avoca.

"Creator," she whispered.

She was preparing herself to take on another hit, when the energy around her morphed once more. But, instead of sizzling with intensity and the electrical zap of power, the air seemed to expand outward. Then, with a pop, the darkness shifted, and a figure was standing in their midst.

Cyrene rose to her feet, watching the darkness diminish and the figure step into the light.

The Nokkin had found them.

"Hello, pet," the Nokkin said.

"I am not your pet," she snapped at it.

"Are you ready to meet my master? It is long past time."

"I know what you are now," Cyrene said, controlling the shudder that ran through her at its presence.

"Clever," the thing said in a bored tone. "But my master is impatient. Though you were so delicious last time. May I have another taste?" he asked the question and then jolted toward her.

She focused on her magic and blasted him backward with her energy. Whatever had brought the two halves of her being together had opened up a world inside her. She was truly new. And, for the first time, she felt utterly connected to herself. She was not lost. She was not fighting herself. She was ready.

The Nokkin blocked her assault, not giving an inch. She honed her energy, throwing a fireball at the creature. It batted it away, as if it was no more concerning than raindrops falling from the sky.

It reached for her, and she shifted. Magic hit her, but she stayed on her feet.

"Tell your master, whoever he is, to leave me alone," she said, blasting through its defenses and landing a hit.

The Nokkin stumbled backward a few feet. "She."

"What?" Cyrene asked with furrowed brows.

"My master is a she—a goddess in fact. Great and all powerful. She will peel your skin from your bones and eat them like candy. Roast you like a pig on a spit. Pick apart your brain until nothing remains."

"Not really giving me incentive to meet her," Cyrene countered, releasing another blast of energy.

The Nokkin evaded that hit and sent one of its own at her. Cyrene pivoted but still caught a hit to the hip. She grunted and doubled over on impact.

"You need incentive?" the creature spat at her.

Then, it shifted, disappearing into a blend of shadows and darkness. Cyrene whirled around in a circle, trying to figure out where the thing had gone. Then, she heard a piercing scream that chilled her bones. She whipped around and saw the Nokkin holding Avoca aloft by the arrow in her shoulder.

"Let her go!" Cyrene shouted, throwing everything she had at the Nokkin.

But he disappeared and reappeared a few feet away. He was still holding Avoca in one hand.

Cyrene was trembling now with fury. Not just fear. Fear was weakness. An emotion that could be forged into something more powerful, into something unstoppable. If she could just overcome it.

Fear wasn't the Nokkin. She could take on the Nokkin.

Fear was losing Avoca forever, and she could not live in that world.

Her hands were clenched into fists at her sides as her blood boiled in her veins. She was drawing on it all. Every ounce. Every drop. Every last piece of magic. She was a siren's call, and she would be destruction.

The Nokkin held Avoca up to Cyrene, and its filthy mouth said, "Incentive?"

Then, with slow, agonizing purpose, the Nokkin lifted its hand and placed it over Avoca's mouth, draining the magic and life force from Cyrene's best friend.

Something cracked inside her.

Shattering at the sight of Avoca dangling from an arrow at the hand of a Nokkin.

No.

The answer was no.

She would not let this happen.

Not again.

She was in control.

She could stop it this time.

Cyrene shut out the madness all around her and centered on that one feeling of being whole. All her magical energy was bottled up inside her. She was the master of her fate.

With a battle cry, Cyrene slammed her fist down into the earth and released all her energy in one powerful arc. The mountains rattled as she blasted through them. The ground under her feet was unsteady. Everything stilled completely as everyone realized what she had done. Even the Nokkin had dropped Avoca, leaving her body crumpled on the ground.

"You will not hurt her," Cyrene said, her voice as cold as ice.

"What are you—"

Cyrene slammed her mind into the ruin of this thing that once had been Doma. It was beast more than man, but she went to work, ripping it apart, shattering it beyond the horrors it had already seen.

It shrieked. An unholy thing.

Then, it lashed out, reaching for her own mind. Trying to grab for her, to drain her power and stop. But it couldn't reach her. She stepped up until she was almost within arm's reach and forced the Nokkin down on its knees before her.

"Your reign is over. It's my turn."

Then, she poured the rest of the power that connected her to this world, that tethered her to Avoca, into her flaming blade. She felt something click. A connection within herself. As her soul opened up and she was one with herself. She thrust up through the empty place where its face should have been and then blasted outward, nearly knocking herself off her feet.

The Nokkin collapsed into a pile of shadows and then blew off into the wind. Whatever she had done finally ended its miserable existence. She didn't know which part of it had been enough.

But she now knew that *she* was enough.

She had always been enough.

"Uh, Cyrene," Basille Selby said, addressing her without a title, which was strange enough, "we need to run."

"What?" she asked, dazed.

"Run!" he said.

Then, Cyrene saw what had him looking so terrified.

"Creator!" she cried. "Avalanche."

And there, barreling down toward them, was a wall of snow, picking up speed and threatening to destroy them all.

The Guild members must have already realized what was happening, and however many of them that were still alive were racing back out of the Pass. But her friends hadn't moved. They hadn't abandoned her.

Orden hoisted Avoca's broken body up onto the nearest horse, but most of the other horses had already scattered. They didn't have another choice. Her powers had set off this chain reaction, and she didn't think that she could stop this, like she had been able to stop the hurricane. She had used up most of her magic, and stopping it could kill her.

With the limited horses, they swung up, one or two to a mount, and raced down the side of the mountain. Cyrene kept checking behind her, anxious to see how far away the snow was. They had barely made it a quarter of the way down when she knew for certain that there was no way she could outrun this. None of them could.

She pulled up her horse and jumped off its back. Then, she smacked its rump and sent it down after her friends. Planting her feet in the snow, she built up a shield with what remained of her powers, desperate and clinging to life.

There was no blood magic to replenish her now. There was only her Doma energy and whatever she had left in reserves. There was only the here and now.

Casting a wide net, she threw a wall up across the path to her friends. They could get out. They could survive this. She just needed to buy them time.

The first impact was like a sprinkle spitting against her shield. The second hit, with the full force of the avalanche, was like a downpour.

She grunted and dug in deeper. She could do this. She could hold back tons of snow from crushing everyone and everything.

The snow kept coming. The weight on her shoulders grew heavier. It was as if her arms and back and shoulders were physically holding up the snow as it climbed ever higher. Then, it pushed over her shield, and she had to adjust it upward.

Her knees buckled, and she went down hard. Part of her shield disintegrated and then another section on the other side. Snow was sliding past her now, heading down toward Alba.

Then, out of nowhere, both sides were reinforced. Matilde and Vera grasped her hands and pushed back on the snow with her. When they helped her hold off the coming snow and ice, it was like taking a breath.

"We need to divert it," Vera said through her teeth.

"Left," Matilde said.

Then, they swung as one, shoving the snow off the main path. It went cascading down the side of the mountain and through the trees, shredding everything in its way and creating a whole new path in its wake.

By the time the snow settled, Cyrene was shaking. She felt as if she could barely catch her breath. But, when she looked up at the thirty-foot wall they had created, she was amazed that the three of them had been able to do it.

"We…we did it," Cyrene gasped. "We did it."

Matilde and Vera shared a worried look.

"What?" Cyrene asked.

They remained silent, but their eyes traveled down to where the others were waiting for them. Orden and Basille were hovering over a body. Ahlvie was on his knees in the snow. Avoca lay on her back, not moving.

Cyrene jumped to her feet, somehow finding energy. She raced down to where they were and skidded to Avoca's side.

"Avoca!" she yelled. She frantically shook her friend.

The Nokkin had stolen her magic, and she had lost a lot of blood, but she couldn't be gone. She just couldn't. Cyrene had saved them. She had to have saved them.

"Give her some space," Orden said, reaching for her.

She pushed him off as Matilde and Vera approached. "Save her. You know how to heal."

"Cyrene," Vera said softly.

"No!" she shouted. "No! Save her. Do it!"

Ahlvie looked up at them all with horrified, lost eyes. As if he couldn't believe what he was seeing before him.

"We have to cut out the arrow and then dress the wound. We need to... to give her our magic. We need to make this right," Cyrene gasped.

"Cyrene, please," Matilde said just as soft and calm.

"Don't you dare!"

Tears poured out of her eyes as she leaned over Avoca and reached for the bond between them.

"You repaid your debt a hundredfold," Cyrene cried, "but don't leave me. Please, don't leave me. I need you. I love you."

But Avoca was gone.

Sixty One

THE FIGHT

—DEAN—

Brigette stood in the center of the chamber room of the Privy Council. She was dressed head to toe in Ellison blue and silver. Her hair was dark in a tight twist, and her tan skin glowed from whatever cosmetics had been administered to her. She looked ethereal, regal, cunning, manipulative, elegant…a queen.

"I, Brigette Ellison, Bride of the Sea, have come to reclaim my throne," she said with a powerful lilt in her voice.

The Privy Council was assembled before her, and they all began to speak at once.

Dean felt like a pompous prick behind her in Eleysian silks and his prize captain's sword, but he knew that Brigette wanted them to make an appearance. They'd spent the last week shoring up alliances, and this was the final test. This was her official claim to the throne.

Darmian nodded at him as the whispers grew. He'd already said that he wasn't worried about this meeting. Brigette was the rightful ruler of Eleysia. And that was that.

Unfortunately, Dean understood politics too well to be as confident as him. Already, the Anders and Mayhews were jostling for position. Their choice brats—Cassia Anders and Teena Mayhew—stood and glared down at Brigette.

They believed Brigette an imposter with a false crown. Apparently, Dean was to blame for most of it. He had apparently found some choice girl in the street who looked like his sister and made her be queen, as if the very idea wasn't outrageous…and treason.

"Enough," Brigette said with the simple composure of a ruler. "We have more important things to discuss than my throne. The matter is settled. We need to consider the real threat—Byern."

"I call for a vote of no confidence," Cassia Anders spat.

"I second the motion," Teena Mayhew called out.

"I…we," Cassia amended, "do not believe you are the rightful ruler of Eleysia. Even if you are Brigette Ellison, your time is over. You allowed the destruction of our most sacred capital. We no longer wish you to be our queen."

The Privy Council erupted in outrage. Dean watched everything they had worked for spiral out of control. They had known this was a possibility, but to actually have those words uttered to Brigette's face…it was repulsive.

Eventually, a vote was called.

Dean held his breath. He had never heard of such a vote actually taking place against a sovereign. If she lost, she would have to fight for her throne alongside these imbeciles. Creator only knew how long that would take to achieve. By then, Byern and Kael Dremylon's magic could destroy the world.

The vote went around the room. One by one, a man or woman raised or lowered their hand for Brigette.

And, when it was all said and done…she lost.

"The Privy Council will reconvene tomorrow morning to discuss the proceedings to choose a new queen for Eleysia," Nobleman Aurthur Anders, head of the Privy Council, said.

His eyes were glittering with delight at the possibilities. But Brigette didn't waver. She didn't storm out of there in anger. She nobly inclined her head and then swept from the room. She didn't say a word as she walked out of the Chamber Room or the whole ride to their new residence. Thankfully, they wouldn't be living in squalor any longer now that Brigette had officially announced herself.

But, once they were back in their quarters, she buried her head in a pillow and screamed at the top of her lungs. Dean couldn't help but laugh. Not at the situation because it was shit. There was no other word for it. But, seeing his sister *act* like his sister, it lightened something in him, if only briefly.

"It'll be fine, Brigette," Dean told her. "You'll have the people behind you, and that will be the way to win this. You know that Cassia and Teena don't hold a candle to you."

Brigette looked up at him and nodded. "I know, but I didn't want it to go this way. With Aurthur head of the Privy Council, Cassia is bound to be a favorite as well. This will be a fight for my life. And…I just wish Mother and

Father were here."

"Me, too," he said softly.

It was the first time Brigette had said anything remotely related to grief in the time that they'd been together. She was all business. But, now that her throne was on the line, there were cracks in her armor.

"And Susann and Karin and Lissa, Lara, Livia, and Ruthe and Hether, Therese and Tifani…even Alise," she said with a harsh laugh. "I miss them all. All our sisters."

"I know. I miss them every second. How could there be so many of us, and now, there are only two?"

Brigette shook her head. "Unfathomable."

They sat in silence. Both feeling the deep loss of nearly their entire family. To have once been so prosperous that the Ellisons had had eleven subsequent daughters in line…to just Brigette. It was devastating. And Dean knew that she would have to think about marrying right away to secure her throne.

"We're going to need something more than us to win," she muttered. "We're going to need so much more to go up against Byern. And I honestly don't know what it is."

"We'll figure it out."

"Will we? Because, from where I'm sitting, I don't see what can do it."

Dean frowned and glanced away from her penetrating stare. He knew exactly what could turn the tide for them. What could make them the victors.

Byern couldn't go unpunished, but if he had to face what he had seen in the Mirror to enact his justice, then so be it.

"Get some rest. I know you haven't been sleeping. We'll figure it out," Dean told her before disappearing from her room.

He moved into the adjoining bedroom where Darmian was standing like a sentinel, awaiting him. His bodyguard from a young age and now best friend. Dean had always been adventurous as a child, and instead of keeping him from his mischief, his parents assigned someone to make sure he would come back in one piece. Now, Darmian was the closest thing he had to a brother.

"You are planning something foolish," Darmian said once Dean closed the door.

Dean grinned. "How can you tell?"

"I've been wondering when you would admit it. You've had the look about you since you arrived."

"I have to leave this place. There is something I need to do for us to win this war."

"You wish to leave your sister *now*? She's facing the entire Privy Council. She is going up in a queens war! She needs you."

"I know," he said guiltily, "but she will win with or without me. I am sure of it. It doesn't change the necessity of what I must do."

"And that is?"

Dean sighed. "I can't tell you. Promise to take care of her?"

Darmian held out his hand, and they shook. "Promise to take care of yourself."

They both knew that he wouldn't.

Leaving Brigette in the position she was in without even a good-bye was heartbreaking. Dean knew that she would be upset. He knew that she needed him. He knew that she would see it as another loss. He only hoped he could prove her wrong.

Because, when he had made the grave mistake of looking into the Mirror of Truth in Aonia, he'd gotten more than he bargained for. His brain still felt addled, as if someone had shaken his insides until they were out of order.

He was a good enough actor to pretend like he was completely in his right mind, but sometimes, it would explode out of him. Witnessing the massacre of his homeland was bad enough. Seeing Kael's and Edric's gleeful faces as they killed thousands and left his beautiful home a wasteland was enough to make anyone crazy.

But it was more than that.

It was more than death and destruction that fueled him now.

That brought him to this moment.

That had driven him out of Rasine, past the now destroyed capital, and to the pirate hold of Ika Roa. The island was overgrown with vegetation. Palm fronds and coconuts littered the white sandy beaches. Gulls squawked overhead. No one would guess that the place had once been inhabited by a fierce warrior nation. No one would guess that anyone at all lived here.

The pirates themselves stuck to the eastern cove where treasure was rumored to be buried, but even the pirates didn't venture into the forest. Even pirates feared what had happened to the residents and anyone who chose to claim it as its own.

Dean knew the consequences. He had seen innumerable years of history of this island. All the faces of the people who had come here and died. He followed the track branded into his mind, slicing through undergrowth and clearing his own path through to the center of the island.

The forest crowded in around him, blocking his way back, as if to say he had already sealed his fate. He belonged to the island now. Not the other way around.

Then, he reached it.

The heart of Ika Roa.

A pool of glittering water with three sea nymphs swimming, undisturbed, at its center. Each as gold as the sun shimmering overhead with glitter in their hair and stars sparkling in their eyes.

"A boy!" the first squealed.

"So long since we've seen a boy," the second one said.

"I do like the looks of this one," the third one said.

Dean bowed low with deep respect for each of these creatures. "I do not come to claim but only to pass through."

"You can pass for a kiss," the first said with a sly grin. "One for each of us is our price."

"My heart belongs to another. She claimed it long ago and will claim it forever more. A kiss is a price I cannot pay."

"Honorable," the second said, slithering to the other side of her sister.

"How will you cross without a heart?" the third asked with a giggle.

"I will know that she holds it in safekeeping and trust that it will bring me back to her."

"Your heart then," the third said, holding out her hand. "If she is to keep it safe for you, then that is our price."

Dean faltered. "And will you give it back when I return?"

"If you return," the second said, "yes."

"Deal."

Dean knelt at the bank of the pond and watched in horror as the first thrust her hand into his chest and removed his beating heart. He clutched his chest, expecting to keel over and die, but nothing happened. He was still functional. He could still move. But, in truth, his heart was to be guarded while he was away.

"Only one worthy of crossing could survive this," the first said. "Sisters."

The girls swam to the middle of the pool, grasped hands, and then, suddenly, miraculously, a bridge materialized before him.

The bridge of legend.

The bridge, once crossed, could transform him into something more… something better…something earned.

Or it could kill him.

Only time would tell if it was worth it.

He set his feet on the edge of the bridge and slowly walked across it. When he reached the other side, his body squeezed, as if being stuffed into a small box, and then he was through and in a whole new world.

Sixty Two

THE HOPE
—KALIANA—

Kaliana could fix this.

She was sure of it.

Edric wasn't too far gone that she couldn't slow down all the madness that had been happening in her court. They had gotten away from the Affiliate and High Order system. Hardly anyone was training anymore. All the members in residence were eating feast after feast and reveling in ball after ball. It was as if decadence and debauchery had become the new norm. All in a matter of months, their court was splintering.

She knew that she had the key to make it right again. She needed to speak with Edric. To find a way to reach him.

Merrick answered the door when she knocked. The idea of him sleeping on a pallet in Edric's living quarters for security was so foreign to her. They'd never had to worry about that before. Now, Edric was always anticipating an attack.

"What do you want?" Merrick asked darkly.

"I'm here to see my husband," she said, raising her chin.

"He doesn't wish to see you."

"I *need* to see him," she told him with a taste of her old fire. "You're dismissed for the evening."

He shot her a deadly glare that said, *As if you could dismiss me.*

"Now!" she shouted.

Merrick slammed the door in her face without preamble. She was furious and getting ready to bang on the door until he reappeared and let her in.

"Edric is aware of your presence. You may enter."

Kaliana took a deep breath and then brushed past Edric's personal guard. The man made her shiver with disgust. There was something off about him.

But her mind left Merrick as soon as she found Edric sprawled on his bed, shirtless. Her mouth watered, and flashes of all the nights she had spent in that bed surfaced. Their relationship had always been…strained. She pushed too hard, but it was anger over being forced into the marriage and then, later, her inability to produce a child. Still, they'd had some good memories. Before Cyrene.

She shook off her thoughts and approached him.

"Hello, wife," Edric said. He had his arms above his head and was grinning like a Cheshire cat.

"Husband," she said.

"Merrick said you wished to speak with me."

"Indeed."

"Is Alessia all right?"

"Yes, our daughter is well."

"Then, what is it you wanted to discuss with me?"

Kaliana swallowed and then proceeded forward. "It's about the court. Everything has changed so quickly. With Eren's death—"

"Are you questioning my judgment?" he asked, sitting up and swinging his legs off the bed.

"I'm not," she lied. "I simply wondered when we were going to get the Affiliates and High Order back to work."

"We are on the verge of war, Kaliana. Even you should be able to see the importance of what we're doing here."

She didn't. And she thought the war was idiotic. They had made their point. There was no need to drag more innocent people into this vendetta.

She was about to open her mouth to say that very thing when the secret passageway that led to the consort's adjoined chambers shifted. Kaliana jumped, expecting to see a ghost. But, of course, it wasn't Daufina. And it obviously wasn't Cyrene. She didn't know if things would be better or worse if Cyrene were here.

"Kael," Kaliana said in confusion.

Of course he knew of the passageways. He had played in them with Edric and their sister, Jesalyn, as children. But what was he doing here?

"Oh, Kaliana," Kael said with a shake of his head. "This is unfortunate."

"Brother," Edric said with a reserved smile.

Before she or Edric could say another word, Kaliana was thrown backward against the stone wall of the bedchamber. Her body slammed into the hard surface, her head smacking with the impact. She cried out, and tears immediately came to her eyes. She went to reach up to touch her aching head but found she couldn't move. Not an inch.

Her eyes were wild as she looked up at Kael. "What have you done?"

"What is necessary," Kael said. His smile was devious. His eyes bright and deadly. In that moment, there was more predator to him than man.

To consider she had ever cared for him…

Her eyes swung to Edric, who was standing at his bedside.

"What are you playing at?" Edric asked.

Kael arched an eyebrow. "I believe I've finally decided to stop playing."

Edric's limbs went ramrod straight, as if an invisible string had tugged him into place. "Release me!"

"Did you think I would be satisfied as your lap dog, brother?" Kael asked. He paced the bedroom with a feline grace. "Did you think, with all the power at my command, that I would actually let you get all the glory?"

"We had a deal," Edric ground out.

"Oh, yes, you didn't kill me in that prison, so things would go back to the way they were. But things could never go back to the way they were. You see, Father chose me," Kael spat. "He chose me. I am the rightful ruler of Byern. I am the one willing to do what needs to be done. You might have inherited the throne, dear brother, but I inherited this."

Kael held aloft a small worn book.

"A book?" Edric asked.

"The book of the Dremylons, passed down from Viktor himself. Every ruler who has come before you had it in their possession and used it to hold on to our power. Viktor Dremylon killed his first child all those years ago to get the blood magic that now courses through my veins. Our own father sacrificed our mother for that same power."

"Why?" Edric's plea was laced with hysteria as the tension mounted.

Kaliana remained strapped where she was, unable to do anything but watch as this all unfolded.

"Why?" Kael laughed. "Because we are to keep Doma magic from resurfacing. We are in charge of fate. And, today, I'm giving in to my fate."

"Brother," Edric said, "please. Whatever you think, know that I have always loved you. Our relationship has never been perfect, but you and I are connected."

Kael reached for the sword at his waist. He removed it from its sheath and admired the steel glinting in the candlelight. A wry smile played on his features. A hint of madness. A glance of desperation.

Then, he shoved it straight through his brother's heart.

"I know," he told Edric. "It is our connection that I need right now."

Edric sputtered, gasping for life. Kaliana couldn't breathe. She couldn't see. Tears streamed down her cheeks, unbidden. Sobs racked her chest as she watched the end of her husband, the very man she had always believed would rule this land peacefully and in prosperity.

He was now…dead.

And at his brother's hand.

"Why?" she wheezed, whimpering in pain as her heart constricted.

Kael seemed to be breathing in Edric's death. His very essence seemed to expand, as if he was sated from the death. Pleased by the outcome.

"Because there is no greater magic than blood."

"Are you going to kill me, too?" she sniffled.

Kael waved his hand, and she dropped like a stone onto the floor.

"Please," she pleaded. She didn't care how pathetic she sounded. "Please don't kill me, too."

Kael stared down at her, unseeing, lost to another world.

"For our child," she begged, admitting the thing she had refused to admit before this moment.

"Our child?" he asked.

"Alessia is yours."

He grinned. "I know."

"Spare her. Spare me. She needs a mother." She prostrated herself before him. She would do anything for her child. Even if she wanted to take up the sword and shove it through *his* chest. She wanted to show him as much mercy as he had shown Edric.

Oh, Edric!

Another sob hit her fresh at the loss.

Then, Kael bent forward and lifted her face to look at him. "I will spare you and my daughter."

"Thank…thank you!" she gasped.

"Because you won't remember any of this."

Then, her mind went blank, and she fell forward into the pool of blood at Kael's feet.

Sixty Three

THE BAD

"**A**voca is gone, Cyrene," Vera said. "The Creator has taken her home."

Cyrene shook her head. *No. Creator, no! That isn't possible.* With a mind to bring Avoca back, Cyrene delved deep into her magic. She found that place where her tether with Avoca was. It was gone.

She screamed, aching for that lost place. *Why?* When she had lost Edric's bond, she assumed it was because the bond had been fulfilled. She couldn't lose Avoca's, too. That meant, there was only Kael left, and that was unacceptable. She had just gotten Avoca. She couldn't lose her.

Cyrene searched deeper. It had to be there. It had to.

People were reaching for her, speaking to her, but she was lost deep into that well of magic. Deep into that place where she had found her oneness against the Nokkin. She had to find Avoca. She couldn't endure another death. Not so soon after Maelia and then her own parents.

Only Ahlvie didn't stop her. He stared into her blank eyes and then reached for her hand. Only he could understand the true depth of her despair. Avoca was the love of his life. Cyrene knew no one could ever compare.

She settled into the snow, linked between Avoca and Ahlvie, and fought for her friend. Maybe she couldn't heal her. Maybe she had no talent in medicine. But she knew Avoca.

Cyrene knew the way she'd laugh when she let her guard down. And the sharp look she would give when Cyrene talked too much. Or her trained fighting stance when her instincts had gone on high alert. She knew how she'd liked to braid her hair and the way she would hone her ice-white blades. She knew all the little pieces of her heart that belonged to Eldora. Cyrene knew Avoca's struggle with the idea of becoming queen and the honor she had known it would have been. And, most of all, she knew the feel of her magic. The way they'd linked, creating power that couldn't exist separately.

That was what she searched for.

That grasp of connection.

That power that linked them.

With a sigh, she felt it.

"Creator," she whispered, "she's still here."

"Cyrene, she's not," Vera said gently.

Cyrene didn't care what she'd said or that Vera knew more about healing than Cyrene ever would. Avoca's bond was still in place. It was faint, practically nonexistent. If Cyrene hadn't delved so deep into herself, she might have believed it was completely gone forever. That whatever the Nokkin had done by stripping her magic had really killed her.

Cyrene wrapped her magic around that barely there bond. "I sense it."

Vera went back to work, using her magic to see what Cyrene meant. She gasped. "I've never…I've never seen anything like it."

"What does that mean?" Ahlvie demanded.

"She might be alive, but she is not in this world," Vera said. "Her body might be of the living, but her mind might never recover."

Cyrene shook her head. She wouldn't accept that. "We need to get her somewhere safe. Where do we go?"

Vera turned to Matilde, who nodded. "Onward."

"Might I remind you that the Pass is blocked?" Basille said, swinging his arm toward the avalanche that had run its course. "Not to mention, we have six people and an unconscious girl and only four horses. We'll never make it through the Pass at this rate."

"We're not going through the Pass," Matilde said. "We're going to the Black Mountain."

"We can't—" Basille began.

"You will take us there, or so help me Creator," Cyrene snapped at him.

Whatever he must have seen in her eyes stopped him in his tracks. He huffed and went with Orden to organize the horses. Cyrene stayed with Avoca while the others made a makeshift litter for Avoca in between two of the horses. Orden and Basille each took their own horse while Cyrene and Ahlvie shared, and the twins took the other horse.

The procession back up the mountain was slow-going. There was no path now. They had to make do with Basille's and Orden's good instincts. Cyrene could hardly pay attention to what they were doing or how it was being done. Her focus remained on Avoca, making sure she was still alive. Never dropping her magic in fear that Avoca would disappear if she did.

Cyrene had no idea what it would mean if her body was living but her mind was elsewhere. The only thing she could think was if it was like when she had been lost to the blood magic in Fen. They had thought she was dying, but she had been brought back from the brink. She never asked Avoca what the bond had felt like. If she had seemed like this. Or if this was worse. It felt so much worse.

"Here," Matilde said with glee.

Vera gasped. "The avalanche shifted the Pass."

"I've never been through here," Basille said uncertainly.

"We have," Matilde said.

"A long, long time ago," Vera said, her voice laced with tears.

They continued on. Cyrene didn't have it in her to ask where they were going. She only thanked the Creator that something was going right. If the path had shifted, then perhaps they could find these caves the twins had mentioned. Perhaps, there, someone could heal whatever was wrong with Avoca.

It was nightfall by the time they reached the first cave. It was enormous. The size of a house that opened up into the mountainside. It was tremendous to think that the snow and ice had obscured this from view for all this time. It was almost as if it had been done on purpose.

Cyrene's heart leaped at the thought. They had made it. They had actually made it. The lost ones had to be here. The piece of the puzzle that had eluded her thus far. The place Serafina had claimed she had to be to master her magic and win this long-fated war.

Their horses clattered against the stone as Matilde and Vera directed them through the cave. Once they were deep enough, they lit their Doma Fire and sent it down the tunnels, lighting lanterns bracketed on the wall. It was clear it was not the first time they had done it.

Cyrene's anticipation only grew as they moved deeper into the dragons' lair. She didn't know what to expect to find. A firedrake's gold hoard. Jewels and treasure beyond comprehension. Glittering scales and fire-breathing horrors as big as the walls they were walking through. Her imagination ran off with her.

They entered an enormous room with a ceiling raised to the heavens, and Matilde and Vera stopped.

"They should be here," Vera whispered.

"Can they be somewhere else?" Cyrene asked.

Matilde frowned. "Possibly."

"There's something at the end of the room," Ahlvie said.

They all took their horses across the giant room, and as they crossed the space, Cyrene realized that it appeared to be a training facility. All sorts of weapons were hanging on the walls—swords, knives, maces, and more. Chain mail and leather gear was nearby. And all manner of other objects she had never seen in use.

But, when they found what Ahlvie had pointed out, her blood went cold. This couldn't be right. There was a man lying in a glass case on top of a slab of granite, fast asleep.

Matilde dismounted, a choked sob catching in her throat. "Is that…"

"Creator," Vera whispered.

"What?" Orden asked. "Who is it?"

Matilde lifted the glass case, and it eased open on rusted hinges that squeaked and shrieked. She gently placed her hand over the man's heart and finally let the tears fall down her cheeks. "Mikel."

Cyrene and Ahlvie shared a glance. The moment felt too intimate for anyone else to watch it.

"You know him?" Basille asked obviously.

"He was…is my husband," Matilde said. "I thought he'd died two thousand years ago after the dragons disappeared from Emporia."

Cyrene's mouth fell open. Matilde was *married?* She had thought for so long that her husband was dead, yet he was here all along…sleeping?

"Can you wake him?" Cyrene asked. She hoped for Avoca's sake that it was possible.

Matilde shuddered, and Vera went to her. They stood on either end of him and then breathed their magic into him. The rest of them dismounted, eager to find out what would happen. A few seconds passed before Mikel coughed and coughed. Then, he opened his stunning green eyes and smiled.

"It took you long enough, Mati."

"Mikel," Matilde said, collapsing over him.

"There, there, love. It's all right. I'm here." He slowly eased up and smiled at Vera. "Sister," he said with a nod.

She returned it with tears streaming down her face. "Brother."

Then, his eyes found Cyrene. "Sera, I thought you would never come. We all feared that Viktor would end up wooing you after all."

Cyrene opened and closed her mouth.

"I am not Serafina," Cyrene said.

Mikel's brows furrowed. "I don't…understand."

"Mikel, darling, how long do you think you were under the sleeping spell?" Matilde asked.

"Not long," Mikel said. "Only a couple of months. Long enough for the dragons to get away while they could."

"No, my love," Matilde whispered.

"What?" Mikel asked.

"Serafina was murdered by Viktor two thousand years ago," Vera told him. "Magic fell, as was predicted. We have been in hiding. The mountains have been covered. No one has been in or out. No one has seen a dragon since."

Mikel stared at them, stunned. His honey-colored skin paled, and his dark brows rose and then fell and then scrunched together. He seemed to be taking it all in.

"Two thousand years," he repeated.

"Yes," Matilde told him. "And this is Cyrene. The one from the prophecy."

"The prophecy," he said, dazed.

"But…where are the dragons?" Cyrene asked. "We came all the way across the world for this. I need them to help me bring back my friend. She's lost. And I need…I was told I needed the dragons."

Mikel's eyes seemed to clear, and then he shook his head. "I'm sorry that you came all this way. But there are no dragons here or…anywhere in Emporia. I cannot help you."

"No!" she shouted, unable to control herself. "We were sent here! The dragons have to be here. We should check the rooms. We should look everywhere. They have to be here. They have to help Avoca." Her voice quavered on the last word.

"They left. All of them. You can check, but they're gone. I volunteered to stay behind to speak for them."

Cyrene cursed and flung her arms wide. "Then, what was the point? Why would Serafina send me to find the dragons to save the world if there were no dragons?"

"Serafina sent you?" Mikel asked, glancing at Matilde.

"She is training in spirit. She can cross the divide."

"Incredible," he whispered. "When have we ever had someone with such talents?"

"We're not sure," Vera said. "Cyrene is…extraordinary."

"Well, if Sera said the dragons would help, it can only be because of the Society," Mikel guessed.

"But the Society doesn't exist anymore," Vera said. "We three are the last of its kind. Without dragons in Emporia, the ancient dragon society is no more."

"There might not be any in Emporia but perhaps…elsewhere," Mikel said.

"You aren't suggesting…" Matilde said.

"I will do anything to right these wrongs," Cyrene said vehemently. "Anything to save Avoca."

"But will you risk Alandria?" Mikel asked with an arched eyebrow.

Cyrene didn't care what or who Alandria was. She would stop at nothing to do what needed to be done.

Her world might be broken.

It might have problems and tyrannical leaders and blood magic.

It might have taken one friend and attempted to take another.

But she wouldn't let it fall to the darkness.

She might not have wanted the burden on her shoulders. She might have once wished for a quiet life. But she would go to the ends of the earth and back to save her friends.

"Bring it," she swore.

To Be Continued...

Acknowledgments

Cyrene's dark times are a testament to finding your own inner strength. Our actions and more importantly our failures shape us. They mold us into the hero that we need to become. They're not easy. They make you second guess yourself. They make you question everything. But when you come out on the other side, you're stronger. You can tell the world to 'Bring it.' just like Cyrene.

So, I'll start by thanking the darkness that I dealt with to get to this place. And the light at the end of the tunnel that pulled me out.

Especially the friends who were there through it all in this book—Anjee, Rebecca K, Rebecca G, and Katie. All the times I had to tell you that I'm killing someone else today and not thinking me totally insane. For loving my bad boys and Cyrene more than anything else. Also to Robin for letting me kill you off.

As always, thanks to Sarah Hansen at Okay Creations for the stunning cover. Lauren Perry at Perrywinkle Photography for the picture of Cyrene on the cover. It completely captures her coming into her own. Jovana Shirley at Unforeseen Editing for last minute edits and the beautiful formatting of the interior! Also, my agent, Kimberly Brower, for loving everything I write even when I come up with crazy ideas. For being 100% in my corner no matter what. Danielle Sanches, my amazing publicist, who probably loved this series first and sends me grabby hands gifs as I go. KP Simmon for your unfailing guidance and joy.

To all the author friends that have supported this series with me and keep me going year after year—Jillian Dodd, Jenn Sterling, Wendy Higgins, Susan Dennard, AL Jackson, SC Stephens, Gennifer Albin, Bethany Hagen, and Molly McAdams.

To my husband, Joel, who listens to all my insane ideas and doesn't think me any crazier than I am. For long walks to help me plot and for believing in Cyrene. And my two writing puppies—Riker and Lucy. All the love. <3

K. A. LINDE grew up as a military brat, traveling the United States and even landing for a brief stint in Australia. She created fantastical stories based off of her love for Disney movies, fairy tales, and *Star Wars*. In her spare time, she loves traveling, *Supernatural*, playing piano, and dancing. She currently lives in Lubbock, TX with her husband and two super adorable puppies.

Kyla is a USA Today bestseller of more than twenty adult novels, but does not encourage anyone younger than eighteen to pick those up.

K. A. Linde loves to hear from her readers!

Visit her online at www.kalinde.com and on Facebook, Twitter, and Instagram @authorkalinde.

Join her newsletter at www.kalinde.com/subscribe for exclusive content, free books, and giveaways every month.